HISPANIC CLASSICS
ISSN 0953 797 X

RAINY DAYS
Días de lluvia

Short Stories by Contemporary Spanish Women Writers

Edited, with an Introduction and Notes
by
Montserrat Lunati

Short stories translated
by
Marilyn Myerscough

ISBN 0 85668 635 2 cloth
ISBN 0 85668 636 paper

British Library Cataloguing-in-Publication Data
A catalogue record for this book is available from the British Library.

The publishers gratefully acknowledge the financial assistance of the
Dirección General del Libro y Bibliotecas of the Ministerio de Cultura de España
with this translation.

Printed and published in England by
Aris & Phillips Ltd, Teddington House, Warminster, Wiltshire BA12 8PQ

Contents

Acknowledgements

The first word of acknowledgement should go to all the authors of each of the texts collected in this anthology, both for their talent in writing the stories and for their generosity in allowing me to include them in this book. I owe a most particular debt of gratitude to Professor Catherine Davies whose comments, suggestions and recommendations I found extremely helpful and illuminating. I would also like to thank Lucinda Phillips for commissioning me to prepare this book and for being always such a supportive and enthusiastic publisher, and to all the staff in Aris & Phillips, especially Janet Davis, who have been so patient and courteous. Thanks are also due to my former colleagues Dr Catrin Redknap and Dr Jean Andrews, and most especially to my colleague Dr Charles Kelley who is always willing to offer me his good humoured support. My appreciation is also due to Marilyn Myerscough who translated the stories with her usual care. And last but not least, I want to express my deepest gratitude to Jordi who has helped me in many ways through the lengthy process and to Roger for coping so well with a working mother.

Montserrat Lunati   Cardiff, June 1997

Ese género de tan difícil definición, tan huidizo en sus múltiples aspectos, y en última instancia tan secreto y replegado en sí mismo, caracol del lenguaje, hermano misterioso de la poesía en otra dimensión del tiempo literario.

This *genre* which is so difficult to define, so elusive in its manifold aspects, and in the final instance so secret and folded in on itself, a caracole of language, mysterious sibling of poetry in another dimension of literary time. (Julio Cortázar)

Cuanto más te internas en el mar remoto de lo femenino, más mujeres te encuentras: hembras fuertes o sutiles, gloriosas o insufribles, pero todas ellas interesantes. Las aguas del olvido están llenas de náufragas y basta con embarcarse para empezar a verlas.

The further you wade out into the far off Sea of Women, the more women you encounter: strong or subtle females, glorious or insufferable, but all of them interesting. The Waters of Oblivion are full of castaways and you only have to set sail to see them.

(Rosa Montero)

Introduction

WOMEN WRITERS IN POST-FRANCO SPAIN: WRITING AS TRANSGRESSION?

To illustrate an article by Rosa Pereda, 'El pensamiento posfeminista' (6), the Spanish newspaper *El País* used a photograph from 1914 in which the suffragette Emmeline Pankhurst is being arrested by a uniformed policeman who carries her in his arms, presumably away to the police station, as though she were a naughty child caught in a mischievous act. It could be argued that the picture was an appropriate choice to accompany Pereda's reflection that, after the 1980s, new strategies had to be found to keep alive the fight for women's rights because of the new, trendy conservatism threatening to undermine women's achievements. This conservatism was manifested in campaigns against abortion, increasing and much publicized mistrust of day-nurseries, claims that women were fed up with trying to be Superwoman and were missing out on life's natural pleasures, like motherhood.

It was as though the snapshot was used as a reminder of how difficult the struggle had been. But we could also read this picture of Emmeline Pankhurst (who looks admirably full of dignity in such uncomfortable circumstances) as being in keeping with the general, popular perception of the self-confessed feminist as someone who is eccentric almost to the point of ridicule. What I am referring to here is the kind of patriarchal attitudes which, however great the success of women in public and private spheres, still dominates the lives and ways of thinking of a majority of people, whatever their race, gender or class. 'El masclisme és interclassista [macho culture cuts across social class],' said the last socialist Director of the Instituto de la Mujer, the Catalan Marina Subirats, in an interview (Alberola, 38) before the March 1996 election in Spain gave power to the conservative Partido Popular.

Despite the many social and political gains made by women over the last century, which have been sanctioned by law in most democratic countries, the resilience of these all-pervasive patriarchal values, often presented as 'natural', justifies a gathering of texts written by women. Since language was dressed in men's clothes for so long, a collection of women's texts is, to some extent, a small step towards a more equal society, a type of positive discrimination, no less political for being literary. Spanish critics and authors have often displayed a tendency to scorn

collections of women's writing, dismissing them as either a hysterical response to perceived victimization on the part of feminist writers and academics, who are accused of sexism (although the same people never question anthologies featuring a majority of, or exclusively, men writers), or the product of marketing surveys carried out by commercially-minded publishers, since women writers nowadays sell very well and most of their readers are women.[1] Ignacio Soldevila-Durante states:

> ¿Se hace realmente el mayor favor posible a las escritoras publicando monografías sobre su obra, o incrementando en los estudios globales el porcentaje respectivo de la atención a ellas dedicada? Es ésta cuestión de estricta justicia compensatoria, ya que debido a las condiciones reales en que la mujer ha vivido hasta el fin del franquismo, y con la honrosa excepción de los breves años de gobierno de izquierda entre 1936 y 1939 *[sic]*, hacer un recuento de los catálogos de la Biblioteca Nacional en dos apartados — hombres y mujeres — dará como resultado un porcentaje más o menos equivalente al 10% de mujeres escritoras. (Soldevila-Durante, 609)

This is a very low percentage indeed, and evidence of just how marginalized women have been in terms of cultural production in Spain up to the present day.

Joan L. Brown surveys the presence of women writers in what has been traditionally considered the canon in Spanish literary history, dividing it into three — somewhat debatable — periods: 'before Franco (1100-1936), during the Franco era (1936-1975) and after Franco (1975 to the present)' (Brown 1990, 553-60).[2] Although the number of women writers increases considerably from one period to another, she finds that only six women from the first period, spanning eight centuries, have been consistently included in most literary histories and anthologies: Teresa de Jesús (sixteenth century), María de Zayas y Sotomayor (seventeenth century), Cecilia Böhl de Faber who used a male penname: 'Fernán Caballero', Gertrudis Gómez de Avellaneda, Rosalía de Castro, and Emilia Pardo Bazán (nineteenth century). By stressing that only six were officially maintained at the centre of the literary establishment, Brown is signalling that equally, if not more, important is the number of women writers who have been forgotten. The pernicious effect of such an approach was pointed out by Elaine Showalter in 1977 when dealing with English writers:

> Criticism of women novelists, while focussing on these happy few [Austen, George Eliot, the Brontës, Woolf], has ignored those who are not 'great', and left them out of anthologies, histories, textbooks, and theories. Having lost sight of the minor novelists, who were the links in the chain that bound one generation to the next, we have not had a very clear understanding of the continuities in women's writing, nor

any reliable information about the relationships between the writers'
lives and the changes in the legal, economic, and social status of
women. (Showalter, 7)

The general position of traditional Hispanism, that of taking seriously only one
small group of women writers accorded the same, or nearly the same, critical
consideration as their male counterparts, is the result of what Chris Weedon
accurately deconstructs as

the liberal-humanist criticism which claims to address both the unique
individual and the universally human, but its gender blindness has
created the conditions for a discourse which is profoundly
conservative and patriarchal in its implications. The individual and the
human nature for which it speaks are both normatively male, and the
meaning and values which it privileges naturalize the social power
relations of patriarchy. (Weedon, 139)

A rough calculation of the number of women poets, novelists and playwrights of
the first period — the eight-century time-span as established by Brown — gathered
in a sample of female-only bio-bibliographic source books (Pérez 1988 and 1996;
Gould Levine, Engelson Marson and Feiman Waldman 1993; the anthologies edited
by Susan Kirkpatrick 1992 and Ángela Ena Bordonada 1989; and those *Mujeres del
27* included in *Ínsula*'s monographic issue of 1993, though some of their
publications spill over into the second period) amounts to one hundred women
writers. The disparity between these figures — six as opposed to one hundred —
needs no comment. Besides, this figure of one hundred could very easily double if
we were to take into account earlier collections.[3] Indeed, however long the list turns
out to be, we shall be always consigning to oblivion those whose literary output
never reached publication, or those whose social status as women prevented them
from 'attempting the pen'.[4]

Nowadays the situation has changed enormously. Unlike other occupations
where women find it difficult in practice to combine successfully the role of
professional and mother, in spite of a certain amount of social improvement,[5] female
literary production is beginning to be highly coveted. Women writers sell well and
that makes them attractive to publishers.[6] This is a relatively recent and extremely
relevant factor which has no doubt helped the female author to become less invisible.
The process started in the thirties and, after a relapse in the immediate aftermath of
the Civil War, gathered momentum — thanks mainly to writers like Carmen Laforet,
Ana María Matute, Carmen Martín Gaite, Elena Quiroga or Dolores Medio[7] and,
later on, to those respected older figures who were re-entering the Spanish scene
after coming back from exile, such as Mercè Rodoreda or Rosa Chacel, as well as
other important names who started publishing in the late sixties, such as Ana María

Moix, or Esther Tusquets, whose first novel dates from 1978 — and took off with the splendid mushrooming of new names in the 1980s and 1990s, of whom, unfortunately, only twelve are represented in this anthology. However, for all the talent and the powerful presence of many of the women writers, the panorama is far from ideal. The number of pages devoted to them in influential reference books has increased steadily but very slowly.[8] At the same time, as Brown points out,

> Consonant with such low representation is the condescending manner in which [...] literary histories describe and categorize literature by women [...], [they] take pains to emphasize (though rarely to define) the 'feminine' nature of all literature by women. By inference, this label is understood to signify sentimentality. (Brown 1990, 555)

Here she is referring to criticism prior to 1975, and we might be tempted to believe that things are now so much better that there is hardly any need to complain; that well prepared critics, familiar with new theoretical trends, have put an end to all these discriminative and patronizing readings, and that Spanish literature written by women has received the attention it deserves.[9] Some of this is certainly true. Nevertheless, certain interesting points could be raised if we were to look at one of the most prestigious collections of essays on Spanish literary history published in the 1990s, the ninth volume of the *Historia y Crítica de la Literatura Española* (whose general editor is Francisco Rico): *Los nuevos nombres: 1975-1990* (edited by Darío Villanueva). This encyclopedic volume covers the exact period of time during which the number of women writers in Spain has flourished. We should welcome the fact that the 'condescending manner' in which previous criticism used to deal with women's literature has entirely disappeared from this volume, and yet the inequality persists. Only 88 women writers are included as opposed to 560 male authors. The gender balance of scholars and academics contributing to this major collective work is also lop-sided: 17 are female while 63 are male.[10] But the fact that of the 88 women writers only 17 (19.2%) are studied in some depth, and only 64 (11.4%) of the 560 male writers are considered interesting enough to be discussed at some length, provides us with rather ambivalent information: either the criteria for including men have been wider (writers at the beginning of their career or those with only one book), or women writers, in spite of being a lesser presence, have been given more individual attention. Both explanations, somehow contradictory, seem valid. Moreover, if we take into account the number of women writers active[11] during the years covered by the volume who might have been included in it, we have to accept that not many names are missing.[12] This leads us to a grim conclusion: although the population is surprisingly gender-balanced — 51% is female in Spain, and 52% in the world (Navarro, 14), there are still fewer women than men writers, as there are fewer female Members of Parliament than male ones.[13] Circumstances which enable women to develop to their full potential may have improved

significantly, and the willingness to neutralize patronising attitudes towards literature written by women might be less hard to find than in previous decades, but the process towards parity is far from over.

Also enlightening in this respect is what Laura Freixas (a writer who knows the Spanish publishing milieu well) states in the introduction to *Madres e hijas*, a ground-breaking anthology of short stories written by women:

> en el mundo editorial de aquí y ahora las mujeres *funcionan*; hay que añadir que ese reconocimiento suele ir acompañado de cierta condescendencia (se las llama *las chicas*), y que si están presentes (aunque, insistimos, de forma muy minoritaria) en la publicación y en los premios comerciales, su reconocimiento académico es harina de otro costal. De la Real Academia están prácticamente ausentes[14] así como de la nómina de los grandes premios institucionales; y como ha mostrado Geraldine Nichols,[15] las historias de la literatura española las ignoran o rebajan sistemáticamente. (Freixas, 18)

To this we could add that all too often academic papers still show unnecessary prejudice: in *Ínsula*'s recent issue dedicated to contemporary narrative, two different contributors use in their respective articles these somewhat derisory subheadings: "Mujeres y autonómicos" (Gracia, 30), and "Mujeres: una lista" (Chicharro Chamorro, 15). Literary debates organized by otherwise serious academic journals or cultural magazines reveal the same degree of unevenness. Looking at a few examples in recent years, we come across the same old tokenism: in 1986 *El Urogallo* brought together six writers for a discussion on 'Narradores de hoy', and only one of them was a woman; in 1988 *Ínsula* published a debate on 'El cuento' held in the Casona de Verines (Pendueles, Asturias) the previous year, and among twenty-eight writers and academics, only five were women; in 1994, five writers and one academic who acted as coordinator were invited by *Ínsula* to debate 'De últimos cuentos y cuentistas', but only one was a woman; six men — authors and critics — were asked to participate in the debates on *¿Qué va a ser de la literatura?* organized in 1996 by the cultural magazine *Lateral* both in Madrid and in Barcelona, but only one woman writer was invited. We could go on.

Thus, for all the positive signs in publishing circles (for example, more series dedicated to female writers — the latest publisher to enter the fray, at the time of writing this introduction, is the influential Anagrama, with two series with Flaubertian titles: 'La educación sentimental' and 'La educación sentimental Serie Mayor'), the real issue at stake is the development of a new consciousness about women and gender, and the recognition by the literary establishment of women writers' success, not only as a sociological phenomenon, but also as a literary one. This recognition should lead to something more than just the mere addition of a few

names to the canon. It should challenge the whole concept of the canon itself, a canon that, if it is to remain at all, should be a non-hegemonic one. [16]

Some women writers seem to believe that the situation is slowly improving though it still leaves a lot to be desired. Others, on the contrary, deny that there is any discrimination against female authors, for example, Cristina Fernández Cubas, who, at the same time, acknowledges the significance of their presence in post-Civil War narrative:

> Tenemos los mismos problemas que los hombres. Y además en España siempre ha habido mujeres escritoras. Cuando yo era pequeña estaban Carmen Laforet, Ana María Matute, poco más tarde Carmen Martín Gaite. Mujeres de éxito, que ganaban premios muy prestigiosos en la misma competencia con los hombres, en iguales condiciones. A nadie se le ocurría, en ningún momento, hacer una antología de esas tres mujeres. A nadie se le ocurrió decir 'son femeninas', en absoluto. Esta es una cosa posterior. Hemos nacido en un país en el cual ser escritora era una cosa natural. (Carmona, 158)

Or Soledad Puértolas:

> Nunca he creído [...] que las mujeres tengan mayores problemas para escribir que los hombres. Nunca se me ha ocurrido que las cosas deban plantearse de ese modo. Tampoco parece que tengan especiales dificultades para publicar sus textos. ¿Dónde reside la discriminación, si es que la hay? (Puértolas 1993, 60)

The debate, though, if such a debate exists, should be set within a larger framework: that of the women writers' approach to literature and the politicization of their writing.[17]

The fight against gender inequalities has been tackled in different ways and with many strategies. In a collective interview Mercedes Abad made this highly significant point:

> Durante cuarenta años la literatura se dedicó casi exclusivamente a la lamentación organizada. Y no sólo la literatura, sino otros modos y otros movimientos, pongo por ejemplo a las mujeres. Yo, desde luego, no me dedico a lamentarme. ('Narradores de hoy', 20)

A few years later, at the University of California, Abad, Fernández Cubas and Puértolas agreed on one thing: 'literatura y feminismo no tienen nada que ver' (Carmona, 158).

There is a widespread reluctance to accept any form of what Rosa Montero calls 'literatura utilitaria' (Davies 1993, 383). A reluctance that reveals the profound mistrust for politics and the power of art to transform reality embedded in a society which had to cope with a dictatorial régime for so long. Adelaida García Morales, a committed socialist[18] and a writer whose fiction is dominated by complex female figures and gender relations, is also adamant that 'La lucha política y la literatura son cosas completamente distintas. [...] La literatura es un territorio imaginario' (Cano, 100).

Although I am aware of the risks of drawing general conclusions, I would suggest that recent Spanish history, and the way pre-1975 currents in Spanish cultural production were influenced by it, still cast a shadow over contemporary writers' views on literature. In 1939 the outcome of a bloody Civil War which lasted three years brought to power a military régime led by General Franco. The dictatorship lasted until his death in 1975. The adversity and political isolation which Spaniards endured for four decades affected every single aspect of their lives. They were denied basic democratic rights and the former pluralistic society of pre-war Spain became, in the 1940s, one in which diversity was perceived as a threat to an illusory fascist sense of unity.[19] After the brutal repression which followed the Civil War, a short period of the so-called *realismo existencial* gave way in the 1950s to political commitment as the predominant feature in literature — and in art in general. Many *engagé* writers, male and female, viewed literature as an instrument for political and social change — their inspiration, in some cases, was not just Sartre or Italian neo-realism, but also Spanish writers and artists living in exile. The literature — narrative, theatre, poetry — produced as a result of this closeness between the world and the text, responded to the creed of what has been labelled *realismo social* or *realismo crítico*: a testimonial writing strongly influenced by leftist thought.[20] A willingness to expose the hardship suffered by the people under Franco's authoritarian régime shaped most of the literary output of those years despite the strict censorship in force at the time. Writers tried to be 'objective' in their attempts both to depict social injustice and political repression, and to avoid the red pen of the censors. As the public and the writers themselves grew tired of *realismo social,* some of them, such as Luis Martín Santos and Juan Goytisolo, questioned and escaped from its limitations without being any less critical of contemporary Spain. From the 1960s until the mid 1970s experimental literature flourished, both as a reaction to a frequently short-sighted belief in *objetivismo* and as a result of the influence of French structuralism and its insistence on the non-referentiality of literature. Many so-called 'anti-novels' were written. Formal experimentation was back in fashion at the expense of storytelling. The subversive potential of irony was cleverly exploited, and together with a questioning of the very nature of language and its conventional use in fiction, this allowed writers to distance themselves from the naive attempts at 'objectivism' of the previous decade. Writers still set out to destroy 'the images of security and wholeness sustained by the [Franco] Regime'

(Herzberger, 253), but now language itself, and hence narration, became the *locus* for this new *avant-garde*, élitist struggle against totalitarianism. As Jo Labanyi says,

> novelists and critics' increasing insistence that the writers duty was to revolutionize language implied that no other revolution was possible; indeed it became fashionable to praise writers for the suicidal act of 'destroying language'. (Graham and Labanyi, 296)

Since the mid 1970s, diversity and a postmodern license to break free from any remaining dominant trends have been the most obvious features of Spanish narrative, along with a renewed fondness for storytelling. The democratic press took over the former testimonial role of literature, and writers today reject 'literatura militante', to use Montero's words again (Davies 1993, 383), because, among other possible reasons, it reminds them of what was fashionable and yet so restrictive only a few decades ago.

Some writers have no qualms about admitting that they are feminists, others are more reluctant to be labelled as such, as indeed they are about any labelling exercise. Among the first group we find Lourdes Ortiz (Porter, 144), Maruja Torres (10) or Laura Freixas (Fidalgo, 60), whose introductory words in *Madres e hijas* offer a convincing comment on the issue of *literatura femenina*. Freixas emphasizes that *literatura femenina* is different from that produced by male writers and takes into account the French feminist notion of *écriture féminine*, which does not automatically exclude men's writing for biological reasons and, we may add, does not guarantee any writing with a female signature immediate inclusion in the alternative space of femininity. Ideally, her words should put an end to all those hopeless, and frequently biased, discussions in the Spanish press about 'the sex of literature' (for example, quizzes in which the readers are supposed to discover the 'sex' of the writers of different anonymous pieces). As the Catalan writer Marta Pessarrodona once rightly said:

> La literatura més que sexe, té gènere (masculí, femení), fonamentalment per raons socials. [Literature has gender (masculine, feminine), rather than sex, basically for social reasons]. (Serra, 76)

Some authors feel definitely uneasy about the appropriation of their condition as women writers by certain critics, and demand to be free from political burdens. Rejection of what is seen as narrow-minded feminism, an imposition rather than a personal option, is clear in the following words of Paloma Díaz-Mas:

> me resulta especialmente molesto que por el hecho de ser mujer te exijan que escribas en reivindicación femenina *[sic]* [...]. Me parece perfectamente lícito que algunas escritoras elijan como tema la

condición de la mujer, pero que no sea obligatorio porque eso me parece paternalismo por parte de las mujeres hacia las mujeres. Ya hemos estado bastante tuteladas durante siglos para que ahora nos vengan a tutelar los movimientos de liberación de la mujer. (Diéguez, 88)

These words are not far from what Suzanne Moore recently wrote *à propos* of the issue of women and their access to political power: 'Women want nothing more and nothing less than the privilege that men take for granted — that their gender is not constantly noted' (Moore, 6).

This is a claim which, in literary terms, is similar to that made by Puértolas, a writer who, on the other hand, has always insisted on favouring the androgynous approach (See Puértolas 1993, 155):

Lo perturbador es que de la mujer se espere, sobre todo eso, el peculiar punto de vista femenino. ¿No resulta raro que pensemos que no puede ser tan amplio y diverso como el punto de vista masculino? Porque hombres hay de todas clases. Escritores de todas clases. ¿Acaso las mujeres y, dentro de esta categoría, las escritoras, están condenadas a ser extremadamente parecidas? (Puértolas 1993, 60-1)

Puértolas touches on an important issue, that of an alleged single female experience, both in writing and history, which feminist criticism is increasingly challenging. Julia Kristeva had already stressed in 'Women's Time' (first published in 1979) the plurality of female expressions and preoccupations. As Helen Graham writes: 'Gender cannot denote a single experience because it is always bisected by socio-economic class and other competing cultural and political identities' (Graham and Labanyi, 183).

Chris Weedon, on the other hand, had acknowledged such a risk in women's literature:

the danger in formulating general laws about women's writing is that they render differences and contradictions invisible, differences which are at least as important as similarities and which tell us more about the precise discursive structuring of gender at any particular historical moment. (Weedon, 157)

But she also insisted that to study women's writing in isolation from male-authored books is beneficial for our understanding of patriarchy, since

The socially and historically produced concerns of women writers as depicted in fiction help to form a map of the possible subject positions

open to women, what they could say or not from within the discursive
field of femininity in which they are located. (Weedon, 157)

As Maggie Humm points out (2), the way something is spoken about reveals how
power relations operate. Socially- and historically-constructed gendered roles for
men and women reveal themselves through language. Critics such as Gonzalo
Navajas also advocate that women's literature needs to be treated separately because
of gender-based literary dissimilarities (the mainly French feminist 'reading for
difference' approach):

> Lo que justifica la autonomía del estudio de la literatura femenina es la
> especificidad de una estética dentro de la cual quedan interpeladas
> epistemológica y metodológicamente la literatura y la novela
> femeninas. Hay una distintividad del discurso femenino en general que
> afecta a la naturaleza del texto escrito por mujeres y que hace, además,
> que la textualidad femenina ocupe un emplazamiento especial dentro
> del paradigma de la literatura en general. (Navajas, 38)

However, it is not textual indications of women's, or men's, alleged essential
natures that we should be searching for, but the exposure of the social construction
of gender. Furthermore, it is not the author, nor a possible identification between the
author and the text, nor the author and the characters, that should be addressed, but
the text itself. And texts escape authorial control when they enter the reader's
domain. Since Roland Barthes certified 'the death of the author' in his influential
essay of the late sixties, and questioned once and for all unitary intentional
subjectivity and the notion of an author pre-ordaining possible interpretations of the
text, we understand that reading is a constantly deferred process of creating meaning,
an open, historically placed dialogue between the reader and the text. Readers
activate dormant intertextual presences, not always the result of the author's
intention, identify different discourses, and explore possible interpretations from
textual evidence. The post-structuralist approach, with its stress on the interactive
role of the reader and on intertextuality, challenges and diffuses the notion of
'authority'. Texts should be read as proposals rather than as authorial statements, and
the limits of interpretation are those imposed only by the reader or by the text itself.
    Rosa Montero's writing is exemplary in this. She refuses to call her own work
'feminist literature' (Davies 1993, 383), possibly to avoid pigeon-holing it [21] and
although her novels, short stories and journalistic work are too complex, ironic and
multi-layered to be interpreted simply as feminist tracts, they show particular
sensitivity to all kinds of discrimination, especially discrimination suffered by
women. Therefore we can read her from this perspective, as Catherine Davies does:

Fiction by women in Spain which articulates female experience is necessarily non-hegemonic. And if the writer supports the general objectives of the Women's Movement, that is, she critiques patriarchy and sexism, and questions the ideological underpinnings of femininity, if she is engaged in the transformation of dominant power relations in society and considers the practice of writing a means of doing this, then she is perforce a feminist writer. (Davies 1994, 5)

Whether we agree or not with Navajas when he says that '[es] la perspectiva genérico-sexual la que produce la especificidad estética, el elemento diferenciador con relación a formas convencionales vinculadas con una perspectiva humanista de raigambre masculina' (Navajas, 38), women writers enrich the plurality of alternative discourses because they carry with them a gender-branded history.

Postmodernism, with its decentering of hegemonic values, has allowed marginal voices to speak their differences. The activity of female writers is of crucial importance, not only 'when they perform the reflexive act of looking at themselves, an act of representation which legitimately collapses the distance between subject and object' (Pietropaolo and Testaferri, xi), but also because their increasing self-assurance and their access to certain mechanisms of cultural production are transforming the literary *status quo*, and this, in itself, is a development of historical relevance that needs to be acknowleged.

Cristina Peri Rossi, Uruguayan born but who has lived in Barcelona since 1972, thinks that the time has come 'para empezar a vender las transgresiones femeninas que, además, son transgresiones a normas que no han sido fijadas por ellas' (Peri Rossi, 5). Women's writing has the potential for trangression just by being there, by trying to share an equal space with the writings of a competitor whose only advantage is that he got there first.

THE CONTEMPORARY 'PROSE TALE':
A STORY OF PLURALITY AND FRAGMENTATION

The number of collections of Spanish short stories[22] published in the last decade reflects the amount of attention which the *genre* has received. This interest is to be attributed not to a comeback as such of this narrative form, but rather to the new critical awareness of it and the challenging way in which a significant number of Spanish authors are employing it.

Nowadays, when *genres* cross boundaries, blurring the differences that have traditionally existed among them, it might seem inappropriate to identify generic peculiarities for the short story; yet, since the underlining of its importance in

relation to the novel is still felt to be necessary to do it justice,[23] perhaps it is useful to deal with the issue again, however briefly.

A distinction has been established between the popular, usually fantastic tale, firmly rooted in the oral tradition — tales of anonymous origin included in medieval collections, or tales which have surpassed their creator's fame (Perrault, Andersen, Hoffman, the Grimm brothers) — and the modern short story that is clearly identified with an author. This distinction, though, between *cuento popular* and *cuento culto* may be seen as rather reductive. Fantasy, for example, once the domain of folk tales, has become a multifunctional strategy: 'esa inquietud que surge de lo cotidiano' (Fernández Cubas quoted in Moret 1994, 32), especially after the beneficial influence of Latin-American writers such as Jorge Luis Borges and Julio Cortázar. It is the textual space where natural and supernatural meet in Cristina Fernández Cubas, José María Merino or Juan José Millás, or the instrument for parody in Laura Freixas, to mention only some of the writers keen to explore the fantastic in unusual ways. A practice potentially subversive since, as Mary Eagleton points out, 'To query the truth, coherence and resolution of realism is to undermine the symbolic order' (Hanson, 58), a statement which could be related to the connection established by Hanson between the short story as the most appropriate *genre* to offer the other side of 'the official story', and fantasy as 'another mode of expression for repressed desire or knowledge' (Hanson, 6).

The literary history of the *cuento*, on the other hand, reflects the significance of the oral tradition and the close relationship between popular and authored short narrative. The first well-known collections of *cuentos* in fourteenth-century European literature kept the oral component as a narrative device to string the stories together, and provide evidence of how traditional tales, *fabliaux* (short narrative poems popular in France from the twelfth to the fourteenth century), fables and popular legends entered the world of the written word. In Boccacio's *Decameron* ten Florentines, after taking refuge from the plague in a villa outside the city, relate one tale each for ten days; in Chaucer's *Canterbury Tales* pilgrims on the road to Canterbury tell stories to entertain each other, and in Don Juan Manuel's *El Conde Lucanor* (or *Libro de los enxiemplos del Conde Lucanor et de Patronio*), different from both of these because of its oriental Jewish and Moslem influence, the young nobleman Lucanor seeks the advice of his steward Patronio, and is answered with *enxiemplos* (exemplary stories). The catharsis experienced by the listeners to the tales — which the reader shares too — in all these earlier collections is also present in some contemporary works such as *El cinturón traído de Cuba*, by Pilar Cibreiro. Soledad Puértolas finds a fascinating explanation for the origin of the *cuento* in its power to transform events rather than to chronicle them, and relates it to the oral tradition, to 'la necesidad fabuladora del hombre, acaso más fuerte que su necesidad de ser testigo de la realidad' (Puértolas 1991, 172).

In a debate on 'De cuentos y cuentistas', five well-known short-story writers (Ignacio Martínez de Pisón, Pedro Zarraluqui, Juan Miñana, Cristina Fernández

Cubas and Enrique Vila-Matas) agreed on the importance of orality in storytelling: 'Lo primero que yo recuerdo no es un libro, sino la narración de historias' (Fernández Cubas in Valls 1994, 5). As Walter Benjamin put it in 'The Storyteller': 'Experience which is passed on from mouth to mouth is the source from which all storytellers have drawn' (Benjamin, 94).

After those first medieval examples many Spanish authors — Cervantes and María de Zayas among them — turned to short narrative in the centuries which followed. It was in the nineteenth century, however, and thanks to the key role played by the press (regular sections in newspapers and magazines) that the *genre* blossomed. Gustavo Adolfo Bécquer, Emilia Pardo Bazán, Cecilia Böhl de Faber, Leopoldo Alas 'Clarín', Juan Valera, Armando Palacio Valdés and Pedro Antonio de Alarcón are among those writers whose short stories went a long way to gain literary respect for the *cuento literario*.[24]

At the turn of the century and until the early 1930s, the short story — together with the *novella* — was very much in fashion. The first book ever published by Pío Baroja, *Vidas sombrías* (1900), was a collection of *cuentos*, and Valle-Inclán won several prizes, not always without controversy, in the many *certámenes de cuentos* organized in those days; some of them were sponsored by periodicals such as *El Cuento Semanal* (1907-12), which awarded the prize to Gabriel Miró in 1907. The role of this successful publication in popularizing the genre and in providing a model for others of a similar kind — *Los Contemporáneos* (1909-26), *La Novela Corta* (1916), *La Novela Semanal* (1921-5), *La Novela Mundial* (1926-8), to name just a few — has been widely recognized.

At the same time, and along with older writers, some *avant-garde* figures such as Ramón Gomez de la Serna, Benjamín Jarnés or Samuel Ros were also devoted to the short story as were many women writers of different political persuasions who showed, possibly for the first time in Spanish literary history, a new professional, rather than just personal, approach to writing.[25]

But it was in the 1950s, when testimonial writing was the dominant trend and after a period of virtual stagnation, that the *genre* made a spectacular comeback. Realist novelists seemed to realise the potential of short narrative prose as a suitable form to 'portray' a *tranche de vie*, and some writers, such as Ignacio Aldecoa, Medardo Fraile or Daniel Sueiro, made their names through their quasi-exclusive dedication to the *cuento*. Other significant novelists who started writing stories in those years are Juan Benet, Rafael Sánchez Ferlosio, Alfonso Grosso, Juan García Hortelano, Juan Marsé, Jesús López Pacheco, Jesús Fernández Santos,[26] not forgetting an important group of women writers to whom we will refer later, and those living in exile since 1939 such as Max Aub, Francisco Ayala, Arturo Barea, Rosa Chacel, María Teresa León, Mercè Rodoreda, Ramón J. Sender and the Catalan writer Pere Calders, whose works produced abroad were not to be fully distributed in Spain until the arrival of democracy.

It could be argued that from the 1950s onwards the short story has not experienced any serious relapse, although it has proved difficult for the *genre* to achieve the same critical recognition as the novel. However, since the early 1980s the appeal of the short story for many authors of the so-called *nueva narrativa* has led to its renovation and made critics and public more aware of it. The favourable reception granted to it by both public and critics[27] should also be taken into account when discussing its present preeminence. And yet, it is still commonplace to complain that the short story is the Cinderella of narrative prose, and to bemoan the dearth of scholarly work it has inspired — although some exceptions are readily acknowledged, such as Baquero Goyanes's seminal study *El cuento español en el siglo XIX* (first published in 1949), Anderson Imbert's *Teoría y técnica del cuento* (1970), Erna Brandenberger's *Estudios sobre el cuento español contemporáneo* (1973), Catharina V. de Vallejo's *Teoría cuentística del siglo XX (Aproximaciones hispánicas)* (1989), or Ana Rueda's *Relatos desde el vacío* (1992).[28] Such observations are somewhat surprising since there are now clear signs of critical attention: journals publish monographic issues on the *cuento* (*Ínsula*, for instance, in 1988 and 1994 and *Las Nuevas Letras, República de las Letras* and *Monographic Review* also in 1988); [29] *Lucanor, Revista del cuento literario*, a journal devoted entirely to the short story, was launched in 1988 and is now well established; publishers (Aguaclara, Alfaguara, Anagrama, Cátedra, Hierbaola, Libertarias, Lumen, Sirmio / Quaderns Crema, Tusquets and so on) are increasingly less reluctant to endorse collections of short stories, especially by successful writers, who pave the way for others; newspapers and magazines also publish short stories thereby continuing a nineteenth-century practice which helped popularize the *genre*; and, most important, writers are turning to it with conviction.[30] Santos Alonso has noted that a writer's dedication to the *genre* is not an obstacle to achieving literary recognition (Alonso, 44), as proved among others by Mercedes Abad, Agustín Cerezales, Pilar Cibreiro, Cristina Fernández Cubas, Ignacio Martínez de Pisón, Quim Monzó, Antonio Pereira, María Eugenia Salaverri or Juan Eduardo Zúñiga. The writers themselves talk and write about the *genre*, as if they felt the need to persuade the reader of its value and to legitimize it once and for all. They do so by engaging in a combination of creative writing and aesthetic reflection pioneered by Edgar Allan Poe and used by other *cuentistas* in the Hispanic tradition, such as Pardo Bazán, 'Clarín', Julio Cortázar or Horacio Quiroga, which finds in Carmen Martín Gaite's *El cuento de nunca acabar* (1983) one of its finest contemporary examples.

In 1842, when reviewing Nathaniel Hawthorne's *Twice-Told Tales*, Poe listed some of the features he thought essential for the 'prose tale'. It required 'to be read at one sitting', 'from a half-hour to one or two hours in its perusal', because 'of the immense force derivable from *totality*' (Poe, 107). With no interruptions in the act of reading, he thought, 'the author is enabled to carry out the fullness of his intention' and 'the soul of the reader is at the writer's control' (108). Even if nowadays we are

rather skeptical about the validity of such statements, brevity — intrinsically related to the possibility of reading without interruptions — is the chief characteristic of this form of narrative. Brevity also suggests that the tautness of the language brings the short story closer to the poem, its selection of words being more demanding than in the novel. Poe's comment on Hawthorne's stories could be applied to the *genre* itself: 'Every word *tells*, and there is not a word which does *not* tell' (112).

This idiosyncratic trait of the short story is still the one that best defines it according to contemporary writers such as José María Merino, who believes the *cuento* to be 'narración pura, en que lo sintético predomina sobre lo analítico, que tiende a la máxima expresividad en el menor espacio dramático posible' (Merino, 21), or Antonio Muñoz Molina, who compares the short story to the sonnet, because of '[la] concentración absoluta y casi químicamente pura de sus normas, sus tareas y sus artificios' (Muñoz Molina, 152). The philosopher and writer Fernando Savater also claims that the *cuento* is

> *domus aurea* de la creación verbal, menos sujeto a la retórica que la poesía, más concentradamente intenso que la novela, sin los requisitos espectaculares del drama teatral, capaz de una complejidad de contenido que no alcanza ni el chiste ni el aforismo [...]. (Savater, 6)

'Short', though, could also imply different things to today's reader. It could imply 'fragmented', that is, the awareness of the impossibility of an undisputed, totalizing discourse. In 1906 Chesterton had already pointed out similarities between the brevity of the form and the modern experience of being alive:

> Our modern attraction to the short story is not an accident of form; it is a sign of a real sense of fleetingness and fragility; it means that existence is only an impression, and, perhaps, only an illusion. We have no instinct of anything ultimate and enduring beyond the episode. (Chesterton quoted in Shaw, 17)

Contemporary writers and critics have broadened this early perception of the short story and see it as the ideal literary form to translate the broken and multifaceted nature of experience: 'Su fragmentariedad casa bien con la sensibilidad contemporánea, formada en la percepción de elementos aislados' (José Antonio Millán quoted in Alonso, 44).

José Luis Martín Nogales, editor of *Lucanor*, focusses his analysis of the contemporary short story entirely on what he calls the 'teoría de la fragmentariedad'. As opposed to the multifaceted linguistic nature of the novel and the complexity of its diachronic progress, the short story offers just a glimpse, an enlightening but self-consciously limited perspective: 'si la novela es la reconstrucción de una globalidad, el cuento supone la captación de algo fragmentario' (Martín Nogales, 34). In the

twilight of ideologies 'el cuento se ha mostrado como el cauce literario adecuado para recoger los fragmentos dispersos de un mundo escindido' (34). Asked about the appropriateness of the *genre* to translate thematically and structurally today's world, the five writers mentioned above who commented on *cuentos* and *cuentistas* were of the same opinion. 'El cuento responde a esa versión fragmentaria de la realidad', said Martínez de Pisón, and Zarraluqui added: 'El ser fragmentario no le impide ser también muy global. [. . .] es un territorio realmente poderoso y lleno de misterio. Quizá por ello tiene esa extraña y leve relación con la poesía' (Valls 1994, 4).

As mentioned previously, narrativity has been, along with plurality, one of the most distinctive features of the *nueva narrativa española* since 1975. One of the literary critics of *El País* stated, perhaps too categorically, that: 'Los experimentalismos se baten en retirada, la metaficción ha dejado de tener el papel que tenía y, aun cuando el espectro temático sea variado, la narratividad impone sus líneas con firmeza' (García-Posada, 32).[31]

Among narrative *genres*, the short story is precisely the most ambitious in terms of its technical and thematic diversity as, given its high degree of self-consciousness, it easily accomodates all types of formal experimentation whilst sharing with the novel the ability to generate the enjoyment associated with the telling and reading of stories.

In 1990 Agustín Cerezales, one of the most innovative of short-story writers, described the situation thus:

> En España se escribe con más libertad que nunca [...]. No me refiero sólo a la libertad ideológica, sino a la estética. [...] No hay escuela que valga. El resultado es variedad, profusión, riesgo, respuesta acorde a la urgencia de la demanda. [...] Estamos inmersos en una espléndida aventura. (Cerezales quoted in Alonso, 45)

This adventure is made even more exciting by the influence of Latin-American writers, with their undisputed talent for storytelling. If novelists, with remarkable exceptions such as Eduardo Mendoza,[32] have been reluctant to accept that there has been a beneficial dialogue between Spanish and Latin-American narrative, most short-story writers (and novelists who are also short-story writers) pay constant tribute to Jorge Luis Borges, Alejo Carpentier, Adolfo Bioy Casares, Julio Cortázar, Carlos Fuentes, Mario Vargas Llosa, Gabriel García Márquez, Juan Carlos Onetti, Juan Rulfo and authors of the so-called 'boom' whose works have been published in Spain with enormous success since the 1960s, thanks to publishers such as Alianza, Salvat or Seix Barral. Fernando Valls acknowledges:

> Parece que nos reconciliamos con el género gracias a los hispanoamericanos [...]. Ellos nos mostraron un modelo mucho más

rico y brillante [...], que el cuento podía ser un género apropiado para
hablar del mundo contemporáneo. (Valls 1994, 4)

The diversity afforded by the *cuento* and its current 'expansión plural' (Carrillo,
9-11) have been made possible by the porosity of the *genre*, its readiness to absorb
new techniques and structural innovations. From stories which follow Poe's
preference for 'tales of effect' to those which incorporate elliptical cinematic
strategies, with surprising or unremarkable endings, either conforming to or
transgressing traditional models, contemporary short stories display a wide range of
executions.

COLLECTING THIS ANTHOLOGY

The stories collected in this anthology follow a rich and diverse tradition of female-
authored short-story writing which goes back to the seventeenth century and to the
short novels written by María de Zayas, and almost two centuries later, to Rosario de
Acuña, Emilia Pardo Bazán (the most prolific of nineteenth-century writers, with
more than five-hundred stories to her credit), Cecilia Böhl de Faber and María del
Pilar Sinués. Clare Hanson, stressing the suitability of the *genre* as the vehicle for an
alternative discourse, suggests that 'the short story has been from its inception a
particular appropriate vehicle for the expression of the ex-centric, alienated vision of
women' (Hanson, 3).[33] This notion could be confirmed by looking into the work of
women writers of the first decades of the twentieth century who turned to the short
story. Among these we find Caterina Albert (who used the male penname of 'Víctor
Català') and a young Mercè Rodoreda, both writing in Catalan, Carmen de Burgos
(whose favourite *nom de plume* was significantly a female one: 'Colombine'), Eva
Carmen Nelken (hers was 'Magda Donato'), Concha Espina, Sofía Casanova,
Blanca de los Ríos, Margarita Nelken, Pilar Millán Astray, Federica Montseny,
María Teresa León, as well as the contributions of Rosa Chacel's *cuentos* in *Revista
de Occidente*, and those of María de la O Lejárraga (who signed most of her works
with her husband's name, 'Gregorio Martínez Sierra') to the popular periodical *El
Cuento Semanal*.
     After the Spanish Civil War writers such as Carmen Martín Gaite or Ana María
Matute, who at the beginning of their careers were associated with *realismo social*,
successfully cultivated the *genre*, as did many others, such as Josefina (Rodríguez)
Aldecoa, Concha Alós, Eulalia Galvarriato, Carmen Kurtz, Carmen Laforet, Dolores
Medio, Elisabeth Mulder, Marta Portal, Elena Quiroga and Elena Soriano. Over the
last twenty years the short story has appealed to almost every woman writer, and
female author and generic form have become allied in the struggle to achieve
unreserved literary recognition.

Diversity and eclecticism are indeed the main features of Spanish women's short-story writing and they should be enough to counter any essentialist or prescriptive views on it. However, it is worth noting that a greater number of female central characters, female narratorial voices and female internal focalizations are found in woman-authored texts, a fact which has a clear impact on the way many issues are dealt with. Although by no means a female prerogative, further common ground is to be observed in the preference of some authors to write short stories for children, an activity in which Gloria Fuertes, Carmen Martín Gaite, Ana María Matute, Rosa Montero, Lourdes Ortiz and Soledad Puértolas, among others, have excelled.

Contemporary women writers have made the most of the *cuento*'s generic technical flexibility, as evidenced by those selected for this collection. They display a wide range of narrative strategies which include: first person narrators (Abad, Fernández Cubas, Díaz-Mas, García Morales, Puértolas, Salaverri); narratorial voices with internal focalization (Freixas, Ortiz, Torres); stream of consciousness techniques, underlining the absence of any intervening narratorial voice (Mayoral); ironically detached narrators (Abad, Montero); stories with linear structures (Díaz-Mas, García Morales, Montero) or circular structures (Torres); stories with unexpected endings (Abad, Díaz-Mas), closed endings (Fernández Cubas) or open endings (Cibreiro, Freixas, García Morales, Mayoral, Montero, Ortiz, Puértolas, Salaverri, Torres); metafictional narratives which defamiliarize cultural conventions (Ortiz) or use parody to subvert generic ones (Freixas); evocative stories with no plot (Cibreiro) or with a clear dramatic unity (Fernández Cubas); stories where anecdote is central to the diegetic progress towards 'effect' (Abad, Fernández Cubas, Díaz-Mas) or those where anecdote is at the service of a character's paradigmatic situation (Freixas, García Morales, Mayoral, Montero, Ortiz, Puértolas); stories in which the linearity of events enhances the suspense of a magical atmosphere (Fernández Cubas) and those in which the immediacy of linearity is used for testimonial purposes (García Morales, Montero).

Plurality is equally obvious when literary tradition and familiar themes and motifs are intertextually explored in order to convey new concerns: realist and testimonial tales coexist with fantastic ones, meditations on the nature of fiction and textuality cohabit with psychological introspections or decentered discourses on women and history.

This anthology offers representative examples also of the thematic diversity of the contemporary *cuento*. It includes stories which use fantasy as an instrument to gain access to a child's perspective and to the enigmatic side of experience (Fernández Cubas), and those in which fantasy becomes a feminist strategy (Freixas); testimonial stories exploring the margins of a ruthless society where no compassion is shown towards poverty and homelessness (García Morales) or old age (Montero); self-referential narratives in which intertextual presences are both highlighted and questioned in order to make new polemical or subversive statements, either by revising literary myths from a feminist perspective (Ortiz), by

humorously incorporating literary references as part of a character's memory (Freixas), or by using artistic ones — a painting — to draw attention to the impossible quest for any lasting fulfilment, and to the importance of the way something — or somebody — is looked at in a story which could be read as a metaphor for the reader's interactive role (Díaz-Mas).

There are stories with middle-aged, alienated female characters who, after a lifetime of serving everyone except themselves and having outgrown their role as wife and mother, overcome the demonizing labels of 'frustrated women' and 'social outcast' in different ways: by angrily refusing sexual conformity and passive domesticity (Ortiz), by leaving home — the space of inner-exile — and seeking a new centre, a new life away from an oppressive existence which has gradually become empty (Torres), or by voicing their unhappiness almost tenderly, by 'writing her body' (Mayoral), although, ultimately, the private rebellions of these three female characters are hindered by the same cultural structures that they refuse to conform to.

There are stories about couples, all of them told by a female narrator who is an ironic, but not altogether detached observer (Abad), an observer who is much more involved than at first appears (Puértolas), or the wife who endures the contradictions and infidelities of the husband (Salaverri); uncompromising yet unromanticized love stories where women find themselves swept away by prevailing male fantasies (Abad), powerless because traditional rules of sexual behaviour give men the privilege of initiative (Puértolas), or trapped in a routine that nevertheless leads to epiphanic moments of self-discovery (Salaverri); stories of lost and unrequited love, sometimes collectively fantasized (Cibreiro), or with irretrievable moments of fulfilment experienced by a male narrator (Díaz-Mas); stories where issues of troubled identities and the search for the self are paramount, either embodying the equation of memory and identity in one individual character (Freixas), in a collective one (Cibreiro), with characters who struggle to identify an imaginary self beyond experiences inflicted upon them (Salaverri), or with characters trying to resist imposed values (García Morales, Mayoral, Ortiz, Torres).

Finally, the emphasis on multiple and dynamic perspectivism confirms the postmodern conviction that events and characters are constructed through language, in plural and unfixed discourses.

Juan José Millás once said that every tale leads to another through a secret door (quoted by Fernández Cubas in Moret 1994, 32). This is especially evident in an anthology, where stories gathered together establish unprecedented links between each other: similarities are underlined, alternative strategies confront each other, a multi-layered perspective on comparable issues emerges, differences are celebrated and ultimately the reader has the power to explore any possible passage from one text to another, interconnecting threads, themes and preoccupations.

The twelve authors included in this anthology, all of them associated with the post-transition years, provide a sample of young, or relatively young, contemporary

Spanish women writers. Nevertheless, the collection is inevitably selective. Excellent writers had to be excluded — not only the great names already known before 1980, but also interesting new ones, such as Luisa Castro, Belén Gopegui, Almudena Grandes, Ana María Navales, Beatriz Pottecher, Clara Sánchez or Mercedes Soriano, to name but a few. It is difficult to find a reason other than limited space.

Attempts to apply objective criteria were made when preparing the book: a) diversity of the authors (writers with different professional backgrounds: journalism, teaching, and so on; writers from different parts of Spain, some also publishing in Catalan or Galician; writers with an already established reputation selected alongside others with only one promising book); b) formal and thematic variety of the stories; c) period in which the stories were first published (the 1980s and early 1990s); d) language in which the stories were originally written (in spite of the variety of regions represented by the authors, all the stories selected were first written in Spanish: this is a bilingual collection and it seemed fitting to reproduce the original in *lenguaje creado,* rather than in a Spanish translation).

In addition to these objective criteria, personal preference and enjoyment also played a key role in the selection process, an enjoyment it is hoped will be shared with the readers of this book.

Comprehensive introductory notes and selected bibliographies are provided for every author. However, the number of items in these vary considerably according to author's age, the number of books published and the amount of academic attention she has attracted. A few titles dealing with more than one author are included in every relevant 'further reading' list, to make it easy for further research.

The stories are presented in chronological order. There is only one exception: 'Días de lluvia'. This story, which gives the book its title, is the one that is situated at the beginning because it so fittingly evokes both the power of literature to create worlds with words and the oral tradition of storytelling — a tradition in which women have been so instrumental.

NOTES

1   This current situation is mainly due to two factors: first, women in Spain, as in many other
     countries, have been more actively involved in literary production than in any other area
     of cultural production (see Weedon, 144; Graham and Labanyi, 383-4), and secondly,
     reading is Spanish women's main cultural activity, in which they are far ahead of men,
     according to an invaluable survey carried out by the sociologist Enrique Gil Calvo
     (1992a), *La era de las lectoras: El cambio cultural de las mujeres españolas*. This is an
     important study whose conclusions coincide with several opinion polls on the subject
     published by the Spanish press, and also with a survey carried out by the magazine *Lire* on
     the femininization of reading habits in France (quoted in Serra, 75). Gil Calvo highlights
     some relevant findings, like the fact that even at the 'turning point' (58) of women's life,
     when they become mothers, and most of their other cultural activity is affected, their
     book-reading rates do not seem to decrease at all, along with evidence about 'la evidente
     superioridad del menú cultural de las activas respecto a los activos' (92) or figures which
     show the undeniable reality of the 'inequívoco avance que supone el desarrollo
     modernizador del comportamiento cultural femenino' (49).

2   The issue is also addressed by Brown in 'Women Writers of Spain: An Historical
     Perspective', in *Women Writers of Contemporary Spain: Exiles in the Homeland* (1991,
     13-25).

3   See Janet Pérez (1988, 1-7) for bibliography on earlier accounts of Spanish women
     writers.

4   See the poem by Anne Finch, Countess of Winchelsea, quoted in Sandra Gilbert and
     Susan Gubar (3).

5   Enrique Gil Calvo (1992b) analizes the social and economic reasons which directly
     reinforce discrimination at home and in the workplace (different salaries according to the
     worker's sex: an average of 25% less for women, as recent figures published by the ILO
     show; unequal opportunities for promotion; unequal allocation of job perks, and so on),
     preventing a more egalitarian distribution of tasks and keeping women and men trapped in
     the vicious circle of patriarchy.

6   Those publishers whose criteria have not been purely commercial, but literary or political
     (Anthropos, La Sal, Lumen, Tusquets), have also played an important role in the diffusion
     of women's writing.

7   The first women who started publishing after the Civil War had been born in the 1920s
     and early 1930s. They were brought up in a country which, with all its failures and
     political turmoil, was not the one that emerged after 1939 where the main role assigned to
     women was to stay at home and look after the family. This may account for women's
     early presence in the literary scene in spite of the hostile environment. This suggestion,
     already made by María del Carmen Riddel (7), coincides with José-Carlos Mainer's clever
     redistribution of the periodization of post-Civil War Spanish literature in *De postguerra
     (1951-1990)*:

> En algún lugar he negado que la contienda de 1936 sea mojón de un nuevo período cultural:
> tras el final de las batallas y hasta 1950, más o menos, he creído ver que se extiende un
> período soterradamente epigonal cuyas claves se asientan en los años republicanos.
> (Mainer, 9)

8   Joan L. Brown gives useful percentages of the number of female authors and pages
    dedicated to them in the most consulted histories of twentieth-century Spanish literature
    published between 1956 (29 pp. out of 815) and 1985 (120 pp. out of 440). (1990, 554)
9   Apart from those journals which are dedicated to women's literature, like *Letras
    Femeninas*, or the recent *Lectora. Revista de dones i textualitat* (Universitat Autònoma de
    Barcelona), several others have published monographic issues on Spanish women writers:
    > *Litoral* 169-170 (1986)
    > *Anales de la Literatura Española Contemporánea* 12/1-2 (1987)
    > *Ventanal* 14 (1988)
    > *Revista de Estudios Hispánicos* 22 (1988)
    > *Revista Canadiense de Estudios Hispánicos* 14/3 (1990)
    > *Monographic Review* 8 (1992)
    > *Ínsula* 557 (1993)
    > *Quimera* 123 (1994)
    > *Bulletin of Hispanic Studies* 72 (1995)

    A considerable number of multi- or single-authored books dealing with different women
    writers or with the representation of women in literature has also been published in recent
    years, the most significant being:
    > Concha Alborg, *Cinco figuras en torno a la novela de posguerra: Galvarriato, Soriano,
    >   Formica, Boixadós y Aldecoa* (Madrid, 1993).
    > Isolina Ballesteros, *Escritura femenina y discurso autobiográfico en la nueva novela
    >   española* (New York, 1994).
    > Joan L. Brown (ed.), *Women Writers in Contemporary Spain. Exiles in the Homeland*
    >   (Newark, London and Toronto, 1991).
    > Lou Charnon-Deutsch, *Gender and Representation: Women in Spanish Realist Fiction*
    >   (Amsterdam, 1990).
    > ———, *Narratives of Desire: Nineteenth-Century Spanish Fiction by Women*
    >   (Pennsylvania, 1994).
    > ———and Jo Labanyi (eds), *Culture and Gender in Nineteenth-Century Spain* (Oxford,
    >   1995).
    > Lisa Condé and Stephen M. Hart (eds), *Feminists Readings on Spanish and Latin-American
    >   Literature* (Lewiston, Queenstown and Lampeter, 1991).
    > Catherine Davies, *Contemporary Feminist Fiction in Spain. The Work of Montserrat Roig
    >   and Rosa Montero* (Oxford and Providence, USA, 1994).
    > Myriam Díaz-Diocaretz and Iris M. Zavala (eds), *Breve historia feminista de la literatura
    >   española (en lengua castellana)*, (Barcelona and Madrid) [two volumes published to
    >   date: *Teoría feminista* (1993) and *La mujer en la literatura española. Modos de
    >   representación desde la Edad Media hasta el siglo XVII* (1995)].
    > María Ángeles Durán and M. D. Temprano, 'Mujeres, misóginos y feministas en la literatura
    >   española' in *Actas de las IV Jornadas de Investigación Interdisciplinaria* (Madrid and
    >   Zaragoza, 1986), 412-484.
    > Elena Gascón Vera, *Un mito nuevo: La mujer como sujeto/objeto literario* (Madrid, 1992).
    > Francisca López, *Mito y discurso en la novela femenina de posguerra en España* (Madrid,
    >   1995).
    > Roberto C. Manteiga, Carolyn Galerstein and Kathleen McNerney (eds), *Feminine Concerns
    >   in Contemporary Spanish Fiction by Women* (Potomac, MD, 1987).
    > María Jesús Mayans, *Narrativa feminista española de posguerra* (Madrid, 1991).
    > Beth Miller (ed.), *Women in Hispanic Literature. Icons and Fallen Idols* (Berkeley, 1983).
    > Geraldine C. Nichols, *Escribir, espacio propio: Laforet, Matute, Moix, Tusquets, Riera y
    >   Roig por sí mismas* (Minneapolis, 1989).
    > ———, *Des/cifrar la diferencia: Narrativa femenina de la España contemporánea* (Madrid,
    >   1992).
    > Elizabeth Ordóñez, *Voices of Their Own. Contemporary Spanish Narrative by Women*
    >   (Lewisburg, London and Toronto, 1991).
    > María del Carmen Riddel, *La escritura femenina en la postguerra española* (New York,
    >   1995).

Elizabeth A. Scarlett, *Under Construction. The Body in Spanish Novels* (Charlottesville and London, 1994).
Noël Valis and Carol Maier (eds), *In the Feminine Mode. Essays on Hispanic Women Writers* (Lewisburg, London and Toronto, 1990).
[The list does not include the numerous articles on the subject in journals specializing in Hispanic studies.]
There have also been contributions on Spanish women writers in books or journals with a European approach:

Biruté Ciplijauskaité, 'Lyric Memory, Oral History, and the Shaping of the Self in Spanish Narrative', in *Forum for Modern Language Studies*, 24/4 (1992) [monographic issue dedicated to *The Language of a Thousand Tongues: Contemporary European Fiction by Women*, ed. and with a 'Foreword' by C. Davies].
Catherine Davies, 'Feminists Writers in Spain since 1900: From Political Strategy to Personal Enquiry', in Helena Forsås-Scott (ed.), *Textual Liberation. European Feminist Writing in the Twentieth Century* (London, 1991), 192-226.

and studies with a similar trans-national scope:

Biruté Ciplijauskaité, *La novela femenina contemporánea (1970-1985). Hacia una tipología de la narración en primera persona* (Barcelona, 1988).

[See also Bibliography on every single author included in this anthology.]

10 As far as the number of pages is concerned, it is difficult to be precise since some of the authors are mentioned only once and often among contemporaries with whom they share some characteristics, therefore it cannot be said that the page is dedicated to one of them.

11 The volume also refers to books published between 1975 and 1990 by writers who were known before 1975 and who, strictly speaking, were not 'new names'.

12 Bearing in mind that the volume was published in 1992, before new writers such as Enriqueta Antolín, Gabriela Bustelo, María Ángeles Caso, Maite Dono, Susana Fortes, Belén Gopegui, María Eugenia Salaverri, Ana Santos, and others were known, the most striking absences are those of Maruja Torres, who had already published her first satirical novel in the 1980s and was a leading figure in Spanish journalism, and Carme Riera, who is mentioned four times always in relation to her scholarly work while nothing is said about her creative writing (other Catalan writers translated into Spanish are mentioned: Mercè Rodoreda, Montserrat Roig). Other possible names which could have been included are Aurora de Albornoz, Gloria Fuertes, Carmen Gómez Ojea, Julia Ibarra, Elena Martín Vivaldi, María Luz Melcón, Concha Lagos, Elena Santiago, Elena Soriano, Acacia Uceta, Arantxa Urretavizcaya and Concha Zardoya, all of them with books published between 1975 and 1990 which are neither more nor less important than those by some of their male counterparts which merited inclusion.

13 According to J.M. Calvo (1995, 18), the world's number of women MPs reached in 1988 its highest point since the struggle for female suffrage began: 14,8%. In 1995 it was reduced to 11,3%, in spite of the encouraging fact that female presence in parliaments is four times what it was in 1945 (figures, though, must have improved with the spectacular increase in the number of women MPs in the British Parliament after the May 1997 General Election). The situation in Spain as far as the number of women in key positions of power is concerned has never been exemplary, but now, after the Conservative Partido Popular won the general election in March 1996, it has definitely worsened:

José María Aznar ha presumido de que en su Consejo de Ministros hay cuatro mujeres [but] el PP no ha nombrado a ninguna secretaria de Estado [all 21 are men] y sólo a dos directoras generales [27 are men] y 12 secretarias generales. El último Gobierno de Felipe González tenía tres ministras, cinco subsecretarias de Estado, tres subsecretarias y 38 directoras generales. (Casqueiro 1996, 22)

14 Carmen Conde, a poet of the so called *Generación de 1936*, was appointed to replace the playwright Miguel Mihura in 1978, and she became the first woman ever to be a member of the Real Academia de la Lengua, to be followed by Elena Quiroga in 1984. After Conde's death in January 1996 she was replaced by the novelist Ana María Matute, but female presence in the institution is still intolerably scarce.

15 She refers to Geraldine C. Nichols's *Escribir, espacio propio: Laforet, Matute, Moix, Tusquets, Riera y Roig por sí mismas* (1989). Nichols's comments are not dissimilar to Brown's in this respect. Elizabeth J. Ordóñez also addresses the issue and draws the conclusion that '[a] number of well-known and respected studies of contemporary Spanish fiction during the last two decades seemed uneasy about where or how to include works by women' (Ordóñez, 15).

16 See Lou Charnon-Deutsch (1-12) for a highly interesting discussion of the notion of canon, this 'unstable concept determined by political and social contingencies, religious and moral beliefs, literary and aesthetic tastes, and, especially, the dynamics of a literary economic system' (3).

17 Both Monica Threlfall (1985) and Catherine Davies (1994) have competently addressed the issue.

18 See her article 'La primavera socialista, a pesar de todo', *El País*, 24 February 1996, published during the 1996 Spanish General Election campaign.

19 For further reading on the situation of women before, under and after Franco, see:

Concha Borreguero, et al., *La mujer española: de la tradición a la modernidad (1960-1980)* (Madrid, 1986).
Anny Brooksbank Jones, 'Women, Politics and Social Change in Contemporary Spain', *Tesserae*, 1/2 (1995), 277-294.
María Rosa Capel, *El trabajo y la educación de la mujer en España (1900-1931)* (Madrid, 1982).
Lidia Falcón, *Mujer y poder político* (Madrid, 1992).
Pilar Folguera (ed.), *El feminismo en España: Dos siglos de historia* (Madrid, 1988).
Helen Graham and Jo Labanyi (eds), *Spanish Cultural Studies: An Introduction. The Struggle for Modernity* (Oxford and New York, 1995).
Olga Kenyon, 'Women under Franco and PSOE: The Discrepancy Between Discourse and Reality', in Bernard McGuirk and Mark I. Millington (eds), *Inequality and Difference in Hispanic and Latin American Cultures* (Lewiston, Queenstown and Lampeter, 1995).
Carmen Martín Gaite, *Usos amorosos de la postguerra española* (Barcelona, 1987).
Monica Threlfall, 'The Women's Movement in Spain', *New Left Review*, 151 (1985), 44-73.

20 By no means homogeneous (some literary historians even prefer to distinguish between *neorrealismo* and *realismo social), realismo* encompassed young writers of the generation of 1950, for whom the Civil War had been a childhood experience and were generally committed to social and political change, and those of the generation of 1936, who experienced the Civil War as young adults, some of them on Franco's side, such as Camilo José Cela — a novelist with aesthetical rather than social concerns — or writers of a Christian persuasion, such as Miguel Delibes.

21 An understandable reluctance since certain Spanish critics tend to be overzealous when it comes to labelling and packaging authors.

22 Some anthologies are notable for the comprehensive list of contemporary authors included:

Ángeles Encinar and Anthony Percival (eds), *Cuento español contemporáneo* (Madrid, 1993).

Joséluis González and Pedro de Miguel (eds), *Últimos narradores: Antología de la reciente narrativa breve española* (Pamplona, 1993).

Juan Ramón Masoliver (ed.), *The Origins of Desire* (London, 1993).

Fernando Valls (ed.), *Son cuentos* (Madrid, 1993).

Among the anthologies of stories written by women, and after the pioneering example of *Doce relatos de mujeres,* by Ymelda Navajo (ed.), (Madrid, 1982) the most significant are:

Ángeles Encinar (ed.), *Cuentos de este siglo* (Barcelona, 1995).

Laura Freixas (ed.), *Madres e hijas* (Barcelona, 1996).

23 See Fietta Jarque, 'Varios autores celebran en El Escorial el auge del cuento', *El País*, 7 August 1966.

24 Literary criticism on the nineteenth-century Spanish short story is abundant, but I would especially recommend the following titles:

Mariano Baquero Goyanes, *El cuento español en el siglo XIX,* (Madrid, 1949). [There is a revised edition by Ana L. Baquero Escudero: *El cuento español: del Romanticismo al Realismo* (Madrid, 1992).

Lou Charnon-Deutsch, *The Nineteenth-Century Spanish Story: Textual Strategies of a Genre in Transition* (London, 1985).

25 For further reading on the Spanish short story in the decades prior to the Civil War, see:

Ángela Ena Bordonada (ed.), *Novelas breves de escritoras españolas 1900-1936* (Madrid, 1989).

Lily Litvak, *El cuento anarquista* (Madrid, 1982).

José María Martínez Cachero (ed.), *Antología del cuento español 1900-1939* (Madrid, 1982).

Federico Carlos Sáinz de Robles, *La promoción de"El Cuento Semanal"* (Madrid, 1975).

26 See the following anthologies for good collections of mid-20th century short stories:

Medardo Fraile (ed.), *Cuento español de posguerra* (Madrid, 1992).

Alicia Redondo Goicoechea (ed.), *Relatos de novelistas españolas (1939-1969)* (Madrid, 1993).

27 Unusual for collections of short stories, the ones recently published by Javier Marías, *Cuando fui mortal* (Madrid, 1996) and Almudena Grandes, *Modelos de mujer* (Barcelona, 1996), as well as the one mentioned above edited by Laura Freixas, have been in the best-seller lists for weeks.

28 Critical theory on the short story is more abundant in the Anglo-Saxon tradition. The following titles may provide useful further reading for those interested in the *genre*:

Rosa M. Grillo de Filippo, *Racconto spagnolo. Appunti per una teoria del racconto e le sue forme* (Salerno, 1985).

Clare Hanson (ed.), *Re-reading the Short Story* (New York, 1989).

Peter Fröhlicher and Georges Güntert (eds), *Teoría e interpretación del cuento* (New York, 1995).

Susan Lohafer, *Coming to Terms with the Short Story* (Baton Rouge and London, 1983).

—— and Jo Ellyn Clarey (eds), *Short Story Theory at a Crossroads* (Baton Rouge and London, 1989)

Charles E. May (ed.), *Short Story Theories* (Athens, Ohio, 1976).
————, *The New Short Story Theories* (Athens, Ohio, 1994).
Vladimir Propp, *Morphologie du conte* (Paris, 1970).
Ian Reid, *The Short Story* (London and New York, 1977).
Valerie Shaw, *The Short Story: A Critical Introduction* (London and New York, 1992).

29 *Ínsula,* issues 495 and 568, respectively; *Las Nuevas Letras,* 8; *República de las Letras,* 22; *Monographic Review,* vol IV.

30 Fernando Valls and Nuria Carrillo (1991) carried out a survey on the number of collections of short stories published in Spanish in Spain between 1975 and 1990, and came up with figures which clearly indicate a progression: 12 in 1975, 33 in 1989 and 32 in 1990.

31 Although the tendency highlighted by García-Posada seems to be the dominant one, it would be wrong to conclude that the explicitly metafictional novel has gone out of fashion: the influential Nadal Prize for 1997 has been awarded to Carlos Cañeque for the novel *Quién*, 'un juego metaliterario a la sombra de Borges [que] reflexiona sobre la literatura y la autoría de los libros' (Moret 1997, 30).

32 See Miguel Riera, 'El caso Mendoza. Entrevista', *Quimera*, 66-67 (n.d.), 42-7.

33 See Mary Eagleton's discussion of 'Gender and Genre' in *Re-reading the Short Story*, edited by Clare Hanson (55-68).

REFERENCES

Alberola   Miquel Alberola, '"El masclisme és interclassista"' [Interview with Marina Subirats], *El Temps*, 27 June 1994, 38-41.

Alonso   Santos Alonso, 'Poética del cuento. Los escritores actuales meditan sobre el género', *Lucanor* 6 (1991), 43-54.

Anderson Imbert Enrique Anderson Imbert, *Teoría y técnica del cuento* (Buenos Aires, 1970).

Baquero Goyanes Mariano Baquero Goyanes, *El cuento español en el siglo XIX* (Madrid, 1949).

Barthes   Roland Barthes, 'The Death of the Author', in *Image—Music—Text*, trans. by S. Heath (London, 1977), 142-8.

Benjamin   Walter Benjamin, 'The Storyteller', in *Illuminations*, trans. by H. Zohn (London, 1992), 83-107.

Brandenberger   Erna Brandenberger, *Estudios sobre el cuento español contemporáneo* (Madrid, 1973).

Brown 1990   Joan L. Brown, 'Women Writers in Spanish Literary History: Past, Present and Future', *Revista Canadiense de Estudios Hispánicos*, 14/3 (1990), 553-60.

Brown 1991   Joan L. Brown (ed.), *Women Writers of Contemporary Spain: Exiles in the Homeland* (Newark, London and Toronto, 1991).

Cano   Soledad Cano, '"El giro a la derecha supone un retroceso": Adelaida García Morales', *Cambio 16*, 25 March 1996, 100-1.

Calvo   José M. Calvo, 'El número de mujeres parlamentarias en el mundo es menor que hace siete años', *El País*, 28 August 1995.

Carmona et al. Vicente Carmona, Jeffrey Lamb, Sherry Velasco and Barbara Zecchi, 'Conversando con Mercedes Abad, Cristina Fernández Cubas y Soledad Puértolas: "Feminismo y literatura no tienen nada que ver" ', *Mester*, 20/2 (1991), 157-65.

Carrillo   Nuria Carrillo, 'La expansión plural de un género: el cuento 1975-1993', *Ínsula*, 568 (1994), 9-11.

Casqueiro   Javier Casqueiro, 'Escaparate de mujeres', *El País*, 26 May 1996.

Charnon-Deutsch Lou Charnon-Deutsch, *Narratives of Desire: Nineteenth-Century Spanish Fiction by Women* (Pennsylvania, 1994).

Chicharro Chamorro Antonio Chicharro Chamorro, 'Del periodismo a la novela', *Ínsula*, 589-590 (1996), 14-7.

Davies 1993   Catherine Davies, 'Entrevista a Rosa Montero (Madrid, 22 de enero de 1993)', *Journal of Hispanic Research*, 1/3 (1993), 383-8.

Davies 1994   Catherine Davies, *Contemporary Feminist Fiction in Spain. The Work of Montserrat Roig and Rosa Montero* (Oxford and Providence, USA, 1994).

Diéguez   María Luz Diéguez, 'Entrevista con Paloma Díaz-Mas', *Revista de Estudios Hispánicos,* 22/1 (1988), 77-91.

28   REFERENCES

Ena Bordonada   Ángela Ena Bordonada, *Novelas breves de escritoras españolas (1900-
                 1936)* (Madrid, 1989).
Fidalgo   Feliciano Fidalgo, 'Laura Freixas, Soledad, Almudena, Clara... escritoras',
                 El País, 25 February 1996.
Freixas   Laura Freixas, 'Prólogo', in *Madres e hijas* (Barcelona, 1996), 11-20.
García-Posada   Miguel García-Posada, 'Nuevos paradigmas', *El País*, 6 January 1995.
Gil Calvo 1992a Enrique Gil Calvo, *La era de las lectoras: El cambio cultural de las
                 españolas* (Madrid, 1992).
Gil Calvo 1992b Enrique Gil Calvo, 'A cargo del hogar', *El País*, 24 December 1992.
Gilbert and Gubar Sandra M. Gilbert and Susan Gubar, *The Madwoman in the Attic: The
                 Woman Writer and the Nineteenth-Century Literary Imagination* (New
                 Haven and London, 1979).
Gould Levine et al. Linda Gould Levine, Ellen Engelson Marson and Gloria Feiman Waldman
                 (eds), *Women Spanish Writers: A Bio-Bibliographical Source Book*
                 (Westport, CT and London, 1993).
Gracia   Jordi Gracia, 'Novela y cultura en el fin de siglo', *Ínsula*, 589-590, (1996),
                 27-30.
Graham and Labanyi Helen Graham and Jo Labanyi (eds), *Spanish Cultural Studies: An
                 Introduction. The Struggle for Modernity* (Oxford and New York, 1995).
Hanson   Clare Hanson (ed.), *Re-reading the Short Story* (New York, 1989).
Herzberger   David K. Herzberger, 'History, Apocalypse, and the Triumph of Fiction in
                 the Post-War Spanish Novel', *Revista Hispánica Moderna*, 44 (1991),
                 247-58.
Humm   Maggie Humm, *Border Traffic: Strategies of Contemporary Women
                 Writers* (Manchester and New York, 1991).
Ínsula   *Ínsula*, 557 (1993) [monographic issue dedicated to *Mujeres del 27*].
Kirkpatrick   Susan Kirkpatrick (ed.), *Antología poética de escritoras del siglo XX*
                 (Madrid, 1992).
Kristeva   Julia Kristeva, 'Women's Time', in *The Kristeva Reader*, ed. by Toril Moi
                 (Oxford, 1987), 187-213.
Mainer   José-Carlos Mainer, *De postguerra (1951-1990)* (Barcelona, 1994).
Martín Gaite   Carmen Martín Gaite, *El cuento de nunca acabar (Apuntes sobre la
                 narración, el amor y la mentira)* (Barcelona, 1983).
Martín Nogales   José Luis Martín Nogales, 'De la novela al cuento: el reflejo de una
                 quiebra', *Ínsula*, 589-590 (1996), 33-5.
Merino   José María Merino, 'El cuento: narración pura', *Ínsula*, 495 (1988), 21.
Moore   Suzanne Moore, 'If I whirled the rules...', *The Guardian*, 19 July 1996.
Moret 1994   Xavier Moret, 'Cristina Fernández Cubas relata "la inquietud que surge de
                 lo cotidiano" ', *El País*, 14 May 1994.
Moret 1997   Xavier Moret, 'Carlos Cañeque gana el Premio Nadal con un juego
                 metaliterario a la sombra de Borges', *El País*, 7 January 1997.
Muñoz Molina   Antonio Muñoz Molina, 'Contar cuentos', *Lucanor*, 6 (1991), 152.
'Narradores de hoy' [unassigned] 'Narradores de hoy', *El Urogallo*, 2 (1986), 18-25.
Navajas   Gonzalo Navajas, 'Narrativa y género. La ficción actual desde la mujer',
                 Ínsula, 589-590 (1996), 37-9.
Navarro   Ana Navarro, 'La mujer y el nuevo paradigma', *El País*, 12 August 1993.

REFERENCES

Ordóñez	Elizabeth J. Ordóñez, *Voices of Their Own: Contemporary Spanish Narrative by Women* (Lewisburg, London and Toronto, 1991).
Pereda	Rosa Pereda, 'El pensamiento posfeminista', *El País* (Babelia), 23 October 1993.
Pérez 1988	Janet Pérez, *Contemporary Women Writers of Spain* (Boston, MA, 1988).
Pérez 1996	Janet Pérez, *Modern and Contemporary Spanish Women Poets* (New York, 1996).
Peri Rossi	Cristina Peri Rossi, 'Escribir como transgresión', *Lectora*, 1 (1995), 3-5.
Pietropaolo and Testaferri	Laura Pietropaolo and Ada Testaferri (eds), *Feminisms in the Cinema* (Bloomington and Indianapolis, 1995).
Poe	Edgar Allan Poe, *The Complete Works of Edgar Allan Poe*, ed. by James A. Harrison, vol.XI (New York, 1965).
Porter	Phoebe Porter, 'Conversación con Lourdes Ortiz', *Letras Femeninas*, 15/1-2 (1990), 139-44.
Puértolas 1991	Soledad Puértolas, 'La gracia de la vida, la inmortalidad', *Lucanor*, 6 (1991), 172.
Puértolas 1993	Soledad Puértolas, *La vida oculta* (Barcelona: 1993).
Riddel	María del Carmen Riddel, *La escritura femenina en la postguerra española* (New York, 1995).
Rueda	Ana Rueda, *Relatos desde el vacío* (Madrid, 1992).
Savater	Fernando Savater, 'Cuentos', *El País Semanal*, 13 August 1984, 6.
Serra	Montserrat Serra, 'Llegir, verb de dona', *El Temps*, 20 November 1995, 74-7.
Shaw	Valerie Shaw, *The Short Story: A Critical Introduction* (London and New York, 1992).
Showalter	Elaine Showalter, *A Literature of Their Own: From Charlotte Brontë to Doris Lessing* (London, 1991) [1st ed. 1977].
Soldevila-Durante	Ignacio Soldevila-Durante, 'Sobre la escritura femenina y su reivindicación en el conjunto de la historia de la literatura contemporánea en España. (A propósito de un reciente libro de Janet Pérez)', *Revista Canadiense de Estudios Hispánicos*, 14/3 (1990), 606-22.
Threlfall	Monica Threlfall, 'The Women's Movement in Spain', *New Left Review*, 151 (1985), 44-73.
Torres	Maruja Torres, 'Luchas de mujer', *El País Semanal*, 9 June 1996, 10.
Vallejo	Catharina V. de Vallejo, *Teoría cuentística del siglo XX (Aproximaciones hispánicas)* (Miami, 1989).
Valls and Carrillo	Fernando Valls and Nuria Carrillo, 'El cuento español actual. Cronología', *Lucanor*, 6 (1991), 83-92.
Valls 1994	Fernando Valls, 'De últimos cuentos y cuentistas', *Ínsula*, 568 (1994), 3-6.
Villanueva	Darío Villanueva (ed.), *Los nuevos nombres: 1975-1990*, vol. IX, *Historia y Crítica de la Literatura Española*, ed. by Francisco Rico (Barcelona, 1992).
Weedon	Chris Weedon, *Feminist Practice and Poststructuralist Theory* (Oxford, 1987).

PILAR CIBREIRO

PILAR CIBREIRO was born in 1952 in the Galician town of Vilaboa. She has lived in El Ferrol and London and is now based in Madrid. She writes poetry in Galician and has published two collections of poems, *O vasalo da armadura da prata* [*El vasallo de la armadura de plata*] (1987) and *Feitura do lume* [*Hechura del fuego*] (1994), although she is better known for her prose fiction in Spanish.

Cibreiro's first book, *El cinturón traído de Cuba* (1985), is a collection of short stories which, according to one critic, can be described as 'la memoria de una Galicia ausente', the Galicia of a century ago. Due to its increasing reputation, *El cinturón traído de Cuba* has become a major work of reference in the collective memory of Galicians and compulsory reading in many Galician schools. The stories from *El cinturón* have been translated into French and Italian and some of them have appeared in three German anthologies. They also feature prominently in recent collections of contemporary Spanish short-story writing.

The *cuento* which has been selected for this Anthology is the one which gives it its title. The pre-television days of the small Galician village, whose collective biography is narrated throughout the stories of *El cinturón traído de Cuba*, could also be the *rainy days* of many characters who people other stories of this present collection. *Rainy Days* reminds us of the oral tradition of storytelling passed on from generation to generation, the verbal strategy of keeping memories alive whilst they are slowly woven into a fabric of fiction. Pilar Cibreiro is currently preparing a new edition of the book with her own illustrations.

In 1990 Pilar Cibreiro published *Arte de acecho*, a novel set in seventies London in which a young Galician female narrator embarks on a journey of self-discovery. She has also published some stories in magazines and academic journals, for example 'Pilar de Campos', in *Ínsula*, 469 (1986), 16.

36

FURTHER READING ON PILAR CIBREIRO

Azancot, Leopoldo, 'El cinturón traído de Cuba', ABC, 22 June 1985.

Carrillo, Nuria, 'La expansión plural de un género: el cuento 1975-1993', Ínsula, 568 (1994), 9-11.

Couceiro, Mario, 'Pilar Cibreiro y su cinturón traído de Cuba', La Voz de Galicia, 9 May 1985.

Díez, Luis Mateo, 'Biografía de una aldea', Guía del Ocio, 5 August 1985, 38.

Encinar, Ángeles, 'Tendencias en el cuento español reciente', Lucanor, 13 (1995), 103-18.

Fajardo, José Manuel, 'Narradores para el fin de siglo', Cambio 16, 21 October 1985, 130-6.

G., J., 'Deixalo chover: El cinturón traído de Cuba', Cambio 16, 10 June 1985, 183.

González, Juan Manuel, 'La narrativa española, o el auge deseado de lo nuevo', El Urogallo, 60 (1991), 24-31.

González Gómez, Xesus, 'Las razones de un descubrimiento', Quimera, 46-47 (1985), 108.

M., N., 'Tierras de la memoria: El cinturón traído de Cuba', El País (Libros), 16 June 1985.

Mayrata, Ramón, 'Más allá de la bruma', La Gaceta del Libro, 15 May 1985, 5.

Morales Villena, Gregorio, 'Tres nuevos autores: Infancia y primera novela', Ínsula, 473 (1986), 5.

Obiol, María José, 'El juego de las similitudes y las diferencias. Madurez en el oficio de contar', El País (Libros), 28 July 1985.

—————, 'Pilar Cibreiro, ecos de La Habana en Vilaboa', La Gaceta del Libro, 15 May 1985, 4-5.

Reyzábal, María Victoria, 'El cinturón traído de Cuba. Primera andadura narrativa', Reseña, 159 (1985), 10.

Sánchez Arnosi, Milagros, 'El cinturón traído de Cuba', Ínsula, 468 (1985), 19.

Talbot, Lynn K., 'Entrevista con Pilar Cibreiro', Letras Peninsulares, 2/3 (1989), 435-40.

Valls, Fernando, 'El renacimiento del cuento en España (1975-1990)', Lucanor, 6 (1991), 27-42.

Rainy Days

Días de lluvia

Original Spanish text from
El Cinturón traído de Cuba (Madrid: Alfaguara 1985), 56-9.

Días de lluvia

¡ Cuánto se aprendía de la lluvia y del paso de sus días, de la calma que imponía y de su silencio, sólo interrumpido por el goteo del agua sobre los tejados, los charcos y los árboles!
Llovía durante muchos días, mansamente y sin cesar. La humedad formaba una cortina de vapor que se espesaba a lo lejos hasta nublar el horizonte de los campos y las colinas, oscureciéndolo y envolviéndolo todo en su neblinoso velo gris.
Dentro de la casa, al abrigo del fuego, alguien desgranaba las doradas espigas del maíz y con los granos iban cayendo las palabras hasta formar historias que yo recogía con ávida fruición y también, alguna vez, con espanto.
Historias de mujeres que lucharon con hombres y vencieron, de amantes sorprendidos en la pasión culminante, de huidas y saltos por la ventana con la ropa en la mano, de burlas en los *Antroidos, esfollas* y *fías*; relatos de escarceos juveniles en los pajares y en los caminos, de agravios, de venganzas, de amor y de desamor, de galanteos, de mozas orgullosas y bien plantadas, de galanes valientes y de bonita voz; historias de emigrantes, de su fortuna y de su fracaso, relatos de visiones, difuntos y aparecidos, de jóvenes suicidas y mujeres poseídas por un espíritu extraño; relatos que hablaban de la vida y de la muerte, entremezcladas.
Cuando me cansaba de palabras subía al fayado a explorar lo ignoto: muebles y ropas caídas en desuso, arcas repletas de trigo que escondían en

Rainy Days

How much we learned from the rain and the passing of rainy days, from the sense of calm it instilled and from its silence, broken only by the steady drip of water onto rooftops, into puddles, onto trees!

It would go on raining for days at a time, gently and on and on. The dampness would form a curtain of vapour which grew thicker in the distance, shutting out the light of the sun from the horizon of fields and hills and casting everything into darkness, enveloping all around in a grey misty veil.

Inside the house, warm near the fireside, someone was stripping the grains from golden ears of maize, and as the grains fell so did words, tumbling on until they became stories which I would glean with avid enjoyment and, occasionally, fear.

Stories about women who fought with men and won, of lovers surprised at the height of their passion, escaping and leaping through windows, clothes in hand, the jokes in the *Antroidos, esfollas* and *fías*;[1] tales of young lovers' fumblings in hay lofts and in country lanes; tales of people wronged, of revenge, about falling in and out of love, of courtships, and haughty fine-looking girls, of brave and handsome young men with silken voices; stories about emigrants, their good fortunes and their failures; tales of visions, the dead and apparitions, of young suicides and women possessed by spirits; stories that spoke of life and death, all jumbled together.

When I grew tired of words I'd climb up to the lumber room at the top of the house to explore the unknown – pieces of furniture and old clothes fallen

---

[1] *Antroidos, esfollas* **and** *fías:* Three Galician words which mean Carnival *(Antroidos)*, the rituals and parties which accompany the stripping of maize leaves *(esfollas)*, and the celebrations which take place at the time of the flax harvest *(fías)*.

su morena superficie la invitación de las nueces y manzanas allí guardadas, la persecución de los ratones, las casas y caminos vecinos vistos desde lo alto y tamizados por la llovizna y los libros, sobre todo los libros.

Había varios de Historia y de Gramática, unos con ilustraciones en blanco y negro y otros en color, pero el más dotado de magia era un libro de viajes redactado en forma epistolar. Cada carta ofrecía un modelo distinto de letra —gótica, inglesa— y otras que no sabía diferenciar, ni siquiera descifrar. Se hablaba allí de los diferentes países y razas, en los dibujos aparecían las calles de Singapur o los minaretes de Tánger, a cada lugar le correspondía su estampa. Libros todos que me descubrían otros mundos lejanos y desconocidos, otras tierras, otras gentes, otras palabras.

Había también revistas de la época traídas por no sé quién. Allí, abandonadas entre viejos colchones de pluma de maíz, entre los bolillos para el encaje y los chalecos raídos, estaban las imágenes de Gary Cooper y su esposa en viaje a España; el Che fumando un puro descomunal cuando era ministro en Cuba y todavía no había sido ensalzado y devorado por el mito, años más tarde; Brigitte Bardot —la melena espesa y rubia, los pantalones blancos y ajustados—, y Mao rodeado de un montón de chinos idénticos e indiferenciables.

El desván estaba lleno de cosas misteriosas y tentadoras. Afuera la lluvia y la niebla eran también un misterio indescifrable.

into disuse, wooden chests full of wheat, their dark surfaces hiding the appetizing walnuts and apples carved there, hunting for mice, the houses and neighbouring roads viewed from on high and filtered through a haze of rain. And the books, above all the books.

There were a number of History and Grammar books, some of them with illustrations in black and white, others in colour, but the one most endowed with magic was a travel book written as a series of letters, each presented in a different typeface – gothic script, roman type – and others I couldn't identify or even decipher. The letters told me about different countries, different races. The illustrations depicted the streets of Singapore or the minarets of Tangiers, each place having its own illustration. All these books opened up distant, unknown worlds to me, other lands, other peoples, other words.

There were also some magazines of the period, but I never knew who'd left them there. Lying where they'd fallen among old mattresses stuffed with corn silks, among the lace-making bobbins and threadbare waistcoats, were pictures of Gary Cooper[2] and his wife on a visit to Spain; Che[3] smoking an enormous cigar in the days when he was still a minister in Cuba, before he'd been elevated and devoured by the myth years later; Brigitte Bardot[4] —the thick cloud of blonde hair, her trousers white and close fitting— and Mao,[5] surrounded by a crowd of Chinese, all dressed the same and wearing identical expressions.

The attic was full of tempting, mysterious objects. And outside, the rain and the mist were another unfathomable mystery.

---

[2]   **Gary Cooper:** US born film actor (1901-61). A star for thirty years and winner of two Oscars for Best Actor, he received a Special Academy Award in 1960 for his many celebrated performances, most of them as the archetypal hero of Westerns.

[3]   **Che:** Ernesto Che Guevara (1928-67). Born in Argentina, he fought in the Cuban Revolution (1956-9), and then he held government posts under Fidel Castro until 1965, when he left Cuba to become a guerrila leader in South America. He was killed in Bolivia.

[4]   **Brigitte Bardot:** French film actress born in 1934. She was an international sex-symbol for fifteen years after her success in *Et Dieu créa la femme* (1956), directed by her husband at the time, Roger Vadim. She is well known for her commitment to the cause of endangered animal species.

[5]   **Mao:** Mao Zedong or Mao Tse-tung (1893-1976). Leader and main theorist of the Chinese Communist Revolution which won national power in China in 1949. He held the posts of Chairman of the Chinese Communist Party and President of the People's Republic of China until his death. He is associated with policies to develop rural industry and provide infrastructure for agriculture, and with the Cultural Revolution, which he launched in 1966 as a radical mass movement to prevent the Chinese Revolution from stagnating.

Llovía morosamente y la humedad lo impregnaba todo: el cuerpo, las paredes, los objetos. Si salíamos las zuecas chapoteaban y se hundían en el suelo mojado, en los caminos embarrados.

Dentro, en los hogares, se desgranaban las espigas y, a su ritmo, seguían cayendo las palabras, pacientes, lentas, repetidas. Eran las mismas historias una y otra vez, como un cuento siempre nuevo e interminable.

No se salía al campo en esos días. Sólo Antonio da Farruca, encapuchado en un saco de esparto, recorría febrilmente su regadío con la azada en la mano y desatascaba regatos o abría nuevos senderos de agua, indiferente a la lluvia, a la semioscuridad del día, al letargo.

De él se decía que emigrando a Cuba muy mozo se enamoró allá de una mulata habanera y que ella no lo quiso. Y Antonio regresó, loco de amor, trastornado para siempre por el desdén de la cubana.

Desde hacía años pasaba por los caminos inaccesible y vestido de remiendos —no lo trataba bien la Farruca, su madre— o recogía colillas a la puerta de "La Maravilla" desconociendo a todos sus vecinos, portando en su caminar de mendigo atolondrado un enigma imposible.

Alto y pacífico, Antonio, el del triste Viaje Sin Suerte y el del Amor Sin Fortuna, el que todo lo hacía con prisa, ensimismado y movido por un secreto furor, mientras hablaba a Mercedes, la perdida al otro lado del mar y recobrada luego en la locura, su mulata hermosa y fatal, nuestra mulata de figura ignorada y por algunos maldecida.

It rained gently but steadily, and the dampness permeated everything: your body, the walls, the things around you. If we went out our wooden clogs would squelch and sink into the wet earth and the muddy paths.

Inside the houses, ears of corn were stripped, and words —patient, slow, repetitive— would come tumbling out to the same rhythm. They were the same stories over and over again, like a tale that was forever new and unending.

Nobody would go out into the fields on rainy days. Only Antonio da Farruca went out, covering himself with a sack made of esparto grass, feverishly plying his way back and forth across his plot of land, hoe in hand, unblocking the channels for the water to flow, or making new ones, indifferent to the rain, the half darkness of the day, and the lethargy.

People said he'd emigrated to Cuba as a very young boy and fallen in love with a *mulata* from Havana, who didn't requite his love. Antonio had returned home, crazy with love, his life forever turned upside down by the Cuban girl's disdain.

For years he'd just drifted around in a world of his own, dressed in rags —la Farruca, his mother, didn't look after him— picking up cigarette stubs in the doorway of "La Maravilla" and ignoring his neighbours, carrying around with him an impossible enigma, in his confused beggar's wanderings.

Tall and unaggressive, Antonio, the man of the Great Misadventure, the man who was Unlucky in Love, the one who did everything in a rush, lost in a dreamworld and driven by a secret fever while he talked to Mercedes, the girl he lost on the other side of the ocean and then, in his madness, won back again, his beautiful and deadly *mulata*, our *mulata*, of the unknown countenance, cursed by some.

CRISTINA FERNÁNDEZ CUBAS
Photograph © Jerry Bauer

CRISTINA FERNÁNDEZ CUBAS was born in 1945 in Arenys de Mar, a seaside town near Barcelona. After studying Law and Journalism she spent some time travelling and living abroad. In 1973 she went to South America and stayed there for two years. She first published two books of short stories, *Mi hermana Elba* (1980), very well received by both public and critics, and *Los altillos de Brumal* (1983), which confirmed her preference for setting events in an ambivalent space, where the natural seems to meet the supernatural and the fantastic requires the involvement of the reader's imagination. Her first novel, *El año de Gracia* (1985), was an adventure story which plays intertextually with *Robinson Crusoe* and one where parody and metafiction perform a decisive role. She continued her exploration of the fantastic as a particular kind of anxiety emerging from ordinary objects, people and events of everyday life in two new collections of stories, *El ángulo del horror* (1990) and *Con Ágatha en Estambul* (1994). They have established Fernández Cubas as a leading figure among those Spanish writers whose dedication to the *cuento* has contributed to the perception of it as a *genre* in its own right, as younger short-story writers such as Ignacio Martínez de Pisón have publicly recognized.

In *El columpio* (1995), her latest novel, Fernández Cubas goes back to some of her recurrent themes: the lasting power of dreams and childhood memories. She has also published other short stories in anthologies and periodicals, including 'Algunas de las muertes de Eva Andrade', in *Gimlet*, 3/5/1981, 26-33; 'Omar, amor', in *Doce relatos de mujeres*, edited by Ymelda Navajo (1982), translated into English and included in the collection edited by J. A. Masoliver, *The Origins of Desire* (1993); and the autobiographical text, 'Elba: el origen de un cuento', in *Lucanor*, 6 (1991), 113-6, of which the story included in this volume is reminiscent.

FURTHER READING ON CRISTINA FERNÁNDEZ CUBAS

Alborg, Concha, 'Cuatro narradoras de la transición', in Ricardo Landeira and Luis T. González del Valle (eds), *Nuevos y novísimos. Algunas perspectivas críticas sobre la narrativa española desde la década de los 60* (Boulder, COL, 1987), 11-27.

Amorós, Andrés, 'Penúltimas novelistas', *ABC*, 19 September 1981.

Asís Garrote, Ma. Dolores de, *Última hora de la novela en España,*(Madrid, 1996).

Ayala-Dip, J. Ernesto, 'El deseo de seducir: cinco relatos cortos de Cristina Fernández Cubas', *El País* (Babelia), 21 May 1994.

Azancot, Leopoldo, 'Aires nuevos: 1984-1985', in Darío Villanueva (ed.), *Los nuevos nombres: 1975-1990* (Barcelona, 1992), 392-3.

Bellver, Catherine G. , 'Two New Women Writers From Spain', *Letras Femeninas*, 8/2 (1982), 3-7.

——————, 'El año de Gracia and the Displacement of the Word', *Studies in Twentieth-Century Literature,* 16/2 (1992), 221-32.

——————, 'El año de Gracia: El viaje como rito de iniciación', *Explicación de Textos Literarios*, 22/1 (1993-4), 3-10.

Bretz, Mary Lee, 'Cristina Fernández Cubas and the Recuperation of the Semiotic in *Los altillos de Brumal*', *Anales de la Literatura Española*, 13/3 (1988), 177-88.

Carmona, V., J. Lamb, S. Velasco and B. Zecchi, 'Conversando con Mercedes Abad, Cristina Fernández Cubas y Soledad Puértolas: "Feminismo y literatura no tienen nada que ver"', *Mester*, 20/2 (1991), 157-65.

Carrillo, Nuria, 'La expansión plural de un género: el cuento 1975-1993', *Ínsula,* 568 (1994), 9-11.

Encinar, Ángeles, 'Escritoras españolas actuales: una perspectiva a través del cuento', *Hispanic Journal,* 13/1 (1992), 181-91.

——————, 'Tendencias en el cuento español reciente', *Lucanor*, 13 (1994), 103-8.

Fajardo, José Manuel, 'Narradores para el fin de siglo', *Cambio 16*, 21 October 1985, 130-6.

García Ortega, Adolfo, 'Españoles traducidos. Hacia la normalización', *El Urogallo*, 23 (1988), 10-3.

Glenn, Kathleen M., 'Authority and Marginality in Three Contemporary Spanish Narratives', *Romance Languages Annual*, 2 (1990), 426-30.

——————, 'Gothic Indecipherability and Doubling in the Fiction of Cristina Fernández Cubas', *Monographic Review*, 8 (1992), 125-41.

——————, 'Back to Brumal: Fiction and Film', *Romance Languages Annual*, 4 (1992), 460-5.

——————, 'Conversación con Cristina Fernández Cubas', *Anales de la Literatura Española Contemporánea,* 18/2 (1993), 355-63.

Gleue, Julie, 'The Epistemological and Ontological Implications in Cristina Fernández Cubas' *El año de Gracia'*, *Monographic Review*, 8 (1992), 142-56.

Goñi, Javier, 'Propuestas (en español) para una primavera', *El Urogallo*, 48 (1990), 43-5.

Ingenschay, Dieter and Hans-Jörg Neuschafer (eds), *Abriendo caminos. La literatura española desde 1975* (Barcelona, 1994).

Lottini, Otello, 'Il segni del tempo: la letteratura spagnola del post-franchismo', in *Diálogo. Studi in onore de Lore Terracini* (Roma, 1990), vol.I, 311-26.

Margenot, John B., 'Parody and Self-Consciousness in Cristina Fernández Cubas' *El año de Gracia'*, *Siglo XX/20th Century*, 11/1-2 (1993), 71-87.

Moret, Xavier, 'Cristina Fernández Cubas relata "la inquietud que surge de lo cotidiano"', *El País*, 14 May 1994.

Murillo, Enrique, 'Introducción', in Cristina Fernández Cubas, *El año de Gracia. Mi hermana Elba* (Barcelona, 1992), 7-13.

Núñez Esteban, Carmen and Neus Samblancat Miranda, 'Los espejos del yo en la narrativa de Cristina Fernández Cubas', *Lectora*, 1 (1995), 89-93.

Obiol, María José, 'El juego de las similitudes y las diferencias. Madurez en el oficio de contar', *El País* (Libros), 28 July 1985.

——————, 'El sueño de la mujer despierta: Cristina Fernández Cubas reaparece con cuatro cuentos cinco años después', *El País* (Libros), 10 June 1990.

——————, 'La escritora y el secreto: Cristina Fernández Cubas vuelve a la novela con *El columpio'*, El País (Babelia), 25 March 1995.

Ortega, José, 'La dimensión fantástica en los cuentos de Fernández Cubas', *Monographic Review*, 8 (1992), 157-63.

Pérez, Janet, *Contemporary Women Writers of Spain* (Boston, MA, 1988), 170-1.

Reboiras, Ramón F., ' "Cada historia es volver a empezar": Con *Agatha en Estambul* [sic] vuelve otra vez Cristina Fernández Cubas, una de las narradoras más personales y fantásticas de los últimos tiempos', *Cambio 16*, 30 May 1994, 95.

Rueda, Ana, 'Cristina Fernández Cubas: una narrativa de voces extinguidas', *Monographic Review*, 4 (1988), 257-67.

Salado, Ana, 'Entrevista a Cristina Fernández Cubas', *La Gaceta del Libro*, 22 May 1985, 6.

Sarret, Josep, 'Cuatro nuevos valores de la narrativa en castellano', *Quimera*, 6 (1981), 51-4.

Suñén, Luis, 'La realidad y sus sombras: Rosa Montero y Cristina Fernández Cubas', *Ínsula*, 446 (1984), 5.

Talbot, Lynn K., 'Journey Into the Fantastic: Cristina Fernández Cubas' *Los altillos de Brumal'*, *Letras Femeninas*, 15/1-2 (1989), 37-47.

Valls, Fernando, 'El renacimiento del cuento en España (1975-1990)', *Lucanor*, 6 (1991), 27-42.

—————, 'De últimos cuentos y cuentistas', *Ínsula*, 568 (1994), 3-6.

—————, 'De las certezas del amigo a las dudas del héroe: Sobre "La ventana en el jardín", de Cristina Fernández Cubas', *Ínsula*, 568 (1994), 18-9.

Zatlin, Phyllis, 'Tales from Fernández Cubas: Adventure in the Fantastic', *Monographic Review*, 3/1-2 (1987), 107-18.

—————, 'Amnesia, Strangulation, Hallucination and Other Mishaps: The Perils of Being a Female in Tales of Cristina Fernández Cubas', *Hispania*, 79/1 (1995), 36-44.

The Clock from Baghdad

El reloj de Bagdad

Original Spanish text from
Mi hermana Elba y Los altillos de Brumal
(Barcelona: Tusquets, 1988), 115-130; first ed. 1983.

El reloj de Bagdad

Nunca las temí ni nada hicieron ellas por amedrentarme. Estaban ahí, junto a los fogones, confundidas con el crujir de la leña, el sabor a bollos recién horneados, el vaivén de los faldones de las viejas. Nunca las temí, tal vez porque las soñaba pálidas y hermosas, pendientes como nosotros de historias sucedidas en aldeas sin nombre, aguardando el instante oportuno para dejarse oír, para susurrarnos sin palabras: "Estamos aquí, como cada noche". O bien, refugiarse en el silencio denso que anunciaba: "Todo lo que estáis escuchando es cierto. Trágica, dolorosa, dulcemente cierto". Podía ocurrir en cualquier momento. El rumor de las olas tras el temporal, el paso del último mercancías, el trepidar de la loza en la alacena, o la inconfundible voz de Olvido, encerrada en su alquimia de cacerolas y pucheros:

—Son las ánimas, niña, son las ánimas.

Más de una vez, con los ojos entornados, creí en ellas.

¿Cuántos años tendría Olvido en aquel tiempo? Siempre que le preguntaba por su edad la anciana se encogía de hombros, miraba por el rabillo del ojo a Matilde y seguía impasible, desgranando guisantes, zurciendo calcetines, disponiendo las lentejas en pequeños montones, o recordaba, de pronto, la inaplazable necesidad de bajar al sótano a por leña y alimentar la salamandra del último piso. Un día intenté sonsacar a Matilde. "Todos los del mundo", me dijo riendo.

La edad de Matilde, en cambio, jamás despertó mi curiosidad. Era vieja también, andaba encorvada, y los cabellos canos, amarilleados por el agua de colonia, se divertían ribeteando un pequeño moño, apretado como una

The Clock from Baghdad

I was never afraid of them, nor did they ever do anything to frighten me. They were just there, next to the kitchen range, mingling with the crackle of the firewood, the taste of bread rolls fresh from the oven, the swish of the old women's skirts. I was never afraid of them, perhaps because in my dreams I pictured them as pale and lovely, hanging like us on the thread of tales set in nameless villages, waiting until the time was right to make themselves heard, to whisper wordlessly to us: "Here we are, just like every night." Or else take refuge in the heavy silence that would presage: "Everything you're listening to is true. Tragically, painfully, sweetly true." It could happen at any minute. The low murmur of the waves after the storm, the passing of the last goods train, the rattle of the crockery in the larder, or the unmistakable voice of Olvido, locked away in her alchemy of pots and pans:

"They're the souls of the dead, child, the souls of the dead.'

More than once, my eyes half closed, I believed in them.

How old would Olvido have been at that time? Whenever I asked her about her age the old lady would shrug her shoulders, cast a sideways glance at Matilde, and carry on impassively shelling peas, darning socks, arranging lentils in little heaps, or would suddenly remember some all-pressing need to go down to the cellar for firewood and stoke up the central-heating stove on the top floor. One day I tried pumping Matilde for some information. "All the years in the world," she told me, laughing.

Matilde's age, on the other hand, never aroused my curiosity. She too was old, she walked with a stoop, and her white hair, stained yellow by eau de cologne, joyously peeped from the edges of a little bun, tight as a ball,

bola, por el que asomaban horquillas y pasadores. Tenía una pierna renqueante que sabía predecir el tiempo y unas cuantas habilidades más que, con el paso de los años, no logro recordar tan bien como quisiera. Pero, al lado de Olvido, Matilde me parecía muy joven, algo menos sabia y mucho más inexperta, a pesar de que su voz sonara dulce cuando nos mostraba los cristales empañados y nos hacía creer que afuera no estaba el mar ni la playa, ni la vía del tren, ni tan siquiera el Paseo, sino montes inaccesibles y escarpados por los que correteaban hordas de lobos enfurecidos y hambrientos. Sabíamos —Matilde nos lo había contado muchas veces— que ningún hombre temeroso de Dios debía, en noches como aquéllas, abandonar el calor de su casa. Porque ¿quién, sino un alma pecadora, condenada a vagar entre nosotros, podía atreverse a desafiar tal oscuridad, semejante frío, tan espantosos gemidos procedentes de las entrañas de la tierra? Y entonces Olvido tomaba la palabra. Pausada, segura, sabedora de que a partir de aquel momento nos hacía suyos, que muy pronto la luz del quinqué se concentraría en su rostro y sus arrugas de anciana dejarían paso a la tez sonrosada de una niña, a la temible faz de un sepulturero atormentado por sus recuerdos, a un fraile visionario, tal vez a una monja milagrera... Hasta que unos pasos decididos, o un fino taconeo, anunciaran la llegada de incómodos intrusos. O que ellas, nuestras amigas, indicaran por boca de Olvido que había llegado la hora de descansar, de comernos la sopa de sémola o de apagar la luz.

Sí, Matilde, además de su pierna adivina, poseía el don de la dulzura. Pero en aquellos tiempos de entregas sin fisuras yo había tomado el partido de Olvido, u Olvido, quizá, no me había dejado otra opción. "Cuando seas mayor y te cases, me iré a vivir contigo." Y yo, cobijada en el regazo de mi protectora, no conseguía imaginar cómo sería esa tercera persona dispuesta a compartir nuestras vidas, ni veía motivo suficiente para separarme de mi familia o abandonar, algún día, la casa junto a la playa. Pero Olvido decidía siempre por mí. "El piso será soleado y pequeño, sin escaleras, sótano ni azotea." Y no me quedaba otro remedio que ensoñarlo así, con una amplia cocina en la que Olvido trajinara a gusto y una gran mesa de madera con tres sillas, tres vasos y tres platos de porcelana... O, mejor, dos. La compañía del extraño que las previsiones de Olvido me adjudicaban no acababa de encajar en mi nueva cocina. "Él cenará más tarde", pensé. Y le saqué la silla a un hipotético comedor que mi fantasía no tenía interés alguno en representarse.

through which bobby pins and hairgrips poked out. She had a gammy leg which knew how to forecast the weather and a number of other skills as well, which, as the years have gone by, I can no longer remember as clearly as I'd like. But compared with Olvido, Matilde seemed much younger to me, not quite as wise and much more inexperienced, in spite of the fact that her voice sounded soft whenever she pointed out the steamed-up windows to us and made us believe there was no sea outside, nor any beach, nor any train track, not even the Paseo, but only craggy and inaccessible mountains over which packs of rabid and hungry wolves roamed. We knew — Matilde had told us so time and again — that no God-fearing man should abandon the warmth of his hearth on nights like that. For who but a sinful soul, condemned to wander amongst us, would dare defy such darkness, such cold, such terrifying groans from the bowels of the earth? And then Olvido would take up the tale. Slowly, deliberately, confident and aware that from that moment on she would hold us in the palm of her hand, that very soon the light of the oil lamp would focus on her face and the wrinkles of the old woman would turn into the apple blossom skin of a child, the terrible face of a grave digger tormented by his memories, a visionary friar, perhaps some miracle-working nun... Until firm footsteps or clicking heels would announce the arrival of some tiresome intruder. Or that they, our friends, using Olvido as a mouthpiece, would suggest it was time for us to rest, to eat our bland soup made with semolina or time to put out the light.

Yes, Matilde, in addition to her prophesying leg, possessed the gift of gentleness. But in those days of wholehearted commitment, I had taken Olvido's side, or perhaps Olvido had left me with no other option. "When you're older and get married, I'm going to live with you." And, sheltered in the lap of my protectress, I couldn't imagine what that would be like, a third person wanting to share our lives, or see a good enough reason to move away from my family or some day to abandon the house next to the beach. But Olvido always decided for me. "The flat will be sunny and small, with no stairs, no basement and no roof terrace." And there was nothing else for it but to dream of it like that, with a spacious kitchen where Olvido would bustle about to her heart's content, and a big wooden table with three chairs, three glasses and three china plates... Or better still, two. The company of the outsider assigned to me in Olvido's prophesies didn't quite fit into my new kitchen. "He'll have his dinner later," I thought. And I removed his chair to a hypothetical dining room my imagination had no interest whatsoever in conjuring up.

Pero en aquel caluroso domingo de diciembre, en que los niños danzaban en torno al bulto recién llegado, me fijé con detenimiento en el rostro de Olvido y me pareció que no quedaba espacio para una nueva arruga. Se hallaba extrañamente rígida, desatenta a las peticiones de tijeras y cuchillos, ajena al jolgorio que el inesperado regalo había levantado en la antesala. "Todos los años del mundo," recordé, y, por un momento, me invadió la certeza de que la silla que tan ligeramente había desplazado al comedor no era la del supuesto, futuro y desdibujado marido.

Lo habían traído aquella misma mañana, envuelto en un recio papel de embalaje, amarrado con cordeles y sogas como un prisionero. Parecía un gigante humillado, tendido como estaba sobre la alfombra, soportando las danzas y los chillidos de los niños, excitados, inquietos, seguros hasta el último instante de que sólo ellos iban a ser los destinatarios del descomunal juguete. Mi madre, con mañas de gata adulada, seguía de cerca los intentos por desvelar el misterio. ¿Un nuevo armario? ¿Una escultura, una lámpara? Pero no, mujer, claro que no. Se trataba de una obra de arte, de una curiosidad, de una ganga. El anticuario debía de haber perdido el juicio. O, quizá, la vejez, un error, otras preocupaciones. Porque el precio resultaba irrisorio para tamaña maravilla. No teníamos más que arrancar los últimos adhesivos, el celofán que protegía las partes más frágiles, abrir la puertecilla de cristal y sujetar el péndulo. Un reloj de pie de casi tres metros de alzada, números y manecillas recubiertos de oro, un mecanismo rudimentario pero perfecto. Deberíamos limpiarlo, apuntalarlo, disimular con barniz los inevitables destrozos del tiempo. Porque era un reloj muy antiguo, fechado en 1700, en Bagdad, probable obra de artesanos iraquíes para algún cliente europeo. Sólo así podía interpretarse el hecho de que la numeración fuera arábiga y que la parte inferior de la caja reprodujera en relieve los cuerpos festivos de un grupo de seres humanos. ¿Danzarines? ¿Invitados a un banquete? Los años habían desdibujado sus facciones, los pliegues de sus vestidos, los manjares que se adivinaban aún sobre la superficie carcomida de una mesa. Pero ¿por qué no nos decidíamos de una vez a alzar la vista, a detenernos en la esfera, a contemplar el juego de balanzas que, alternándose el peso de unos granos de arena, ponía en marcha el carillón? Y ya los niños, equipados con cubos y palas, salían al Paseo, miraban a derecha e izquierda, cruzaban la vía y se revolcaban en la playa que ahora no era una playa sino un remoto y peligroso desierto. Pero no hacía falta tanta arena. Un puñado, nada más, y, sobre todo, un momento de silencio. Coronando la

But on that warm Sunday in December, as the children danced around the recently arrived package, I kept my eyes firmly fixed on Olvido's face and it seemed to me there was no room left for even one new wrinkle. She was strangely stiff, taking no notice of the calls for scissors and knives, not joining in the fun the unexpected gift had unleashed in the hallway. The words "All the years in the world" came to mind, and for a moment I was possessed by the certainty that the chair so hastily removed to the dining room was not that of the hypothetical, future and still indistinct husband.

They had delivered it that very morning, all done up in thick wrapping paper, tied round with string and ropes like a prisoner. Stretched out like that on the rug it looked like a giant brought low and having to tolerate the dancing and screeching of excited, restless children, convinced right up to the very last minute that the colossal plaything was intended for them. My mother, showing all the guile of a pampered she-cat, stood close by and watched the efforts at unveiling the mystery. A new cupboard? A sculpture? A lamp? But no, of course not. This was a work of art, a curio, a bargain. The antique dealer must have been out of his mind. Or perhaps it was old age, a mistake, other things to worry about. Because the price had turned out to be absurdly low for such a wonderful thing. We just had to rip off the last bits of sticky tape, the cellophane protecting the most fragile parts, open the little glass door and hook in the pendulum. A free-standing clock almost ten feet tall, with gold-plated numbers and hands and a simple yet perfect mechanism. We would have to clean it up, make sure it stood level, varnish over the inevitable wear and tear that comes with age. Because it was a very old clock, bearing the date 1700, and it had been made in Baghdad, probably by Iraqi craftsmen for some European customer. This was the only interpretation that could be put on the fact that the numerals were in Arabic and the lower part of the casing was embossed with a group of human figures in festive mood. Dancers? Guests at a banquet? The years had worn their features smooth, the folds of their clothing, the delicacies that could still be made out on the worm-eaten surface of a table. How was it that not one of us made the decision to raise our eyes, to let them dwell on the clock-face, to gaze at the set of balances that set the chimes in motion when they were altered by the weight of a few grains of sand? And now the children, armed with buckets and spades, were going out to the promenade, looking to right and left, crossing the railroad track and turning somersaults on the beach that was no longer a beach but a remote and dangerous desert. But there was no need for so much sand. One handful, no more and, above all, a moment of silence. Crowning the face of the clock, covered in dust, appeared the final

esfera, recubierta de polvo, se hallaba la última sorpresa de aquel día, el más delicado conjunto de autómatas que hubiéramos podido imaginar. Astros, planetas, estrellas de tamaño diminuto aguardando las primeras notas de una melodía para ponerse en movimiento. En menos de una semana conoceríamos todos los secretos de su mecanismo.

Lo instalaron en el descansillo de la escalera, al término del primer tramo, un lugar que parecía construido a posta. Se le podía admirar desde la antesala, desde el rellano del primer piso, desde los mullidos sillones del salón, desde la trampilla que conducía a la azotea. Cuando, al cabo de unos días, dimos con la proporción exacta de arena y el carillón emitió, por primera vez, las notas de una desconocida melodía, a todos nos pareció muchísimo más alto y hermoso. El Reloj de Bagdad estaba ahí. Arrogante, majestuoso, midiendo con su sordo tictac cualquiera de nuestros movimientos, nuestra respiración, nuestros juegos infantiles. Parecía como si se hallara en el mismo lugar desde tiempos inmemoriales, como si sólo él estuviera en su puesto, tal era la altivez de su porte, su seguridad, el respeto que nos infundía cuando, al caer la noche, abandonábamos la plácida cocina para alcanzar los dormitorios del último piso. Ya nadie recordaba la antigua desnudez de la escalera. Las visitas se mostraban arrobadas, y mi padre no dejaba de felicitarse por la astucia y la oportunidad de su adquisición. Una ocasión única, una belleza, una obra de arte.

Olvido se negó a limpiarlo. Pretextó vértigos, jaquecas, vejez y reumatismo. Aludió a problemas de la vista, ella que podía distinguir un grano de cebada en un costal de trigo, la cabeza de un alfiler en un montón de arena, la china más minúscula en un puñado de lentejas. Encaramarse a una escalerilla no era labor para una anciana. Matilde era mucho más joven y llevaba, además, menos tiempo en la casa. Porque ella, Olvido, poseía el privilegio de la antigüedad. Había criado a las hermanas de mi padre, asistido a mi nacimiento, al de mis hermanos, ese par de pecosos que no se apartaban de las faldas de Matilde. Pero no era necesario que sacase a relucir sus derechos, ni que se asiera con tanta fuerza de mis trenzas. "Usted, Olvido, es como de la familia." Y, horas más tarde, en la soledad de la alcoba de mis padres: "Pobre Olvido. Los años no perdonan".

No sé si la extraña desazón que iba a adueñarse pronto de la casa irrumpió de súbito, como me lo presenta ahora la memoria, o si se trata, quizá, de la deformación que entraña el recuerdo. Pero lo cierto es que Olvido, tiempo antes de que la sombra de la fatalidad se cirniera sobre nosotros, empezó a adquirir actitudes de felina recelosa, siempre con los oídos alerta, las manos crispadas, atenta a cualquier soplo de viento, al

surprise of the day, the most delicate set of automata that we could ever imagine. Heavenly bodies, planets, tiny little stars waiting for the opening notes of a tune to set them going. In less than a week we would know all the secrets of its mechanism.

It was installed on the stair landing, at the top of the first flight, a place that looked as if it had been specially built for it. It could be admired from the hallway, from the first floor landing, from the big comfortable chairs in the living room, from the trap-door that led out onto the roof terrace. When, after a few days, we had worked out the exact amount of sand and the chimes had for the first time sounded the notes of some unfamiliar tune, we all thought it looked even taller and more beautiful. The Baghdad Clock had arrived. Arrogant, majestic, its muffled tick measuring every one of our movements, the breaths we took, our childish games. It felt as if it had been in that same place from time immemorial, as if it were the only thing that had ever stood in its place, such was the haughtiness of its bearing, its confidence, the respect it commanded in us when, as night fell, we gave up the peaceful kitchen to climb the stairs to our bedrooms on the top floor. Nobody remembered how bare the old stairway used to be. Visitors declared themselves enchanted by it and my father never stopped congratulating himself on his good luck and astuteness in acquiring it. A unique find, a thing of beauty, a work of art.

Olvido refused to clean it. She claimed to be afraid of heights, she pleaded migraines, old age and rheumatism. She hinted at problems with her sight, she who could distinguish a grain of barley in a sack of wheat, the head of a pin in a heap of sand, the tiniest pebble in a handful of lentils. Scaling a step ladder was no job for an old lady. Matilde was much younger, and anyway she'd been in the house for a shorter length of time. For she, Olvido, enjoyed the privilege of seniority. She had brought up my father's sisters, had been there at my birth, at the births of my brothers, that pair of freckled faces who never left Matilde's side. But she didn't have to harp on about her rights so much, or hold on so tight to my plaits. "You, Olvido, are like one of the family." And hours later, in the solitude of my parents' bedroom: "Poor Olvido. The years are taking their toll."

I don't know if the strange sense of unease that was soon to take over the house erupted suddenly, which is how my memory makes it feel now, or if it's to do, perhaps, with the distortion that lies at the heart of memory. But one thing was certain, which was that Olvido, some time before the shadow of fate started to hang over us, began to take on the appearance of a suspicious cat. Her ears were always pricked, her hands would twitch, alert

menor murmullo, al chirriar de las puertas, al paso del mercancías, del rápido, del expreso, o al cotidiano trepidar de las cacerolas sobre las repisas. Pero ahora no eran las ánimas que pedían oraciones ni frailes pecadores condenados a penar largos años en la tierra. La vida en la cocina se había poblado de un silencio tenso y agobiante. De nada servía insistir. Las aldeas, perdidas entre montes, se habían tornado lejanas e inaccesibles, y nuestros intentos, a la vuelta del colegio, por arrancar nuevas historias se quedaban en preguntas sin respuestas, flotando en el aire, bailoteando entre ellas, diluyéndose junto a humos y suspiros. Olvido parecía encerrada en sí misma y, aunque fingía entregarse con ahínco a fregar los fondos de las ollas, a barnizar armarios y alacenas, o a blanquear las junturas de los mosaicos, yo la sabía cruzando el comedor, subiendo con cautela los primeros escalones, deteniéndose en el descansillo y observando. La adivinaba observando, con la valentía que le otorgaba el no hallarse realmente allí, frente al péndulo de bronce, sino a salvo, en su mundo de pucheros y sartenes, un lugar hasta el que no llegaban los latidos del reloj y en el que podía ahogar, con facilidad, el sonido de la inevitable melodía.

Pero apenas hablaba. Tan sólo en aquella mañana ya lejana en que mi padre, cruzando mares y atravesando desiertos, explicaba a los pequeños la situación de Bagdad, Olvido se había atrevido a murmurar: "Demasiado lejos". Y luego, dando la espalda al objeto de nuestra admiración, se había internado por el pasillo cabeceando enfurruñada, sosteniendo una conversación consigo misma.

—Ni siquiera deben de ser cristianos —dijo entonces.

En un principio, y aunque lamentara el súbito cambio que se había operado en nuestra vida, no concedí excesiva importancia a los desvaríos de Olvido. Los años parecían haberse desplomado de golpe sobre el frágil cuerpo de la anciana, sobre aquellas espaldas empeñadas en curvarse más y más a medida que pasaban los días. Pero un hecho fortuito terminó de sobrecargar la enrarecida atmósfera de los últimos tiempos. Para mi mente de niña, se trató de una casualidad; para mis padres, de una desgracia; para la vieja Olvido, de la confirmación de sus oscuras intuiciones. Porque había sucedido junto al bullicioso grupo sin rostro, ante el péndulo de bronce, frente a las manecillas recubiertas de oro. Matilde sacaba brillo a la cajita de astros, al Sol y a la Luna, a las estrellas sin nombre que componían el diminuto desfile, cuando la mente se le nubló de pronto, quiso aferrarse a las

to every breath of wind, the least noise, doors creaking, the passing of the goods train, the fast through-train, the express, or the everyday rattle of saucepans on shelves. Only now it wasn't the souls who were calling for prayers, or sinful friars condemned to wander the earth for years on end. Life in the kitchen was invaded by a tense and oppressive silence. It was no use going on about it. The remote villages in the mountains had turned into far off and inaccessible places, and when we came home from school our efforts to tease out new tales were left as questions to which no replies were given, floating in the air, hovering amongst them, vanishing into nothing, along with the smoke and the whispers. Olvido seemed a prisoner inside herself, and although she pretended to be absorbed in scrubbing the bottoms of kitchen pans, in varnishing cupboards and larders, or whitening the grouting between the mosaic tiles, I knew she would be moving through the dining room, cautiously mounting the bottom treads, standing still on the little landing and just looking. I would imagine her just standing there looking at it with the courage that came from not really being there in front of the bronze pendulum, but instead safe in her world of cooking pots and frying pans, a place where the ticking of the clock didn't reach and where the sound of the inevitable chimes could easily be drowned out.

But she scarcely spoke. Only on that now distant morning when my father, crossing seas and traversing deserts, explained to the children where Baghdad was, Olvido had dared to mutter: "Too far away." And then, turning her back on the object of our admiration she had made her way along the corridor, shaking her head grumpily, talking to herself as she went.

"They can't even be Christians," she then added.

In the beginning, and even though I regretted the sudden change that had taken place in our lives, I attached no great importance to Olvido's ramblings. The years seemed to have suddenly come crashing down on the old woman's fragile body, on those shoulders which were determined to grow more and more hunched as the days went by. But a chance event proved the final straw for the rarified atmosphere of those days. To me, with my child's mind, it was an accident; to my parents, it was a piece of bad luck; to old Olvido, it was the confirmation of her suspicions. Because it had taken place alongside the noisy faceless group in front of the bronze pendulum, facing the little gold-plated hands. Matilde was bringing up the shine on the little box of heavenly bodies, the Sun and the Moon, the nameless stars which made up the tiny procession, when her mind suddenly

balanzas de arena, apuntalar sus pies sobre un peldaño inexistente, impedir una caída que se presentaba inevitablemente. Pero la liviana escalerilla se negó a sostener por más tiempo aquel cuerpo oscilante. Fue un accidente, un desmayo, una momentánea pérdida de conciencia. Matilde no se encontraba bien. Lo había dicho por la mañana mientras vestía a los pequeños. Sentía náuseas, el estómago revuelto, posiblemente la cena de la noche anterior, quién sabe si una secreta copa traidora al calor de la lumbre. Pero no había forma humana de hacerse oír en aquella cocina dominada por sombríos presagios. Y ahora no era sólo Olvido. A los innombrables temores de la anciana se había unido el espectacular terror de Matilde. Rezaba, conjuraba, gemía. Se las veía más unidas que nunca, murmurando sin descanso, farfullando frases inconexas, intercambiándose consejos y plegarias. La antigua rivalidad, a la hora de competir con su arsenal de prodigios y espantos, quedaba ya muy lejos. Se diría que aquellas historias, con las que nos hacían vibrar de emoción, no eran más que juegos. Ahora, por primera vez, las sentía asustadas.

Durante aquel invierno fui demorando, poco a poco, el regreso del colegio. Me detenía en las plazas vacías, frente a los carteles del cine, ante los escaparates iluminados de la calle principal. Retrasaba en lo posible el inevitable contacto con las noches de la casa, súbitamente tristes, inesperadamente heladas, a pesar de que la leña siguiera crujiendo en el fuego y de que de la cocina surgieran aromas a bollo recién hecho y a palomitas de maíz. Mis padres, inmersos desde hacía tiempo en los preparativos de un viaje, no parecían darse cuenta de la nube siniestra que se había introducido en nuestro territorio. Y nos dejaron solos. Un mundo de viejas y niños solos. Subiendo la escalera en fila, cogidos de la mano, sin atrevernos a hablar, a mirarnos a los ojos, a sorprender en el otro un destello de espanto que, por compartido, nos obligara a nombrar lo que no tenía nombre. Y ascendíamos escalón tras escalón con el alma encogida, conteniendo la respiración en el primer descansillo, tomando carrerilla hasta el rellano, deteniéndonos unos segundos para recuperar aliento, continuando silenciosos los últimos tramos del camino, los latidos del corazón azotando nuestro pecho, unos latidos precisos, rítmicos, perfectamente sincronizados. Y, ya en el dormitorio, las viejas acostaban a los pequeños en sus camas, niños olvidados de su capacidad de llanto, de su derecho a inquirir, de la necesidad de conjurar con palabras sus inconfesados terrores. Luego nos daban las buenas noches, nos besaban en la frente y, mientras yo prendía una débil lucecita junto al cabezal de mi cama, las oía dirigirse con pasos

went blank, she made a grab for the sand balances, tried to position her feet on some non-existent step, to prevent a fall which looked inevitable. But the fickle step ladder refused to support that wobbling body any longer. It was an accident, a fainting fit, a momentary blackout. Matilde didn't feel well. She had been saying so just that morning as she was getting the little ones dressed. She felt sick, her stomach was upset, it could have been last night's dinner, who was to say it wasn't a secret and treacherous glass of wine taken by the warmth of the fire. Yet it was impossible to make yourself heard in that kitchen dominated by dark omens. And now it wasn't just Olvido. To the old lady's unnameable fears had been added Matilde's spectacular terror. She would pray, she would ward off spirits and she would wail. They were more united than ever, muttering ceaselessly, jabbering unconnected phrases, exchanging advice and prayers between themselves. The rivalry of yesterday, the pitting of their arsenal of marvels and terrors against each other, was now a thing of the distant past. You might say those stories which used to make us quake with excitement were no more than games. Now, for the first time, I felt that they were afraid.

During that winter I gradually took longer and longer to get home from school. I would linger in the empty squares, in front of cinema posters, in front of the bright shop windows in the high street. I would put off for as long as possible the inevitable contact with nights at home, suddenly sad, unexpectedly icy, in spite of the fact that the firewood still crackled in the hearth and the aroma of freshly baked rolls and popcorn still floated out of the kitchen. My parents, long immersed in getting ready for a trip, appeared to be unaware of the sinister cloud that had gathered over us. And they left us alone. A world of old ladies and children left alone. Climbing the stairs Indian file, holding hands, not daring to speak, to catch each other's eye, to catch the other in a burst of terror that, by being shared, might compel us to name that which had no name. And we would go on up, step after step, our hearts in our mouths, holding our breath on the first landing, running as fast as we could to the next, pausing for a few seconds to catch our wind, continuing on the last few treads of the stairway in silence, the beating of our hearts pounding in our chests — precise, rhythmic, perfectly synchronized beats. And, once in the bedroom, the old ladies would put the children to bed, children who had forgotten their capacity for tears, their right to ask questions, their need to stave off their unconfessed terrors with words. Then they would bid us goodnight, kiss us on the forehead and, as I was lighting the little night light by the side of my bed, I would hear them shuffling along

arrastrados hacia su dormitorio, abrir la puerta, cuchichear entre ellas lamentarse, suspirar. Y después dormir, sin molestarse en apagar el tenue resplandor de la desnuda bombilla, sueños agitados que pregonaban a gritos el silenciado motivo de sus inquietudes diurnas, el Señor Innombrado, el Amo y Propietario de nuestras viejas e infantiles vidas.

La ausencia de mis padres no duró más que unas semanas, tiempo suficiente para que, a su regreso, encontraran la casa molestamente alterada. Matilde se había marchado. Un mensaje, una carta del pueblo, una hermana doliente que reclamaba angustiada su presencia. Pero ¿cómo podía ser? ¿Desde cuándo Matilde tenía hermanas? Nunca hablaba de ella pero conservaba una hermana en la aldea. Aquí estaba la carta: sobre la cuadrícula del papel una mano temblorosa explicaba los pormenores del imprevisto. No tenían más que leerla. Matilde la había dejado con este propósito: para que comprendieran que hizo lo que hizo porque no tenía otro remedio. Pero era una carta sin franqueo. ¿Cómo podía haber llegado hasta la casa? La trajo un pariente. Un hombre apareció una mañana por la puerta con una carta en la mano. ¿Y esa curiosa y remilgada redacción? Mi madre buscaba entre sus libros un viejo manual de cortesía y sociedad. Aquellos billetes de pésame, de felicitación de cambio de domicilio, de comunicación de desgracias. Esa carta la había leído ya alguna vez. Si Matilde quería abandonarnos no tenía necesidad de recurrir a ridículas excusas. Pero ella, Olvido, no podía contestar. Estaba cansada, se sentía mal, había aguardado a que regresaran para declararse enferma. Y ahora, postrada en el lecho de su dormitorio, no deseaba otra cosa que reposar, que la dejaran en paz, que desistieran de sus intentos por que se decidiera a probar bocado. Su garganta se negaba a engullir alimento alguno, a beber siquiera un sorbo de agua. Cuando se acordó la conveniencia de que los pequeños y yo misma pasáramos unos días en casa de lejanos familiares y subí a despedirme de Olvido, creí encontrarme ante una mujer desconocida. Había adelgazado de manera alarmante, sus ojos parecían enormes, sus brazos, un manojo de huesos y venas. Me acarició la cabeza casi sin rozarme, esbozando una mueca que ella debió suponer sonrisa, supliendo con el brillo de su mirada las escasas palabras que lograban aflorar a sus labios. "Primero pensé que algún día tenía que ocurrir," masculló, "que unas cosas empiezan y otras acaban..." Y luego, como presa de un pavor invencible, asiéndose de mis trenzas, intentando escupir algo que desde hacía tiempo ardía en su boca y empezaba ya a quemar mis oídos: "Guárdate. Protégete... ¡No te descuides ni un instante!"

to their bedroom, opening the door, whispering to one another, complaining and sighing. And then to sleep, without bothering to turn off the weak light cast by the bare light bulb, restless dreams that loudly announced the hushed-up reason for their daytime worries, the Unnamed Lord, the Master and Owner of our lives in old age and in childhood.

My parents' absence lasted no more than a few weeks, time enough though for them to find the house annoyingly altered when they returned. Matilde had left. Some message, a letter from the village, a sister in trouble anxiously demanding her presence. But how could that be? Since when did Matilde have sisters? She never talked about one, yet she still had a sister in the village. Here was the letter: on the scrap of squared paper a trembling hand explained the details of the unforeseen occurrence. They only had to read it. Matilde had left it with this aim in mind: that they might understand that what she'd done, she had done because there was no alternative. But it was a letter without a postage mark. How could it have got as far as the house? A relative had delivered it. A man appeared at the door one morning with a letter in his hand. And that curious and affected wording? My mother looked amongst her books for an old guide to good manners and social etiquette. Those little notes of condolences, of congratulations, some change of address, the communication of an unhappy event. She had read that letter before. If Matilde wanted to leave us, she had no need to resort to ridiculous excuses. But she, Olvido, could not answer. She was tired, she felt poorly, she had waited until they came home before saying she was ill. And now, stretched out on the bed in her room she wanted nothing more than to rest, to be left in peace, for them to stop trying to get her to eat a little something. Her throat refused to swallow any food or to take even a sip of water. When it was agreed it would be a good idea if the little ones and I should spend a few days with some distant relatives, I went up to say goodbye to Olvido, and I thought I was standing before a woman I didn't know. She had lost an alarming amount of weight, her eyes looked enormous, her arms were all bones and veins. She stroked my head almost without touching me, twisting her face into what she must have thought was a smile, making up for the few words that managed to fall from her lips with the glitter of her eyes. "At first I thought it had to happen one day," she mouthed, "that certain things would begin and others come to an end..." And then, as if in the grip of some invincible dread, she grasped at my plaits, trying to spit out something that had been burning in her mouth for a long time and now began to burn in my ears: "Be on your guard. Look after yourself... Don't be careless for even a second! "

Siete días después, de regreso a casa, me encontré con una habitación sórdidamente vacía, olor a desinfectante y colonia de botica, el suelo lustroso, las paredes encaladas, ni un solo objeto ni una prenda personal en el armario. Y, al fondo, bajo la ventana que daba al mar, todo lo que quedaba de mi adorada Olvido: un colchón desnudo, enrollado sobre los muelles oxidados de la cama.

Pero apenas tuve tiempo de sufrir su ausencia. La calamidad había decidido ensañarse con nosotros, sin darnos respiro, negándonos un reposo que iba revelándose urgente. Los objetos se nos caían de las manos, las sillas se quebraban, los alimentos se descomponían. Nos sabíamos nerviosos, agitados, inquietos. Debíamos esforzarnos, prestar mayor atención a todo cuanto hiciéramos, poner el máximo cuidado en cualquier actividad por nimia y cotidiana que pudiera parecernos. Pero, aun así, a pesar de que lucháramos por combatir aquel creciente desasosiego, yo intuía que el proceso de deterioro al que se había entregado la casa no podía detenerse con simples propósitos y buenas voluntades. Eran tantos los olvidos, tan numerosos los descuidos, tan increíbles las torpezas que cometíamos de continuo, que ahora, con la distancia de los años, contemplo la tragedia que marcó nuestras vidas como un hecho lógico e inevitable. Nunca supe si aquella noche olvidamos retirar los braseros, o si lo hicimos de forma apresurada, como todo lo que emprendíamos en aquellos días, desatentos a la minúscula ascua escondida entre los faldones de la mesa camilla, entre los flecos de cualquier mantel abandonado a su desidia... Pero nos arrancaron del lecho a gritos, nos envolvieron en mantas, bajamos como enfebrecidos las temibles escaleras, pobladas, de pronto, de un humo denso, negro, asfixiante. Y luego, ya a salvo, a pocos metros del jardín, un espectáculo gigantesco e imborrable. Llamas violáceas, rojas, amarillas, apagando con su fulgor las primeras luces del alba, compitiendo entre ellas por alcanzar las cimas más altas, surgiendo por ventanas, hendiduras, claraboyas. No había nada que hacer, dijeron, todo estaba perdido. Y así, mientras, inmovilizados por el pánico, contemplábamos la lucha sin esperanzas contra el fuego, me pareció como si mi vida fuera a extinguirse en aquel preciso instante, a mis escasos doce años, envuelta en un murmullo de lamentaciones y condolencias, junto a una casa que hacía tiempo había dejado de ser mi casa. El frío del asfalto me hizo arrugar los pies. Los noté desmesurados, ridículos, casi tanto como las pantorrillas que asomaban por las perneras de un pijama demasiado corto y estrecho. Me cubrí con la manta y, entonces, asestándome el tiro de gracia, se oyó la voz. Surgió a mis

Seven days later, when I got home, I found a room that was meanly empty, smelling of disinfectant and chemist's cologne, the floor shining, the walls whitewashed, not one single object or item of personal clothing in the wardrobe. And at the far end, under the window that looked out over the sea, all that was left of my beloved Olvido: a bare mattress, rolled up on top of the rusty bed-springs.

But I scarcely had time to feel her absence. Disaster had decided to vent its spleen on us without allowing us pause for breath, denying us the rest that was proving so imperative. Objects fell from our hands, chairs broke, food went off. We felt nervous, agitated, worried. We had to make an effort to pay greater attention to everything we did, to afford maximum care to whatever activity, however trifling and routine it might appear to us. But even so, in spite of the fact that we fought to combat that growing disquiet, I sensed that the process of deterioration to which the house had succumbed could not be stopped by resolution and good will alone. There were so many things we forgot to do, so numerous the oversights, so incredible the mistakes we made time and again that now, with hindsight, I look back on the tragedy that blighted our lives as a logical and inevitable event. I never knew whether we forgot to take out the braziers that night, or whether we did so in a hurry, like everything else we did in those days, neglectful of some tiny ember hidden amongst the flaps of the table that had the heater under it, between the fringes of some tablecloth carelessly flung down... But, with shouts and screams, they plucked us from our beds, wrapped us in blankets, and we rushed down the terrifying staircase, suddenly filled with dense, black, choking smoke, as if we were suffering from some fever. And then, safe now, a few yards away, in the garden, there was a huge and unforgettable sight. Violet, red, yellow flames, eclipsing the early dawn light with their glow, competing with one another to see which could reach the greatest height, bursting through windows, cracks in the brickwork, skylights. There was nothing that could be done, they said, all was lost. And thus it was that, immobilized by panic, as we stood there watching the hopeless battle against the fire, it seemed as if my life was about to be extinguished at that very instant, at just twelve years old, enveloped in a murmur of lamentations and expressions of sympathy, beside a house that had ceased to be my home some time ago. The cold of the asphalt made me scrunch my feet. They looked enormous, ridiculous, to me — almost like the calves of my legs that were sticking out from my too short and too tight pyjama bottoms. I covered myself up with the blanket and then, dealing me the *coup de grâce*, I heard the voice. It came from behind

espaldas, entre baúles y archivadores, objetos rescatados al azar, cuadros sin valor, jarrones de loza, a lo sumo un par de candelabros de plata.

Sé que, para los vecinos congregados en el Paseo, no fue más que la inoportuna melodía de un hermoso reloj. Pero, a mis oídos, había sonado como unas agudas, insidiosas, perversas carcajadas.

Aquella misma madrugada se urdió la ingenua conspiración de la desmemoria. De la vida en el pueblo recordaríamos sólo el mar, los paseos por la playa, las casetas listadas del verano. Fingí adaptarme a los nuevos tiempos, pero no me perdí detalle, en los días inmediatos, de todo cuanto se habló en mi menospreciada presencia. El anticuario se obstinaba en rechazar el reloj aduciendo razones de dudosa credibilidad. El mecanismo se hallaba deteriorado, las maderas carcomidas, las fechas falsificadas... Negó haber poseído, alguna vez, un objeto de tan desmesurado tamaño y redomado mal gusto, y aconsejó a mi padre que lo vendiera a un trapero o se deshiciera de él en el vertedero más próximo. No obedeció mi familia al olvidadizo comerciante, pero sí, en cambio, adquirió su pasmosa tranquilidad para negar evidencias. Nunca más pude yo pronunciar el nombre prohibido sin que se culpase a mi fantasía, a mi imaginación, o a las inocentes supersticiones de ancianas ignorantes. Pero la noche de San Juan, cuando abandonábamos para siempre el pueblo de mi infancia, mi padre mandó detener el coche de alquiler en las inmediaciones de la calle principal. Y entonces lo vi. A través del humo, los vecinos, los niños reunidos en torno a las hogueras. Parecía más pequeño, desamparado, lloroso. Las llamas ocultaban las figuras de los danzarines, el juego de autómatas se había desprendido de la caja, y la esfera colgaba, inerte, sobre la puerta de cristal que, en otros tiempos, encerrara un péndulo. Pensé en un gigante degollado y me estremecí. Pero no quise dejarme vencer por la emoción. Recordando antiguas aficiones, entorné los ojos.

Ella estaba allí. Riendo, danzando, revoloteando en torno a las llamas junto a sus viejas amigas. Jugueteaba con las cadenas como si estuvieran hechas de aire y, con sólo proponérselo, podía volar, saltar, unirse sin ser

me, from between trunks and filing cabinets, things rescued at random, worthless pictures, earthenware jugs, the best things a pair of silver candlesticks.

I know that for the neighbours gathered on the promenade it was only the untimely chime of a beautiful clock. But to my ears it had sounded like a sharp, treacherous, perverse shout of laughter.

That same early morning the ingenuous conspiracy of poor memory started its plotting. Of life in the village we were to recall only the sea, the walks along the beach, the striped summer bathing tents. I pretended to adapt myself to the new times, but in the days that followed I never missed a word of what was said in my unheeded presence. The antiques dealer dug his heels in about taking the clock back, advancing reasons of dubious credibility. The mechanism had deteriorated, the woodwork was worm-eaten, the dates had been fiddled with... He denied ever having at any time owned such an unduly large object in such out-and-out bad taste, and advised my father that he should sell it to a rag-and-bone man or get rid of it on the nearest rubbish tip. My family ignored the words of the absent-minded dealer, and instead acquired an astonishing calmness in order to deny the obvious. I could never again speak the proscribed name out loud without my fantasy, my imagination or the innocent superstitions of ignorant old women getting the blame. But on St John's Eve,[6] when we turned our backs forever on the village where I'd spent my childhood, my father ordered the hired car to stop near the main street. And then I saw it. Through the smoke, the neighbours, the children gathered round the blazing bonfire. It looked smaller, forsaken, sad. The flames hid the figures of the dancers, the set of automata had sprung from the casing and the dial was hanging down, motionless, on top of the glass door which had at one time enclosed the pendulum. It reminded me of a decapitated giant and I shivered. Yet I didn't want to allow my emotions to get the better of me. Remembering former fondnesses, I screwed up my eyes.

She was there. Laughing, dancing, fluttering round the flames with her old friends. She was playing with the chains as if they were made of air and by just thinking of it she could fly, leap, merge without being seen with the

---

[6]   **St John's Eve**: on the night of 23rd June, the eve of St John's Day, the beginning of summer is celebrated with bonfires in some areas of Spain (e.g. Catalonia and Alicante).

vista al júbilo de los niños, al estrépito de petardos y cohetes. "Olvido," dije, y mi propia voz me volvió a la realidad.

Vi cómo mi padre reforzaba la pira, atizaba el fuego y regresaba jadeante al automóvil. Al abrir la puertecilla, se encontró con mis ojos expectantes. Fiel a la ley del silencio, nada dijo. Pero me sonrió, me besó en las mejillas y, aunque jamás tendré ocasión de recordárselo, sé que su mano me oprimió la nuca para que mirara hacia el frente y no se me ocurriera sentir un asomo de piedad o tristeza.

Aquélla fue la última vez que, entornando los ojos, supe verlas.

whoopings of the children, with the tremendous noise of firecrackers and rockets. "Olvido," I said, and my own voice brought me back to reality.

I watched how my father was banking up the pyre, stoking the fire and returning to the car, out of breath. On opening the car door he found himself looking into my expectant eyes. True to the law of silence, he said nothing. But he smiled at me, kissed me on both cheeks and, though I shall never have occasion to remind him of it, I know his hand pressed the back of my neck to make me look straight ahead and it didn't cross my mind to feel the slightest trace of pity or sadness.

Through half-closed eyes, that was the last time I succeeded in seeing them.

PALOMA DÍAZ-MAS
Photograph © Colita fotografía

PALOMA DÍAZ-MAS was born in Madrid in 1954, and graduated in Romance Philology and Journalism from the Universidad Complutense. After spending six years as a researcher on Sephardic Language and Literature at the CSIC, in Madrid, she now teaches Spanish Golden Age and Sephardic Literature at the Universidad del País Vasco in Vitoria. She spent two short periods, in 1988 and in 1990, as a visiting scholar at the University of Oregon, Eugene (USA).

In 1973 she published a collection of short stories written when she was only seventeen, *Biografías de genios, traidores, sabios y suicidas, según antiguos documentos*. Venturing into different genres, she won several prizes: the Ciudad de Cáceres for her novel *Tras las huellas de Artorius* (1984), and the Ciudad de Toledo for her play *La informante* (1984).

Her following novel, *El rapto del Santo Grial* (1984), was shortlisted for the prestigious Premio Herralde in 1983, after which her literary career took off. Since then she has published *Nuestro milenio* (1987), a book of short stories for which she was shortlisted for the Premio Nacional de Narración the following year, *Una ciudad llamada Eugenio* (1992), in which she amusingly reflects on the 'American way of life' she experienced during her stay in the United States, and *El sueño de Venecia* (1992), for which she won the tenth Premio Herralde. This is a mature and well-crafted novel in which intertextuality and an intrahistorical reading of history shape the journey of a seventeenth-century painting to contemporary Spain.

Other short stories include: 'En busca de un retrato', in *Nuevas letras*, 8 (1988), also collected in *Cuento español contemporáneo*, edited by A. Encinar and A. Percival (1993); 'La discreta pecadora, o ejemplo de doncellas recogidas', in *Cuentos eróticos*, edited by Laura Freixas (1988), later included in *Relatos eróticos*, edited by Carmen Estévez (1990); 'Me sé todos los cuentos', in *Lucanor*, 1 (1988), 37-43; and 'La niña sin alas' in *Madres e hijas*, edited by Laura Freixas (1996).

Reflecting on her own work as a fictional writer she contributed with 'Los nombres de mis personajes' to *El oficio de narrar*, edited by Marina Mayoral (1990), and as a result of her scholarly work, she has published *Los sefardíes: Historia, lengua y cultura* (1986 and 1993), translated into English by George K. Zucker: *Shephardim. The Jews from Spain* (Chicago, 1992), and has edited early Spanish poetry, *Romancero* (1994), as well as Sephardic poetry, *Poesía oral sefardí* (1994). Paloma Díaz-Mas is currently working in collaboration with other scholars on an annotated edition of the fifteenth-century play *La Celestina*.

FURTHER READING ON PALOMA DÍAZ-MAS

Altares, Guillermo, 'Premios literarios', *El Urogallo*, 90 (1993), 62-4.

Asís Garrote, Ma. Dolores de, *Última hora de la novela en España* (Madrid, 1996).

Azancot, Leopoldo, *'El rapto del Santo Grial'*, *ABC*, 23 June 1984.

Diéguez, María Luz, 'Entrevista con Paloma Díaz-Mas', *Revista de Estudios Hispánicos*, 22/1 (1988), 77-91.

Estévez, Carmen, 'Introducción', in Carmen Estévez (ed.), *Relatos eróticos* (Madrid, 1990), 7-26.

Hernández, Juana Amelia, 'La postmodernidad en la ficción de Paloma Díaz-Mas', *Romance Languages Annual*, 2 (1990), 450-4.

Gil Casado, Pablo, *La novela deshumanizada española (1958-1988)* (Barcelona, 1990).

Martín, Salustiano, *'El sueño de Venecia*. La verdad, el error y la memoria histórica', *Reseña*, 237 (1993), 28.

Myers, Eunice, 'The Quixerotic Quest: Paloma Díaz-Mas's "La discreta pecadora, o ejemplo de doncellas recogidas" ', *Monographic Review*, 7 (1991), 146-55.

Navajas, Gonzalo, 'Narrativa y género. La ficción actual desde la mujer', *Ínsula*, 589-590 (1996), 37-9.

Obiol, María José, 'El juego de las similitudes y las diferencias. Madurez en el oficio de contar', *El País* (Libros), 28 July 1985.

Ordóñez, Elizabeth J., 'Parody and Defiance. Subversive Challenges in the Texts of Díaz-Mas and Gómez Ojea', in *Voices of Their Own. Contemporary Spanish Narrative by Women* (Lewisburg, London and Toronto, 1991), 150-73.

Pérez, Janet, 'Characteristics of Erotic Brief Fiction by Women in Spain', *Monographic Review*, 7 (1991), 173-95.

───────── 'Contemporary Spanish Women Writers and the Feminized Quest-Romance', *Monographic Review*, 8 (1992), 36-49.

Samblancat Miranda, Neus, *'El sueño de Venecia* o el guiño de los clásicos', *Lectora*, 1 (1995), 105-10.

Vidal-Folch, Ignacio, 'Introducción', in Paloma Díaz-Mas, *El rapto del Santo Grial. Nuestro milenio* (Barcelona, 1993), 7-13.

Zatlin, Phyllis, 'Women Novelists in Democratic Spain: Freedom to Express the Female Perspective', *Anales de la Literatura Española Contemporánea*, 12 (1987), 29-44.

The Masterpiece

La obra maestra

Original Spanish text from
Nuestro milenio (Barcelona: Anagrama, 1987), 109-117.

La obra maestra

Pese a todas las apariencias, Amal era una isla en nuestro mundo. A primera vista, tenía un aire de tópico galán, de dandy un poco demodé. Pero tras sus trajes de impecable corte —lana inglesa en invierno, alpaca o lino en verano—, tras sus zapatos italianos y sus corbatas de seda, tras sus pañuelos bordados con una A que se retorcía en sombreadas volutas blancas, tras la conversación cortés y brillante, tras las sienes prematuramente plateadas y la barba impecable, tras las manos aristocráticas nunca teñidas por el halo azafranado de la nicotina, tras sus estudios en un par de universidades norteamericanas, tras su formación artística en Italia y Alemania, tras su dominio de cuatro o cinco idiomas occidentales, tras sus colonias varoniles y su cartera repleta de tarjetas de crédito, tras todos esos signos en los que había adoptado lo más exquisito, relumbrante e incluso snob de Europa y parte de América, se ocultaban unos sentimientos, unas convicciones y una moral que a todos se nos antojaban ancestrales, casi anacrónicas y, desde luego, incomprensibles en un hombre como él.

Apenas sabíamos más que retazos de su historia: alguna alusión a un anciano progenitor rico y lejano que desde algún menudo país desértico —del cual nunca pudimos recordar el nombre, tan pequeño era— enviaba puntualmente cheques de muchas cifras a las instituciones encargadas de la larga formación intelectual y artística de su hijo (una formación que había comenzado en la adolescencia inglesa y llegaba casi a una cuarentena cosmopolita); vagas evocaciones de usos, costumbres y paisajes variopintos por él bien conocidos; y, siempre, la convicción de que cada vez que mencionásemos un país, una ciudad, un monumento, un río, Amal había

The Masterpiece

In spite of all appearances, Amal was an island in this world of ours. At first sight, he might have been taken for a stereotypical ladies' man, a slightly *démodé* dandy. Yet behind his suits of impeccable cut — English wool in winter, alpaca or linen in summer — behind his Italian shoes and his silk ties, behind his handkerchiefs embroidered with an A which would twirl into shadowy white scrolls, behind the polite sparkling conversation, behind the prematurely silvered temples and the impeccable beard, behind the aristocratic hands which had never been stained with the saffron-coloured halo of nicotine, behind his studies at a couple of American universities, behind his artistic training in Italy and Germany, behind his mastery of four or five Western languages, behind his manly colognes and his wallet stuffed full of credit cards, behind all these signs that he had adopted the most exquisite, dazzling, even snobbish, things that Europe and part of America had to offer, there lay hidden from view certain sentiments, certain convictions and a morality that we felt belonged to a bygone age, almost anachronistic, and of course incomprehensible in a man such as he.

We scarcely knew anything more than snippets of his background: some allusion to an aged rich and remote father who from some insignificant desert country — whose name none of us could ever remember, it was so small — would regularly send cheques for large sums of money to the institutions entrusted with the lengthy intellectual and artistic education of his son (an education which had commenced during an English adolescence and had continued until he was approaching a cosmopolitan forty-something); blurred evocations of miscellaneous fashions; customs and landscapes with which he was well acquainted; and always the conviction that whenever we referred to a country, a city, a monument, or a river, Amal

estado allí, había paseado sus calles, había contemplado su arquitectura, había recorrido su ribera.

Desarrollaba su trabajo con la misma aristocrática ligereza con que sostenía una conversación mundana o emprendía viaje a un país lejano. Y, pese a eso —o tal vez por eso mismo— era uno de los pintores más cotizados de aquel momento, el que se disputaban los marchantes, las galerías de arte y las instituciones públicas deseosas de dar premios o hacer encargos. Ninguna técnica parecía tener secretos para él: lo mismo dibujaba con mano segura que preparaba un grabado o empastaba colores con acierto, y a su sabiduría pictórica eran igualmente dóciles el óleo y la témpera, la sanguina y el lápiz de plata, el clarión y la punta seca. En un principio cultivó unos paisajes despiadados pese a su aparente amenidad, y luego pareció cansarse de ellos para sumirse en unos impresionantes bodegones hiperrealistas de angustiosa viveza, y por fin había derivado a un no figurativismo de enorme fuerza expresiva: líneas onduladas como olas o sierpes llenaban a veces sus cuadros de un movimiento frenético, y otras eran laberínticas multitudes de formas geométricas diminutas que, entrelazándose o cruzándose, sumían al espectador en un dédalo sugerente en el que parecía haber figuras, sin haberlas.

Desde allí había enlazado con su tradición más antigua y venerable, aquélla que nos parecía anacrónica y contradictoria con su imagen de exquisito occidental hombre de mundo; sus cuadros se poblaban cada vez más de unas líneas cursivas y elegantes que, sin serlo, recordaban poderosamente la escritura cúfica, la que decoraba los paramentos de mármoles y estucos de los palacios, mezquitas y madrasas de su país natal. Y los fondos habían ido adquiriendo progresivamente tonalidades marmóreas, o recamados de oro y plata como las orlas que adornan las copias medievales de los coranes de lujo, o rojizos relieves de cordobán, o iridiscencias metálicas como las de las heréticas telas persas.

Pues, en efecto, eran para él heréticos, pese a su belleza, aquellos tapices pavonados y verdes en los que desfilaban ordenadamente ejércitos enteros, doncellas semiveladas, monstruos terrestres, pájaros fantásticos; y que incluso se atrevían a representar al mismísimo Profeta arrebatado al cielo por un caballo volador de rostro humano, o descendedor a los siete círculos infernales por una escala nunca hollada por el hombre. Porque Amal, el pintor de moda en las subastas y en los salones, era un musulmán

would have been there, would have walked through its streets, would have gazed on its architecture, would have travelled its shores.

He went about his work with the same aristocratic ease with which he would hold a worldly conversation or undertake a journey to a far-off land. And yet in spite of this — or perhaps because of this — he was one of the painters most in demand at that time, the one over whom art dealers, galleries and public institutions seeking to hand out prizes or award commissions, would fight. It seemed that no technique held any secrets for him; he would sketch with the same sure hand he used to prepare an engraving or skilfully apply colours; oils and tempera, sanguine and silver point, chalks and etching — all were equally tamed by his artistic know-how. Initially, he cultivated landscapes which were merciless despite appearing agreeable, but then he seemed to grow tired of these and immersed himself in striking hyper-realistic still-lifes of distressing intensity, finally drifting towards a non-figurative style of enormous expressive power: sometimes undulating lines like waves or serpents filled his pictures with frenetic movement, and at other times labyrinthire multitudes of tiny geometric shapes, intertwining and criss-crossing, plunged the spectator into a thought-provoking maze in which it looked as if there were figures without any actually being there.

From this point he had followed his own older and more venerable tradition, the one that to us seemed anachronistic and contradictory to his image as a refined Western man of the world; his canvasses became filled with cursive and elegant lines which, even though they were not, strongly reminded us of the Kufic script that decorated the marble and stucco façades of the palaces, mosques and places of learning of the country of his birth. And the backgrounds had gradually taken on marmoreal hues, or been embroidered with gold and silver like the borders that adorn medieval de luxe copies of the Koran, or the red-brown relief work of Cordovan leather, or metallic iridescent spectra like those found in heretical Persian fabrics.

Because, in fact to him they were heretical, in spite of their beauty, those tapestries in peacock blues and greens in which whole armies paraded in an orderly fashion, young girls with veils half-covering their faces, terrestrial monsters, fantastic birds; some of them even daring to show the Prophet himself being carried up to heaven by a flying horse with a human face, or descending into the seven circles of Hell via a ladder which had never been set foot on by man. Because Amal, the fashionable painter in auction houses and salons, was a deeply-religious, pious and strict Muslim. And precisely

convencido, piadoso y estricto. Precisamente por eso nunca había pintado una figura humana, y aseguraba que no la pintaría jamás.

Alguna vez alguien pretendió burlarse: ¿cómo era posible que él, un hombre culto e instruido, un pintor inspirado y de sólida formación, renunciase al figurativismo pura y simplemente por una superstición, por una prohibición coránica dictada hace trece siglos para evitar la idolatría, y hoy carente de sentido? Los ojos de Amal relumbraron de ira y de desprecio, los dedos se crisparon sobre el vaso de zumo que bebía —era, creo, en el cóctel de inauguración de su quinta exposición en solitario— y por un momento temimos todos una escena desagradable. Pero no pasó nada. El silencio cargado de violencia que siguió fue suficiente para que el contertulio imprudente se deslizase del grupo y saliera de nuestro círculo casi sin hacerse notar. Nadie volvió a hacerle a Amal una observación por el estilo. Sin embargo yo, a raíz de aquel incidente que sin duda todos olvidaron, llegué —de forma irracional y sin ningún motivo real para pensarlo— a la convicción de que en el fondo Amal deseaba pintar una figura y, aún más, que tal vez estuviera ya intentándolo a escondidas.

Pasó el tiempo y olvidé aquella idea que me había cruzado, como una estrella fugaz, por la mente una o dos veces. Y cuando ya la tenía olvidada, vino a verme Amal.

Era presa de una agitación inusual en él, siempre tan mesurado. Nunca lo había visto tan excitado, tan inquieto. Balbuciendo, por primera vez alterado e inseguro, me lo confesó todo: llevaba años trabajando en el proyecto, lo había conseguido al fin, que no se lo dijera a nadie, le había costado mucho decidirse, muchas veces había destruido el trabajo ya hecho, había tenido múltiples· y constantes dudas de conciencia, creía haber encontrado por fin la solución, había pensado mantenerlo oculto, era yo la única persona a quien lo había dicho, se dio cuenta de que no podía ocultarlo, necesitaba la opinión de alguien, alguien capaz de guardar un secreto, debía jurarle que jamás lo diría, era imprescindible que le diese mi opinión, con una sola opinión le bastaba, pero necesitaba al menos una, sólo me daría oportunidad de verlo una vez, no debía (de nuevo) contárselo a nadie.

Naturalmente, había pintado una figura.

Me llevó a un lugar en el que yo nunca había estado: una pequeña buhardilla en un barrio viejo de la ciudad. Era una sola habitación pequeña,

because of this he had never painted a human figure, and he swore he never would.

Somebody once tried to taunt him: how was it possible that he, a cultivated and learned man, an inspired painter with a good education, could turn his back on figurative painting purely and simply because of some superstition, some Koranic prohibition issued thirteen centuries ago to avoid idolatry and that had no relevance today? Amal's eyes flashed with anger and scorn, his fingers closed tight around the glass of juice he was drinking — it was, I think, at the cocktail party held to launch his fifth one-man exhibition — and for a moment we were all afraid there would be an unpleasant scene. But nothing came of it. The ensuing silence, charged with violence, was enough for the imprudent guest to slip away from the group and leave our circle virtually without anyone noticing him go. Nobody ever made such a remark to Amal again. Nevertheless, as a result of that incident, which everybody else undoubtedly forgot, I became convinced — irrationally and without any real motive for believing so — that deep down Amal wanted to paint a figure and, what was more, was perhaps secretly already attempting to do so.

Time went by and I forgot all about this idea that had flashed across my mind once or twice like a shooting star. And when I had completely forgotten about it, Amal came to see me.

He was caught up in a state of unusual agitation, this man who was always so calm. I had never seen him so excited, so anxious. Looking for the first time disturbed and unsure of himself, he stammeringly confessed everything to me: he had spent years working on the project, had finally managed to finish it, I mustn't say a word to anybody; it had been very difficult for him to make up his mind to do it, he had destroyed again and again the work he had done, had many persistent crises of conscience, he believed he had finally found the solution, had thought about keeping it hidden, and I was the only person to whom he had said anything; he had realized he could not hide it, that he needed someone else's opinion, someone who was capable of keeping a secret, I would have to swear to him that I would never say a word, that it was vital I should tell him what I thought about it, one single opinion would be enough for him, but he needed at least one, he would only let me see it once, I must not (that word again) say a word to anybody.

He had, of course, painted a figure.

He took me to a place where I had never been before: a little garret in an old quarter of the city. It was just one small room, but it was very well lit

pero muy luminosa gracias a una mansarda que se abría sobre un mar de tejas verdinosas; olía intensamente a pintura, a aguarrás, a los inconfundibles olores de un estudio de pintor en el que se ha trabajado durante muchos meses. El lugar de trabajo conocido de Amal estaba en la otra punta de la ciudad, y era evidente que aquel había constituido hasta entonces su otro lugar, su refugio secreto.

En la pared del fondo, enfrente de la mansarda, estaba colgado el cuadro. Al mirarlo, dudé si mi amigo se había vuelto loco, o simplemente se estaba burlando de mí: era un cuadro bellísimo, sin duda, con una armonía especial en el movimiento de las líneas y una deliciosa sensibilidad en la combinación de los diversos tonos de las gamas del terracota y el rosa. Pero no era figurativo, no había en él ningún cuerpo, ningún rostro: sólo una amalgama de pinceladas de color.

Le miré con sorpresa. Pero antes de que yo pudiera balbucir nada, Amal me indicó que me sentase frente al cuadro, en un gran almohadón que había en el suelo; y, recobrado ya el sereno aplomo de gentilhombre que le acompañaba siempre como una aura, me susurró dulce e irónicamente: "¿cómo podremos gozar de la belleza sin la virtud de la paciencia?" Y, dicha la frase, que me sonó a aforismo de un sabio musulmán más antiguo que él, me dejó solo, frente a frente con su pintura.

Transcurrieron horas, que pasé ensimismado en aquella maraña de líneas ondulantes y de colores mórbidos que tenían, sin que se pudiera saber bien por qué, un encanto que entonces me atreví a calificar —no sabía cuán acertadamente— de erótico. Empezó a caer la tarde y un resplandor rojizo que emanaba de las nubes del horizonte, por encima del oleaje de los tejados, comenzó a entrar por la mansarda. Primero fue como un rayo bermellón y luego toda la estancia se fue coloreando de un irreal tinte rosado que parecía conferir un latido de vida y de sangre a las mismas paredes.

Entonces la ví: era una mujer y estaba desnuda, levemente recostada, con las manos abandonadas blandamente sobre el regazo. La carne rosada que parecía palpitar se distinguía sólo ligeramente de su cabello de destellos rojizos, y rojizo era también el vello de su sexo, y las arreboladas mejillas se fundían casi con el color del pelo y sobre la piel de rosa apenas destacaban los labios un poco más bermejos. Parecía arder en su reposo, como una rosa incandescente y febril. Era la mujer más irrealmente bella que había visto jamás.

La contemplación sólo pudo durar unos minutos: los de la puesta de sol. Porque poco a poco la luz rosada del atardecer fue tornándose malva y

thanks to a skylight that opened onto a sea of tiles moss-green with age. It smelt strongly of paint, of turpentine, all those unmistakeable smells one finds in a studio where a painter has been working for many months. Amal's regular workplace was on the other side of the city, and it was clear that this had until now been his other place, his secret hideaway.

The painting was hanging on the back wall, facing the skylight. As I looked at it, I wondered if my friend had gone mad or was simply having fun at my expense. It was undoubtedly a very beautiful painting, with a special harmony in the movement of the lines and a delightful sensitivity in the way the range of different shades of terracotta and pink combined. But it was not a figurative work, it had no body, no face: only an amalgam of coloured brush-strokes.

I looked at him in surprise. But before I could stammer anything, Amal indicated that I should sit down in front of the canvas on a large cushion which lay on the floor; and having by now recovered that serene gentleman's aplomb which he wore at all times like an aura, he whispered to me softly and ironically: "How can we enjoy beauty without the virtue of patience?" And, having uttered this phrase, which sounded to me like an aphorism from some wise Muslim much older than himself, he left me alone, face to face with his painting.

The hours went by and I spent them engrossed in that tangle of wavy lines and morbid colours which, without being able to work out exactly why, cast a spell that at the time I dared to describe — I didn't know how right I was — as erotic. Dusk began to fall and the ruddy glow that emanated from the clouds on the horizon, above the swell of the rooftops, began to seep through the skylight. At first it was like a vermilion streak and then the whole room was gradually tinged with an unreal pinkish hue that seemed to bring the very walls to life, to put blood in them.

Then I saw her: it was a woman and she was naked, slightly reclining with her hands resting tenderly in her lap. One could hardly distinguish her almost living flesh from her hair with its burnished glow; her pubic hair was reddish too, and her rosy cheeks virtually melted into the colour of her hair while her lips, only slightly red, scarcely stood out from her pink skin. She appeared to burn in her repose, like an incandescent and febrile rose. She was the most unreally beautiful woman I had ever seen.

My contemplation of her could only last a few minutes: the minutes it took for the sun to set. Because little by little the rosy light of the sunset was

luego de un azul hondo y denso, y según se producían estos cambios la belleza se iba diluyendo en una amalgama de trazos confusos, hasta que por fin la figura se hundió en la tela como se hunde una moneda que arrojamos a un estanque profundo: la vamos viendo cada vez más pequeña, cada vez más difusa entre las ondas metálicas que ella misma forma, hasta que sólo queda un brillo lejano y luego, de repente, el brillo desaparece ante nuestros propios ojos y no la vemos más.

Y no la vi más. Porque Amal nunca más me la enseñó. Apenas atendió a mis barboteos de inefable entusiasmo: estaba tan seguro de que era perfecta que tal vez ni siquiera quería una opinión, sino sólo un testigo.

Creo que no la vio nadie más, aunque estuvo mucho tiempo expuesta: primero, en la galería de arte más prestigiosa de la ciudad, bajo unos focos despiadados incapaces de poner de manifiesto su misterio. Se vendió bien y creo que el comprador fue una entidad bancaria que instaló el cuadro como una joya en el vestíbulo de su oficina principal. Allí permanecerá, silenciosa y oculta, la más bella mujer que he visto: en un lugar donde nunca entra la luz incandescente del atardecer.

turning into mauve and then into a dark, dense blue, and as these changes were taking place so the beautiful woman was melting into an amalgam of confused strokes until at last the figure sank into the canvas like a coin tossed into a deep pond: we watch it getting smaller and smaller, more and more diffuse amidst the metallic waves which it makes, until the only thing that remains is a distant glow and then, suddenly, the glow disappears before our very eyes and we see it no more.

And I didn't see her any more. Because Amal never showed her to me again. He scarcely listened to my babblings of ineffable enthusiasm; he was so sure she was perfect that maybe he did not even want an opinion, only a witness.

I do not think anybody else ever saw her, although she was on exhibition for a long time: initially in the most prestigious art gallery in the city, under merciless lights incapable of revealing her mystery. The painting sold for a good price and I believe the buyer was a bank which installed it like a jewel in the entrance to its head office. There she will remain, silent and hidden away, the most beautiful woman I've ever seen: in a place where the incandescent light of the sunset never penetrates.

ADELAIDA GARCIA MORALES

ADELAIDA GARCÍA MORALES was born in Badajoz, and at the age of eleven went to live in Seville, the city from which her parents came. She graduated in Philosophy in 1970 from the Universidad Complutense, Madrid, and went on to study cinematography. She has been a secondary schoolteacher of Spanish language and literature as well as of philosophy. She has also worked as a translator, as a model and an actress.

Her first book comprised two short novels, *El sur* and *Bene* (1985). *El sur*, an intense exploration of a father-daughter relationship, won her acclaim even before it was published. Written in 1981, it provided the basis for the film of the same title made in 1983 by García Morales's husband, the director Víctor Erice. In 1985 she won the Premio Herralde with the novel *El silencio de las sirenas* (1985), a tale of romantic love in which an Adèle Hugo-like female character is observed by a bemused girl friend, narrator of the story. In 1985 García Morales also won the Premio Ícaro, awarded to the best literary newcomer of the year by the newspaper *Diario 16*.

After a quiet period of five years, her next novel, *La lógica del vampiro* (1990), continues her exploration of the feminine world, as does *Las mujeres de Héctor* (1994). *La tía Águeda* (1995), like her first two *novellas*, revolves around childhood, solitude and the painful process of growing up.

Nasmiya (1996) ventures into a more exotic territory: the questioning of alternative values to Western's concepts of love, bigamy and jealousy in a couple converted to Islam. In her latest book, *Mujeres solas* (1997), she focusses on the problems that women confront in middle age.

Adelaida García Morales is well respected outside Spain and her books have been widely translated, two of them into English: *The Silence of Sirens* (1988) and *The South and Bene* (1992).

86
FURTHER READING ON ADELAIDA GARCÍA MORALES

Asís Garrote, Ma. Dolores de, *Última hora de la novela en España* (Madrid, 1996).

Bayón, Miguel, 'Mujeres escritoras: la mirada que ve desde el rincón', *Cambio 16*, 24 November 1986, 149-52.

Cano, Soledad, 'Adelaida García Morales: "El giro a la derecha supone retroceso"', *Cambio 16*, 25 March 1996, 100-1.

Ciplijauskaité, Biruté, 'Una historia de amor desde la perspectiva kafkiana', *Ínsula*, 488-489 (1987), 24.

——————, *La novela femenina contemporánea (1970-1985). Hacia una tipología de la narración en primera persona* (Madrid, 1988).

——————, 'Intertextualidad y subversión en *El silencio de las sirenas* de Adelaida García Morales', *Revista Hispánica Moderna*, 41/2 (1988), 167-74.

Compitello, Malcom Allan, 'Making *El Sur*', *Revista Hispánica Moderna*, 46/1 (1993), 73-86.

Echevarría, Ignacio, 'Lo innombrable: Adelaida García Morales aborda con delicadeza la fantasía y el terror', *El País* (Libros), 3 June 1990.

García Ortega, Adolfo, 'Españoles traducidos. Hacia la normalización', *El Urogallo*, 23 (1988), 10-3.

Jehenson, Yvonne, 'Adelaida García Morales', in Linda Gould Levine, Ellen Engelson Marson and Gloria Feiman Waldman (eds), *Spanish Women Writers: A Bio-Bibliographical Source Book* (Westport, CT and London, 1993), 211-8.

Lottini, Otello, 'Il segni del tempo: la letteratura spagnola del post-franchismo', in *Diálogo. Studi in onore di Lore Terracini* (Roma, 1990), vol.I, 311-26.

Malaxechevarría, Coro, 'Mito y realidad en la narrativa de Adelaida García Morales', *Letras Femeninas*, 17/1-2 (1991), 43-9.

Manteiga, Roberto, 'From Empathy to Detachment: The Author-Narrator Relationship in Several Spanish Novels by Women', *Monographic Review*, 8 (1992), 19-35.

Mazquiarán de Rodríguez, Mercedes, 'The Metafictional Quest for Self-Realization and Authorial Voice in *El silencio de las sirenas*', *Romance Languages Annual*, 2 (1990), 477-81.

——————, 'Gothic Imagery, Dreams, and Vampirism: The Haunting Narrative of Adelaida García Morales', *Monographic Review*, 8 (1992), 164-82.

Montero, Isaac, '¿Nuestra realidad ausente?', *República de las Letras*, 18 (1987), 64-8.

Morris, Barbara, 'Father, Death and the Feminine: The Writer's "Subject" in Adelaida García Morales' *El sur*', *Romance Languages Annual*, 1 (1989), 559-64.

Navajas, Gonzalo, 'Narrativa y género. La ficción actual desde la mujer', *Ínsula*, 589-590 (1996), 37-9.

——————, *Más allá de la posmodernidad. Estética de la nueva novela y cine españoles* (Barcelona, 1996).

Obiol, María José, 'El juego de las similitudes y las diferencias. Madurez en el oficio de contar', *El País* (Libros), 28 July 1985.

Oleza, Joan, 'Un realismo posmoderno', *Ínsula*, 589-590 (1996), 39-42.

Ordóñez, Elizabeth J., 'Writing Ambiguity and Desire: The Works of Adelaida García Morales', in Joan L. Brown (ed.), *Women Writers of Contemporary Spain. Exiles in the Homeland* (Newark, London and Toronto, 1991), 258-77.

——————, 'Beyond the Father: Desire, Ambiguity, and Transgression in the Narrative of Adelaida García Morales', in *Voices of Their Own. Contemporary Spanish Narrative by Women* (Lewisburg, London and Toronto, 1991), 174-92.

Peña, Luis de la, 'Sobre la fragilidad del amor', *El País* (Babelia), 2 March 1996.

Pérez, Janet, *Contemporary Women Writers of Spain* (Boston, MA, 1988), 173-4.

Sánchez Arnosi, Milagros, 'Adelaida García Morales: La soledad gozosa', *Ínsula*, 472 (1986), 4.

Scarlett, Elizabeth A., 'Nomads and Schizos: Postmodern Trends in Body Writing', in *Under Construction. The Body in Spanish Novels* (Charlottesville and London, 1994), 166-85.

Thompson, Currie K., 'Adelaida García Morales' *Bene* and That Not-So-Obscure Object of Desire', *Revista de Estudios Hispánicos*, 22/1 (1988), 99-106.

——————, '*El silencio de las sirenas*: Adelaida García Morales' Revision of the Femenine "Seescape" ', *Revista Hispánica Moderna*, 45/2 (1992), 298-309.

A Chance Encounter

El encuentro

Original Spanish text
first published in *Sur Express*, 3 (1987), and
subsequently collected in *Relatos de mujeres*
(Madrid: Popular, 1988), 51-66.

El encuentro

De vez en cuando, forzado por el paso descontrolado del tiempo por mi vida, trato de detenerme con el fin de evaluar, clasificar, o simplemente recordar, mis actividades de la última semana. Pero un turbulento marasmo, constituido por retazos de lo vivido, entremezclados y confusos, aislados unos de otros, se adueña de mi memoria. Siempre recuerdo, más o menos, lo mismo: voy de aquí para allá, me dejo caer por el bar de la esquina, por el café de Milagros o por la cervecería de la plaza. A veces busco encuentros fortuitos por el barrio, forzando tontamente el azar, o bien me otorgo el derecho de introducirme en conversaciones ajenas. Si algo no puedo soportar es el silencio. No estoy capacitado para resistir un día entero sin hablar, sin decir cualquier cosa, lo que sea. Aunque no me importa reconocer que carezco de empatía y que tampoco soy de esos hombres que poseen una vocación definida. A pesar de las apariencias, detesto a los charlatanes y, de ningún modo, he decidido esta dispersión callejera a la que ya me he resignado. Lo que sucede es que para la otra alternativa, la de permanecer en mi estrecha vivienda así, sin más, sin un televisor siquiera, sin ocupaciones y obligado a un mutismo absoluto, no me veo con aptitudes. Y menos aún ahora que acabo de renunciar a la comida diaria que me ofrecía mi hermana entre consejos y reprobaciones. Me había convertido en el blanco de todas las iras familiares. Incluso mis sobrinos más pequeños habían aprendido, imitando a sus padres, a juzgarme con parcialidad por cualquier menudencia. No pienso volver a visitarles. Que se peguen entre ellos. He cumplido los treinta años y, dados los tiempos en que vivimos, se me puede considerar todavía un joven parado. Aunque mi cuñado, azuzado por la hostilidad que me profesa, asegura que mi desocupación nada tiene que ver con el paro actual. Afirma que lo mío es de otra índole, que son motivos muy diferentes a los comunes los que me mantienen alejado del

A Chance Encounter

From time to time, forced by the hurtling passage of time in my life, I endeavour to slow down a bit so as to evaluate, classify, or simply recall what I did the week before. But a turbulent paralysis comprising snippets of personal experience all jumbled together and in no particular order, one isolated from the other, takes hold of my memory. I always remember more or less the same thing: I'm on my way from here to there, I drop in at the bar on the corner, the Milagros café or the pub in the square. Sometimes I'm on the lookout for chance encounters around the neighbourhood, stupidly pushing my luck, or else awarding myself the right to barge my way into somebody else's conversation. If there's one thing I can't stand it's silence. I'm just not capable of going a whole day without speaking, without saying something, anything. I don't mind admitting, though, I have no empathy, neither am I one of those men who have some definite vocation. In spite of appearances, I detest smooth-talking tricksters and there's no way this wandering the streets I've resigned myself to now was my decision. The thing is, the other alternative — the one of staying put like this in my cramped room, with nothing else, not even a television, nothing to do and forced into total silence, I'm not capable of that. And even less so now that I've just given up the meal my sister used to provide me every day along with advice and reprimands. I'd become the target for all the family's wrath. Even the youngest of my nephews, copying their parents, had learned to sit in prejudiced judgement on me for every little thing. I don't think I'll go and see them again. Let them fight among themselves. I've reached the age of thirty and, given the times we live in, I might still be regarded as a young man who's out of work. Though my brother-in-law, egged on by the hostility he bears towards me, claims my not having a job's got nothing to do with the current unemployment statistics. He says that in my case it's something else, that the reasons that keep me out of a job are very different

trabajo. Yo diría que, por la animadversión con que me habla y por la delectación con que me insulta, cree haber descubierto móviles delictivos en mi infortunio. Hace apenas dos días nos enzarzamos en una enconada discusión, a raíz de mi inasistencia a una cita que él mismo había concertado. Me negué a acudir sólo por dignidad. Estaba convencido de que aquel supuesto conocido suyo, del que lo único que sabía era que se apellidaba Núñez, tampoco dispondría de un empleo para mí en su Agencia. Ya a las últimas entrevistas que me había impuesto, me presenté desesperanzado, sin cambiar mi atuendo de costumbre, vestido al desgaire, sin preocuparme por lucir la indumentaria correcta. Finalmente, aunque guardé la tarjeta de visita, por si acaso, tuve el coraje de responderle verbalmente a sus ofensas y de despedirme jurando que, en lo sucesivo, sería para ellos sólo un muerto.

Aquella misma noche, gracias a las vicisitudes de la suerte, conecté con un viejo enjuto y barbicano, merodeador de papeleras públicas, basuras y otros desechos. Casi tropiezo con él. Su deslucida figura se irguió de pronto ante mí, como surgiendo de entre grandes cubos repletos de desperdicios. El movimiento de sus dedos, casi vertiginoso, me retuvo a su lado, admirándole durante varios minutos. Estoy seguro de que en aquellos momentos no le incomodó mi curiosidad. Incluso me atrevería a afirmar que le complacía el disponer de un espectador ante el que exhibir la destreza de malabarista con que hizo volar el contenido íntegro de un cajón de madera. Pensé que el virtuosismo de aquellos dedos, tan extraño a la torpeza general del resto de su cuerpo, no podía ser sino el resultado de un prolongado y pertinaz entrenamiento. "¡Nada, no hay nada!" protestó mientras, con un ademán rutinario de mendicidad, me tendía la mano hasta casi rozarme. Le di las buenas noches con agrado y permanecí inmóvil junto a él, como si acabara de llegar a una cita. El viejo murmuró algo a guisa de saludo y se arregló el nudo de la corbata que, a falta de cinturón, le sujetaba los pantalones. Debido a que no era un trasnochador y al quebrantamiento de mi ánimo por la ruptura familiar, pese a la independencia que ésta suponía, volví a desearle buenas noches, ahora con el fin de despedirme y continuar el camino hacia mi casa. "¡Espera, no te vayas! ¡Quédate conmigo hasta que se apaguen las luces de las calles, hasta que se haga de día!" Al escuchar su voz suplicante pensé que era un loco y aún así, me detuve. No me sentía capaz de salir corriendo sin responderle, sin mirarle siquiera, y menos aún de pasar la noche vagando a su lado por el asfalto. Enseguida intuí que no me resultaría fácil torcer su voluntad. Así

to the usual ones. I'd say that from the animosity he shows when he talks to me and the delight he takes in insulting me, he thinks he's uncovered criminal motives behind my misfortune. Scarcely two days ago we got involved in a heated row because I'd failed to turn up to some appointment he himself had set up. I refused to turn up solely out of self-respect. I was convinced that that so-called acquaintance of his, about whom the only thing I knew was that his name was Núñez, didn't have a job for me in his agency anyway. At the last interviews he'd forced down my throat I turned up without any real expectations, without altering the way I usually looked, without bothering to change the slovenly way I usually dressed, without bothering to wear the "right" sort of clothes. Finally, and even though I kept the visiting card just in case, I found the courage to tackle him to his face about his offensive remarks, and then I left swearing that the next time they saw me I'd be in my coffin.

That same night, thanks to the vicissitudes of fortune, I bumped into a gaunt old man with a grey beard, a forager of public litter bins, rubbish tips and other sources of garbage. I nearly collided with him. His shabby figure suddenly reared up before my very eyes as if surging up from the midst of great bucketfuls of refuse. The giddy movement of his fingers held me at his side marvelling at him for several minutes. I'm convinced that during that time my curiosity didn't bother him. I'd even go so far as to say he was pleased to have an audience before which to exhibit how he could make the full contents of a wooden box vanish with all the dexterity of a juggler. I thought the great virtuosity of those fingers, so strangely at odds with the general clumsiness of the rest of his body, could only be the result of some extended and dedicated training. "Nothing, there's nothing!" he complained, meanwhile stretching out his hand in a routine begging gesture until he was almost grazing me. I wished him a cheery good evening and stood still beside him, not moving a muscle, as if just turning up for an appointment. The old man muttered something by way of a greeting and arranged the knot of the tie that in the absence of a belt was holding up his trousers. Since I was not a night owl, and as my spirits were pretty low after the family bust-up, despite the independence this implied, I again wished him good night, planning now to take my leave of him and continue on my way home. "Wait, don't go! Stay with me 'till they turn out the street lights, 'till the morning comes!" Hearing his pleading voice I thought he was crazy, but even so I stopped. I felt I couldn't just run off without giving him an answer, without even looking at him, and even less spend the night wandering the streets with him. I guessed straightaway that it wouldn't be easy for me to

que, abocado sin remedio a postergar la despedida, le invité a que me acompañara en mi recorrido. Su abrumador agradecimiento me forzó a precisar con descortesía que sólo andaríamos juntos hasta mi puerta. ¿Qué necesidad tenía yo de agobiarme creando compromisos en un encuentro tan insignificante? Pero, observando su lánguida figura, frente a mí, encogiéndose resignada en el interior de su chaqueta, estuve tentado a prolongar el paseo, pues nos hallábamos a pocos pasos de mi domicilio. No obstante, supe contenerme.

Emprendimos así una silenciosa marcha que a él debió parecerle un perfecto fraude, ya que, al detenerme para introducir la llave en la cerradura, sin esperar mi consentimiento, a modo de represalia, me comunicó que subiría conmigo. "¡Nada de eso!" le dije con visible fastidio. Y, enseguida, mecánicamente, para suavizar mi negativa, añadí que no había ascensor y que, además, vivía en el ático. "¡Mejor!" exclamó el viejo, aclarando sin tardanza que despreciaba todos los aparatos eléctricos en general, pero que a los ascensores precisamente no los soportaba. Jamás se había dejado elevar por ninguno de ellos. No me importaba demasiado mostrarme grosero con él, o mezquino, o incluso duro, pero tampoco su presencia me repelía hasta el punto de dejarme enredar en un forcejeo que, tal vez, se prolongara durante toda la madrugada. Por otra parte, no encontré, en aquellos momentos, ninguna razón contundente que me impulsara a emplear la violencia con un pobre estólido. Y, ante todo, no se puede olvidar que era la primera vez en mi vida que alguien se empeñaba con testarudez en conseguir mi compañía. Claro que tal extravagancia, más que complacido, me dejó desconcertado e indefenso ante aquel vagabundo que me observaba ansioso, casi con temor, como si esperase de mí algo parecido a una sentencia.

Emprendimos el ascenso a un ritmo normal hasta que, a mitad de la escalera, se detuvo jadeante. Ya en el último tramo tuve que transportarle, colgado por completo de mi cuello. Por fortuna, su cuerpo parecía consistir sólo en un esqueleto o armazón de alambre, cubierto directamente por la ropa. Atravesamos la azotea, sin prisa, hasta alcanzar mi propiedad: un estrecho rectángulo situado en una de las esquinas. Al entrar en la salita, el viejo se reanimó de golpe. Y como si hubiera sido impulsado por un resorte oculto, se entregó sin perder un instante, a lo que sin lugar a dudas, parecía ser la razón misma de su existencia. Todas sus facultades se pusieron, de inmediato, al servicio de sus dedos. Escrutó, palpó y tiró cuanto alcanzaron sus ojos. Nada podía satisfacerle. Y, como en cumplimiento de una misión fatídica, hizo volar un cenicero vacío, una bufanda, un peine mellado, unos

change his mind. So, forced into agreeing to delay the leave-taking, I invited
him to accompany me as I walked. His overwhelming gratitude drove me to
make it rudely clear that we would only be walking together as far as my
door. What need did I have to overburden myself by creating awkward
situations in such a meaningless encounter? Yet watching his languid figure
in front of me, resignedly cringing inside his coat, I was tempted to prolong
the walk since we were by this time just a few steps away from where I
lived. Nevertheless, I managed to contain myself.

   Thus we set off on a silent walk that to him must have seemed a complete
farce, because when I stopped to put the key in the lock, without waiting for
my consent, by way of a reprisal, he said he'd come up with me. "Oh no you
won't!" I told him with visible annoyance. And then, almost immediately,
mechanically, so as to smooth over my having said no, I added there was no
lift and what was more I lived in the attic. "All the better!" cried the old
man, clarifying this without further ado by explaining that he had no time for
electrical apparatus in general but it was lifts in particular he really couldn't
abide. He'd never allowed himself to be carried up in one. I didn't care very
much about how rude or mean or even callous I appeared to him, yet neither
did his presence repel me to the point where I would allow myself to get
embroiled in some struggle that might well go on into the early hours of the
morning. On the other hand just then I found no convincing reason to drive
me to use violence against a poor blockhead. Above all you mustn't forget
this was the first time in my life that anybody had been so pig-headedly
determined to seek out my company. Of course, such extravagance, rather
than making me feel pleased, left me bewildered and defenceless in the
presence of this tramp who was watching me anxiously, almost fearfully, as
if he were expecting something approaching a verdict from me.

   We started our climb at a normal pace until halfway up the stairs he
paused for breath. By the time we got to the last flight I w`s already having
to carry him, his whole weight hanging from my neck. Fortunately his body
seemed to be nothing more than a skeleton or wire framework covered only
by his clothes. We made our unhurried way across the flat roof until we
reached my place: a narrow rectangle situated at one of the corners. As we
entered the tiny room the old man suddenly recovered his wind. And as if
driven by some hidden force, without another second's ado, he set about
what appeared to be the undoubted reason for his very being. All his talents
were immediately at the service of his fingers. He examined, he felt and
threw aside everything his eyes lit upon. There was no satisfying him. And
as if in fulfilment of some fateful mission he sent an empty ashtray flying, a

calcetines, un frasquito de colirio, una caja de zapatos, recibos, periódicos y otros objetos abandonados sobre la gran mesa que ocupa, con exactitud geométrica, la mitad de la habitación. Después, pasó al otro lado, encaramándose con un pie en la butaca y el otro en el velador del rincón. En esa postura tenía acceso a una estantería, cuyo contenido: unos pocos libros y un plato de cerámica rudimentaria, tampoco logró interesarle. Bajó contrariado, murmurando algo y cayendo directamente en el cuarto contiguo: mi dormitorio. Su afán desenfrenado de búsqueda, su vertiginoso registro, no se detuvo ante mis pertenencias más íntimas. No respetaba nada, incluso llegó a levantar el colchón de mi cama. Una vez hubo convertido mi hogar en una gigantesca papelera, se echó al suelo con el propósito de levantar las baldosas más inestables. Entonces creí adivinar sus verdaderos móviles en medio de tanto teatro. No es ningún inocente, me dije, busca dinero. Y, saliendo al fin de mi estupor, le increpé: "¡Menudo sinvergüenza está usted hecho, amigo!" "¡Nada, no hay nada!" protestaba él por su cuenta, invulnerable a mis insultos. Le llamé ratero varias veces y, abriendo la puerta con autoridad, le ordené salir inmediatamente, mientras le señalaba la oscura intemperie de la azotea. Incluso le amenacé con denunciarle a la policía si no abandonaba mi vivienda. Me aclaró entonces, con una vehemencia desproporcionada, que ante todo deseaba evitar que le confundieran con un ladrón. Por eso, rara vez buscaba entre los objetos en venta de las tiendas o de los puestos de mercadillos. Temía, por encima de cualquier otra desventura, que le recluyeran de nuevo en lo que llamó un presidio infantil. Sus palabras me confundieron, me desconcertaron, incluso lograron que me avergonzara de mi crueldad. "Entonces ¿qué anda usted buscando?" le pregunté. Pero ya no me respondió. Sentándose en la butaca de la salita, me miró con fijeza, igual que si tuviera ante sí un ilimitado vacío. Por primera vez tuve ocasión de observarle con detenimiento. La huella de una antigua ferocidad permanecía en sus facciones. Bajo sus pobladas cejas, una mirada rota, desvanecida tras una película blanquecina, prestaba a su rostro el gesto perdido de un ciego. Ni siquiera me veía. Cerró los ojos e, inmediatamente, sin ningún proceso previo, sin que pasara el tiempo, comencé a escuchar los estertores de su respiración. Y digo "estertores" porque más que a un sosegado reposo, su sueño se asemejaba a una agitada agonía. Pensé que estaría enfermo, muy enfermo.

A la mañana siguiente, al despertarme, ya tenía el firme propósito de arrojar de mi vida a aquel individuo sin sentido, imagen viva de la mala fortuna que me acechaba. Era la encarnación misma de un mal

scarf, a comb with some of its teeth missing, some socks, a little bottle of eyedrops, a shoe box, receipts, newspapers and other things scattered about the big table that with geometric precision takes up half the room. Then he crossed to the other side of the room, perching with one foot on the armchair and the other on the small table in the corner. In this position he could reach a shelf, the contents of which — a few books and a crude ceramic dish — also failed to catch his interest. Annoyed, he got back down, muttering something, and immediately fell on the adjoining room: my bedroom. His uncontrolled urge to search, his mind-boggling rummaging, didn't stop even when he got to my most intimate belongings. He respected nothing, even going so far as to lift up the mattress on my bed. Once he'd turned my home into one huge waste bin, he threw himself onto the floor so that he could start lifting up some of the looser tiles. At this point I thought I guessed the real motives behind this pantomime of his. This is no simpleton, I told myself, he's looking for money. And coming out of my stupor at last I upbraided him: "You cheeky devil, you!" "Nothing, there's nothing," he complained, ignoring me, unmoved by my insults. I called him a sneak thief several times, and holding open the door with authority I ordered him to get out there and then, all the time showing him the inclement darkness outside on the flat roof. I even threatened to report him to the police if he didn't leave my home. He then pointed out to me with a vehemence out of all proportion that what he wanted above anything else was to avoid being taken for a thief. That was why he rarely rummaged through things on sale in shops or on stalls. More that any other misfortune, he feared that they would lock him away again in what he called a young offenders institution. His words confused me, bewildered me, even managed to make me feel ashamed at how cruel I'd been. "So what are you looking for?" I asked him. But this time he didn't answer. Sitting in the armchair in my tiny room he stared at me, as if he were peering into some boundless void. For the first time I had a chance to examine him carefully. The mark of some former ferocity was still etched on his features. Under his heavy brows the broken look in his eyes, masked over with a whitish film, gave his face the lost expression of a blind man. He didn't even see me. He closed his eyes and immediately, without further ado, without any time elapsing, I began to hear the death rattle in his throat. And I say "death rattle" because instead of peaceful repose his sleep resembled agitated death throes. I thought he must be ill, very ill.

The next morning when I woke up I'd already made up my mind to throw this absurd old man out of my life, this vivid image of the bad luck that was lying in wait for me. He was the very incarnation of a bad premonition. I

presentimiento. Le zarandeé sin cuidado y le fui despabilando por el camino, mientras cruzaba la azotea, cargando a medias con él sobre mis hombros. En cuanto pisamos la acera, le tendí la mano en señal de despedida. Pero él me negó la suya. Se había agarrado al borde de mi chaqueta para formular lo que muy bien podría ser una invitación. Al punto supe que comía casi a diario en una institución de caridad. Pretendía que yo le acompañara con el fin de que aprendiera el camino y así poder beneficiarme, en el futuro, de su misma fuente de alimentación. Ni me sorprendió, ni me molestó que me hubiera tomado por un igual. Nada tenía de extraño. Con el tiempo y las contrariedades, me he vuelto perezoso, abúlico, descuidando hasta límites inadmisibles mi aspecto externo. Quién sabe la apariencia que puedo yo ofrecer ahora a alguien que carezca de la mirada indulgente con que, en virtud de tantos años de convivencia, me aceptan los vecinos de mi barrio. Pese a la insistencia del viejo infortunado, rechacé su propuesta con desdén, desabrido, tal vez por temor a ir cayendo, poco a poco, solapadamente, en su misma forma de desamparo si frecuentaba lugares de mendicidad. Así pues, me despedí de él alegando que tenía un compromiso. Debía acudir a una entrevista importante, una cuestión de trabajo. Saqué de mi bolsillo la tarjeta de visita que había recibido de mi cuñado y se la enseñé. No pretendía que la leyera, ni tampoco que la mirase. Me bastaba con nombrarla, con exhibirla como prueba incuestionable de nuestras diferencias, como señal inequívoca de que yo no era de los suyos. Y, para convencerme de que aquella desvalida criatura no era precisamente mi espejo, me alejé con la intención de ignorarle en lo sucesivo.

Nos hallábamos en una de esas calles céntricas y angostas, en las que la irrupción del tiempo moderno se manifiesta reduciendo a mero estorbo todo cuanto albergan. Allí mismo, en una esquina cualquiera, en medio de un agitado trasiego, se detuvo el viejo, aceptando mi desprecio con naturalidad. Adosado a la fachada porosa, adherido a ella como si la sucia superficie penetrara su cuerpo traslúcido, extendió su mano mendicante, armonizando con cuanto le rodeaba, igual que una mancha de humedad o un desconchado en un edificio en ruina.

Minutos más tarde, entré en la Agencia que dirigía el señor Núñez, siguiendo las indicaciones que colgaban en la puerta: "Entre sin llamar". Asimismo logré introducirme, con la tarjeta de visita en la mano, en su propio despacho sin que nadie tratara de impedírmelo. El director, a pesar de su atuendo juvenil, era un hombre maduro y castigado. Primero me miró

shook him roughly and roused him out of his sleep all the while walking, crossing the roof terrace with him half-slung over my shoulders. As soon as we stepped onto the pavement I stretched out my hand towards him in a gesture of farewell. But he refused to give me his. He'd grabbed the edge of my coat to formulate what might well have been an invitation. I instantly learned that he ate virtually every day at some charitable institution. He tried to get me to go with him so that I would know the way and thus in future be able to take advantage of this same source of food. It neither surprised nor bothered me that he'd taken me to be an equal. There was nothing odd about that. Over the years, with all the setbacks I've suffered, I've grown lazy, apathetic, intolerably careless about my appearance. Who knows how I might look now to anybody who might lack the indulgent eye with which my neighbours in the district, by dint of the many years we lived so close to each other, accept me. Despite the hapless old man's persistence, I turned down his offer scornfully, a little sharply, possibly out of fear I would fall, gradually and insidiously, into the same helpless state were I to frequent those places where the beggars roamed. And so I took my leave of him claiming I had an appointment. I had to attend some important interview, it was to do with work. I took the visiting card I'd got from my brother-in-law out of my pocket and showed it to him. I didn't want him to read it or even look at it. It was enough for me to mention it, to hold it up as unquestionable proof of the difference between us, as an unmistakable sign that I was not the same as him. And in order to convince myself that that destitute creature was not my mirror image, I walked away with the intention of ignoring him from then on.

We found ourselves in one of those downtown narrow streets where the inrush of modern times manifests itself by reducing everything that such areas cherish to just a nuisance. At that very spot, on some corner or other, in the midst of frenetic to-ings and fro-ings the old man stopped still, accepting my contempt as if it were the most natural thing in the world. With his back against the porous facade, stuck to it as if the dirty surface were biting into his translucent body, he stretched out his begging hand, blending in with his entire surroundings like a damp stain or a place where the plaster has come away from a dilapidated building.

Minutes later I entered the agency run by Señor Núñez, following the instructions hanging on the door: "Enter without knocking." With the visiting card in my hand I likewise managed to get into his own office without anybody trying to stop me. In spite of the youthful way he was dressed, the manager was a mature and careworn man. Initially he looked

con sobresalto. Después, al escuchar mis lacónicas palabras de identificación, dijo impertinente: "¡Ah, eres tú!" Contuve a tiempo la tentación de excusarme. Pues ¿qué le iba a decir, lo siento pero soy yo? ¡De ningún modo! Arrostrando su injusta incomodidad ante mi presencia, le informé sobre el motivo de mi visita. "¿Qué sabes hacer?" me preguntó expeditivo. "Si se trata de menudencias... tareas simples... no sé... cualquier cosa." Percibí al punto que mi respuesta no satisfizo y, además, que conmigo sólo deseaba ahorrar: tiempo, palabras, saludos, sonrisas, amabilidad e incluso ademanes, pues me observaba mirándome de lado, a hurtadillas, en una postura rígida y manifiestamente incómoda, negándome la mínima deferencia de girar para hablarme abiertamente de frente.

"¿Sabes taquigrafía?" Por el tono de su voz, más que una pregunta, sus palabras me parecieron una adivinanza. "Pues... no la considero demasiado difícil" respondí yo, dispuesto a no dejarme humillar. "Pero ¿sabes o no sabes?" Ante su insistencia articulé un movimiento de hombros y cabeza, un gesto incalificable, que logró acrecentar su desprecio. "¿Hablas inglés?" "Si me empeño..." "¿Qué quieres decir?" "Pues que si me lo propusiera..." "En fin —protestó— ahora no hay nada, pero se te hará una ficha." Llamó entonces a uno de sus empleados y, sin la menor dilación, se abrió la puerta para dejar paso, no a la persona solicitada, sino a la desvencijada figura del viejo callejero. Había entrado inocentemente, avanzando hasta el centro de la habitación. Allí se detuvo y me dedicó una inoportuna risita de júbilo, como si pretendiera congratularse con mi fracaso. Ante un individuo así, impertinente, osado, fuera de cualquier regla de juego, nada más lógico que una reacción brusca y despectiva. Mientras el director, indignado, trataba de expulsarle, yo me mantenía a distancia, indiferente, disimulando nuestro reciente trato. Ni siquiera intervine cuando le agarró con violencia por un brazo, lastimándole, para conducirle hasta la salida. Tampoco me sumé, como hubiera sido lo natural, a los comentarios del oficinista en cuyas manos me dejó el señor Núñez. Sin llegar a darme más pistas sobre el posible trabajo, sin dejarme entrever ni la menor esperanza de conseguirlo, sin despedirse siquiera, me abandonó precipitadamente, dispuesto a recuperar el tiempo perdido entre mi visita y la del intruso. No es difícil comprender que, viéndome en el trance de rellenar una ficha en esas condiciones y convencido de su ineficacia para justipreciar mis capacidades, cayera en un hondo abatimiento.

taken aback. Then on hearing my terse words of identification he said peevishly: "Oh, it's you!" I managed to curb the temptation to apologize in time. After all, what was I going to say to him, "Sorry, but yes, it's me?" Not likely! Braving his unjust irritation at my being there, I told him of the reason for my visit. "What can you do?" he promptly asked me. "If you're talking about bits and bobs... simple jobs... I don't know... anything." I immediately realized my reply was unsatisfactory and that anyway he only wanted to save things — time, words, greetings, smiles, being friendly, gestures even — for he was looking at me out of the corner of his eye, pretending not to, in a stiff and obviously uncomfortable posture, denying me even the basic courtesy of turning round to speak to me face to face.

"Can you do shorthand?" From the tone of his voice, his words sounded like a guessing game to me rather than a question. "Well... I don't consider it too difficult," I replied, unwilling to allow myself to be humiliated. "Well, do you know how to or don't you?" In view of his insistence I sketched a movement with my shoulders and head, a gesture into which nothing could be read, and which managed to deepen his scorn. "Do you speak English?" "If I try hard enough..." "What do you mean?" "Well if I were to really put my mind to it..." "Well," he stated, "at the moment there's nothing, but we'll fill out a form for you." Then he called one of his employees and, without delay, the door opened to let somebody into the room, not the person he'd asked to come in but the broken-down figure of the old man who lived on the streets. He'd entered innocently enough, advancing to the middle of the room. There he stopped and let out an untimely snigger of jubilation in my direction as if to congratulate himself on my failure. Faced with someone like that — impertinent, daring, beyond any set of rules — the only logical thing was a rude and contemptuous reaction. While the manager, who was angry by now, tried to throw him out I kept my distance, indifferent, concealing the fact of our recent dealings. I didn't even intervene when the director seized him roughly by the arm, hurting him, so as to lead him to the way out. Nor, as would have been the natural thing to do, did I add my voice to the comments made by the clerk in whose hands Señor Núñez left me. Without giving me any clues about the potential job, without allowing me the least glimmer of hope of landing it, without even saying goodbye, he rushed off and left me, seeking to make up for the time that had been wasted on my visit and that of the intruder. Finding myself at the critical point of filling in a form under such circumstances and convinced that it wouldn't effectively appraise my capabilities, it's not hard to understand why I should fall into a deep depression.

De nuevo en la calle, no me extrañó descubrir al viejo esperándome con una inexplicable sonrisa de satisfacción, casi de regocijo. No le reprendí, ni le exigí que justificara su comportamiento. No le dije nada. Me abandoné a la deriva, conducido por él, ignorando que ahora había tomado un rumbo fijo. Supe que nos hallábamos en su territorio cuando, al entrar en un bar, siguiendo siempre su iniciativa, un camarero le saludó, llamándole por su nombre: Simón. Y, no obstante haberle advertido sobre mi imposiblidad de pagar, pidió con entusiamo una botella de buen vino y dos vasos. Inmediatamente, antes incluso de empezar a beber, quiso abonar el importe. De un bolsillo de su chaqueta extrajo una cartera de piel desgastada y, ante mi estupor, la hizo bailar entre sus dedos hasta dejarla abierta en mis manos. Contenía una considerable cantidad de dinero. Se la devolví enseguida, desconcertado, incapaz de admitir que mi compañero, por llamarle de alguna manera, había sido el artífice, él solo, de tan importante hurto. Y, mientras barajaba con su habilidad de malabar el resto del botín: unos pocos papeles y algunos documentos, se me apareció fugazmente el rostro severo del señor Núñez, enmarcado en una pequeña fotografía. De golpe, aunque por breves instantes, me alarmé. Si éste no disponía de otras referencias sobre mi persona que las que hubiera podido recibir de mi cuñado, estaba perdido. Por fuerza haría recaer sobre mí toda la culpabilidad. Claro que este mal presagio se desvaneció muy pronto. Pues ¿acaso no resultaba a todas luces evidente que el sospechoso era el otro, el viejo pordiosero que había logrado colarse en su oficina con tanta desfachatez? Una vez tranquilizado, le di unas palmadas en la espalda a guisa de reconocimiento y ¿por qué no decirlo? también de admiración. No se puede negar que, dadas las circunstancias en que se produjo y conociendo, por otra parte, sus temores, semejante intrepidez exigía un talante heroico. Y así, aquella vida en ruina que, hasta entonces, me había sugerido su miserable figura, de súbito se me apareció transfigurada, como un paisaje desconocido, inquietante, incluso amenazador. Sin embargo, cuando, algo más tarde, le oí murmurar de nuevo: "¡Nada, no hay nada!" mientras hurgaba en la cesta de una vendedora de tabaco, le zarandeé impaciente y le hablé como a un loco: "¡Dígame qué está buscando, hombre, yo puedo ayudarle!" Nos hallábamos en un pasadizo subterráneo, un paso de peatones que conducía, además, a las taquillas del metro. Le había seguido hasta allí sólo por inercia, porque no pensaba asistir más a la comida en casa de mi hermana, porque no tenía, en aquellos instantes, un punto más atractivo al que dirigirme. No sé por qué, me sentía con derecho

Back on the street again it didn't surprise me to find the old man waiting for me with an inexplicable smile of satisfaction, and almost of delight, on his face. I didn't reprimand him, neither did I demand an explanation for his behaviour. I didn't say a word. I allowed myself to be drawn along, following where he led, unaware that he had now taken a fixed course. I knew we were in his territory when, on entering a bar and, always following his lead, a waiter greeted him, addressing him by his name: Simón. And notwithstanding the fact that I had warned him I couldn't possibly pay, he enthusiastically called for a bottle of good wine and two glasses. Immediately, before we even began to drink, he wanted to settle the bill. He took a battered leather wallet out of a pocket in his jacket and, as I watched in astonishment, made it twirl a couple of times between his fingers before laying it open in my hands. It contained a good deal of money. I immediately gave it back to him, disconcerted, unable to admit that my companion, for lack of a better word, had been the sole architect of such a sizeable theft. And as he, with his juggler's skill, was shuffling the remains of the haul: a few papers and some documents, the severe features of Señor Núñez appeared fleetingly before my eyes, framed in a little photograph. Suddenly, albeit for only a few brief seconds, I was alarmed. If the manager had no other references about what sort of person I was other than those he'd been able to get from my brother-in-law, I was sunk. The full blame would necessarily fall on me. However, this strong sense of foreboding soon evaporated. Wasn't it blatantly obvious that the suspect should be the other man, the old beggar who had managed to gatecrash his office so brazenly? Once I'd calmed down, I patted him once or twice on the back in acknowledgement and — why not admit it? — admiration too. You can't deny that given the circumstances it took place under and, on the other hand, knowing about his fears, such an intrepid action called for an heroic disposition. And now, the ruined life that up until that moment had been suggested by his miserable figure, suddenly appeared to have been transfigured, like an unknown landscape, disturbing, menacing even. Nonetheless, when a little while later I heard him again mumble: "Nothing, there's nothing!" as he was rummaging through a tobacco vendor's basket, I shook him impatiently and spoke to him as if to a mad person: "Tell me what you're looking for — I can help you!" We were in an underground passage, a pedestrian subway that also led to the ticket office for the Metro. I had followed him thus far out of sheer inertia, since I wasn't planning to go to eat at my sister's house any more, and because just then I had nowhere better to go. I don't know why but I felt I had the right to wheedle it out of

a sonsacarle. Pero en aquel trance no se mostraba receptivo a ninguna pregunta. Tal vez ni siquiera me había escuchado. Y tampoco parecía dispuesto a desvelar a nadie el secreto de su extravagancia. Finalmente, la vendedora, que por su tolerancia podría ser una antigua conocida, perdió la paciencia: "¡Bueno, ya está bien!" "¡Mira cómo me está poniendo todo!" Simón soltó malhumorado una caja de cerillas y nos dio la espalda. Ignorándonos a ambos, cruzó la multitud de peatones con dificultades, abriéndose paso en dirección perpendicular a la de ellos. Le observé mientras se alejaba, flotando entre los transeúntes, como una forma sólo ligeramente humana, como un simulacro de hombre, como si su búsqueda imposible, entre desechos y objetos insignificantes, no fuera más que un puro desmoronamiento convertido en acción, una manera activa de disparatar. "¡Otro!" exclamó la vendedora de tabaco mirándome a mí, no con desprecio sino con un deje de lástima y de conmiseración tal que me hizo sentir frío. Su "otro" me reflejaba, como un espejo resquebrajado, una imagen mía descompuesta e irreconocible, pero tremendamente familiar a un tiempo. "Una cosa que le dé la suerte. Eso es lo que busca" me aclaró la vendedora arrugando la nariz en una mueca de desprecio, molesta conmigo, como si pensara que yo le había obligado a decir una tontería. Tenía el pelo canoso y rizado en una permanente pasada de moda. Mientras se arreglaba el peinado, ajustándose bien las horquillas, me dijo en son de burla que también yo podría encontrar la cosa, sí, la cosa que me daría suerte y cambiaría mi vida. Sólo tenía que estar atento, hurgar en todas partes, incluso en los lugares más insólitos, incluso en los más repugnantes. Hablaba con tal desprecio que, de haberla escuchado en otras circunstancias, me habría pronunciado en defensa del viejo, habría improvisado algún gesto de solidaridad con él. Pero en aquel preciso instante sus palabras sólo me inspiraron un pesado aburrimiento. Alcé mi voz bruscamente, por encima de la suya, decidido a hacerla callar. No me faltaba más que enredarme en una conversación tan insensata. En aquel momento pude haberme marchado, salir al exterior y reintegrarme al ritmo natural de mis días. Pero no lo hice. Me dispuse a buscar a Simón con el propósito de despedirme una vez más. No tardé mucho en encontrarle. Se había acomodado en el suelo, junto a un hombre pulcro y maduro que informaba de su miseria por escrito, con letras mayúsculas, en un cartón que le colgaba del cuello. Me detuve a su lado, mirándole desde arriba y separado de él por una línea

him. But at that juncture he didn't look as if he'd be receptive to any questions. Perhaps he hadn't even been listening to me. And neither did he seem ready to reveal the secret of his extravagance to anybody.

Finally, the tobacco vendor, who from the way she put up with him could have been a very old acquaintance, lost patience: "OK, that's enough now! Look what a mess you're making of everything!" With a show of bad temper, Simón let go of a box of matches and turned his back on us. Ignoring both of us he made his way with difficulty through the crowd of pedestrians, cutting a vertical line through their mass. I watched him as he moved farther and farther away, floating amongst the passers-by like a shape that was only vaguely human, a semblance of a man, as if his impossible search amongst the rubbish and worthless things were no more than a straightforward breakdown converted into action, an active way of behaving absurdly. "Another one!" exclaimed the tobacco vendor looking at me, not scornfully but with such a hint of sadness and commiseration that it made my blood run cold. Her "another one" reflected back to me, as if from some cracked mirror, an image that was distorted and unrecognizable, yet at the same time very familiar. "Something that will bring him luck. That's what he's looking for," explained the woman selling the tobacco, wrinkling her nose in a grimace of scorn, offended with me as if she thought I'd forced her into saying something silly. She had greying hair that was curled into an outdated perm. Whilst she sorted out her hair-do, carefully adjusting the kirby-grips, she told me in a taunting voice that I too would be able to find the thing, yes, the very thing that would bring me luck and change my life. I only had to be observant, to rummage everywhere, even in the most unwonted, the most repugnant, places. She was saying this with such derision that, had I been listening under any other circumstances, I would have spoken up in defence of the old man, would have improvised some gesture of solidarity with him. But at that precise instant her words inspired in me nothing more than a heavy sense of boredom. I raised my voice rudely above hers, resolved to make her shut up. That was all I needed, to get myself involved in such a stupid conversation. I could have stalked off right then, gone outside and reintegrated myself into the natural rhythm of my days. But I didn't do it. I got ready to go in search of Simón so I could say my farewells one more time. I didn't have to wait long before I found him. He was settled on the ground, next to a tidily dressed middle-aged man who was advising the world of his poverty in writing, in capital letters, on a piece of cardboard that was hanging round his neck. I stopped next to him, looking down at him from above, separated from him by an imaginary but

imaginaria pero perfectamente definida. Allí estaba el viejo, entonando una canción inclasificable, una suerte de quejido, tal vez un torpe simulacro de saeta. Había extendido ante sí una cartulina con varias estampas pegadas. Todas eran de la virgen de Triana. Rocé con mi pie, suavemente, el bolsillo de su chaqueta, abultado por la cartera recién adquirida. "¿No te basta con esa suerte?", le pregunté tuteándole, sin pensarlo, por vez primera. "Eso es otra cosa", me respondió distraído, con indiferencia. Entonces me dejé deslizar por la pared, poco a poco, hacia abajo, doblando las rodillas hasta caer a su lado, en aquel suelo de asfalto, inaccesible para mí sólo unos segundos antes. Fue como si hubiera resbalado en el límite mismo de lo que siempre había considerado la normalidad. Y sentí que el mundo entero se desplomaba allá arriba, desvaneciéndose en mi cabeza, dentro de ella. Durante breves minutos, fugaces e irrepetibles, me entregué a un descanso impensable. Una moneda vino rodando hasta mis rodillas. Nadie la reclamó.

perfectly defined line. Here was the old man, intoning some song you couldn't quite identify, in a kind of wailing, perhaps some ungainly sham of a *saeta*.[7] He had a piece of thin cardboard laid out in front of him on which various holy pictures had been stuck. All showed the Virgin of Triana. I used my foot to brush gently against the pocket of his jacket, which was bulging with the recently acquired wallet. "Isn't that luck enough for you?" I asked, using the familiar form of address for the first time without thinking. "That's another matter," he replied distractedly, indifferently. Then I let myself gradually slide down the wall, bending my knees until I was down at his side, on that concrete ground, a place that had been inaccessible to me just a few seconds earlier. It was as if I had slipped on the very edge of what I had always regarded as normality. And I felt that the whole world was coming crashing down from above, dispersing itself onto my head, inside it. For a few short fleeting and unrepeatable minutes I consigned myself to an unthinkable rest. A coin came rolling towards my knees. Nobody picked it up again.

---

[7]   *saeta* : a short flamenco verse sung at the passing of a procession during Holy Week in southern Spain.

LOURDES ORTIZ
Photograph © Albert Chust

LOURDES ORTIZ was born in Madrid in 1943. A novelist and a short-story writer as well as a poet and an occasional playwright, she also publishes scholarly essays on literature, communication theory and art, and has translated from French (Jean Jolivet, Jacques Le Goff, Flaubert, Marquis of Sade, Georges Bataille, Michael Tournier) and Italian (Aleksander R. Luría). She is currently the Director of the Real Escuela de Arte Dramático in Madrid, where she teaches art history.

Although she is mainly known for her novels, her prolific and versatile work includes essays: *Escritos políticos de Larra* (1967), *Comunicación crítica* (1977), *Conocer Rimbaud y su obra* (1979), and *Camas* (1989), plays: *Las murallas de Jericó* (1980), *Fedra, Penteo, Electra, Pentesilea, El local de Bernardeta A., Cenicienta* (1988), *Yudita* (1991), and books for children.

She has published one collection of short stories, *Los motivos de Circe* (1988), and a number of others in various periodicals and anthologies: 'Paisajes y figuras', in *Doce relatos de mujeres*, edited by Ymelda Navajo (1982); 'Alicia', in *Cuentos eróticos*, edited by Laura Freixas (1988), later included in *Relatos eróticos*, edited by Carmen Estévez (1990); 'El espejo de las sombras' in *Diario 16* (1991), also collected in *Cuento español contemporáneo*, edited by A. Encinar and A. Percival (1993); and 'El inmortal', in *Cuentos de este siglo*, edited by Ángeles Encinar (1996).

So far she has seven novels to her credit. *Luz de la memoria* (1976), an excellent example of a polyphonic novel, is a complex exploration of a male character whose experiences during the political struggle against Franco's dictatorship lead to disillusionment. Her second novel, *Picadura mortal* (1979), is a thriller and incorporates what was in those days the novelty of a female detective whose image echoes that of those liberated young women of early post-Franco Spain. *En días como éstos* (1981) is a book where terrorism and violence engage the reader in a somewhat experimental narrative, while *Urraca* (1982), with its alternative discourse on Spain's history located in a female voice, is a good example of an historiographic metafictional novel. It is based on the twelfth-century Castilian queen of the same name, who was locked in a cell by her own son, the future king Alfonso VII. *Arcángeles* (1986) is a self-reflexive attempt to recreate

the aggressiveness of the postmodern world and the problems of the writer in finding the appropriate language for doing so.

Antes de la batalla (1992) and *La fuente de la vida* (1995) have the same testimonial approach as some of her earlier works. *Antes de la batalla* is a book somewhat reminiscent of a 1950s novel, with its host of characters and its bitter portrayal of the complacency prevailing, under the Socialist government, amongst people who had once been freedom-fighters against Franco's dictatorship. The travels of one of the main characters provide an opportunity to discuss contemporary problems such as the Israeli-Palestinian conflict. In *La fuente de la vida,* set against a political and economic background, mainly of Peru and Rumania, both the third-world Latin-American country and the post-Communist one are exploited by the opulent West through the illegal trafficking of children, either for adoption or for organ-transplants.

FURTHER READING ON LOURDES ORTIZ

Ackers, John C., 'The Generation of Spanish Novelists After Franco', *The Review of Contemporary Fiction*, 8/2 (1988), 292-9.

Alborg, Concha, 'Cuatro narradoras de la transición', in Ricardo Landeira and Luis T. González del Valle (eds), *Nuevos y novísimos. Algunas perspectivas críticas sobre la narrativa española desde la década de los 60* (Boulder, COL, 1987), 11-27.

Alonso, Santos, 'La transición: hacia una nueva novela', *Ínsula*, 512-513 (1989), 11-2.

Alonso Martín, Antonio, 'Los avatares de la novela española última', *Liminar*, 2 (1979), 54-7.

Amorós, Andrés, 'Penúltimas novelistas', *ABC*, 19 September 1981.

Asís Garrote, Ma. Dolores de, *Última hora de la novela en España* (Madrid, 1996).

Ballesteros, Isolina, *Escritura femenina y discurso autobiográfico en la nueva novela española* (New York, 1994).

Bobes Naves, María del Carmen, 'Novela histórica femenina' in José Romera Castillo, Francisco Gutiérrez Carbajo and Mario García-Page (eds), *La novela histórica a finales del siglo XX* (Madrid, 1996), 39-54.

Ciplijauskaité, Biruté, *La novela femenina contemporánea (1970-1985). Hacia una tipología de la narración en primera persona* (Madrid, 1988).

————, 'Historical Novel from a Feminine Perspective: *Urraca*', in Roberto C. Manteiga, Carolyn Galerstein and Kathleen McNerny (eds), *Feminine Concerns in Contemporary Spanish Fictions by Women* (Potomac, MD, 1987), 29-42.

————————, 'Lyric Memory, Oral History, and the Shaping of Self in Spanish Narrative', *Forum for Modern Language Studies*, 28/4 (1992), 390-400.

Conte, Rafael, 'Policías y ladrones o el juego que quería ser real', *El País* (Libros), 5 August 1984.

————————, 'En busca de la novela perdida', *Ínsula*, 464-465 (1985), 1,24.

Encinar, Ángeles, 'La sexualidad y su significación en la novelística española actual', *Asclepio*, 42/2 (1990), 63-74.

————————, '*Luz de la memoria* de Lourdes Ortiz', in *Novela española actual: la desaparición del héroe* (Madrid, 1990), 112-27.

————————, 'Escritoras españolas actuales: una perspectiva a través del cuento', *Hispanic Journal*, 13/1 (1992), 181-91.

————————, '*Urraca*: una recreación actual de la historia', *Letras Femeninas*, 20/1-2 (1994), 87-99.

Estévez, Carmen, 'Introducción', in Carmen Estévez (ed.), *Relatos eróticos* (Madrid, 1990), 7-26.

Gil Casado, Pablo Gil, *La novela deshumanizada española (1958-1988)* (Barcelona, 1990).

González Santamera, Felicidad, 'Introducción', in Lourdes Ortiz, *Los motivos de Circe. Yudita* (Madrid, 1991), 7-41.

Hart, Patricia, 'The Picadura and the Picardía of Lourdes Ortiz', in *The Spanish Sleuth. The Detective in Spanish Fiction* (London and Toronto, 1987), 172-81.

Janzon, Anjouli, '*Urraca*; un ejemplo de metaficción historiográfica' in José Romera Castillo, Francisco Gutiérrez Carbajo and Mario García-Page (eds), *La novela histórica a finales del siglo XX* (Madrid, 1996), 265-73.

León-Soleto, Trinidad de, 'Entrevista a Lourdes Ortiz', *ABC*, 11 May 1986.

Manteiga, Roberto, 'From Empathy to Detachment: The Author-Narrator Relationship in Several Spanish Novels by Women', *Monographic Review*, 8 (1992), 19-35.

Molinaro, Nina L., 'Resistance, Gender, and the Mediation of History in Pizarnik's *La condensa sangrienta* and Ortiz's *Urraca*', *Letras Femeninas*, 19/1-2 (1993), 45-54.

Morales Villena, Gregorio, 'Entrevista con Lourdes Ortiz', *Ínsula*, 479 (1986), 1, 10.

————————, 'Lourdes Ortiz y Álvaro Pombo, ópera quinta', *Ínsula*, 480 (1986), 13.

Moreno Moreno, Jesús, 'Lourdes Ortiz: La voz del lenguaje', in *Seis calas en la narrativa española contemporánea*, (Alcalá de Henares, 1989).

Navajas, Gonzalo, 'Narrativa y género. La ficción actual desde la mujer', *Ínsula*, 589-590 (1996), 37-9.

Ordóñez, Elizabeth J., 'Reading Contemporary Spanish Narrative by Women', *Anales de la Literatura Española Contemporánea*, 7 (1982), 237-51.

—————, 'Inscribing Difference: *L'Écriture féminine* and New Narrative by Women', *Anales de la Literatura Española Contemporánea*, 12/1-2 (1987), 45-58.

—————, 'Writing "Her/story": Reinscriptions of Tradition in Texts by Riera, Gómez Ojea, and Ortiz', in *Voices of Their Own: Contemporary Spanish Narrative by Women* (Lewisburg, London and Toronto, 1991), 127-48.

Pérez, Janet, *Contemporary Women Writers of Spain* (Boston, MA, 1988), 165-7.

—————, 'Characteristics of Erotic Brief Fiction by Women in Spain', *Monographic Review*, 7 (1991), 173-95.

Porter, Phoebe, 'Conversaciones con Lourdes Ortiz', *Letras Femeninas*, 15/1-2 (1990), 139-44.

Pulgarín, Amalia, 'La necesidad de contar por sí misma: *Urraca* de Lourdes Ortiz', in *Metaficción historiográfica: la novela histórica en la narrativa hispánica posmodernista* (Madrid, 1995), 153-201.

Ragué, María José, 'Penélope, Agave, y Fedra, personajes femeninos griegos, en el teatro de Carmen Resino y Lourdes Ortiz', *Estreno. Cuadernos del Teatro Español Contemporáneo*, 15/1 (1989), 23-34.

Rodríguez, Jesús, 'Historia de un desengaño: los hijos de Federico Sánchez', *Cuadernos de Aldeeu*, 9 (1993), 255-66.

Sanz Villanueva, Santos, 'Generación del 68', *El Urogallo*, 26 (1988), 28-60.

Sobejano, Gonzalo, 'Ante la novela de los años setenta', *Ínsula*, 396-7 (1979), 1, 22.

—————, 'La novela poemática y sus alrededores', *Ínsula*, 464-465 (1985), 1, 26.

Spires, Robert C., 'A Play of Difference: Fiction after Franco', *Letras Peninsulares*, 1/3 (1988), 285-98.

—————, 'Lourdes Ortiz: Mapping the Course of Postfrancoist Fiction', in Joan L. Brown (ed.), *Women Writers of Contemporary Spain. Exiles in the Homeland* (Newark, London and Toronto, 1991), 198-216.

Suñén, Luis, 'Escritura y realidad', *Ínsula*, 464-465 (1985), 5.

Talbot, Lynn K., 'Lourdes Ortiz' *Urraca*: A Re-Vision/Revision of History', *Romance Quarterly*, 38/4 (1991), 437-48.

Tébar, Juan, 'Esforzada vocación de la novela policiaca española', *El País* (Libros), 27 March 1983.

—————, 'Novela criminal española de la transición', *Ínsula*, 464-465 (1985), 4.

Torres, Maruja, 'Un cadáver en la bañera', *El País Semanal*, 15 November (1981), 19-23.

Villanueva, Darío, 'La novela, 1976', in *El año literario español 1974-1979* (Madrid, 1980), 331-45.

Villarín, Juan, 'Viaje por nuestra ignorada novela policiaca', *Alfoz*, 86 (1992), 123-6.

Penelope

Penélope

Original Spanish text from
Los motivos de Circe. Yudita
(Madrid: Castalia / Instituto de la Mujer, 1991), 75-85; first ed. 1988.

Penélope

"Vuélvete a tu habitación. Ocúpate de las labores que te son propias, el telar y la rueca, y ordena a las esclavas que se apliquen al trabajo... y del arco nos ocuparemos los hombres y principalmente yo, cuyo es el mando de esta casa".

Son palabras de Telémaco. Ella, Penélope, acata y se repliega: veinte años permitiendo que Atenea, la de los ojos de lechuza, ponga a sus ojos un plácido sueño. Duerme sin cesar... duerme y teje una tela inacabable de deseos insatisfechos. Allá, en lo alto de la magnífica casa, contempla cómo se vence su carne mientras se indigna ante la desvergüenza joven de las esclavas que aprovechan la fiesta y los hombres que acuden al panal siempre oferente de un lecho que se hurta y se brinda.

Penelope

"Go back to your room. Attend to your own work – the loom and the distaff – and order the slaves to get on with theirs... and we men will look after the bow, and especially I who am master of this house." [8]
These words are spoken by Telemachus.[9] She, Penelope,[10] obeys and withdraws: twenty years of permitting Athene,[11] she of the owl-like gaze, to bathe her eyes in a peaceful sleep. She sleeps without end... she sleeps and weaves an endless fabric of unsatisfied desires. There, high up in that magnificent house, she ponders on how her flesh is getting older while she gets angry at the youthful brazenness of the female slaves who are taking advantage of the holiday and the men who are flocking round the ever-tempting honeycomb of a bed that is both snatched away and offered.

---

[8]   See *Odyssey,* XXI, 350-354.
[9]   **Telemachus:**   the son of Odysseus, King of Ithaca, and Penelope.
[10]   **Penelope:**   the wife of Odysseus. She waited for her husband for ten years, while he fought in the Trojan War, and ten more while he travelled home. For three years she avoided the pleas of over a hundred suitors by pretending to weave a shroud for her father-in-law, Laertes, but actually unravelled it by night. Odysseus returned secretly and slaughtered all the suitors. Penelope has come to symbolize faithfulness and loyalty beyond endurance.
[11]   **Athene:**   also known as Pallas Athena and identified by the Romans with Minerva, is the virgin goddess of arts, crafts and war. Patroness of Athens, she is believed to have created the olive-tree and her symbol is the owl.

"Pretendíamos a la esposa de Odiseo —cuenta Anfimedonte, al llegar al lugar donde reposan los muertos— y ella ni rechazaba las odiosas nupcias, ni quería celebrarlas".

Ni rechazaba, ni aceptaba: sólo el sueño sobre ese lecho de olivo labrado por el marido, lecho inamovible, cinturón de castidad adornado con oro y con marfil, como promesa de un regreso que condena a una espera cubierta de fantasmas. Recluida en la noble casa, en aquella hacienda confortable que labrara el esposo antes de la partida. Esposa fiel, que se deja tentar, mientras tasa con los ojos semi-abiertos y una sonrisa apenas perceptible de Core, eternamente joven, a los hombres que acuden y compiten por ella. Recatada y triste, tejiendo y recordando las palabras, los cuentos del incansable narrador, aquel diestro en embustes que rompió su doncellez y le hizo un hijo, ese hijo que ahora crece, como imagen del padre, frente a ella y que vuelve a recordarle una y otra vez quién es el amo:

"Vuélvete a tu habitación..."

Habitación poblada por los hilos tenues de un sudario que es sudario de la propia carne; paños mojados de una túnica precursora que deja huellas como de bronce, cinceladas sobre una piel que ya ha olvidado las delicias del abrazo, piel guardada en alcanfor, bañada en la nostalgia... anhelante, como una flor de cardo que apenas desprende aroma y recogida, resguardada en un rechazo pertinaz, cabezón e inútil que la va convirtiendo en estatua que conserva la calidez sedosa del mármol más pulido.

Ellos, los pretendientes, llenan la casa con sus gritos, sus borracheras y sus modos de hombre. Ella desde su alcoba huele el deseo de los varones, se estremece con sus risotadas, presiente el recorrido ávido de sus manos sobre el cuerpo limpio y fragante de las esclavas jóvenes. Al anochecer, a la luz de las antorchas, ascienden las voces y la música de agua que no deja de manar de la cítara, sube el olor caliente del sebo quemado, de la grasa

"We were suitors for the hand of Odysseus's wife," [12] says Amphimedon [13] when he arrives at the place where the dead repose, "and she didn't reject the odious nuptials, nor want to celebrate them."

She neither rejected, nor accepted: only the dream on that olive-wood bed carved by her husband, the unmoveable bed, chastity belt decorated with gold and ivory, like the promise of a return that condemns her to a period of waiting, full of ghosts. Shut away in that noble house, on that comfortable estate worked by her husband before his departure. The faithful wife, who allows herself to be tempted, while with half-open eyes and a scarcely perceptible Core-like[14] eternally-young smile she weighs up the men who come and compete for her hand. Modest and sad, weaving and recalling the words, the tales of the indefatigable narrator, that expert in telling lies who ruptured her maidenhead and created a child in her, that child who is today growing up, in the image of his father, in front of her and who reminds her again and again who is the master: "Go back to your room..."

A room full of the slender threads of a shroud which is a shroud for her own flesh; damp pieces of cloth of a robe foretelling death, which leaves marks as if of bronze, engraved on a skin which has now forgotten the delights of an embrace, skin preserved in camphor, bathed in nostalgia... eager, like the flower of the thistle that hardly gives off any aroma, and secluded, shielded in prolonged, obstinate and useless rejection that is turning her into a statue that retains the silky quality of the most highly polished marble.

They, the suitors, fill the house with their shouts, their drunkenness and their men's ways. She, from her room, smells the desire of the males, she trembles at their guffaws, can imagine them avidly running their hands over the clean, sweet-smelling bodies of the young slave girls. When night falls, in the light of the torches, their voices rise as does the watery music which never stops flowing from the zither. The warm smell of burnt grease and the

---

[12]   **Odysseus** : the king of Ithaca and hero of Homer's *Odyssey*, the account of his journey back to Ithaca after being in the Trojan War. Also known as Ulysses or Ulixes, his Latin name. He left his homeland to help the Greek Prince Menelaus when his wife Helen was abducted by the Trojan Prince Paris. Helen was considered the most beautiful woman in the world and her many suitors – Odysseus had been one of them before he married Penelope – agreed among themselves that whoever she eventually married would be defended by all the others. When Paris carried Helen off to Troy, the Greek leaders organized the expedition against Troy which lasted ten years. During the Trojan War Odysseus was respected for his intelligence and wiliness.

[13]   **Amphimedon**: one of Penelope's suitors; see *Odyssey* XXIV, 125-7.

[14]   **Core** : or Kore, means Maid; the enigmatic smile refers to the Archaic Greek statues of young girls also known as Cores.

chisporreante de la carne recién asada... hay un olor untuoso y turbio de sudor y cuerpos entremezclados, como en un friso de bruscos ademanes, donde centauros lúbricos atenazan a las doncellas no espantadas, sino complacientes y, mientras se vacían las cubas y se llenan las cráteras, ella puede escuchar aún la melopea lánguida de las canciones.

Ha aprendido a distinguir las voces... la voz segura y firme de Antínoo... Conoce bien sus chanzas y sus valentonadas... el más diestro y agudo, el más hermoso de los pretendientes; la voz delicada, casi femenina de Eurímaco que regala sus oídos con tiernos elogios que a veces le hacen olvidar que el tiempo pasa...; la voz sensata, madura de Anfínomo... Oye desde lejos sus charlas y siente un temblor que la hace refugiarse y encogerse entre las pieles de cabra cuando oye el relato desvergonzado de las hazañas amorosas.

Les ve jugar al atardecer en el patio, ante el umbral de la casa. Y conoce y distingue cada músculo de sus cuerpos, tensos al tirar la jabalina o el disco: la precisión de Antínoo, la dulzura, que es casi debilidad, de Eurímaco, la seguridad protectora de Anfínomo... Todos allí, día tras día, sólo por ella... acechando, esperando el momento en que se presente una vez más en el umbral, enmarcada por sus doncellas, como en una comitiva sacra para la entrega de un peplo, y se coloque ante ellos en silencio, siempre altiva, con el velo cubriéndole el rostro, disimulando y ocultando las arrugas... allí, entre las columnas, mientras siente el látigo acuciante de las miradas y se sabe señora de voluntades, insinuando y desmintiendo.

"A todos les da esperanzas —cuenta Antínoo— y a cada uno en particular le hace promesas y le envía mensajes".

De tarde en tarde se cruza con cualquiera de ellos y baja los ojos como si se sonrojara... tal vez tú... y luego se retira llevándose a la alcoba el roce de esos dedos que por un instante... el calor de aquel aliento que... la procacidad descarada, provocativa de la risa de Antínoo, la broma burda del que intentó retenerla contra el muro, aquellos labios que durante un segundo...

Al anochecer desciende al calor del hogar y aguarda en silencio, sintiéndose observada, admirada, presintiendo... mientras los hombres escuchan la voz templada del aedo que canta las hazañas de aquéllos que

crackling fat of recently roasted meat rises... there's an unctuous and murky smell of sweat and bodies intermingled, like in a frieze depicting rough movements, where lewd centaurs grip young virgins who are not afraid but obliging and, while the barrels are emptied out and the drinking vessels are filled up, she can still hear the languid *melopoeia* of the songs.

She has learned to distinguish the voices... the firm, assured voice of Antinous... she knows all about his jokes and bluster... the most shrewd and witty, the most handsome of the suitors; the delicate, almost feminine, voice of Eurymachus who regales her ears with tender eulogies that at times make her forget that time is passing...; the sensible, mature voice of Amphinomus...[15] She listens from afar to their talk and feels a shiver that makes her seek refuge and shrink between the goatskins when she hears the shameless story of amorous exploits.

She sees them as night falls gambolling in the garden, in front of the house. And she knows and can distinguish every muscle of their bodies, taut as they throw the javelin or the discus: the accuracy of Antinous, the gentleness, which is almost weakness, of Eurymachus, the protective security of Amphinomus... All of them there, day after day, just for her... watching, waiting for the moment when she shows herself once more at the front of the house, framed by her ladies in waiting, as if in a sacred procession to hand over a *peplos*,[16] and she stations herself before them in silence, ever haughty, with a veil covering her face, disguising and hiding the wrinkles... there, between the pillars, while she feels the piercing whiplash of their eyes and knows herself to be mistress of their wishes, teasing and rejecting.

"She gives hope to everybody," says Antinous, "and she makes promises and sends messages to each one individually."

Now and then she comes face to face with one or other of them and lowers her eyes as if she was blushing... perhaps you... and then she moves away taking back to her room with her the brush of those fingers that for just an instant... the warmth of that breath that... the brazen cheek of Antinous' provocative laugh, the coarse joke of the man who tried to pin her against the wall, those lips that for a second...

When night comes she goes down to the warmth of the hearth and waits there in silence, feeling herself observed, admired, full of foreboding... while the men listen to the tuneful voice of the *aedos* [17]who sings of the feats of

---

[15] **Antinous, Eurymachus and Amphinomus**: three of Penelope's suitors.
[16] **Peplos:** an outer robe or shawl worn by women in Ancient Greece.
[17] *aedos:* minstrel.

debieron partir, esa historia oída ya mil veces, donde se narran las aventuras de los héroes, de aquel Odiseo, su esposo, que marchó un día camino del Ilión... y entonces esas dos lágrimas como de ámbar, la representación de una tristeza de coribante, expresada con la serenidad del rito, que no puede ocultar la rebelión y un cierto aburrimiento:

"¡Femio! Pues que sabes otras muchas hazañas de hombres y de dioses que recrean a los mortales y son celebradas por los aedos, canta algunas de ésas, sentado ahí en el centro y óiganlas todos silenciosamente y bebiendo vino; pero deja ese canto triste que constantemente me angustia el corazón en el pecho..."

Y envuelta en su dolor como en un manto sepulcral vuelve a su alcoba y teje.

Veinte años que ella cuenta en los metros de hilo, tela de araña que se anuda y se hace densa y en la que puede leerse el tejido rechinante del tiempo; la lanzadera en su ir y venir, ágil entre sus dedos, crea un ritmo de olas, de tempestades y de ausencias mientras ella sueña con barcos que se enfrentan a mares embravecidos, y con prudentes y benévolos mensajeros de los dioses que recorren las nubes y se aproximan a su lecho... Intenta recordarle. A veces, cuando mira a Telémaco cree reconocer los rasgos ya desdibujados del padre bajo aquellas facciones firmes, en los pómulos, bajo aquellos miembros del varón-niño que se arquean en el aire y trazan perspectivas y escorzos entre las recias columnas de piedra blanca. Y cuando él, su hijo, se calza las sandalias y se dobla percibe las piernas duras de Ulises y vuelve a sentir la presión de aquellos muslos firmes contra los suyos, el calor de los tendones prietos, la fortaleza de aquellas piernas preparadas para la carrera y curtidas por todos los vientos. Y entonces repara en los otros: ve la gallardía de Antínoo, la complacencia de Eurímaco, la nobleza de Anfínomo y en el sueño protector que le depara la diosa macho, la diosa guerrera —lo mismo que el escultor va haciendo brotar de la dura piedra los rasgos seguros, sonrientes y serenos del

those who had to depart, that story heard a thousand times already, in which they tell of the adventures of the heroes, of that Odysseus, her husband, who set off one day for Ilium[18]... and then those two amber-like tears, the representation of a corybantic[19] sadness expressed with ritual serenity, that cannot hide the rebellion and a certain boredom:

"Phemius![20] Since you know about many other feats of men and the gods who recreate mortals and who are celebrated by the *aedos*, sing about some of them, sitting there in the middle, and let everybody listen to them in silence and drink their wine; but no more of that sad song that never fails to wring my heart."

And, enveloped in her grief as if in a winding-sheet, she returns to her room and weaves.

Twenty years that she measures out in the metres of thread, a spider's web that gets into knots and gets thicker and in which she can read for herself the creaking weave of time; the shuttle in its plying back and forth, agile between her fingers, creates the rhythm of waves, of storms and of absences while she dreams of boats that confront roaring seas, and of judicious and kindly messengers from the gods who fly through the clouds and come close to her bed... She tries to remember him. Sometimes, when she looks at Telemachus, she thinks she recognises the lines, now blurred, of the father beneath those firm features, in the cheek-bones, under those manly boy limbs that arch in the air and trace perspectives and foreshortenings between the solid pillars of white stone. And when he, her son, puts on his sandals and bends down she can see the strong legs of Ulysses[21] and once again she feels the pressure of those firm thighs against her own, the warmth of the taut tendons, the power of those legs ready for the race and weathered by the wind. And then she notices the others: she sees the gallantry of Antinous, the kindness of Eurymachus, the nobility of Amphinomus and in the protective dream provided for her by the virile goddess, the warrior goddess – in the same way as the sculptor continuously brings forth from the hard stone the sure, smiling and serene features of the adolescent who excels

---

18   **Ilium:** another name for the city of Troy.
19   **Corybantic:** refers to the male attendants of Cybele, the fertility goddess. The Corybantes celebrated the goddess's rites with armed dances during which they clashed spears and shields and beat cymbals. When the infant god Zeus was being hunted by his father, the Corybantes saved him by drowning out his crying with their frenzied din.
20   **Phemius:** a minstrel or *aedos* in Odysseus's household. He was forced to serve Penelope's suitors during his master's absence, but Odysseus spares his life on his return.
21   See note 12.

adolescente que descolla en el pugilato—, ella acaricia con la mente la
materia suave del recuerdo con la que va modelando, perfilando y
corrigiendo los rasgos del esposo perdido y él aparece allí de nuevo, como
un fantasma que regresa del Hades para hablarle y dormir a su lado sobre
aquellas pieles sedosas del carnero que ella mantiene limpias y oreadas
desde que él marchó:

"Pero a mí me envía algún dios pesadillas funestas. Esta misma noche
acostóse a mi lado un fantasma, muy semejante a él, como era Odiseo
cuando partió con el ejército; y mi corazón se alegraba, figurándose que no
era sueño sino veras."

Y en ese momento los brazos duros de Antínoo, la sonrisa de Eurímaco,
la fortaleza de Anfínomo se convierten en bosquejos inacabados, torpes de
aquél que se mantiene intacto con el paso del tiempo, divinal y joven para
ella a través de sus ruegos y ensoñaciones de malcasada. Y luego, como si
un mal espíritu burlón se introdujera en la alcoba, llega hasta ella nítida,
como un crótalo repiqueteante, la risa de Mantinao que se revuelca en el
atrio con cualquiera de los pretendientes y siente unos celos que muerden
sus entrañas desgarrándola y la hace presentir a todas las Circes, las
Calipsos, las posibles mujeres de rasgos exóticos y técnicas maduras,
infinitamente sabias en el arte del amor, mujeres de cabelleras desatadas de
Gorgona insaciable y cree escuchar de pronto los gemidos entrecortados de
Ulises que se mezclan, se superponen a la risa desatada de la doncella y se
levanta del lecho y querría azotar el cuerpo blanco de la niña para castigar
en aquella piel el deseo enloquecido del esposo; huele la semilla del varón
sobre la carne apenas cubierta por la túnica de algodón blanca y gime y

at boxing – in her mind she caresses the smooth material of the memory with which she goes on modelling, profiling and correcting the features of her lost husband and he appears again, like a ghost who has returned from Hades[22] to talk to her and sleep at her side on those silky sheepskins that she has kept clean and aired ever since he went away:

"But some god sends me funereal nightmares. This very night there lay beside me a ghost, who looked a lot like him, like Odysseus used to be when he left with the army; and my heart became happy, imagining that it wasn't a dream but was real."

And at that moment the firm arms of Antinous, Eurymachus's smile, Amphinomus's strength, become unfinished, rough sketches of the man who remains intact with the passage of time, god-like and young for her through her entreaties and fantasies of an unhappily married woman. And then, as if an evil, mocking spirit had come into the bedroom, the laugh of Mantinaos[23] who indulges in amorous pursuits with one or other of the suitors in the inner courtyard, reaches her clearly, like a merrily pealing rattlesnake, and she feels jealous pangs gnawing at her entrails, tearing her apart and causes her to sense the presence of all the Circes,[24] the Calypsos,[25] the potential women with exotic features and mature techniques, infinitely wise in the art of love, women with heads of loose flowing hair like the insatiable Gorgon,[26] and suddenly she thinks she hears the laboured groans of Ulysses that mingle with, superimpose themselves on, the loose laugh of the young virgin and she gets up from her bed and wants to whip the white body of the young girl, to punish in that skin the maddened desire of her husband; she smells the seed of the man on flesh scarcely covered by the white cotton tunic and she

---

[22] **Hades:** the abode of the dead.

[23] **Mantinaos:** although her name is not mentioned in the *Odyssey*, she is supposed to be one of the twelve girls who, having engaged in erotic liaisons with the suitors, are eventually killed by Telemachus.

[24] **Circe:** a sorceress who lived in the island of Aeaea. When returning to Ithaca after the Trojan War, Odysseus stopped at Aeaea. Circe transformed half of his men to stone, but after falling in love with Odysseus she changed his men back to their original form. Odysseus lived with her for a year before resuming his homeward journey.

[25] **Calypso:** a goddess or nymph who lived alone on the island of Ogygia, where Odysseus was washed ashore after being shipwrecked. She fell in love with him and kept him with her for seven years, after which Odysseus, missing his wife and son, resumed his journey to Ithaca.

[26] **Gorgons:** three ugly sea-monsters – the sisters Stheno, Euryale and Medusa – who had their hair laced with snakes.

acude de nuevo al telar, deshace la labor y recomienza, se pierde en los hilos cruzados, en el ir y venir de la lanzadera... y puede verle, escucha el bramido ronco de su garganta y las olas se mezclan con el batir de los remos y se arremolinan las estrellas haciendo perder el Norte, mientras él cabalga como Tritón sobre las olas y la risa argentina de Circe traspasa los muros de piedra y se clava, como aguja del más fino metal, en su vientre, y maldice a las brujas incontinentes que retozan en lechos cubiertos con pieles de animales nunca antes contemplados y beben de un vino obscuro y fuerte que se agarra a los labios y deja manchas rojas sobre el torso del hombre, y siente la sequedad de su carne que se va arrugando como secan los higos dulces en los almacenes, amarilleando, retorciéndose y perdiendo la suavidad de pulpa de la blanca savia perfumada y fresca.

Y entonces convoca a las doncellas y hace que cubran su rostro de arena ocre y perfilen sus ojos, que perfumen de resina su cuerpo y desciende al zaguán y se muestra con un brillo en la retina que incita y reclama, como la hembra del cabrito atrae al macho.

Pero allí observándola, censurándola, alerta siempre cual el cazador que otea la pieza, está Telémaco, ese hijo que habla discretas palabras:

"Vuelve a tu habitación... ocúpate de las labores que te son propias."

Sabe del reproche; conoce la mirada del hijo, pidiendo cuentas: los cuerpos destripados de los cerdos en la continua matanza, como en unas bacanales perpetuas; las vísceras sangrantes de los bueyes devorados, las ancas del animal troceadas y girando noche tras noche en el asador; la hacienda de mi padre... mi herencia; los puercos que se alimentan con bellotas son cuidados con esmero para mi mayoría de edad, mientras tú...

¡Esa puerca de Helena...! Hay orgullo y desprecio cuando piensa en aquélla a la que debe su desgracia. Ella no resistió: se dejó llevar, como cualquier criada por el primero que alabó sus rubios cabellos y puso calambres en sus dedos. Helena. Pero ella, Penélope, juró entonces y ha vuelto a jurar día tras día durante veinte años que habría de lavar la mancha que sobre su pueblo y sobre los suyos cayó desde que el adulterio trajera la

moans and goes back to her weaving, unpicking what she's done and starting again, losing herself in the crossed threads, in the coming and going of the shuttle... and she can see him, hear the rough roar in his throat and the waves mingle with the stroking of the oars and the stars begin to whirl and eddy until the North is lost, while he rides the waves like Triton[27] and the silvery laugh of Circe passes through the stone walls and, like a needle made of the finest metal, penetrates her belly, and she curses the lascivious witches that frolic in beds covered with the skins of animals that have never been seen before and drink of a dark strong wine that clings to the lips and leaves red stains on the torso of the man, and she feels the dryness of her flesh that is becoming wrinkled as sweet figs dry out in store-houses, turning yellow, shrivelling and losing the succulent softness of the perfumed and fresh white sap.

And then she summons the maids and tells them to cover her face with ochre sand and outline her eyes, perfume her body with resin and she goes down to the vestibule and shows herself with a sparkle in her eye that incites and demands attention, as the female goat attracts the male.

But there looking at her, censuring her, ever alert as the hunter stalking his prey, is Telemachus, that son who utters the judicious words:

"Go back to your room... attend to your own work."

She knows it is a reproach; she knows that look of her son, calling her to account: the butchered bodies of the pigs in the continual slaughter, as if in some eternal bacchanalia; the bloody entrails of the devoured oxen, the animal haunches cut up and turning night after night on the spit; my father's estate – my inheritence; the pigs that are fed with acorns and looked after with care for my coming of age, while you...

"That swine Helen...!"[28] There's arrogance and scorn when she thinks about that woman to whom she owes her misfortune. She didn't resist: she allowed herself to be carried away like any little maid by the first man to praise her blonde hair and make her fingers tingle. Helen. But she, Penelope, swore then and has gone on swearing day after day for twenty years that she would have to wash away the stain that fell on her people and on her loved ones after that adulterous act brought shame to the lands of

---

[27]   **Triton:** son of Poseidon and Amphitrite, Triton is a minor sea-god; a merman, he is a fish below the waist and a man above it.

[28]   See note 12.

desdicha a las tierras de Itaca. Ella no cederá. Aguarda como un perro fiel para desmentir a los viejos cantores que manchan sus bocas maldiciendo a la mujer que, como Pandora, abrió la cajita de todos los males... ¡Qué tonto fuiste, Menelao! Porque Helena, la argiva, fue débil y se dejó seducir por el primer forastero, Ulises tuvo que partir. Por eso Penélope desprecia a Helena y se ha encerrado en un largo mutismo que la condena a una soledad, atormentada por los desvelos y las lágrimas.

A veces sube al desván donde guarda las arcas que contienen los ricos peplos y los delicados mantos y acaricia el arco de Ulises. Nadie tras él, ninguna mano se ha atrevido a tocarlo. Era ágil y diestro, y certero con la aguda flecha. Y ella, como el arco, era también flexible y tersa, dócil y manejable, entre las manos suaves y precisas, las manos poderosas del varón. ¡Aquella extraña mezcla de fortaleza y ternura, de agilidad y brío que condensa la serenidad imperecedera y grácil del templo... la ligereza de las columnas, la solidez del mármol!...

Y ahora ha llegado. Dicen que es él, ese hombre anciano sin fuerza en los músculos que viste como mendigo y trae el polvo de los caminos en las sandalias mal curtidas. Y hay un momento de espanto, una vacilación que la hace renegar de aquel tiempo pasado, un miedo... y permanece muda, sin despegar los labios porque tiene el corazón estupefacto. Y entonces, una vez más, Telémaco percibe la vacilación y la reprime con dureza:

"Madre mía... descastada madre, ya que tienes ánimo cruel, ¿por qué te pones tan lejos de mi padre, en vez de sentarte a su lado y hacerle preguntas y enterarte de todo?: Ninguna mujer se quedaría así, con ánimo tenaz, apartada de su esposo, cuando él después de tantos males, vuelve en el vigésimo año a la patria tierra. Pero tu corazón ha sido siempre más duro que una piedra".

Veinte años esperando y ahora aquel anciano...

Ithaca. She will not give in. She stands guard like a faithful dog to contradict the old singers who stain their mouths cursing the woman who, like Pandora,[29] opened the little box containing all the ills of the world... What a fool you were, Menelaus![30] It was because Helen of Argos was weak and allowed herself to be seduced by the first stranger, that Ulysses had to go away. That is why Penelope scorns Helen and has locked herself away in a long silence which condemns her to a solitary existence, tortured by troubles and tears.

Sometimes she goes up into the attic where she keeps the chests that store the rich *peplos* and finely-woven cloaks and she strokes the bow that belongs to Ulysses. Nobody after him, no hand has dared to touch it. He was agile and skilful, and sure with the sharp arrow. And she, like the bow, was flexible and smooth too, docile and yielding, in the soft and experienced hands, the strong hands of the man. That strange mix of strength and tenderness, of agility and verve that is captured in the imperishable and graceful serenity of the temple... the lightness of the pillars, the solidity of marble!...

And now he has arrived. They say it's him, that old man with no power in his muscles, dressed like a beggar, and carrying the dust of the highways on his rough leather sandals. And there is a moment of terror, a hesitation that makes her vigorously deny that time has gone by, a fear... and she remains silent, not opening her lips because her heart remains speechless. And then, once more, Telemachus notices her hesitation and harshly upbraids her:

"Oh mother mine – my cold, indifferent mother, you have a cruel heart now, why do you stand so far apart from my father instead of taking your place at his side and asking him questions and finding out all he has done: No wife would be like that, with such tenacious nerve, separated from her husband when he, after so many bad things, returns to his homeland after twenty years away. But your heart has always been harder than a stone."[31]

Twenty years waiting and now that old man...

---

[29] **Pandora:** according to Hesiod, the first woman made out of clay by Hephaestus and adorned by the gods with special qualities (her name means "all gifts"). Married to Epimetheus, she brought with her a jar or a box with all sorts of evils, which she released on earth, keeping only hope inside.

[30] See note 12.

[31] See *Odyssey*, XXIII, 97-104.

"Ni me encono, ni me tengo en poco, ni me admiro en demasía, pues sé muy bien *cómo eras* cuando partiste de Itaca en la nave de largos remos."

Y Ulises habla y describe morosamente el lecho que tan sólo él podía conocer y Penélope siente un desfallecimiento, un vértigo y, tras recuperarse, balbucea:

"No te enojes conmigo... ya que eres en todo el más circunspecto de los hombres y las deidades nos enviaron la desgracia y no quisieron que gozáramos juntos de la mocedad, ni que juntos llegáramos al umbral de la vejez." Porque los años del esposo le han devuelto sus propios años, esas canas que pintaba y repintaba, esa delgadez de la piel que comienza a separarse de la carne, como sudario prematuro.

Ya no habrá pretendientes que devoren la cosecha y la carne de los animales bien cebados, ya no habrá salmodias, ni canciones al anochecer, ni el juego del eterno ofrecimiento y el rechazo, ni lides en el patio, ni el sudor agrio de los cuerpos desnudos, ni el delirio de la orgía.

Los pretendientes han muerto por la mano de Ulises... Sierva del hijo fue como sierva del padre... Objeto del deseo que puede ser disputado, poseído y conquistado y es anhelado en la medida en que con su fidelidad establecía la mediación. Hay un Otro que no estaba y que en su ausencia seguía poseyendo... Todos, incluso el hijo, que compite por ella en el torneo, querían ocupar el lugar de ese otro... Y cuando el otro, Ulises, vuelve y se asienta en el hogar, Penélope deja de existir y pasa a ser la sombra que trasiega en el cuarto de las mujeres.

Todos los jóvenes de Itaca, los más hermosos han muerto ya. Ahora, por las noches, cuando Atenea, la de los ojos de lechuza, cierra sus ojos y la incita al sueño, recuerda el murmullo de las voces, los encuentros furtivos en las esquinas del patio tras las columnas y acaricia con melancolía la piel reseca y fría del esposo que a su vez sueña con los brazos siempre frescos de Circe, con la juventud de Nausica o el encanto hechicero de Calipso.

"I'm not angry, nor do I think of myself as someone unimportant, but neither do I think too much of myself, because I know full well *how you used to be* when you set off for Ithaca in the ship with the long oars."[32]

And Ulysses talks and slowly describes the bed that he alone was able to know and Penelope feels a faintness coming on, an attack of dizziness, and after recovering herself, she stammers:

"Don't get angry with me... for you are in all things the most circumspect of men and the gods sent us misfortune and didn't want us to enjoy our youth together, or for us to arrive at the threshold of old age together." [33] Because the age of her husband has returned her to her own age, those grey hairs that she would dye and re-dye, that thinness of the skin that is beginning to come away from the flesh, like a premature shroud.

No longer will there be suitors to eat up the harvest and the flesh of well-fattened animals, no longer will there be psalmodies or singing as night falls, nor the game of the eternal offering and refusing, nor fights in the garden, nor the bitter sweat of naked bodies, nor the delirium of the orgy.

The suitors have died at the hand of Ulysses... As she was the slave of the son so she is the slave of the father... Object of desire that can be wrangled over, possessed and conquered and is longed for insofar as her fidelity acted as arbiter. There is Another who was not there and who in his absence continued to possess... Everybody, including her son, who competes for her in the tournament, wanted to take the place of that other... And when that other, Ulysses, comes back and takes his seat at the hearth, Penelope ceases to exist and turns into the shadow that moves about the women's room.

All the young men of Ithaca, the most beautiful ones, have died now. Now, when Athene of the owl-like eyes, closes hers at night and spurs her on to sleep, she recalls the murmur of the voices, the furtive encounters in the corners of the courtyard behind the pillars and sadly she strokes the dry, cold skin of her husband who in turn dreams of the ever young arms of Circe, of the youthfulness of Nausicaa[34] or the bewitching charms of Calypso.

---

[32]   *ibid.* 174-7.
[33]   *ibid.* 209-12.
[34]   **Nausicaa:** daughter of Alcinous, king of the Phaeacians, and Arete. The shipwrecked Odysseus begged assistance of Nausicaa when she was washing clothes at the seashore. She greeted him and told him how to win the help of her parents. Alcinous offered her in marriage to Odysseus, but he refused out of loyalty to his wife.

La divinal Penélope en aquella cama de olivo, que fue su lazo, contempla a Ulises que ha regresado y llora: él tiene tras sí una historia para narrar y ante él una hacienda que reconstruir y un reino que legará a su hijo. Ella, la esposa, que ya no está en edad de volver a ser madre y renunció, cuando era tiempo, al tacto de los cuerpos jóvenes, se refugia en el sueño y deja que los fantasmas de los pretendientes le devuelvan el eco de un goce que ya no puede ser: la risa de Eurímaco... la belleza de Antínoo... la fortaleza de Anfínomo. Y como en un lamento percibe desde el fango caliente de la tierra el rugido denso y quejumbroso de las bacantes y la risa dominadora, seca de Atenea que pone lanzas y esculpe sobre los páramos.

The divine Penelope on that bed of olive-wood that was her snare looks at Ulysses who has come back and she weeps: he has behind him a story to tell and ahead of him an estate to rebuild and a kingdom to leave to his son. She, the wife, who is no longer of an age when she can be a mother again and who, while there was still time, renounced the touch of young bodies, takes refuge in dreams and allows the ghosts of the suitors to give her back the echo of a pleasure that can no longer be: the laughter of Eurymachus... Antinous's beauty... Amphinomus's great strength. And as in a lament, she perceives from the hot mire of the earth the heavy, querulous roar of the Bacchantes[35] and the domineering, dry laughter of Athene that throws down spears and sculpts the waste land.

---

[35]   **Bacchantes:**   also known as Maenads, they are female followers of Bacchus or Dionysos, god of wine and of vegetation in general. As priestesses they also took part in the wild celebrations and orgiastic rites of the festivals of Bacchus.

LAURA FREIXAS

135

LAURA FREIXAS was born in Barcelona in 1958. A former student of the French Lycée, after finishing a degree in Law at the Universitat de Barcelona, she went to Paris for a year, where she attended the École des Hautes Études while studying the Russian feminist Alexandra Kollontai. Back in Barcelona, she worked for a while in a literary agency, until she came to Britain as a Foreign Language Assistant, first at the University of Bradford (1983-4), and then at the University of Southampton (1984-5). She was then offered a post by Grijalbo, a publishing house in Barcelona, and founded a new literary series, *El espejo de tinta* (1987-94), which she used as a vehicle for introducing authors, texts and genres still relatively unknown in Spain: Clarice Lispector, Paul Bowles, Sylvia Plath's letters, the correspondence between Pasternak, Rilke and Tsvietáieva, erotica, etc.

In 1988 she published *El asesino en la muñeca*, a collection of short stories in which the passing of time and its consequences, as the title indicates, is a prominent theme. Commenting ironically on her own book, she states that there is too much evidence of the fact that the author has read Julio Cortázar instead of Teresa de Jesús. Her statement might be correct, but there is no denying that *El asesino en la muñeca* includes some of the most refreshing and original stories ever published in Spain. Stories from *El asesino en la muñeca* have been collected in several anthologies both in Spain and in Britain, and she has also published 'La eterna juventud', in *Lucanor* 3 (1989), 34-7, and 'La intérprete', in *Lucanor* 12 (1994), 24-32.

Freixas has translated the diaries of Virginia Woolf and Elizabeth Smart, and Smart's biography by Rosemary Sullivan, and has written prologues to translations of Beauvoir, Tatiana Tolstói and Dorothy Parker, among others. In 1991 she returned to Paris for a sabbatical year which she spent reading Spanish and French sixteenth-, seventeenth- and eighteenth-century literature.

Laura Freixas now lives in Madrid and is working freelance for several publishers, as well as being a literary critic for *El País, La Vanguardia, Claves, El Europeo, El Urogallo*, etc. She has given a series of lectures on autobiography at the Biblioteca Nacional in Madrid, and has published papers on writers' diaries in *Revista de Occidente*: 'Diarios íntimos españoles: un recuento', 160 (1994), 155-223, and 'Auge del diario ¿íntimo? en España', 182-3 (1996), 5-14, as well as samples of her own diary, 182-3 (1996), 175-80. Freixas has also edited and written

the introduction to a monothematic anthology of short stories by Spanish women writers, *Madres e hijas* (1996), and has recently published her first novel, *Último domingo en Londres* (1997), which follows the epistolary tradition.

FURTHER READING ON LAURA FREIXAS

C., A. ,'(Literatura femenina)', *El País*, 28 February 1996.

Carrillo, Nuria, 'La expansion plural de un género: el cuento 1975-1993', *Ínsula*, 568 (1994), 9-11.

Castilla, Amelia, '14 escritoras cuentan en una antología la relación entre madres e hijas', *El País*, 28 February 1996.

Fidalgo, Feliciano, 'La mirada virgen no existe' [Interview with Laura Freixas], *El País*, 26 February 1996.

Goñi, Javier, 'Novela epistolar a varias voces', *El País* (Babelia), 1 March 1997.

Hernández, Teresa, 'Ventana al futuro: Laura Freixas reúne varios relatos de escritoras españolas', *Diario 16*, 9 March 1996.

Noceda, Nuria G., 'Madres - hijas: Una relación de igual a igual, tensa y ambivalente', *Diario 16,* 3 March 1996.

Masoliver, Juan Antonio, *'El asesino en la muñeca'*, *La Vanguardia Española*, 7 July 1988.

——————, 'La mujer en la creación', *La Vanguardia*, 2 February 1996.

Obiol, María José, 'Una aportación propia', *El País* (Babelia), 2 March 1996.

Sanz Villanueva, Santos, *'El asesino en la muñeca'*, *Diario 16*, 29 October 1988.

Squier, Susan M., 'Fetal Voices: Speaking for the Margins Within', *Tulsa Studies in Women's Literature*, 10/1 (1991), 17-30.

Valls, Fernando, 'Mujeres que cuentan', *El Mundo*, 23 March 1996.

Villalba Alvárez, Marina, 'Vida vs. muerte en la narrativa de Laura Freixas: *El asesino en la muñeca* o la inútil medición del tiempo', in *Actas del IV Simposio Internacional de la Asociación Española de Semiótica: describir, inventar, transcribir el mundo*, José Romera Castillo (ed.), (Madrid, 1992), 845-51.

Memories for Sale

Memoria en venta

Original Spanish text from
El asesino en la muñeca (Barcelona: Anagrama, 1988), 15-26.

Memoria en venta

El día en que cumplió cuarenta años, la señorita Ernestina decidió deshacerse de todos sus recuerdos.

Era ésta, desde luego, una decisión dolorosa, y tanto más incomprensible —a primera vista— cuanto que, hasta entonces, la señorita Ernestina había prodigado a sus recuerdos un cariño y atención sin igual: no sólo había ido acumulando, con los años, un número extraordinario de ellos, sino que los conservaba, además, en impecable estado; pero precisamente por eso, se le habían vuelto una carga demasiado pesada.

Sólo quien tiene una buena colección de recuerdos sabe el trabajo, el tiempo y los desvelos que su mantenimiento requiere. Para empezar, hay que vigilar constantemente su buen orden; pues uno evoca un recuerdo cualquiera y son, por lo menos, cuatro o cinco los que emergen, prendidos al primero por nexos insospechados; y si uno se descuida, dejándose llevar por los tentadores senderos del pasado, serán no cinco o seis, sino hasta veinte o treinta los que salgan de sus escondrijos por sorpresa, recuerdos olvidados uniéndose al cortejo. Es necesario devolverlos luego, con todo cuidado, a sus fechas respectivas, a fin de volver a encontrarlos fácilmente la próxima vez que uno quiera revivirlos. Eso por no hablar de los cuidados sin fin que su conservación exige: quitar cada día el polvo, hacer limpieza a fondo los sábados, y renovar regularmente las bolas de naftalina; de lo contrario, se corre el consabido riesgo —la señorita Ernestina, tan cuidadosa, se enfermaba sólo de pensarlo— de que al ir a buscar un recuerdo un poco antiguo, digamos de la primera infancia, lo encuentre uno mohoso, apolillado, todo descolorido o, lo que es peor, roído hasta la médula por los ratones del olvido.

Mencionemos por último la cuestión del espacio. La capacidad de la memoria es limitada, y la de la señorita Ernestina estaba rebosando. Además de los recuerdos propios —y no eran pocos—, tenía un sinfín de

Memories for Sale

On the day of her fortieth birthday, Miss Ernestina decided to get rid of all her memories.

This was, of course, a painful decision and one, moreover, that at first sight was all the more difficult to understand, given that until that time Miss Ernestina had lavished an unrivalled amount of love and attention on her memories: not only had she been accumulating an extraordinary number of them over the years, she had also kept them in an impeccable condition; but this was precisely why they had now become a burden too heavy to bear.

Only someone who has a fine collection of memories knows the work, the time, and the care needed to maintain them. To start with, constant attention must be paid to keeping them in the right order; one evokes some memory or other, and at least four or five will pop up, each linked to the first by some unsuspected connection; and if you're not careful, and allow yourself to be drawn down the tempting byways of the past, there won't only be five or six but as many as twenty or thirty forgotten memories flushed out of their hiding places and joining the procession. You need therefore to take the utmost care to return them to their respective dates so that you can easily find them again the next time you want to revive them. And that is to say nothing of the endless care demanded in their preservation: dusting them off each day, with a jolly good clean on Saturdays, and regularly renewing the mothballs; were it otherwise, you would run the timeworn risk — Miss Ernestina, so very careful in her ways, would feel ill just thinking about it — that when setting out in search of some rather ancient memory, let's say one from early childhood, you'd find one that was mildewed, moth-eaten, badly faded, or worse, gnawed to the marrow by the mice of oblivion.

Finally let us mention the question of space. The capacity of the memory is limited, and Miss Ernestina's was full to overflowing. In addition to her own memories — and these were not few — she had an endless supply of

ajenos: recuerdos de familia que le legó su madre, por ejemplo, u otros que
le prestaron y cuyo desmemoriado propietario había olvidado reclamarle.
La cosa llegaba hasta tal punto, que en los últimos tiempos la señorita
Ernestina los iba perdiendo por la calle.

—Perdone, señorita —la interpelaba al darle alcance un caballero galante
y sudoroso—. ¿No será suyo este Primer Beso a la Luz de la Luna que
acabo de encontrarme por el suelo? Por poco lo piso, y la verdad, hubiera
sido una lástima... —Se lo mostraba delicadamente en la palma de la mano,
y la señorita Ernestina, reconociéndolo, daba las gracias confusa y se lo
metía en el bolso.

Pero no eran, en definitiva, esos incidentes menores los que habían
determinado la irrevocable decisión de la señorita Ernestina; ni tampoco
trataba, con ella, de ahorrarse trabajo; no la movían, en fin, consideraciones
de orden práctico, sino algo más profundo: le dolían sus recuerdos.
Saboreándolos, como caramelos, los gastaba; y a la vez, se hacían más
bellos: pues es bien sabido que están hechos de una materia indefinible,
frágil y brillante como alas de mariposa, que el tiempo y el uso van tornando
irisada y sutil, casi translúcida, vaga y dramática al igual que los sueños; y
con los años, comienzan traicioneramente a rezumar nostalgia, hasta
volverse amargos. Los placeres de la memoria se envenenan: cuando
pretendía, con ternura, acariciar sus recuerdos preferidos, la señorita
Ernestina se encontraba con un dolor punzante como el mordisco de un
gato.

La señorita Ernestina tenía un amigo novelista; su primera idea fue
cederle en bloque todos sus recuerdos, para que, aplicando las venerables
recetas de la alquimia poética, los mezclase —invocando a las Musas— con
claros de luna y amargos vocativos, sueños robados e ilusiones perdidas; y
añadiendo luego un mechón de pelo blanco de Madame Arnoux, migajas de
cierta famosa madalena y otras sagradas reliquias, los convirtiese en libros.
Mas acabó por descartar tal solución, pues le repugnaba la idea de poner sus
recuerdos, aun así transformados, en millares de manos anónimas y ajenas, y
condenarlos a repetirse eternamente, sin final ni reposo, al capricho de

other people's: family memories which had been bequeathed her by her mother, for example, or others which had been lent her and whose absent-minded owner had forgotten to reclaim. It reached such a stage that Miss Ernestina had of late started losing them in the street.

"Excuse me, Señorita," a polite gentleman bathed in sweat would ask as he caught up with her, "would this be yours, this First Kiss in the Moonlight which I've just found on the ground? I very nearly trod on it, and to tell the truth that would have been a shame..." He would hold it out to her delicately in the palm of his hand, and Miss Ernestina, recognizing it, would thank him, embarrassed, and would put it away in her handbag.

But when all was said and done, it wasn't these minor incidents that drove Miss Ernestina to take her irrevocable decision; neither was she trying to save herself work; at any rate it was not considerations of a practical nature that moved her to act, but something more profound: her memories were causing her pain. Like sweets, savouring them melted them down; and at the same time, they became sweeter: it is, after all, a well known fact that they are made of a substance that is beyond definition, fragile and shimmering like butterfly wings, that time and use make rainbow-hued and subtle, almost transparent, hazy and dramatic just like dreams; and that with the passing of the years, they treacherously start to ooze nostalgia until they turn bitter. The pleasures of the memory become tainted: when she tried tenderly to stroke her favourite memories, Miss Ernestina would experience a sharp pain like the bite of a cat.

Miss Ernestina had a friend who was a novelist: her first idea was to transfer all her memories to him lock, stock and barrel so that by applying ancient recipes from poetic alchemy, he could — by summoning up the Muses — mix them with shafts of moonlight and bitter laments, stolen dreams and lost illusions; and then by adding a tuft of Madame Arnoux's[36] white hair, crumbs from a certain famous madeleine cake[37] and other sacred relics, turn them into books. But she eventually ruled out any such solution because the idea of putting her memories, even transformed in that way, into thousands of anonymous and alien hands and condemning them to be repeated forever, without end, without rest, at the whim of some inattentive

---

[36]   **Madame Arnoux:** a female character from the novel *L'Éducation sentimentale* by the French writer Gustave Flaubert (1821-80).

[37]   **Madeleine cake:** in *Du Coté de Chez Swann,* the first novel of the series *À la recherche du temps perdu* by the French writer Marcel Proust (1871-1922), the taste of a *petite madeleine* (small French sponge cake) dipped in tea triggers the workings of memory for the narrator.

lectores desatentos. Casi era preferible arrojarlos al mar, y dejar que una niña, un día, encontrase, acurrucados en una caracola, los recuerdos de otra niña ya en la tumba. (La señorita Ernestina imaginó también, por un momento, el susto que se llevaría una pescadera cuando al abrir un besugo en el año dos mil hallase en su interior el recuerdo grandioso, deslumbrante y sonoro de una noche en la Ópera).

Repartir sus recuerdos entre los pobres, como sin duda le habría aconsejado su pía bisabuela, le parecía tan ostentoso como donarlos a un archivo o a un museo; sin contar con que los pobres, ya se sabe, son en extremo susceptibles, y el regalo de recuerdos usados podría ofenderles. Así que finalmente, y a falta de mejor solución, la señorita Ernestina optó por poner a la venta sus recuerdos.

Redactó pues el siguiente anuncio, que hizo insertar en el periódico local: "SE VENDEN DIEZ MIL RECUERDOS EN BUEN ESTADO. Al por mayor o al detall. Precios razonables. Curiosos abstenerse."

Y se sentó junto al teléfono en espera de eventuales compradores.

El primero en llamar fue un jeque árabe. Estaba muy interesado, según dijo, en adquirir recuerdos invernales, ya que sólo durante un reciente viaje a Suiza —a fin de concluir un importante negocio de trueque de camellos por relojes de cuco, precisó— había descubierto los encantos del invierno. La señorita Ernestina respondió que tendría algunos.

—¿Con nieve? —preguntó el jeque, esperanzado.

—Bueno —empezó la señorita Ernestina, que era muy servicial—, nieve, lo que se dice nieve..., en mi ciudad no nieva, pero si se conforma con granizo...

—¡Ni hablar! —exclamó el jeque, con voz de hombre importante. He dicho nieve, ¡nada de imitaciones! ¡Y además quiero auroras boreales, esquimales, ventiscas, iglúes, icebergs y trineos tirados por pingüinos!

—Será por renos —corrigió educadamente la señorita Ernestina; pero en ese preciso instante, novecientos treinta y cinco relojes de cuco comenzaron simultáneamente a dar las once (hora de Kuwait). Una terrible maldición islámica fue lo último que oyó. El jeque había colgado.

reader, repelled her. It would almost be better to cast them into the sea and let some little girl some day find, curled up in a shell, the memories of another little girl now in her grave. (Miss Ernestina also imagined for a second a fisherwoman's fright as she slit open a sea bream in the year two thousand and found nestling in its innards a splendid, brilliant and sound-filled memory of a night at the Opera.)

To share out her memories amongst the poor, which is undoubtedly what her pious great grandmother would have advised her to do, seemed to her as ostentatious as donating them to an archive or a museum; this is to say nothing of the fact that the poor, as we already know, are extremely sensitive, and the gift of used memories might offend them. So finally, and in the absence of any better solution, Miss Ernestina opted to put her memories up for sale.

So she compiled the following advertisement and had it inserted in the local newspaper:

"FOR SALE: TEN THOUSAND MEMORIES IN GOOD CONDITION. To be sold as a job lot or piecemeal. Reasonable prices. No browsers please."

Then she sat down by the phone and waited for potential purchasers.

The first person to call was an Arab sheikh. He was very interested, he said, in acquiring memories of winter since it had only been during a recent visit to Switzerland, undertaken to clinch an important deal concerning an exchange of camels for cuckoo clocks, he explained in some detail, that he had discovered the delights of that season. Miss Ernestina replied that she had a few.

"With snow?" asked the sheikh hopefully.

"Well," began Miss Ernestina, who was a very helpful sort of person, "snow, what they call snow..., it doesn't actually snow in my town, but if you don't mind hailstones..."

"Not another word," exclaimed the sheikh, sounding like a man of substance. "I said snow. I don't want any imitations! And besides, I want aurora borealis, Eskimos, blizzards, igloos, icebergs and sledges drawn by penguins!"

"That would be reindeer," corrected Miss Ernestina, politely; but just at that moment nine hundred and thirty five cuckoo clocks all began simultaneously to strike eleven o'clock (Kuwaiti time). A dreadful Islamic curse was the last thing she heard. The sheikh had hung up.

Poco tiempo después telefoneó una dama muy afable, que comenzó preguntando si tendría recuerdos literarios. La señorita Ernestina, llena de buena voluntad, tomó carrerilla y se lanzó a declamar:

—¡Con diez cañones por Mancha, de cuyo nombre no quiero acordarme...! No, me parece que no era exactamente eso —añadió en voz más baja.

La dama, con mucho tacto, aprovechó ese momento de vacilación para continuar:

—No, verá, señorita, lo que sucede es que estoy escribiendo la biografía novelada de una princesa rusa de principios de siglo y me hacen falta recuerdos, cómo le diría yo, pues eso, novelescos. Bueno, pues he visto su anuncio en el periódico y me he dicho, digo, Carmelina, a lo mejor este caballero, o esta señorita, te podrían ayudar. Yo no le podría pagar mucho, la verdad, y claro está que si por casualidad fuese usted una princesa rusa, no vendería sus recuerdos por cuatro pesetas. Pero mire, la cosa está en que yo me conformaría con recuerdos, digamos, de Hamburgo o de Estrasburgo, si no los tiene de San Petersburgo, porque, claro, usted en San Petersburgo no habrá estado nunca, pero mire, si a eso vamos, yo tampoco, pero el lector medio mucho menos, no sé si me entiende, y mientras suene exótico... En fin, que usted me vende los recuerdos que tenga de duelos, collares de esmeraldas, lobos esteparios, amores imposibles, suicidios con daga, adulterios..., me haría un buen precio, ¿verdad?, siendo de segunda mano..., bueno, a lo que iba: yo entonces cambio todos los nombres para que suenen a ruso, si es Martínez, Martinoff, si es García, Garciovsky, y así (licencia poética, le llamamos a eso en nuestra jerga); pongo aquí y allá un grupo de campesinos bailando la balalaica, una horda de bolcheviques feroces con la hoz y el martillo al cinto, y vamos, que me queda bordado. ¿Qué le parece?

La señorita Ernestina dudó un rato.

—¿Amores imposibles dice usted que le sirven? —preguntó por fin—. Porque de eso... —añadió en un murmullo—, de eso alguno tengo.

A little while later a very affable lady telephoned and began by asking if she had any literary memories. Miss Ernestina, willing as ever, took a deep breath and launched into a recital:

"*Con diez cañones por Mancha, de cuyo nombre no quiero acordarme...!*[38] No, I don't think it went quite like that," she added in a lower tone of voice.

The lady most tactfully took advantage of this moment's hesitation to continue:

"No, you see, Señorita, the thing is I'm writing a biography in the form of a novel about a Russian Princess who was living at the beginning of the century and I need some memories that are, how shall I put it, well yes, like something out of a novel. So, having seen your advertisement in the paper I said to myself, Carmelina, I said, this gentleman, or this lady, might be able to help you. In truth I wouldn't be able to pay very much, and of course if you happened by any chance to be a Russian Princess, you wouldn't just sell your memories for peanuts. But look, the thing is this, I would be happy with some memories of, let's say, Hamburg or Strasbourg, if you don't have any of St. Petersburg, because obviously you could never have been to St. Petersburg, but look, if it comes to that, I haven't either, much less the average reader, I don't know if you can follow me, and as long as it sounds exotic... Well, so you sell me any memories you might have of duels, emerald necklaces, wolves on the Steppes, impossible love affairs, people committing suicide with a dagger, adulterous affairs... you'd give them to me for a good price, wouldn't you, their being second hand... Well, as I was saying: I then change all the names so they sound Russian — Martinoff for Martínez, Garciosvky for García and so on (we call that 'poetic licence' in our trade); I pop in a group of peasants here and there dancing to the balalaika, a horde of angry Bolsheviks with hammers and sickles at their belts, hey, I'm making a fantastic job of it. What do you think?"

Miss Ernestina hesitated a moment.

"Do you think impossible love affairs might do?" she asked at last. "Because," she added in a whisper, "I do have some of those."

---

[38]   ***Con diez cañones... acordarme:*** ingenious intertextual combination of the openings of two canonical works of Spanish literature, *Canción del pirata*, a poem by José de Espronceda (1808-42) whose first four lines are: "Con diez cañones por banda, /viento en popa a toda vela / no corta el mar, sino vuela / un velero bergantín", and *El ingenioso hidalgo Don Quijote de la Mancha*, by Miguel de Cervantes (1547-1616), whose famous beginning is as follows: "En un lugar de la Mancha, de cuyo nombre no quiero acordarme...".

—Si es con duques o marquesas, desde luego —respondió la dama con firmeza.

—Ah, no —replicó la señorita Ernestina—. Sólo puedo ofrecerle, si usted no la ha leído, mi recuerdo de *El rojo y el negro*.

—Rojos, por supuesto —respondió su interlocutora, con evidente suspicacia—, pero ¿me quiere usted decir qué pinta un negro en San Petersburgo en 1910?

—Dejémoslo —propuso la señorita Ernestina, algo desanimada.

Telefonearon o escribieron aún varias personas más: el inevitable representante del *Guinness Book of Records*; la directora de un orfelinato de provincias que deseaba adquirir varios lotes de recuerdos de infancia felices con vistas a obtener una subvención del Ministerio; un condenado a cadena perpetua que pedía recuerdos eróticos para entretener la vaciedad de sus noches —pero había que mandárselos disimulados en el relleno de un pastel de chocolate o en el doble fondo de una caja de galletas—; y un ciego de nacimiento, deseoso de comprar recuerdos de colores, especialmente el lila, del que le habían hablado tan bien. A éste, por lo menos, Ernestina pudo enviarle por correo el recuerdo de la espléndida buganvilla que ornaba la fachada de la casa de su bisabuela. Pero pasaban los días, y el grueso de su memoria seguía intacto y sin comprador.

"Qué lástima de recuerdos", meditaba una tarde la señorita Ernestina, tristemente. "Yo me había encariñado con ellos y bien veo que no valen nada... Si antes pretendía venderlos, ahora estaría dispuesta a regalarlos; y si ni regalados los quiere nadie, los quemaré, o los enterraré bien hondo, y yo con ellos."

En ese preciso instante llamaron a la puerta. Era el trapero del barrio. Olía a vinagre y a conejo.

—¿E' aquí 'onde venden recuerdo'? —preguntó sin más preámbulo.

—Sí, aquí es —respondió ella algo desconcertada.

El trapero, que ya se había metido en la sala, les echó un vistazo y propuso rápidamente:

—Ze lo' compro a peso.

—No, no hace falta —respondió la señorita Ernestina, con fatiga—. Ya no los quiero para nada y me hará un favor si se los lleva.

"Only if they involve dukes or marquises, of course," replied the other lady firmly.

"Ah, no," replied Miss Ernestina. "But, if you haven't already read it, I can only offer you my memory of *Scarlet and Black*."[39]

"The Reds, of course," replied the woman on the other end of the phone, clearly suspicious, "but what on earth was a black man doing in St. Petersburg in 1910?"

"Let's just leave it," suggested Miss Ernestina, somewhat discouraged.

Several other people phoned or wrote: the inevitable representative of the *Guinness Book of Records*; the female head of an orphanage somewhere in the provinces who wanted to acquire several batches of happy childhood memories with a view to obtaining some sort of a grant from the Ministry; a man condemned to life imprisonment who was asking for erotic memories to help him fill the emptiness of his nights — although she would have to send them smuggled inside the filling of a chocolate cake or in the false bottom of a box of biscuits; and a man blind from birth, hoping to purchase some memories of colours, particularly lilac, of which he had heard so many nice things. To the latter at least Ernestina had been able to send a letter containing the memory of the wonderful bougainvillaea which had adorned the front of her great grandmother's house. But the days passed, and the bulk of her memory remained intact and without a purchaser.

"What a pity about my memories," mused Miss Ernestina sadly one evening. "I used to be so extremely fond of them and now I can see they're not worth anything ... Even though I was trying to sell them before, now I'd be ready to give them away; and if nobody even wants them as a gift, I'll burn them, or bury them good and deep, and me along with them."

At that very moment there was a knock at the door. It was the local rag-and-bone man. He smelt of vinegar and rabbits.

"Is this where's 'ems selling mem'ries?" he asked without preamble.

"Yes, it's here..." she replied, slightly taken aback.

The rag-and-bone man, who had by now come into the room, cast his eyes over them and soon made his decision:

"I'll buy 'em from ya by weight."

"No, there's no need for that," replied Miss Ernestina wearily. "I don't want them any more, and you'll be doing me a favour if you just take them away."

---

[39]   ***Scarlet and Black:*** *Le Rouge et le noir*, a novel by the French writer Stendhal, pseudonym of Henri Beyle (1783-1842).

Sin perder el tiempo en comentarios, el ropavejero comenzó a recoger recuerdos a puñados, y algunos sueños e ilusiones que había también en el montón, y los fue metiendo hechos un revoltijo en el saco que llevaba.

—Pero, dígame —inquirió tímidamente la señorita Ernestina—, ¿qué hará con ellos?

—Pué verá —contestó el hombre, sin dejar la faena—, tengo un cliente amnézico que zeguramente me comprará tó' er lote, zi ze lo dejo baratito.

—La señorita Ernestina guardaba silencio, admirada por tanto sentido práctico—. Y zi no —concluyó él—, pué' pá' quemá' en la e'tufa o pá' relleno de corchone'.

Y tras recoger los últimos recuerdos desparramados por el suelo —entre los que la señorita Ernestina tuvo tiempo de reconocer el del entierro de su padre y el de un osito de peluche que tuvo de pequeña y al que quería con locura—, el atareado trapero se fue como había venido.

Los meses siguientes, la vida de la señorita Ernestina fue apacible, si no feliz. Dormía a pierna suelta y sin sueños; comía con apetito, y nunca se distraía de lo que estaba haciendo ni se equivocaba de parada de autobús, como antes le sucedía con frecuencia. Por los documentos que había conservado, sabía su nombre, domicilio, fecha de nacimiento y número de cartilla del seguro; nadie le pedía que supiera algo más. En sus ratos libres, miraba arrobada la televisión. Pagaba religiosamente sus impuestos, y creía a pies juntillas las noticias de los periódicos y los discursos de las autoridades. Era, en suma, la ciudadana modelo.

Pero un día sucedió algo extraño. Iba por la calle, atenta a los semáforos y dócil a las indicaciones de los guardias, cuando oyó a alguien gritar: "¡Armando!", y tuvo un terrible sobresalto. Como una iluminación, una voz interior le dijo que Armando era el nombre de su primer amor; pero no le dijo más. En vano buscó ella, detenida y como fulminada en medio de la acera, la historia de aquel amor perdido en su vacía memoria; no halló sino

Wasting no time on niceties, the rag-and-bone man began picking up memories by the fistful, along with a few dreams and illusions that were also included in the heap, and stuffed them higgledy-piggledy into the sack he was carrying.

"But tell me," ventured Miss Ernestina, "what are you going to do with them?"

"Well, see", answered the man, without pausing in what he was doing, "I've gotta client who's lost his mem'ry oo'll surely buy the lot off me if I let 'im 'ave 'em cheap." Miss Ernestina said not a word, marvelling at such common sense. "An' if 'e don't," the man concluded, "well per'aps I'll burn 'em in the stove or use 'em to stuff a mattress."

And having scooped up the final memories scattered about the floor — amongst them one that Miss Ernestina just had time to recognize as her father's funeral, and another of a teddy bear she'd had when she was a little girl and that she'd loved to bits   — the busy rag-and-bone man left as suddenly as he'd arrived.

During the months that followed Miss Ernestina's life was peaceful if not happy. She slept soundly and dreamlessly; she had a good appetite and never got distracted from what she was doing or got off at the wrong bus stop, which was something that had happened before on a number of occasions. From the documents she'd kept she knew her name, address, date of birth and her NHS number; nobody expected her to know anything more. In her free moments she would watch the television, entranced. She religiously paid her taxes, and believed absolutely what she read in the papers and the platform speeches of the authorities. She was, in short, the model citizen.

But then one day something strange happened. She was walking along the street, watching the traffic lights and dutifully obeying the signals of the policemen, when she heard somebody shout: "Armando!" [40] and her heart gave a great lurch. Like an illumination, a voice inside her told her that Armando was the name of her first love; but it didn't tell her anything else. Standing there stock still as if struck by lightning in the middle of the pavement, she cast around in vain in her empty memory for the story of that lost love; she could find nothing more than vague fragments: the echo of a

---

[40] **Armando:** ironic use of a male name with Romantic undertones; Armand Duval and Marguerite Gautier are the main characters in the nineteenth-century French play, *La Dame aux camélias* (1852) by Alexandre Dumas, *fils* (1824-95) based on his own novel of the same title which is the source of Verdi's *La Traviata*.

vagos fragmentos: el eco de una ciudad —París, tal vez— y un ramo de gladiolos de color impreciso.

Desesperada, pues acababa de descubrir que la pérdida de un recuerdo querido duele más que todos los recuerdos juntos, la señorita Ernestina se precipitó a su casa y escribió un nuevo anuncio:

"EXTRAVIADO PRIMER AMOR. Muy cariñoso. Responde al nombre de Armando. Signos distintivos: París y gladiolos. Se gratificará espléndidamente a quien lo devuelva sano y salvo a su desconsolada propietaria."

Esta vez, sin embargo, no tuvo la paciencia de aguardar junto al teléfono. Como también había olvidado la visita del ropavejero, no tenía idea de qué podía haberse hecho de aquel precioso recuerdo, y creyó haberlo perdido esa misma mañana. Volvió, pues, a la calle fatídica, y a gatas por el suelo, comenzó a recorrer los adoquines palmo a palmo.

Al verla rebuscar con tanto ahínco, varios transeúntes se le acercaron solícitos. Los hombres creían que había perdido el reloj o un billete de mil; las mujeres, que se le había roto el collar de perlas buenas; y los niños tiraban del brazo de sus madres para que les dejasen ayudar a la señora a encontrar la canica o la largartija que seguramente andaba buscando. A todos los apartaba con nerviosismo la señorita Ernestina:

—Hagan el favor de no pisar —les decía, irritada—. ¿No ven que estoy buscando un recuerdo, y que podrían aplastarlo?

Entonces, los niños preguntaban: "Mamá, ¿qué es un recuerdo?", y los adultos seguían su camino con ofendida dignidad, disgustados de haber perdido el tiempo.

Por fin, un viejecito que la había estado observando en silencio se le acercó para decirle:

—Debería usted alegrarse, señorita. Créame que la envidio. Usted podrá disfrutar del presente, construir un futuro; no como yo, que atrapado por innumerables recuerdos, vivo con la vista vuelta atrás e inmóvil.

La señorita Ernestina levantó la cabeza:

—¡Cómo que debería alegrarme! —replicó, dolida—. ¡Es el recuerdo de mi primer amor lo que he perdido! ¿Se da cuenta?

El anciano movió la cabeza compasivamente.

—¿Ha probado en el Ayuntamiento? —sugirió, tras un breve silencio.

—¿En el Ayuntamiento? —repitió la señorita Ernestina.

—Sí —dijo el anciano—. En la Oficina de Recuerdos Perdidos podría ser que lo tuvieran.

city — Paris, perhaps — and a bunch of gladioli the colour of which she couldn't make out.

In despair, having just discovered that the loss of a cherished memory hurts more than all the other memories put together, Miss Ernestina rushed home and wrote out another advertisement:

"MISLAID — ONE FIRST LOVE. Very loving. Answers to the name of Armando. Distinguishing features: Paris and gladioli. Handsome reward to the person who returns it safe and sound to its disconsolate lady owner."

This time, however, she didn't have the patience to wait by the phone. Since she'd also forgotten about the visit of the rag-and-bone man, she had no idea what could have become of that precious memory, and believed she'd lost it just that morning. So she went back to the fateful street, and dropping down on all fours she began to go over the paving slabs inch by inch.

Seeing her searching so intently, several passers-by approached and asked if there was anything they could do. The men thought she'd lost her watch or a thousand peseta note; the women that her string of good pearls had broken; and the children tugged at their mother's arms that they might be allowed to help the lady find the marble or the little gecko she was surely looking for. Miss Ernestina nervously shooed them all away:

"Please, don't step here," she told them irritably. "Can't you see I'm looking for a memory and you might trample on it?"

Then the children asked: "What's a memory, mama?" and the adults continued on their way with offended dignity, annoyed at having wasted their time.

Finally, a little old man who'd been watching her in silence went up to her and said:

"You should cheer up, Señorita. Believe me, I envy you. You can enjoy the present, build a future; not like me, trapped in endless memories, I live looking over my shoulder, unable to move."

Miss Ernestina lifted her head.

"What do you mean, I should cheer up!" she answered, hurt. "It's the memory of my first love I've lost! Do you understand?"

The old man nodded his head compassionately.

"Have you tried at the Town Hall?" he suggested after a brief silence.

"At the Town Hall?" repeated Miss Ernestina.

"Yes," said the old man. "The Lost Memories Office might have it."

La señorita Ernestina dio las gracias y corrió al Ayuntamiento. Allí la atendió una señora muy amable.

—Verá —comenzó la señorita Ernestina, sofocada aún por la carrera—, no tiene pérdida: es el recuerdo de un primer amor llamado Armando, con gladiolos rojos, o tal vez blancos o amarillos, y atardeceres en París; por lo que más quiera, dígame: ¿lo han encontrado?

La funcionaria la contempló en silencio, con una mirada que a la señorita Ernestina, sin saber por qué, le pareció triste, y la invitó a seguirla.

Atravesaron varios corredores tenebrosos en cuyas paredes se alineaban, sobre estanterías, recuerdos polvorientos clasificados por orden alfabético. En la sección de la A, y a medida que avanzaban, la señorita Ernestina pudo distinguir recuerdos de abnegación y de abanicos, de acrobacias, achaques y achuchones, de adulterios y alpiste, de Antípodas y arañas, de arenques y arzobispos... Atravesaron varias secciones más, hasta llegar a la P.

—Sección de Primeros Amores Sin Dueño —anunció su guía, con amplio y fatigado gesto—. Usted misma.

Y, dando media vuelta, se marchó.

Hace de esto diez o doce años. La señorita Ernestina lleva examinados alrededor de siete mil recuerdos, lo que representa apenas una décima parte del total. A veces, en un arrebato de desesperanzada furia, lo tira todo por el suelo, y se pone a llamar a voces a su Armando, o a oler el aire, porque está segura de poder reconocer su olor entre millares; pero sólo huele a polvo, y sólo el silencio le contesta.

Miss Ernestina thanked him and hurried along to the Town Hall.   There she was attended by a very kind lady.

"You see," began Miss Ernestina, still out of breath from rushing, "You can't miss it: it's the memory of a first love called Armando, with red gladioli, or perhaps they were white or yellow, and of sunsets in Paris; by all you hold most dear, please tell me: have you found it?"

The clerk gazed at her in silence, with a look that struck Miss Ernestina as sad, though she didn't know why, then invited her to follow her.

They went down a number of gloomy corridors with walls lined with shelves on which were stacked dusty memories filed in alphabetical order. As they made their way along, in the section marked A Miss Ernestina was able to make out memories of abnegation, fans, acrobatics, attacks of ill health and assaults, adulterous affairs and bird-seed, the Antipodes and arachnids, of herrings and archbishops.[41] They went through a number of further sections before they came to the letter F.

"First Loves — no Owners," announced her guide with a sweeping but weary gesture of her hand. "Help yourself!"

And, turning on her heels, she left.

This happened ten or twelve years ago. Miss Ernestina has looked at around seven thousand memories, which scarcely represent a tenth of the total. Sometimes, in a fit of hopeless anger she hurls everything onto the floor, and calls out to her Armando, or sniffs at the air because she's certain she'd be able to recognize his smell amongst thousands; but she is only sniffing at dust, and only the silence answers her.

---

[41]   **Abnegation ... archbishops:** note that in Spanish all these words begin with *A*.

MARINA MAYORAL

MARINA MAYORAL was born in Mondoñedo, Galicia, in 1942. After graduating in Philology at Santiago de Compostela, she moved to Madrid to study for a doctorate on the Galician poet Rosalía de Castro at the Universidad Complutense, while at the same time taking a degree in Psychology at the Escuela de Madrid. She went on to publish several books on the post-Romantic poet: *La poesía de Rosalía de Castro* (1974), her doctoral thesis, *Rosalía de Castro y sus sombras* (1976), *Rosalía de Castro* (1986), and a critical edition of Rosalía's *En las orillas del Sar* (1978). As a literay critic, she has also written *Análisis de cinco comedias* (1977), with Andrés Amorós and Francisco Nieva, and *Análisis de textos* (*Poesía y prosa españolas*) (1977).

In 1978 she was appointed lecturer at the Universidad Complutense where she has been teaching Spanish literature ever since. As a critic, Marina Mayoral has focussed her interest on another Galician woman writer, the nineteenth-century novelist Emilia Pardo Bazán and has published critical editions of *Cuentos y novelas de la tierra* (1984), *Los pazos de Ulloa* (1986), *Insolación* (1987), and *Dulce dueño* (1989).

Mayoral's contributions to academic journals and conferences are numerous, and it is worth noting that while her involvement in literature as a novelist and short-story writer has grown in complexity and dedication, her work as a literary critic has become more introspective. This shift can be detected in her edited work, *El oficio de narrar* (1990), a collection of papers given mainly by well-known novelists at a conference organized by her in Madrid, in which they reflected on one aspect of their craft. Significantly, Mayoral's paper, 'La perspectiva múltiple', is devoted to one of the most distinctive features of her narrative: multiple perspectivism. *El personaje novelesco* (1993) contains papers from another conference on a similar theme also coordinated by her, including her own personal contribution, 'La autonomía del personaje novelesco'.

Although she had been writing short stories for a considerable time and some were later collected in *Morir en tus brazos y otros cuentos* (1989), Mayoral's first novel was not published until 1979. *Cándida, otra vez* (1979, 1992) has a distinctive Galician setting, also present in *Plantar un árbol* (1981) – later revised and translated into Galician as *Unha árbore, un adeus* (1988) – and in *La única libertad* (1982), where the imaginary town of Brétema epitomizes the social

complexities and the long-lasting significance of the place and class into which one is born. Even when her characters move to Madrid they are always very conscious of their Galician origins and upbringing, as is the case in *Al otro lado* (1980), which won the Premio Novelas y Cuentos, and *Contra muerte y amor* (1985), also set in the imaginary Brétema.

In the late 1980s she began to publish in Galician, the first titles being *O reloxio da torre* (1988) – later translated into Spanish as *El reloj de la torre* (1991) – and *Chamábase Lluís* (1989), which won the Premio Losada Diéguez. *Recóndita armonía* (1994), again with the town of Brétema as the main spatial reference, deals with one of her recurrent themes, the friendship between two women, a kind of love and companionship which proves to be far more enduring than sexual or romantic love. In 1994, she also published the novel *Tristes armas* and the collection of stories *Querida amiga*.

Some of her short stories have been collected in anthologies, such as, 'Entonces empezó a olvidar' in *Cuento español contemporáneo,* edited by A. Encinar and A. Percival (1993), and 'En los parques, al anochecer' in *Relatos eróticos* , edited by Carmen Estévez (1990).

Marina Mayoral's latest novel, *Dar la vida y el alma* (1996), is an engaging reflection on love which plays cleverly with the metafictional mode. A female first-person narrator tells the story of a mismatched couple, displaying not only a highly literary knowledge of love, but also the strategies of a scholarly approach, with footnotes and references to secondary criticism. The result is a splendid exploration of what literature is about, and signals a promising new direction in her writing.

FURTHER READING ON MARINA MAYORAL

Alborg, Concha, 'Marina Mayoral's Narrative: Old Families and New Faces from Galicia', in Joan L. Brown (ed.), *Women Writers of Contemporary Spain. Exiles in the Homeland* (Newark, London and Toronto, 1991), 179-97.

————, 'Las artes plásticas en la narrativa de Marina Mayoral: De metaficción a metaarte', *Revista Hispánica Moderna*, 54/1 (1991), 144-9.

————, 'Marina Mayoral', in Linda Gould Levine, Ellen Engelson Marson and Gloria Feiman Waldman (eds), *Spanish Women Writers: A Bio-Bibliographical Source Book* (Westport, CT and London, 1993), 330-6.

Amorós, Andrés, 'Penúltimas novelistas', *ABC*, 19 September 1981.

Asís Garrote, Ma. Dolores de, *Última hora de la novela en España* (Madrid, 1996).

Cadenas, C.B., 'Cuando los personajes lo son', *Nueva Estafeta*, 50 (1983), 94.

Carrillo, Nuria, 'La expansión plural de un género: el cuento 1975-1993', *Ínsula*, 568 (1994), 9-11.

Díaz Castañón, Carmen, 'Historia de una familia', *Cuadernos del Norte*, 12 (1982), 89-90.

Díaz-Mas, Paloma, 'Un itinerario por los sentimientos', *Ínsula*, 535 (1991), 24.

Encinar, Ángeles, 'Tendencias en el cuento español reciente', *Lucanor*, 13 (1995), 103-8.

Estévez, Carmen, 'Introducción', in Carmen Estévez (ed.), *Relatos eróticos* (Madrid, 1990), 7-26.

García Rey, José María, 'Marina Mayoral: la sociedad que se cuestiona en medio de una dudosa realidad', *Cuadernos hispanoamericanos*, 394 (1983), 214-21.

Glenn, Kathleen M., 'Marina Mayoral's *La única libertad*: A Postmodern Narrative', in Juan Fernández Jiménez, José J. Labrador Herraiz and L. Teresa Valdivieso (eds), *Estudios en homenaje a Enrique Ruiz Fornells* (Erie, PA, 1990), 267-73.

Gullón, Germán, 'La perezosa modernidad de la novela española (y la ficción más reciente)', *Ínsula*, 464-465 (1985), 8.

————, 'El novelista como fabulador de la realidad: Mayoral, Merino, Guelbenzu ...', in Ricardo Landeira and Luis T. González del Valle (eds), *Nuevos y novísimos. Algunas perspectivas sobre la narrativa española desde la década de los 60* (Boulder, COL, 1987), 50-70.

Jones, Margaret E. W., 'Different Wor(l)ds: Modes of Women's Communication in Spain's *narrativa femenina*', *Monographic Review*, 8 (1992), 57-69.

Martí-Maestro, Abraham, 'La novela española en 1982 y 1983', *Anales de la Literatura Española Contemporánea*, 9/1-3 (1984), 149-74.

Martín, Salustiano, 'Recóndita armonía. Vivir para contarlo', Reseña, 260 (1995), 27.

Navajas, Gonzalo, 'Narrativa y género. La ficción actual desde la mujer', Ínsula, 589-590 (1996), 37-9.

Noia, María Camino, 'Claves de la narrativa de Marina Mayoral', Letras Femeninas, 19/1-2 (1993), 33-44.

Pérez, Janet, Contemporary Women Writers of Spain (Boston, MA, 1988),156-7.

————, 'Characteristics of Erotic Brief Fiction by Women in Spain', Monographic Review, 7 (1991),173-95.

Saldaña, Francisco, 'Dialogando con las escritoras españolas Marina Mayoral y Ana Rossetti', in Literatura Española Contemporánea (Westminster, CA, 1991), 209-17.

Sánchez Arnosi, Milagros, 'Entrevista a Marina Mayoral', Ínsula, 431 (1982), 4-5.

Sanz Villanueva, Santos, 'Generación del 68', El Urogallo, 26 (1988), 28-60.

Talbot, Lynn K., 'Self-Discovery and History in the Galician World of Marina Mayoral', Letras Peninsulares, 5/3 (1992-93), 451-64.

Tarrío Varela, Anxo, 'Marina Mayoral, una voz para Galicia', Ínsula, 514 (1989), 20.

Valencia, Antonio, 'Prólogo', in Marina Mayoral, Al otro lado (Madrid,1981).

Vivas, Ángel, 'Un paseo con el amor y la muerte', Leer, June (1985), 37-9.

Zatlin, Phyllis, 'Detective Fiction and the Novels of Mayoral', Monographic Review, 3/1-2 (1987), 279-87.

————, 'Women Novelists in Democratic Spain: Freedom to Express the Female Perspective', Anales de la Literatura Española Contemporánea, 12 (1987), 29-44.

Nine Months and a Day [1]

Nueve meses y un día

Original Spanish text from
Morir en tus brazos y otros cuentos
(Alicante: Aguaclara, 1989), 70-73.

© Marina Mayoral, 1989

---

[1] A connection between pregnancy and a prison sentence is established by the title, which incorporates *'and a day'*, the Spanish formula that is added sometimes to the time a condemned person has to spend in jail.

Nueve meses y un día

Todo empezó aquella noche en que le dije a Juan: "hoy no hace falta que te lo pongas". O quizá, para ser más exactos, empezó antes, bastante antes, cuando el médico me dijo que el esterilet me estaba haciendo una úlcera, o antes aún, un día, inclinada sobre la taza del water, mientras me limpiaba las babas con papel higiénico entre arcada y arcada; entonces pensé que tendría que buscar otro procedimiento porque aquellas náuseas me estaban haciendo cogerle asco hasta a los ratitos buenos. Así que la cosa viene de lejos, aunque en sentido estricto empezó aquella noche. A Juan le cayó mal, pero eso tampoco es una novedad, también los otros, Marieta y Juan Carlos, le cayeron como una patada. En cierto modo lo de éste fue más bien extrañeza, "¿estás segura?" dijo y "ya hablaremos", porque ese día tenía reunión de filatélicos y yo creo que con la ilusión de una serie nueva por la que estaba muy interesado se le pasó un poco el susto y lo dejó estar. Peor fue con Marieta. Yo quería decírselo a ella la primera, al fin es mujer y tiene que comprenderlo, así que me armé de valor y se lo dije: "Marieta, nena, vas a tener...". Pero en el último momento me corté. Marieta siempre ha sido muy seca, muy despegada, y de pronto la vi allí tan lejana, comiéndose su filete con patatas fritas sin esperar siquiera a que llegase su padre, pero se me cruzaron las palabras y le dije: "Marieta, nena, vas a tener un hijo". Y ella, sin levantar la vista del plato y de la revista que tenía al lado, engullendo a toda velocidad, me dijo: "no digas tonterías, mamá, es que no he desayunado". Debía haberlo dejado, no era seguramente el momento adecuado, pero con ella nunca se sabe y además siempre viene a escape, de modo que insistí y se lo dije. Se lo tuve que decir dos veces, fue

Nine Months and a Day

It all began that night when I said to Juan: "You really don't need to wear one tonight." Or perhaps, to be more precise, it started before that, quite a long time before that, when the doctor told me the coil was giving me an ulcer, or even before that, one day, crouched over the lavatory bowl as I cleaned up the spittle between one bout of vomiting and the next with toilet paper; and then I thought I'd have to find some other method because those nauseous spells were making me feel sick in the pit of my stomach and spoiling even the good times I enjoyed in bed with him. So it had been going on for some time, though strictly speaking it started that night. Juan didn't take it very well, though that isn't anything new either; the others, Marieta and Juan Carlos, had also come as a bolt out of the blue to him. In a way this third one came as rather a surprise to him, "Are you sure?", he said, and "We'll talk about it later," because he had a meeting of his stamp collectors club that day and I think that because he was looking forward so much to a new issue he was really interested in, the shock wore off a bit and he put it out of his mind. It was worse with Marieta. I wanted her to be the first one I told about it, after all she's a woman and she should understand, so I plucked up my courage and said to her: "Marieta, my darling, you're going to have...". But at the last second I stopped short. Marieta's always been very self-contained, very detached, and all of a sudden I had this vision of her, so distant, eating her steak and chips without even waiting for her Dad to arrive, but the words just kept tumbling out and I said: "Marieta, darling, you're going to have a baby." And without raising her eyes from her plate or the magazine she had next to it, bolting down her food as fast as she could, she said: "Don't talk such rubbish, Mum, it's just that I haven't had any breakfast today." I should have left it at that, it obviously wasn't the right time, but you never know with her and anyway she is always about to dash off, so I persisted and told her. I had to tell her twice, it was really

muy desagradable, me sentí tan avergonzada como si fuera un delito, sin ninguna razón. Marieta ha heredado esa forma de mirar de mi suegra, me acuerdo cuando la conocí, todavía no se me notaba nada, pero tuve la sensación de que la tripa me crecía de repente y me abultaba las faldas, mucho peor que con mi padre, dónde va a dar, mi padre fue quien bajó la cabeza anonadado, yo lo comprendo, no teníamos un real y, además, yo era su niña, dieciocho años eran muy pocos para casarse así, de penalty, pero qué se le iba a hacer. Y Marieta me miró igual que mi suegra, sin ninguna comprensión, sin ninguna simpatía, qué digo de simpatía, sin piedad, yo diría que con el mismo odio, pero ¿por qué, Señor?, ¿qué me reprocha?, ¿qué hay de malo en eso? Yo desde niños se lo expliqué a los dos, se lo conté todo, la verdad, nada de la cigüeña, de una forma bonita, "a los niños los tienen las mamás en un nidito junto al corazón, un poco más abajo" y después, cuando fueron mayorcitos les di un libro muy bien hecho, que lo encargué a Francia a unos amigos porque aquí todavía no había, ni era frecuente hablar a los niños de esas cosas, pero yo quería que lo supieran desde el comienzo, que lo aprendieran bien, no como yo ni como su padre. Y cuando se fue en el verano a Inglaterra hace ya bastantes años, yo le hablé de la píldora, no era agradable para mí, me parecía tan niña, diecisiete años, pero yo sabía por experiencia lo que puede pasar a esa edad y mejor prevenir que lamentar, a los padres siempre nos coge de sorpresa, pero ella me cortó muy seca: "ya tomo mis precauciones, mamá, yo no me voy a casar de penalty". Ni de penalty ni de nada, ya se ve. No sé qué me reprocha, ni cómo tiene el valor de hablarme así. Cuando dijo que se iba a vivir con Pablo ¿qué esperaba que hiciéramos? ¡como para alegrarse, vamos, vaya situación! Aún ahora cuando la gente me pregunta ¿qué les voy a decir?, "pues no, no se ha casado", "pues sí, vive con uno", hasta para presentarlo a los amigos es una complicación no poder decir "mi yerno" o "mi hijo político" o "el marido de Marieta", lo normal; pues no: Pablo para aquí y Pablo para allá y todos disimulando y echando capotes. Y encima tan seca, tan dura, a mí me parece bien que venga a comer, que vengan los dos y que Juan les pase un dinero todos los meses, pero, por Dios, un poco de comprensión con las debilidades de los otros, que yo admito que son

unpleasant, I felt so ashamed, as if it were a crime, though there was no need
to feel like that. Marieta has inherited that look of hers from my mother-in-
law, I remember when I first met her, there was nothing showing yet, but I
had the feeling my belly was suddenly swelling, my skirts were filling out,
much worse than with my Dad, well for goodness sake my Dad was the one
who drooped his head, dumbfounded, I can understand why, we didn't have
a penny to our name, and anyway I was his little girl, eighteen is very young
to get married like that, a shot-gun wedding, but what else could one do?
And Marieta looked at me the same way as my mother-in-law, without the
slightest understanding of what I was feeling, without the slightest sympathy,
sympathy is not the right word, without mercy, I'd say with the same hatred,
but why, Lord? what's she reproaching me for? what's so wrong about this?
Even when they were children I explained things to both of them, told them
everything, told them the truth in a nice way, none of that rubbish about
storks: "Mummies have babies in a little nest next to their hearts, but a little
bit further down" and then, when they were a bit older I gave them a book,
very well written, that I asked some friends to bring back from France
because they still didn't have anything like that here, it wasn't the done thing
to talk to children about those things, but I wanted them to know about it
from the very beginning, so they'd learn properly, not like me or their father.
And when she went off to England that summer some years ago now, I
talked to her about the pill, it wasn't very nice for me, she seemed so young,
just seventeen, but I knew from experience what can happen at that age, and
better safe than sorry, it always catches us parents by surprise, but she just
snapped at me: "I'm already taking my own precautions, Mum, because I
don't want a shot-gun wedding." No shot-gun wedding, no nothing, that's
clear to everybody. I don't know why she's reproaching me, or how she has
the nerve to talk to me like that. When she said she was going to live with
Pablo, what did she expect us to do? Be over the moon about it, come on,
what a situation! Even now when people ask, what am I going to say to
them?, "Well no, they're not married", "Well yes, she lives with somebody",
even introducing him to our friends is complicated. I can't say "my son-in-
law" or "my son by marriage", or "Marieta's husband", the usual things; no:
it's Pablo here and Pablo there and everybody putting on a show and a
pretense. And she is so self-contained, so cold, but it's OK by me if she
comes over here to eat, if they both come, and if Juan slips them money
every month, but, for God's sake, spare me a moment of human frailty, I
admit it is human frailty, but what she has to realize is that I'm not

debilidades, pero tiene que darse cuenta de que no soy una vieja y que tengo las mismas necesidades que ella y que un error lo comete cualquiera.

Pero ella siempre ha sido así, ya me lo esperaba, en cierto modo me ha dolido más lo de Juan Carlos; si le digo que tengo lepra no me mira con más horror. Él fue desde pequeño mucho más cariñoso que la niña, sin comparación, lo que pasa es que en estas cosas me preocupa, hay algo que no va bien, yo no sé si los frailes... no sé, pero no me parece a mí normal tanto desinterés. Yo no soy como mi suegra que quería a su hijo para ella sola, por muy viuda que fuera ya podía suponer que alguna se lo había de llevar un poco antes o un poco después, no era para tomárselo así. A mí me gustaría que Juanca saliese con chicas y, en fin, lo normal a su edad, lo que pide la naturaleza. Cuando se me empezó a notar volvía la vista hacia otro lado, como si fuera algo repugnante y eso que llevaba unos vestidos muy monos y muy disimulones, y ahora igual, le voy a dar un beso y tuerce la cara. Me preocupa este chico y me duele que reaccione así, en el fondo es egoísmo, no querer enterarse de los problemas de una. De modo que si la familia hace eso ¿qué vas a esperar de los de fuera?, "estás loca", "qué insensatez", "¡a estas alturas!". Hasta el médico, "¿ha calculado usted los riesgos?", calculado, qué barbaridad, como si una fuese una máquina; ni una palabra de aliento, nadie. El único Juan, "a lo hecho, pecho", como siempre, no es un gran consuelo, pero tampoco lo de los otros. Más de dos me han recomendado el viaje a Londres, Marieta también. Pero yo eso no lo quiero, no es por ser católica, que sí lo soy, pero me parece horrible, como planear un crimen, a escondidas y en un país con esa lengua que no se entiende nada. Además, le decía yo a Gloria, que ella sí que fue hace años a Londres y es de las que me animaban al viaje, mi abuela tuvo dieciocho hijos, estuvo pariendo casi hasta los cincuenta y no le salió ninguno mal. Y ella me decía, "pero tú qué sabes si de los seis que se le murieron de niños había alguno tonto" y en eso tiene razón, cuando son pequeños se les nota menos y sobre todo antes, que la medicina estaba más atrasada. Pero el mío no, el mío no era tonto. Era un niño hermoso y parecía fuerte. Nació justo a los nueve meses y un día. Nació muerto. Fue en el momento del parto, el chico venía bien, pero tardé mucho en dilatar y después algo falló, no tenía ganas de empujar, no sé por qué sería. Me dio mucha pena. Entonces sí que me sentí vieja, que ya no servía, que ya no sirvo. Porque la verdad es que

an old woman and I've got the same urges as she has and that anybody can make a mistake.

But she's always been like that, I was expecting it, but in some ways Juan Carlos has hurt even more than she has; if I had told him I had leprosy he couldn't have looked at me with more horror. Ever since he was little he's been much more loving than the girl, there's no comparison, but the thing is he worries me in this respect, there's something that's not quite right, I don't know if the monks... I don't know, but such a lack of interest doesn't seem normal to me. I'm not like my mother-in-law who wanted to have her son all to herself, she might well have been a widow, but she must have known that some girl was going to take him away sooner or later, she didn't have to react like that. I'd be happy if Juanca went out with girls, after all it's normal at his age, it's what nature intended. When I began to show he averted his eyes from me, as if it were something repulsive, and although I was wearing pretty dresses that hid everything, and even now if I go to give him a kiss he turns his face away. That boy worries me and it hurts me he reacts like that, it's all down to selfishness, not wanting to get involved in somebody else's problems. So if the family behave like that, what can you expect from other people: "Are you mad?", "How stupid!", "At your time of life!". Even the doctor, "Have you calculated the risks?" Calculated, what a thing to say, as if I were a machine; not a word of encouragement, not from anybody. Only Juan, "Let's try and make the best of it", same as always, he's not a lot of comfort, but he's not as bad as the others. More than one person has recommended the trip to London, including Marieta. But I don't want that, it's not because I'm a Catholic, of course I am, but it seems horrible to me, like plotting a murder in secret, and in a country where they speak a language you can't understand a word of. Besides, I said to Gloria, she's the one who went to London a few years back and who was among those pushing me to go, my grandmother had eighteen children, she went on giving birth until she was almost fifty and they were all OK. And she said to me: "But you don't know if one of the six who died in childhood was backward," and she was right about that, when they're little it's less obvious and anyway, in those days medicine was much less advanced. But not mine, mine wasn't retarded. He was a beautiful boy and he looked strong. He was born at exactly nine months and a day. He was still born. It happened just as he was being born, the baby was coming out alright, but I was very late dilating and then something went wrong, I didn't want to push, I don't know why that should be. It caused me so much sorrow. After that of course I felt old, felt I was useless, that I am useless. Because the truth of it is that I

yo lo quería, quería a ese niño, desde aquella noche, desde antes. Yo me acuerdo de cuántas angustias con Marieta y con Juanca, llegaron y cargamos con ellos, pero lo que se dice quererlos, antes, antes de verlos ya aquí, pues no, no los quería, y después estábamos deseando dejárselos a mi madre, nos apetecía salir, y con sólo una habitación y aquella cocinita tan pequeña y siempre llena de humos, nos arreglábamos muy mal, no nos iba a alquilar un palacio, decía mi suegra... Ahora tenemos una casa grande y un dinerillo ahorrado y una asistenta por horas y yo tengo tanto tiempo libre. Juan se pasa las horas en el estudio o en la obra y después muchos días con los filatélicos, y yo estoy aquí, esperando que aparezca Marieta y me cuente algo, o el chico. Juan se enfada conmigo, dice que no entiende por qué me siento vieja, que él se encuentra en plena forma, está pensando en apuntarse al maratón, siempre le ha gustado hacer deporte. Así que yo vengo aquí, a este cuarto donde pensaba poner la cuna, junto a la ventana, para que al crecer pudiera ver el árbol y los pájaros que vienen algunas mañanas, y me siento aquí, y lloro un rato.

wanted him, I wanted that baby, from that night, from before that. I remember how much distress there was with Marieta and Juanca, they arrived and we were saddled with them, but what you might call wanting them, before, before seeing them born, well no, I didn't want them, and afterwards we wanted to leave them with my mother, we longed to go out and, with just one room and that tiny little kitchen so small and always full of smoke, things were really difficult for us, she wasn't going to rent a palace for us, my mother-in-law used to say... Now we have a big house and a bit of money put by and a daily help and I have so much free time. Juan spends his time in the study or at work and a lot of time at the stamp club, and here I am, waiting for Marieta to show up and tell me something, or the boy. Juan gets cross with me, he says he doesn't understand why I feel old, that he feels on top of the world, he's thinking of putting his name down for the marathon, he's always enjoyed being involved in sport. Anyway, I come in here, into this room where I was thinking of putting the cot next to the window, so that as he got bigger he'd be able to see the tree and the birds that come some mornings, and I sit here and I cry a while.

MERCEDES ABAD
Photograph © Carmen Rosa Pérez

MERCEDES ABAD was born in Barcelona in 1961, where she studied at the French Lycée and graduated in Journalism from the University. A professional journalist and a fine short-story writer, she has been the object of academic interest right from her first controversial book of stories, *Ligeros libertinajes sabáticos* (1986), which won the eighth Premio La Sonrisa Vertical, an award for erotic literature, when she was twenty-four. The book was an immediate best-seller and has been reprinted many times and translated into several languages. Three years later she published another collection of stories, *Felicidades conyugales* (1989), an engaging book that won her acclaim and recognition beyond the restrictions imposed by her success as a *genre* writer.

Abad's short stories have been included in *Litoral Femenino: Literatura escrita por mujeres en la España contemporánea*, edited by Lorenzo Saval and J. García Gallego (1986); in *Relatos eróticos*, edited by Carmen Estévez (1990); in *Los siete pecados capitales* (1990); in *Verte desnudo* (1992), a collection that challenges and reverses the male gaze by giving female authors the opportunity to write about different parts of the male body; and in *Cuentos de este siglo*, edited by Ángeles Encinar (1995). Abad is also the author of a light-hearted essay, *Sólo dime dónde lo hacemos* (1991), which explores in an amusing way alternative places to make love.

More recently, another book has confirmed her subversive sense of humour and her talent for the *cuento* in the best European tradition: *Soplando al viento* (1995), in which some of her best stories display an approach to cruelty similar to Saki's. Some of her articles in *El País* have been included in a collective volume, *Crónicas de cada día* (1996).

Attracted by the theatre which she regards as a real challenge because of the dearth of young playwrights in Spain – as she told the students of the University of California in 1991, Mercedes Abad has written two plays in Catalan: *Pretèrit Perfecte* (1992) and *Si non é vero* (1995).

FURTHER READING ON MERCEDES ABAD

Blanco, María Luisa, 'Mercedes Abad: "Lo pornográfico y lo obsceno son conceptos distintos"', *Cambio 16*, 8 July 1996, 25.

Carmona, V., J. Lamb, S. Velasco and B. Zecchi, 'Conversando con Mercedes Abad, Cristina Fernández Cubas y Soledad Puértolas: "Feminismo y literatura no tienen nada que ver"', *Mester*, 20/2 (1991), 157-65.

Estévez, Carmen, 'Introducción', in Carmen Estévez (ed.), *Relatos eróticos* (Madrid 1990), 7-26.

Lorente, Elena, 'Generaciones cruzadas: Beatriz de Moura / Mercedes Abad', *El País*, 14 August 1996.

Mandrell, James, 'Mercedes Abad and *La Sonrisa Vertical*: Erotica and Pornography in Post-Franco Spain', *Letras Peninsulares*, 6/2-3 (1993), 277-99.

'Narradores de hoy' [round table discussion], *El Urogallo*, 2 (1986), 18-25.

Rueda, Ana, 'Mercedes Abad: *Felicidades conyugales*', *España Contemporánea*, 4/1 (1991), 150-4.

Senabre, Ricardo, '*Soplando al viento* de Mercedes Abad', *ABC*, 10 March 1995.

Pérez, Janet, 'Characteristics of Erotic Brief Fiction by Women in Spain', *Monographic Review*, 7 (1991), 173-95.

Valls, Fernando, 'La literatura erótica en España entre 1975 y 1990', *Ínsula*, 530 (1990), 29-30.

Vosburg, Nancy, 'Entrevista con Mercedes Abad', *Letras Peninsulares*, 6/2-3 (1993), 221-30.

Uncontrolled Passion

Pasión defenestrante

Original Spanish text from
Felicidades conyugales (Barcelona: Tusquets, 1989), 13-21.

172

Pasión defenestrante

A Darlos Icaria

Erase un día tórrido y húmedo, una carretera mal cosida, un coche que anhelaba la jubilación y, en el interior del vehículo, un hombre y una mujer. La mujer —yo— conducía con evidente torpeza a causa de los incesantes manotazos que daba al aire en un vano intento de ahuyentar un enjambre de moscas especialmente tenaces, que absolvían a su compañero de viaje y concentraban en ella toda su furia. La predilección de los insectos hacia mí era cuestión que no lograba explicarme y que había verificado a lo largo de penosos veranos durante los cuales picores y escozores me habían impedido entregarme a cualquier actividad que no fuera la de rascarme el pellejo mientras los bichos, semejantes a una aureola mística, seguían ejecutando su frenética danza en torno a mí.

Ríos de sudor y perversos afluentes estriaban mi rostro. No pude evitar maldecir en voz alta, con la consiguiente ofuscación del hombre que iba a mi lado, un simple desconocido, interesado en la compra de una mansión que ni siquiera me pertenecía. Maldije el momento en que, ignoro si llevada por un masoquismo profundamente arraigado o, simplemente, para demostrar que era capaz de hacerlo, acepté encargarme de todos los asuntos relacionados con la venta de la propiedad que Paula había abandonado meses atrás. Al morir Igor, ella había jurado no volver a poner los pies en aquel extraño lugar, morada fantasmagórica de la demencia del difunto.

Cuando, tras nuestra lenta y dificultosa ascensión, llegamos a lo alto de la colina donde se hallaba la casa, tanto mi posible cliente como yo ofrecíamos un aspecto lamentable: desgreñados, empapados en sudor y cubiertos de polvo. Antes de cruzar la verja que daba acceso a la mansión, y aun a sabiendas de que el impacto de lo real superaría con creces cuanto yo pudiera decir, me dispuse a poner en antecedentes al hipotético comprador

Uncontrolled Passion

To Darlos Icaria

Once upon a torridly hot and humid day, a road in a bad state of repair, a car hankering after retirement, and inside the vehicle a man and a woman. The woman — me — was driving all over the road as the result of taking incessant swipes at the air in a vain attempt to drive away a swarm of particularly tenacious flies that ignored her travelling companion and concentrated all their fury on her. The insects' preference for me was something I never managed to work out, but which had been confirmed during the course of painful summers when bites and stings had prevented me from concentrating on anything other than scratching at my skin while the horrid little creatures, like some mystic halo, continued to execute their frenetic dance around me.

Rivers of sweat and perverse tributaries streaked my face. I couldn't help cursing out loud to the resultant bewilderment of the man at my side, a mere stranger, who was interested in the purchase of a mansion that didn't even belong to me. I rued the day on which — I don't know whether I was driven by some deeply-ingrained masochism or simply to show I could do it — I agreed to take on the responsibility for anything related to the sale of the property that Paula had just up and left some months before. When Igor died she'd sworn she'd never again set foot in that strange place, that haunted abode of the dead man's insanity.

When, after our slow and hard climb, we reached the top of the hill on which the house stood, both my potential client and I looked a sorry sight: dishevelled, bathed in sweat and covered in dust. Before passing through the iron gates that gave access to the mansion, and even though I knew full well the impact of the house itself would far exceed any words I might utter, I wanted to give the would-be purchaser — I seem to recall his name was

—creo recordar que se llamaba Julius Capdefila— acerca de las innumerables virtudes del lugar: precio francamente irrisorio, amplitud del terreno circundante, paisaje idílico salpicado de árboles exóticos y sombras bienhechoras, piscina octogonal con un fauno en el centro haciendo las veces de surtidor y una náyade bañándose en sus aguas, jardín romántico donde se apretujaban más de un centenar de esculturas cuyos estilos eran absolutamente dispares, edificio construido bajo los preceptos de la arquitectura minimalista y una capillita barroca que Igor había transformado en un taller de pintura y cuyos frescos sorprenderían a más de un avezado pornógrafo. El conjunto no podía ser más absurdo. Considerado por separado, cada elemento era bello en sí mismo, pero su arbitraria yuxtaposición hacía imposible cualquier armonía, por heterodoxa que fuera. A causa de ello, y aunque Paula, poco interesada en el dinero que la venta de semejante pastiche pudiera proporcionarle, había bajado el precio una y otra vez, nuestros propósitos de venta se estrellaban contra la previsible reticencia de los visitantes. Desmoralizada como estaba, y absorta en mil y una tretas, tardé en advertir el interés que manifestaba mi acompañante. Mientras inspeccionábamos el interior de la vivienda, Julius Capdefila observaba atentamente cada uno de los objetos que se apiñaban en mesas y estanterías. Me explicó que coleccionaba objetos antiguos o simplemente curiosos y que se hallaba sinceramente sorprendido ante el desapego de la propietaria hacia piezas tan valiosas. Percibí cierto recelo de hombre honesto en su mirada estrábica, como si sospechase que aquellos objetos podían ser producto del robo, y la casa, una hermana gemela de la guarida donde Alí Babá y sus cuarenta compinches ocultaban sus tesoros. Supuse que el precio de auténtico saldo que pedíamos a cambio no hacía sino acentuar semejante impresión y, al ver que el escrupuloso coleccionista permanecía mudo y expectante, a la espera de una explicación plausible que aniquilara de una vez por todas a cualquier gusanillo roedor de conciencias, decidí relatarle las razones que impulsaban a mi amiga Paula a deshacerse de aquella bicoca al precio que fuera.

Cuando Paula conoció a Igor —ya no recuerdo en qué circunstancias, aunque juraría que debieron de ser tan absurdas como todo lo que aconteció después— su primera sensación, según me contó días más tarde, fue que ninguna de las partes que componían la excéntrica personalidad del checo se avenía a integrarse en una totalidad ordenada y coherente. Más adelante yo misma tendría la ocasión de comprobarlo. Igor era caótico, pero también obsesivamente meticuloso en cuestiones de orden, capaz también de mentir con sinceridad, exhibicionista y exageradamente púdico a la vez, y hurón

Julius Capdefila — some background to the innumerable virtues of the place: a price that was frankly laughable, the extensive grounds in which it was set, idyllic landscape dotted with exotic trees and providential areas of shade, an octagonal swimming pool with a faun in the middle that acted as a fountain and a naiad bathing in its waters, a romantic garden where room had been found for more than a hundred sculptures of utterly different styles, a building constructed under the precepts of minimalist architecture, and a tiny Baroque chapel that Igor had transformed into a painter's studio and whose frescoes would surprise more than one experienced pornographer. The whole thing couldn't have been more absurd. Each element taken separately was beautiful in itself, but its arbitrary juxtaposition made any sort of harmony, however heterodox it might be, impossible. As a result, and even though Paula, who was little interested in the money the sale of such a pastiche might yield her, had dropped the price more than once, our sales prospects were dashed on the rocks of the visitors' predictable reluctance. Demoralized as I was, and engrossed in a thousand and one stratagems, I was slow to notice the interest my companion was showing. As we inspected the inside of the house, Julius Capdefila paid careful attention to each and every one of the objects piled together on tables and shelves. He explained that he collected antiques or simply curios and was genuinely surprised at the owner's indifference to such valuable pieces. From his squinting look I noted a certain honest man's mistrust, as if he suspected those objects might have been the proceeds of some robbery and the house a twin sister to the lair where Ali Baba and his forty chums hid their treasure. I supposed that the knock-down price we were asking in exchange could only add to that impression and, noting that the scrupulous collector kept silent and expectant, waiting for some plausible explanation that would lay once and for all whatever prickings of conscience were gnawing at him, I decided to come clean as to the reasons that compelled my friend Paula to rid herself of that plum property at any price.

When Paula first met Igor — I don't now remember under what circumstances, though I'd be willing to swear they must have been as absurd as everything else that subsequently took place — her first reaction, according to what she told me a few days later, was that none of the parts that made up the Czech's eccentric personality had managed to blend into one ordered and cohesive whole. I would later have occasion to verify this for myself. Igor was chaotic, but he was also obsessively meticulous on matters of order, capable, too, of lying with sincerity, an exhibitionist yet at the same time exaggeratedly modest, a shy loner yet the indisputable star of

solitario y estrella indiscutible de todas las fiestas. Era precisamente esa cualidad bífida de su naturaleza la que mayor encanto y poder de seducción le confería. Paula, a quien lo insólito atraía sistemáticamente, no tardó en sucumbir a los turbios encantos del checo y, en vista de que éste correspondía con notable ardor a los galanteos de mi amiga, todo permitía augurarles una inolvidable secuencia de pasión y felicidad. Las cosas, sin embargo, empezaron a torcerse mucho antes de lo previsto.

Muy poco tiempo después del inicio de su relación con Igor, Paula me llamó un día por teléfono y me rogó, sin más aclaraciones, que acudiera a su casa lo antes posible. De su tono de voz deduje que era presa de una viva agitación, de modo que me reuní con ella inmediatamente. Nada más llegar a su casa, me deslumbró la visión de un magnífico clavicordio. Alevosamente, Paula me dejó paladear durante unos instantes mi estupor sin decir palabra; luego señaló hacia un rincón de la sala donde mi atónita mirada tropezó con un inmenso colmillo de elefante. Habida cuenta de la precaria situación económica en que se hallaba mi amiga, la repentina aparición de objetos tan costosos no dejaba de ser sorprendente. Estaba a punto de preguntarle a Paula si le había tocado la lotería cuando ella, llorosos los ojos y temblorosos los labios, me anunció que era Igor quien le había regalado, no sólo el clavicordio y el colmillo, sino un sinfín de otros objetos, aunque de tamaño indudablemente más modesto, que se alineaban an anaqueles antaño desnudos. Paula me contó que todo había empezado un día en que Igor y ella se hallaban en el casco antiguo de la ciudad y pasaron casualmente frente al escaparate del anticuario donde estaba expuesto aquel hermoso clavicordio. Paula se detuvo unos instantes a contemplar el instrumento; luego ambos prosiguieron su paseo. En este punto del relato, mi amiga se empeñó en jurarme que ella nunca había pedido nada a Igor; yo, que la conocía bien, sonreí ante sus intentos de justificación: Paula era la persona menos interesada de cuantas había conocido. Sea como fuere, el clavicordio apareció en casa de Paula al día siguiente, acompañado de una nota en la que Igor le rogaba aceptar aquel humilde presente. Ella, halagada, agradeció el gesto. Sin embargo ese gesto revestiría con el tiempo un significado absolutamente siniestro. Tras aquel primer regalo un auténtico diluvio de ellos invadió la vida de Paula. Todas las sinceras protestas de mi amiga resultaron vanas; no pasaba un solo día sin que, cuando salían juntos, Igor la arrastrara al interior de alguna tienda y la obligara a salir de ella con un montón de objetos que Paula ni siquiera había deseado. Él firmaba cheques con auténtico deleite, como si ésa fuera su

any party. It was precisely this double-stranded quality of his nature that gave him even greater charm and powers of seduction.

Paula, who was systematically attracted by the unusual, lost no time in succumbing to the Czech's dark charms, and given the fact that the latter responded with notable ardour to my friend's flirting, the scene was fully set for an unforgettable sequence of passion and happiness. Things, nevertheless, began to go wrong long before they were expected to.

Shortly after her relationship with Igor had started, Paula called me on the phone one day and, without proffering any further explanation, begged me to go to her house as soon as possible. From her tone of voice I deduced that she was in a real state of turmoil, so I went over to see her immediately. I had scarcely got to her house when I was dazzled by the sight of a magnificent clavichord. Slyly, Paula allowed me to wallow in astonishment for a few seconds without saying a word; then she pointed to a corner of the room where my astounded gaze fell on a huge elephant tusk. Knowing the precarious financial situation my friend was in, the sudden appearance of such costly items couldn't help but come as a surprise. I was on the point of asking Paula if she'd won the lottery when, her eyes filled with tears and her lips trembling, she announced that Igor had given them to her as presents, not just the clavichord and the tusk but an endless list of other things too, though undoubtedly more modest in size, which were now ranged on the hitherto bare shelves. Paula told me it had all started one day when she and Igor had found themselves in the old quarter of the city and had passed by chance in front of an antique dealer's shop window where that beautiful clavichord had been on display. Paula had stopped for a second to look at the instrument; then the pair had continued on their walk. At this point in the story my friend insisted in telling me that she had never asked Igor for anything; I, who knew her well, smiled at her attempts at justification: Paula was the least materialistic person I'd ever known. Be that as it may, the clavichord turned up at Paula's house the next day, accompanied by a note in which Igor begged her to accept that humble present. She, flattered, thanked him for the gesture. Nevertheless, that gesture was, with time, to take on a truly sinister significance. After that first present an absolute deluge of things invaded Paula's life. All my friend's genuine protests proved in vain; whenever they went out together Igor would without fail drag her inside some shop and force her to come out again with a pile of things Paula hadn't even wanted. He signed cheques with true delight as if that were his only

única misión en la vida y, si ella intentaba rehusar los regalos, él se sentía
mortalmente ofendido.

El día que me lo confesó todo, una Paula visiblemente desconcertada me
pedía un consejo que yo no fui capaz de ofrecer; balbuceé torpemente y sin
convicción alguna que los regalos muy bien podían ser un reclamo afectivo,
o tal vez una tradición checa poco conocida en nuestro país o un
experimento psicológico revolucionario. Pasamos horas y horas cavilando
sin que ninguna lucecilla se encendiera en nuestras mentes. Con todo, el
mero hecho de haberse confiado a mí alivió sensiblemente a mi amiga; al
despedirnos, su estado de ánimo, sin ser precisamente el óptimo, había
mejorado de forma ostensible.

Cuando volvimos a encontrarnos, Paula me contó, no sin un mohín
irónico, que se había convertido en una adicta a los regalos; si bien era
cierto que seguían provocándole cierta inquietud acerca de la salud mental
de Igor, si transcurrían un día o dos sin que él le hubiera ofrecido algún
presente, una horrible ansiedad se apoderaba de ella. Entre risas de abierta
complicidad, Paula me dijo que había amenazado a Igor: si no le regalaba
una casa donde cupieran ella y sus regalos, daba por terminada su relación.
Reímos juntas y olvidamos el asunto durante unas horas en las que me
alegré de encontrar de nuevo a la Paula de siempre, confiada, risueña y vital.

El tiempo transcurrió de regalo en regalo. Cuando Igor compró la casa
de la colina para Paula, ella ya había logrado aceptarlo todo sin graves
problemas de conciencia. Las compras compulsivas de Igor se habían
convertido en placentera normalidad. Y por temor a resultar inconveniente,
ella nunca se atrevió a indagar acerca de las fuentes de ingresos del checo;
se contentaba con pensar que, si él despilfarraba el dinero de aquella
manera, era porque sin duda alguna podía permitirse ese lujo. Pero como
las personas felices tienen la peligrosa costumbre de asumir, como algo
evidente e incuestionable, la felicidad de sus seres más queridos, la tragedia
pilló a Paula desprevenida. Cuando Igor, con todas sus cuentas bancarias
agotadas y deudas espectaculares —lo atestiguan ciertos papeles que la
policía encontró en los bolsillos de la chaqueta del cadáver—, saltó por la
ventana del noveno piso de un edificio, el mundo se desmoronó sobre Paula
y los regalos. Un psiquiatra se vio obligado a internarla temporalmente en
una clínica para enfermos de los nervios. Ella no llevó ningún regalo
consigo. Postrada en su cama del hospital, alarmó a todos los médicos y
enfermeras de la clínica con sus delirios, infatigables repeticiones de
misteriosos inventarios de objetos rarísimos entre los cuales destacaba un
clavicordio.

mission in life, and if she tried to refuse the presents he'd feel mortally offended.

On the day she confessed all this to me, a visibly disturbed Paula asked for advice that I was incapable of providing: I stammered awkwardly and without conviction something about how the gifts might very well be a call for her attention, or perhaps a Czech custom not widely known in our country, or a revolutionary psychological experiment. We spent hours and hours going back and forth over it all without any glimmer of light being kindled in our minds. Nevertheless, the mere fact of having confided in me brought my friend significant relief; when we said goodbye to each other her spirits, without exactly being good, had clearly improved.

The next time we met up, Paula, with a grimace, told me that she'd turned into a gift junkie: even though it was true they continued to cause her a certain amount of disquiet about the state of Igor's mental health, if one or two days went by without his proffering her some present or other she'd be seized by a dreadful anxiety. Amid openly complicit laughter, Paula told me that she'd threatened Igor: if he didn't give her a house where she and his presents would fit, their relationship would be over. We laughed together and put the matter to one side for a couple of hours, during which I was happy to rediscover the Paula of old — trusting, smiling and vital.

Time passed from gift to gift. By the time Igor bought the house on the hill for Paula she had already managed to accept the whole thing without any serious problems of conscience. Igor's compulsive purchases had turned into agreeable normality. And fearful of its proving an unwise thing to do she never dared inquire into the sources of the Czech's income: she contented herself with thinking that if he was squandering his money like that it was because he could undoubtedly allow himself that luxury. But since happy people have the dangerous habit of taking for granted the happiness of their loved ones as something obvious and unquestionable, the tragedy caught Paula off guard. When Igor, his bank accounts exhausted and with spectacular debts — these were attested to by certain documents the police found in the pockets of the jacket that the corpse was wearing — jumped through the window of the ninth floor of a building, the world crashed around Paula and the gifts. A psychiatrist was forced to admit her temporarily into a clinic for people undergoing nervous breakdowns. She didn't take a single gift with her. Stretched out on her hospital bed she alarmed all the doctors and nurses at the clinic with her delirious, tireless repetitions of mysterious inventories of extremely rare objects, among which the clavichord stood out.

Cuando Paula, una vez restablecida, salió del hospital, se negó a volver a la casa de la colina; cada uno de los regalos que ahí se amontonaban era un dardo clavado en su cerebro. Me dijo que me regalaba la mansión y, cuando logré hacerla entrar en razón y persuadirla de que lo mejor sería venderla, puso como condición que fuese yo quien se ocupara de todo.

Al concluir mi relato, el semblante de Julius Capdefila, coleccionista desconfiado y hombre intachable y ejemplar, expresaba el más profundo estupor. Todo cuanto había relatado, me dijo, añadía más valor a una casa que, desde el primer momento, lo había seducido. Capdefila quiso aclarar algunos detalles de nuestro trato y la venta quedó acordada. Anochecía ya cuando subimos al coche para iniciar el regreso y, como suele ocurrirme a esa hora del día a menos que interponga una tenaz resistencia, empezó a embargarme la melancolía. La alimenté recordando a Igor y la ansiedad que parecía gobernar todos sus actos, su avidez por la vida, su talante risueño, los accesos de hilaridad que tan frecuentemente lo estremecían y que siempre acababa contagiándonos a Paula y a mí, sus largos y repentinos silencios y su mirada llena de fuego. Y luego los regalos, todos los regalos, desfilaron por mi mente en siniestra comitiva. Había algo en aquella historia que no encajaba: faltaba una pieza en el rompecabezas. Tras la muerte de Igor, esa vaga sospecha me había inducido, sin que Paula lo supiera, a investigar en la vida del checo. Hablé con personas que lo habían conocido, recorrí consulados y departamentos de inmigración y metí la nariz en todos sus papeles, sin encontrar jamás indicio alguno que me permitiera comprender lo que había sucedido. Desanimada, al cabo desistí de mi búsqueda. Pero la pieza seguía faltando y nada podía convencerme de lo contrario.

Tras la firma del contrato de venta de la casa de la colina, Paula tomó el dinero obtenido y, en un gesto tan absurdo como liberador, lo repartió entre todos aquéllos que habían querido a Igor y lamentaron sinceramente su muerte. A modo de desquite, Paula dio a la parte que le había tocado un destino muy peculiar: hizo construir un panteón para Igor en el cementerio más bonito y caro de la ciudad. La pesadilla de Paula se convertía en chiste.

Yo había desistido ya de mi empeño en encontrar la pieza que faltaba en el rompecabezas cuando un día recibí una llamada telefónica de Julius Capdefila. Temerosa de que el coleccionista hubiera tenido algún problema relacionado con la casa, me estremecí al oír su voz, pero él se apresuró a

When Paula, her health now restored, left the hospital, she refused to go back to the house on the hill; every one of the gifts that were piled up there was a dart hammered into her brain. She told me that she was giving the mansion to me, and when I managed to get her to see sense and persuaded her that the best thing would be to sell it, she stipulated that it should be I who took care of everything.

When I got to the end of my story the face of Julius Capdefila, a mistrustful collector and an irreproachable and exemplary man, registered the most profound astonishment. Everything he'd been told, he said, added more value to a house that had seduced him from the very first moment. Capdefila wanted to clarify a few details of our transaction and the sale was agreed. Night was already beginning to fall when we got into the car to start our return journey, and, as usually happens with me at that time of the day unless I put up a really strong resistance, I began to feel overwhelmed with sadness. I fuelled this by remembering Igor and the anxiety that appeared to govern everything he did, his lust for life, his cheerful personality, the fits of mirth that shook him so frequently and always ended up infecting Paula and me, his long and sudden silences and his eyes filled with fire. And then the gifts, all the gifts, filed through my brain in a sinister procession. There was something in that story that didn't fit: a piece of the jigsaw was missing. After Igor's death this vague suspicion, without Paula knowing anything about it, had prompted me to look into the Czech's life. I talked to people who had known him, I scoured Consulates and Immigration Departments, and poked my nose into all his papers without ever finding any clue that would allow me to understand what had happened. Discouraged, I eventually gave up my search. But the piece stayed missing, and nothing could convince me otherwise.

After the signing of the contract for the sale of the house on the hill, Paula took the money and in a gesture as absurd as it was liberating, shared it out between all those people who had loved Igor and who sincerely mourned his death. As a way of making amends, Paula used the share that had come to her for a truly singular purpose: she had a pantheon built for Igor in the most beautiful and expensive cemetery in the city. Paula's nightmare had turned into a joke.

I had already given up my quest for the missing piece in the jigsaw when one day I got a phone call from Julius Capdefila. Afraid that the collector may have run into some problem with the house I trembled when I heard his

tranquilizarme; había encontrado en la rendija de una puerta una carta de Igor dirigida a Paula. Capdefila me rogó que avisara a la destinataria de la misiva y fuéramos inmediatamente a la casa de la colina. Yo protesté aduciendo que Paula no querría volver a aquel lugar, y Capdefila, tan comprensivo como siempre, se avino a que nos encontrásemos en un bar. Paula ya estaba esperando cuando yo llegué; sostenía una copa de vino con mano trémula. Estaba tan pálida y tensa y sus ojos miraban al vacío de una manera tan enajenada que, incluso en un lugar tan repleto de gente como aquel bar, llamaba poderosamente la atención. Julius Capdefila no tardó en aparecer y entregar la carta a Paula. En el interior de un sobre sucio y arrugado había una hoja pequeña de papel y un par de líneas que decían así:

"Querida Paula:
"He pasado media vida buscando un pretexto para suicidarme. No sabes cuánto agradezco tu colaboración. Gracias mil,
"Igor"

voice, but he quickly tried to reassure me; in the crack of some door he'd found a letter from Igor addressed to Paula. Capdefila begged me to let the addressee of the missive know of its existence and said we should go immediately to the house on the hill. I protested that Paula wouldn't want to go back to that place, and Capdefila, as understanding as ever, agreed we should meet in a bar. Paula was already waiting when I got there; she was holding a glass of wine in a trembling hand. She was extremely pale and tense and her eyes looked into space in such a deranged way that, even in a place as crowded with people as that bar was, she caught their attention. Julius Capdefila was not long in showing up and handing over the letter to Paula. Inside a dirty envelope, all crumpled up, there was a little piece of paper with a couple of lines that read as follows:

"Dear Paula:
I've spent half my life looking for a pretext to commit suicide. You can't know how grateful I am for your collaboration. A thousand thanks,
Igor"

ROSA MONTERO

ROSA MONTERO was born in Madrid in 1951. She began to publish in the Madrid press during her university years — she studied Psychology and graduated in Journalism from the Escuela Oficial de Periodismo. She has contributed to many newspapers (*Arriba, Pueblo, Mundo Diario*) and magazines (*Contrastes, Posible, Personas, Hermano Lobo, Fotogramas, Destino, Jano*), but she is mainly associated with *El País*, the newspaper on which she started working in 1977, and whose Sunday Supplement she edited from 1980 to 1982.

What has made Rosa Montero one of the most popular and well-liked journalists in Spain is her series of interviews (a favourite *genre* of hers, see *El País Semanal*, 10/9/95) and her weekly columns and articles. Her journalistic work has been collected in several books of interviews — *España para ti para siempre* (1976), *Cinco años de país* (1982), *Entrevistas* (1996), and articles — *La vida desnuda* (1994).

As in the case of Maruja Torres, another contributor of note to *El País*, Montero's social and politically-minded approach leads her to debate the most controversial issues: terrorism, the horrors of war, linguistic sexism, sexual harassment, abortion, women's rights at work and at home, the pervasive effects of gender-oriented patterns of behaviour, racism, ageism or any kind of violation of civil or human rights. Particularly incisive is her feminist perspective in the series of biographical accounts of real women, first published fortnightly in *El País Semanal* and later collected in *Historias de mujeres* (1995). Of the fifteen women selected some are famous but with hidden facets, like Simone de Beauvoir, Agatha Christie or the Bronte sisters, and some are figures rescued from oblivion in an attempt to do them justice, like María de la O Lejárraga (1874-1956) who actually wrote the works that her husband, Gregorio Martínez Sierra, took the credit for, the sculptress Camille Claudel, or Zenobia Camprubí, Juan Ramón Jiménez's devoted wife. It is written in an austere, very matter-of-fact style, rather different from the humorous, colloquial, often satirical tone that is so characteristic of her journalistic and literary work. The series shows the same conviction that has frequently allowed her to talk about "un buen montón de señoras formidables" who have been victims of the worst kind of discrimination, that of being ignored, wiped out from historical memory.

Rosa Montero has been awarded several prizes for her work in the media, among these the Nacional de Periodismo in 1980 and the Derechos Humanos in 1989. She also worked in TVE for two years and wrote the scripts for a comedy series, *Media naranja*, shown in 1987, which questions the roles of gender in a couple's relationship, and won the Martín Fierro award for the best foreign series on Argentinian television in 1988.

A successful novelist, Rosa Montero has published seven novels between 1979 and 1997, all of them best-sellers and mostly translated into other European languages: *Crónica del desamor* (1979), a testimonial account of the mood of the early days of Spanish democracy, mainly from the perspective of a young professional woman. *La función Delta* (1981) is an existentialist and feminist portrayal of a woman through her diaries (one written when she is thirty and making her début as a film-maker, the other when she is sixty and dying of cancer) whose chapters constantly juxtapose past and present.

A far more ambitious book, *Te trataré como a una reina* (1983), "parodies sleuth fiction and popular romance from a feminist point of view" (Davies 1994, 124-5), creating a grotesque and run-down world where characters are all victims rather than roles with which one can identify. In *Amado amo* (1988) the struggle for power and its ancestral misogynistic echoes meets the careerism of the 1980s in an effective contemporary satire. *Temblor* (1990), another bold step by this versatile writer, deals with Montero's recurrent themes in the form of an epic science-fiction narrative (*Temblor* is likely to be made into an opera by the Centro Nacional de Nuevas Tendencias Estéticas).

Bella y oscura (1993) explores the familiar ground of her previous work, with the action set in a seedy world reminiscent of *Te trataré* and of the short story 'Paulo Pumilio', and uses fantasy as a controversial, disquieting, rather than comforting, presence.

La hija del caníbal (1997), Montero's latest novel, combines the structure of a thriller with elements of the historical novel – when dealing with twentieth-century Spanish anarchism — but it focusses mainly on the existential crisis of a woman that is triggered by her husband's disappearance.

Montero has published several short stories: 'Paulo Pumilio', in *Doce relatos de mujeres*, edited by Ymelda Navajo (1982); 'Parece tan dulce', in *Lucanor*, 11 (1994), 29-33, and later in *Cuentos de este siglo*, edited by Ángeles Encinar (1996); 'El puñal en la garganta', published first in *El País Semanal*, August 1994, and afterwards in *Relatos urbanos* (1994); 'Tarde en la noche', *El País Semanal*, August 1995; and 'Noche de Reyes', in *Este mundo* (1995). Rosa Montero is also the author of a children's novel, *El nido de los sueños* (1991).

FURTHER READING ON ROSA MONTERO

Alba, Narciso, 'Entrevista con Rosa Montero', *Ventanal: Revista de Creación y Crítica*, 14 (1988), 81-100.

Alborg, Concha, 'Cuatro narradoras de la transición', in Ricardo Landeira and Luis T. González del Valle (eds), *Nuevos y novísimos. Algunas perspectivas críticas sobre la narrativa española desde la década de los 60* (Boulder, COL 1987), 11-27.

——————, 'Metaficción y feminismo en Rosa Montero', *Revista de Estudios Hispánicos*, 22/1 (1988), 67-76.

Amell, Alma, 'Una crónica de la marginación: la narrativa de Rosa Montero', *Letras Femeninas*, 18/1-2 (1992), 74-82.

——————, 'El personaje masculino en las novelas de Rosa Montero', *Letras Femeninas*, 18/1-2 (1992), 105-10.

Amell, Samuel, 'El periodismo: su influencia e importancia en la novela del postfranquismo', *Castilla*, 12 (1989), 7-14.

——————, 'El motivo del viaje en tres novelas del posfranquismo', in Juan Fernández Jiménez, José J. Labrador Herraiz and L. Teresa Valdivieso (eds), *Estudios en homenaje a Enrique Ruiz Fornells* (Erie, PA, 1990), 12-8.

——————, 'Tradición y renovación: un difícil balance en la novela española actual', *Crítica Hispánica*, 14/1-2 (1992), 5-11.

Amorós, Andrés, 'Penúltimas novelistas', *ABC*, 19 September 1981.

Arribas, Inés, 'Poder y feminismo en *Amado amo* de Rosa Montero', *Romance Languages Annual*, 3 (1991), 348-53.

Asís Garrote, Ma. Dolores de, *Última hora de la novela en España* (Madrid, 1996).

Ballesteros, Isolina, *Escritura femenina y discurso autobiográfico en la nueva novela española* (New York, 1994).

Bayón, Miguel, 'Mujeres escritoras: la mirada que ve desde el rincón', *Cambio 16*, 24 November (1986), 149-52.

Brown, Joan L, 'Rosa Montero: From Journalist to Novelist', in Joan L. Brown (ed.), *Women Writers of Contemporary Spain. Exiles in the Homeland* (Newark, London and Toronto, 1991), 240-57.

——————, 'Men by Women in the Contemporary Spanish Novel', *Hispanic Review*, 60 (1992), 55-70.

Cabello Castellet, George, Jaume Martí Olivella and Guy H. Wood (eds), *Cine-Lit. Essays on Peninsular Film and Fiction* (Corvalis, 1992).

Chicharro Chamorro, Antonio, 'Del periodismo a la novela', *Ínsula*, 589-590 (1996), 14-7.

Ciplijauskaité, Biruté, *La novela femenina contemporánea (1970-1985). Hacia una tipología de la narración en primera persona* (Barcelona, 1988).

Conte, Rafael, 'Sobre un excepcional discurso narrativo', *El País* (Libros), 11 March 1984.

—————, 'En busca de la novela perdida', *Ínsula*, 464-465 (1985), 1,24.

Davies, Catherine, 'Entrevista a Rosa Montero (Madrid, 22 de enero de 1993)', *Journal of Hispanic Research*, 1/3, (1993), 383-8

—————, *Contemporary Feminist Fiction in Spain. The Work of Montserrat Roig and Rosa Montero* (Oxford and Providence, USA, 1994).

Drinkwater, Judith, 'Postmodern Identities: Writing by Women and Rosa Montero's *Amado amo*', in Ruth Christie, Judith Drinkwater and John Macklin, *The Scripted Self: Textual Identities in Contemporary Spanish Narrative* (Warminster, 1995), 153-66.

Encinar, Ángeles, 'Escritoras españolas actuales: una perspectiva a través del cuento', *Hispanic Journal*, 13/1 (1992), 181-91.

Fernández Santos, Ángel, 'Rosa Montero: Narrar es una inutilidad necesaria', *El País*, 21 November 1983.

Franz, Thomas R, 'Intertexts and Allusions as Aids to Meaning in Monteros's *Temblor*', *Anales de la Literatura Española Contemporánea*, 18/2 (1992), 261-79.

Galán Lorés, Carlos, 'Los más jóvenes de los jóvenes', *Ínsula*, 512-513 (1989), 14-5.

García-Posada, Miguel, 'Una novela de iniciación', *El País*, (Babelia), 17 May 1997.

Gascón Vera, Elena, 'Rosa Montero ante la escritura femenina', *Anales de la Literatura Española Contemporánea*, 12/1-2 (1987), 59-77.

—————, *Un mito nuevo: la mujer como sujeto/objeto literario* (Madrid, 1992).

—————, '*Temblor*: Caos y traición como fuerza de las mujeres', *Cuadernos de Aldeeu*, 8/2 (1992), 153-78.

Gazarian Gautier, Marie-Lise (ed.), 'Rosa Montero', in *Interviews with Spanish Writers* (Elmwood Park, IL, 1991), 208-15.

Giménez, Viviana-Claudia, 'Subversión en *Te trataré como a una reina* de Rosa Montero', *Romance Languages Annual*, 3 (1991) 454-9.

Glenn, Kathleen M., 'Victimized by Misreading: Rosa Montero's *Te trataré como a una reina*', *Anales de la Literatura Española Contemporánea*, 12/1-2 (1987), 191-202.

—————, 'Reader Expectations and Rosa Montero's *La función Delta*', *Letras Peninsulares*, 1/1 (1988), 87-96.

—————, 'Authority and Marginality in Three Contemporary Spanish Narratives', *Romance Languages Annual*, 2 (1990), 426-30.

—————, 'Conversación con Rosa Montero', *Anales de la Literatura Española Contemporánea*, 1/3 (1990), 275-83.

—————, 'Fictions of the Self in *La función Delta y Primera memoria*', in Sixto E. Torres and Carl King (eds), *Selected Proceedings of the Thirty-*

Ninth Annual Mountain Interstate Foreign Language Conference (Clemson, 1991), 197-203.

——————, 'Fantasy, Myth and Subversion in Rosa Montero's *Temblor'*, *Romance Languages Annual*, 3 (1991), 460-4.

——————, *'Temblor'*, *Anales de la Literatura Española Contemporánea*, 16 (1991), 401.

——————, 'Rosa Montero', in Linda Gould Levine, Ellen Engelson Marson and Gloria Feiman Waldman (eds), *Spanish Women Writers: A Bio-Bibliographical Source Book* (Westport, CT and London: 1993), 350-7.

Goñi, Javier, 'El silencio de las ballenas. Lo fantástico, presente en la última novela de Rosa Montero', *El País* (Babelia), 24 April 1993.

Hart, Stephen M., *White Ink. Essays on Twentieth-Century Feminine Fiction in Spain and Latin America* (London, 1993).

Ingenschay, Dieter and Hans-Jörg Neuschafer (eds), *Abriendo caminos. La literatura española desde 1975* (Barcelona, 1994).

Juristo, Ángel, 'Señales de cambio', *El Urogallo*, 85 (1993), 28-31.

Lottini, Otello, 'Il segni del tempo: la letteratura spagnola del post-franchismo', in *Diálogo. Studi in onore de Lore Terracini* (Roma, 1990), vol.I, 311-26.

Manteiga, Roberto, 'The Dilemma of the Modern Woman: A Study of the Female Characters in Rosa Montero's Novels', in Roberto C. Manteiga, Carolyn Galerstein and Kathleen McNerny (eds), *Feminine Concerns in Contemporary Spanish Fiction by Women* (Potomac, MD., 1988), 113-23.

——————, 'From Empathy to Detachment: The Autor-Narrator Relationship in Several Spanish Novels by Women', *Monographic Review*, 8 (1992), 19-35.

Masoliver Ródenas, Juan Antonio, '*Temblor* de Rosa Montero', *Ínsula*, 525 (1990), 19-20.

Miguel Martínez, Emilio de, *La primera narrativa de Rosa Montero* (Salamanca, 1983).

Monegal, Antonio, 'Entrevista a Rosa Montero', *Plaza. Revista de Literatura*, 11 (1986), 5-12.

Myers, Eunice D., 'The Feminist Message: Propaganda and/or Art? A Study of Two Novels by Rosa Montero', in Roberto C. Manteiga, Carolyn Galerstein and Kathleen McNerny (eds), *Feminine Concerns in Contemporary Spanish Fiction by Women* (Potomac, MD., 1988), 99-112.

Navarro, José María, 'El lenguaje coloquial en *Te trataré como a una reina'*, in Karl Heinz Joppich and Wolfgang Hillen (eds), *Actas de las Jornadas Hispánicas de la Asociación Alemana de Profesores/as de Español* (Bonn, 1986), 13-24.

Ordóñez, Elizabeth J., 'Inscribing Difference: *L'Écriture féminine* and New Narrative by Women', *Anales de la Literatura Española Contemporánea*, 12/1-2 (1987), 45-58.

Oropesa, Salvador, 'El encuentro con la otredad: "Estampas bostonianas" de Rosa Montero', in Juan Fernández Jiménez, José J. Labrador Herraiz and L. Teresa Valdivieso (eds), *Estudios en homenaje a Enrique Ruiz Fornells* (Erie, PA, 1990), 472-8.

Oyarzun, Luis A., 'Eroticism and Feminism in Spanish Literature after Franco: *Los amores diurnos* de Francisco Umbral and *Crónica del desamor* de Rosa Montero', *Mid-Hudson Language Studies*, 4 (1981), 135-44.

Pérez, Janet, *Contemporary Women Writers of Spain* (Boston, MA, 1988), 162-4, 200.

Plaza, José María, 'Horror y belleza', *Leer*, 65 (1993), 52-4.

Regazzoni, Susana, *Cuatro novelistas españolas de hoy. Estudios y entrevistas* (Milano, 1984).

Sanz Villanueva, Santos, 'El realismo en la nueva novela española', *Ínsula*, 464-465 (1985), 7-8.

Sarriás, Cristobal, 'Reflexión crítica sobre la última narrativa de España', *Razón y Fe*, 203 (1981), 541-9.

————, 'La juventud en la literatura castellana actual', *Razón y Fe*, 209 (1984), 25-31

Suñén, Luis, 'La realidad y sus sombras: Rosa Montero y Cristina Fernández Cubas', *Ínsula*, 446 (1984), 5.

Talbot, Lynn K., 'Entrevista con Rosa Montero', *Letras Femeninas*, 14/1-2 (1988), 90-6.

Valls, Fernando, 'La literatura femenina en España: 1975-1989', *Ínsula*, 512-513 (1989), 13.

————, 'La última narrativa de Rosa Montero: Notas sobre *Temblor, El nido de los sueños, y Bella y oscura*', *Lectora*, 1 (1995), 95-103.

Zatlin, Phyllis, 'The Contemporary Spanish Metanovel', *Denver Quarterly*, 17/3 (1982), 62-73.

————, 'La reaparición de nuevas corrientes femeninas en la novela española de posguerra', *Letras Femeninas*, 9 (1983), 35-42.

————, '*Crónica del desamor* and *La función Delta*', *Hispanófila*, 84 (1985), 121-3.

————, 'Women Novelists in Democratic Spain: Freedom to Express the Female Perspective', *Anales de la Literatura Española Contemporánea*, 12 (1987), 29-44.

————, 'The Novels of Rosa Montero as Experimental Fiction', *Monographic Review*, 8 (1992), 114-24.

————, 'Gothic Inversion of the Future: Rosa Montero's *Temblor*', *Romance Notes*, 33/2 (1993), 119-23.

The Grandfather

El abuelo

Original Spanish text from
El País Semanal, 29/7/1990,4.

El abuelo

Debería haber sospechado algo por la propina que le dieron: 200 pesetas que el hombre le metió en la mano, con torpe disimulo, mientras aparentaba estar absorto en la contemplación del letrero roto de la gasolinera. Debería haberlo sospechado, porque, además, no tenía la pinta de dar buenas propinas. Con ese aspecto de mirarlo todo por las comisuras de los ojos, y la camisa de manga corta abrochada hasta el gaznate. En cuanto que retiró la manguera, el hombre se metió en el coche como una bala y salió zumbando. Bueno, le costó un poco arrancar. Estaba nervioso: arrancaba y se le calaba, y entonces echaba el cuerpo hacia delante, como intentando impulsar el vehículo con los hombros. Por fin, el utilitario petardeó y allá fueron los tres en el coche encarnado: el tipo que nunca miraba a los ojos, la mujer gorda que se mordía los labios y el niño que, en el asiento de atrás, aplastaba la nariz contra el cristal y bizqueaba. Mariano no sabía por qué, pero se había fijado en ellos. Quizá por las 200 pesetas. Pero más bien porque tenían algo ligeramente raro y especial. Desagradable.

Como era el principio de las vacaciones había mucho movimiento en la gasolinera, de modo que Mariano tardó en darse cuenta. Luego le vio ahí, de pie junto a la puerta de los lavabos. Era un viejo alto y delgado, pulcramente vestido. Llenó Mariano los depósitos de unos cuantos coches y el viejo seguía ahí, tieso como una estaca, aunque le estaba cayendo encima un sol africano. Mariano se enjugó las manos con un trapo y se acercó a él:

—¿Desea usted algo?

El viejo le miró y pestañeó con aire confundido. Tenía la frente cubierta de gotitas de sudor y la calva congestionada y con manchones rojos. Sonrió.

The Grandfather

He should have suspected something from the tip he was given: 200 pesetas, which the man slipped into his hand with awkward dissimulation as he pretended to be absorbed in the broken sign over the petrol station. He should have suspected him anyway because he didn't look like the sort who'd give a good tip. With that way he had of looking at everything out of the corner of his eye and his short-sleeved shirt buttoned fast up to his gullet. As soon as he pulled out the nozzle the man had shot into the car like a bullet and roared off. OK, he had a bit of trouble getting started. He was nervous: he tried to start the car several times and flooded the engine, and then threw his body forward as if trying to propel the vehicle with his shoulders. Finally the engine of the little blood red car back-fired and there they were, the three of them, inside it: the chap who never looked anyone in the eye, the fat woman gnawing at her lip, and the kid in the back seat pressing his nose against the glass and making himself go cross-eyed. Mariano didn't know why, but he had noticed them. Perhaps it was because of the 200 pesetas. But more likely it was because there was something rather strange and special about them. Unpleasant.

Being the beginning of the holidays, there was a lot of coming and going at the petrol station, so it took Mariano a while to realise what was going on. Then he saw him, standing there, next to the door to the toilets. He was a tall, thin elderly man, tidily dressed. Mariano filled up the tanks of a few more cars and the old man went on standing there, stiff as a post, even though the heat of an African sun was beating down on him. Mariano wiped his hands on a rag and went over to him:

"Can I get you something?"

The old man looked at him and blinked as if confused. His brow was covered with droplets of sweat and his balding head was flushed with big red blotches. He smiled.

—Quiero una *coca-cola.*

"Acabáramos," se dijo Mariano; "si no le llego a preguntar, se nos derrite." Abrió el arcón congelador, sacó un bote de *cola* y se lo dio.

—Son 125 pesetas.

—¿Y la pajita? —preguntó el anciano, frunciendo reprobadoramente el ceño.

—Aquí no tenemos pajitas —resopló Mariano mientras miraba las filas de acalorados automovilistas que esperaban para repostar—. Son 125 pesetas.

—Yo no tomo *coca-cola* sin pajita —explicó el viejo con educada firmeza.

—Mire, a mí me dan lo mismo sus costumbres —gruñó Mariano, que era un hombre más bien brusco—. Usted ha abierto el bote y me lo tiene que pagar: 125 pesetas.

El anciano se irguió, digno como un duque. Le sacaba por lo menos media cabeza a Mariano, pero era todo puro pellejo y huesos, una menudencia casi transparente.

—No llevo dinero encima. Tendrá que esperar usted a que vuelva mi hijo.

—¿Su hijo? ¿Y adónde se ha marchado su hijo?

El viejo parpadeó; extendió el brazo y señaló alrededor, con un vago ademán en el que cabía con holgura la inmensidad del mundo. Mariano miró en torno suyo: el páramo en el que estaba instalada la gasolinera refulgía bajo un sol infernal. Tierras desérticas y sucias, sembradas de latas y papeles. Mariano resopló haciendo acopio de paciencia y regresó a los surtidores. Se pasó un buen rato llenando depósitos y el viejo seguía ahí, con toda la solanera en la cabeza, aferrado como un poseso a su lata de *cola.* Y entonces, de pronto, Mariano comprendió. No era un hombre inteligente; sobre todo, no era un hombre de pensamiento rápido. Pero al fin comprendió. Se puso tan nervioso que derramó parte del combustible por el suelo y dejó un automóvil a medio servir. Corrió hacia el anciano:

—¿Cómo es su hijo?

El viejo dio un respingo y le miró con cara de susto.

—¿Y cómo es el coche? Porque venían ustedes en coche, ¿no? —insistió angustiado.

Y entonces, a trompicones, el anciano confirmó sus sospechas. Sí, el coche era rojo; sí, iba con el nieto y con la nuera. Sí, él había entrado a los retretes y...

"I want a *Coca Cola*."

"I get it," said Mariano to himself; "If I hadn't asked him, he'd have melted." He opened the fridge, took out a can of cola and handed it to him.

"That's 125 pesetas."

"What about the straw?" asked the old man, frowning with disapproval.

"We don't have straws here," sighed Mariano, keeping an eye on the rows of tired, hot drivers waiting to have their cars filled up. "That's 125 pesetas."

"I don't drink *Coca Cola* without a straw," explained the old man in a firm well-mannered voice.

"Look, I don't give a damn what you do or what you don't," growled Mariano, who was a rather rude man. "You've opened the can and now you've got to pay me: 125 pesetas."

The old man straightened up, dignified as a duke. He was at least half a head taller than Mariano, but he was all skin and bones, a virtually transparent little man.

"I don't carry any money on me. You'll have to wait until my son comes back."

"Your son? And where's your son gone?"

The old man blinked; he stretched out his arm and made a broad, vague signalling gesture that widely encompassed the immensity of the world. Mariano looked around him: the bleak plateau that formed the setting for the petrol station sparkled under the hellish sun. It was a dirty wasteland littered with tin cans and bits of paper. Mariano sighed. He was doing his best to be patient. He went back over to the petrol pumps. He spent quite a long time filling up tanks and the old man went on standing there, with the full force of the sun beating down on his head, clinging to his can of cola like a man possessed. And then suddenly Mariano understood. He wasn't an intelligent man; and he certainly wasn't a man who could think on his feet. But at last he understood. He got so nervous he spilled some petrol on the ground and left a car he was halfway through filling up. He ran over to the old man:

"What does your son look like?"

The old man gave a start and looked at him with a frightened face.

"And what does the car look like? Because you did come by car, didn't you?" he insisted anxiously.

And then, in fits and starts, the old man confirmed his worst suspicions. Yes, the car was red; yes, he'd been with his grandson and his daughter-in-law. Yes, he'd gone off to the toilet and...

Mariano se pasó la manaza por la cara. Que le tuviera que ocurrir esto a
él. A finales de julio. Con el trabajo que había. Con el calor que hacía. Y
tener que hacerse cargo de un viejo chocho. Le miró con inquina por el
rabillo del ojo: ahí estaba, sudoroso y purpúreo, achicharrado. Ahora sólo
faltaba que el anciano la *palmara* de una insolación. Mariano rugió bajito,
limpió con un trapo la banqueta y la puso en la sombra, pegada a la pared de
la oficina.

—Venga. Siéntese ahí —gruñó.

El viejo obedeció dócilmente y se dejó caer en la banqueta con un
suspiro de alivio. Se mantenía muy serio y erguido, sujetando con toda
majestad su *coca-cola* intacta. Mariano mandó al chico que telefoneara a la
Guardia Civil para que vinieran a recogerle.

—Vamos a la playa —dijo de pronto el viejo con una sonrisa
complacida—. Mi nieto sabe nadar. Mi nieto me quiere mucho. Es un
buen chico.

—Ya.

Se había corrido la voz por la estación y los clientes miraban al anciano
como quien mira la jaula de los monos. A ver si llegan los civiles de una
vez, se dijo Mariano. *Pelona* se acercó al viejo renqueando y le olisqueó
amistosamente con su hocico fino y tembloroso. También ella había
aparecido por allí un buen día, con señales de haber llevado collar y
evidentemente abandonada, medio muerta de hambre y arrastrando una pata
aplastada que nunca llegó a recuperar. Mariano había dejado que la perra
durmiera en la gasolinera, y además la alimentaba, pero, claro, un viejo era
otra cosa.

El anciano parpadeó e inclinó la cabeza hacia él.

—Es que, ¿sabe usted?, tengo un poquitito de incontinencia —explicó en
un penetrante susurro—. Por eso tuve que ir al excusado mientras echaban
gasolina... Claro, yo comprendo que para los demás debe ser muy
cansado...

Por primera vez en muchos años, Mariano pensó: "Menos mal que soy
un solterón". Luego se acercó al congelador, sacó un zumo y arrancó la
pajita que venía adherida al cartón.

—Tenga, su maldita paja —dijo adustamente.

Y el viejo la cogió con avidez, la hundió en el bote y comenzó a chupar,
con un ruidito de lactante y una expresión de dicha absoluta, el caldo
recalentado y pegajoso.

Mariano wiped his broad hand across his face. How could something like this happen to him? At the end of July. With the work he had to do. In this heat. And to have to take charge of some old dodderer. He looked at him with resentment out of the corner of his eye: there he was, sweaty and red in the face, frying to a crisp. All it needed now was for the old man to peg out from sunstroke. Mariano growled, wiped the bench with a rag and moved it over into the shade, hard up against the wall of the office.

"Come on. Sit yourself down here," he grunted.

The old man obeyed meekly and dropped down onto the bench with a sigh of relief. He remained unsmiling and ramrod straight, clinging with full majesty to his untasted *Coca Cola*. Mariano sent the boy off to phone the Guardia Civil for them to come and pick him up.

"We're going to the beach," said the old man suddenly with a happy smile. "My grandson knows how to swim. My grandson loves me very much. He's a good boy."

"Sure he is."

Word had spread around the petrol station and the customers were looking at the old man in the same way as they would a cage of monkeys. "Let's see if the Guardia Civil turn up for once," muttered Mariano to himself. Pelona limped up to the old man and sniffed at him in a friendly way with her sensitive and trembling nose. She too had just turned up there one fine day, with signs of having once worn a collar but now obviously abandoned, half dead from hunger and dragging one crushed paw which had never recovered. Mariano had let the dog sleep in the petrol station and had fed her, but of course an old man was a different matter.

The old man blinked and leaned his head towards him.

"The thing is, you know, I'm a bit incontinent," he explained in a piercing whisper. "That's why I had to go to the toilet while they were filling the tank... Of course, I know it must be very tiresome for everybody else..."

For the first time in many years Mariano thought: "It's not such a bad thing I never got married." Then he went over to the fridge, took out a carton of juice and yanked off the little straw that was stuck to it.

"Here, take your bloody straw," he said gruffly.

And the old man took it eagerly, plunged it into the can and, making little noises like a baby at the breast, he began to suck at the hot, sticky liquid, with an expression of absolute happiness on his face.

MARUJA TORRES

MARUJA TORRES was born in Barcelona in 1943. Widely regarded as one of the best journalists working in the Spanish press today, she has an impressive record of thirty years of experience behind her. Like Montero, she writes from a feminist, politically-minded perspective and is very much associated with *El País*, where she publishes weekly contributions, mainly the prestigious last page column and her regular section in the paper's Sunday Supplement. She occasionally writes series of documentaries, some of them the product of her work as a news correspondent all over the world, a mode of journalism that she has also undertaken for *Cambio 16* and *Diario 16*.

A good example of this type of journalism is one of the few titles in contemporary Spanish travel-writing, *Amor América: Un viaje sentimental por América Latina* (1993), a deeply moving and personal account of her journey by train throughout ten Latin-American countries, in which she combines the chronicle of what she sees with her memories of other journalistic visits to the continent, never resorting to sentimentalism or nostalgia. Especially memorable are the chapters dedicated to Colombia, a country she visited in 1985, after the avalanche caused by the volcano Nevado del Ruiz which buried the city of Armero (also the origin of Isabel Allende's short story 'De barro hemos nacido'), and to Panama, where she had been posted in December 1989, and where Juantxu Rodríguez, a young Spanish photographer covering the information with her for *El País*, was murdered by US marines during the invasion that put an end to the Noriega era. *Amor América* is one of the bravest and most comprehensive visions of contemporary Latin America ever written, as well as being a post-colonialist reflection that denounces the pernicious nature of all kinds of totalitarianism.

America is, no doubt, one of Torres's passions, as is cinema (see her short story 'El cuarto hombre', in *El País Semanal*, 28/7/1996). She regularly contributes to specialist magazines like *Fotogramas* or *Cinemanía*. For years she has also written for popular weeklies, *Garbo* and *Pronto* among them, as well as for satirical periodicals like *Por favor* and *El Papus*, where she has been able to develop her flair for humour, irony and political and social satire that is the hallmark of all her work. Her style is based on a clever reworking of oral communication that keeps the freshness of bold colloquialisms and allows her to address serious issues with a deceptively detached approach.

Torres's first two novels, *Oh, es él* (1986), translated into English as *Desperately Seeking Julio* (1991), and *Ceguera de amor* (1991), are very much connected with her subversive and satirical yet sympathetic treatment of contemporary subculture. In both, the protagonist is Diana Dial, a gossip columnist and a passionate admirer of 'the Faust of our time', Julio Iglesias. In *Oh, es él* she sets off for America to meet and interview her adored singer, represented as a narcissistic ageing playboy who lives in fear of growing bald and lives surrounded by unscrupulous bodyguards, while in *Ceguera de amor* Diana lives dangerously again among the collective madness of the preparations for the Fifth Centenary of Columbus's Discovery of America in 1992.

Both novels, like most of her journalistic work, explore the postmodern erosion of the distinction between high and pop art and revel in a type of irony that can transform itself into sarcasm but never gratuitously or at the expense of the innocent or the genuine characters (see her revealing interview with Pedro Almodóvar, *El País Semanal*, 17/9/1995, where it becomes obvious that their work shares some of these characteristics). A selection of her contributions in *El País* has been collected in *Como una gota* (1996).

Torres has recently published a third novel, *Un calor tan cercano* (1997), a *deseografía*, as she calls it, in which the reworking of some of her own childhood memories in one of Barcelona's poorest districts provides the basis for an engaging fictional account.

FURTHER READING ON MARUJA TORRES

Amell, Samuel, 'El periodismo: su influencia e importancia en la novela del postfranquismo', *Castilla*, 12 (1989), 7-14.

Chicharro Chamorro, Antonio, 'Del periodismo a la novela', *Ínsula*, 589-590 (1996), 14-7.

Mora, Rosa, 'Tres formas de recordar el presente', *El País*, 6 June 1993.

———————, 'Vi América con tus ojos. El largo viaje de Maruja Torres', *El País* (Babelia), 19 June 1993.

———————, 'Un duro viaje a la literatura', *El País* (Babelia), 25 January 1997.

Obiol, María José, 'Artículos para oír y leer', *El País* (Babelia), 3 August 1996.

Santos, Care, 'Soñar América', *El ciervo*, January 1994, 35.

The Woman Who Disappeared

Desaparecida

Original Spanish text from
El País Semanal, 4/4/1993, 4.

'Desaparecida' was later collected in *Como una gota*
(Madrid: El País/Aguilar, 1996), 101–105.

Desaparecida

La mujer hizo una pausa, miró a los otros y continuó su relato: "Resultó increíblemente fácil. Salí del hotel y caminé por la calle Mallorca, hasta Bailén. En un portal vi un anuncio: 'Se alquila piso'. Anoté el teléfono indicado y llamé desde una cabina. Esa misma tarde formalicé el contrato. Lo que iba a ser un fin de semana en otra ciudad se convirtió en 15 años de vida".

Ahora que lo pensaba, se daba cuenta de que la idea había madurado en ella progresivamente, de tal forma que no se sintió culpable cuando, por fin, cuajó, empujándola a realizar un acto tras otro con fría deliberación, como quien añade cuentas a un collar. Había jugado con ello desde que los niños, que ya no eran niños, empezaron a llegar tarde, una noche tras otra, y a encerrarse en sus habitaciones con el teléfono, relacionándose con un mundo propio que se encontraba al otro lado del portal y al que ella no conseguiría nunca pertenecer. Se dio cuenta de que eso no la dolía, sino de que más bien la aliviaba, igual que las frecuentes desapariciones de su marido, que al volver envuelto en perfume ajeno esgrimía reuniones de negocios, sin que ella le preguntara, porque tampoco le importaba en absoluto. Se fue aislando en sí misma cada vez más, y finalmente conquistó un terreno que sólo estaba en su imaginación, pero que la reclamaba día tras día con mayor insistencia. Ociosa, daba vagas instrucciones a la asistenta y se metía en su dormitorio —que sólo era suyo cuando no estaba él y los chicos no irrumpían pidiendo cosas—, encendiendo al principio el pequeño televisor que tenían a los pies de la cama, y viendo de forma ausente

The Woman Who Disappeared

The woman stopped speaking for a moment, looked at the others and then went on with her story: "It turned out to be incredibly easy. I went out of the hotel and walked along Calle Mallorca as far as Bailén.[42] In a doorway I saw a notice: 'Flat to let'. I made a note of the number it gave and called from a phone box. I signed the contract that same afternoon. What started off as a weekend away in another town turned into fifteen years of my life."

When she thought about it now, she realized that she had only thought things out gradually, so she didn't feel guilty when it finally crystallized into shape, propelling her into taking one coldly deliberate step after another, like somebody threading beads on a necklace. She'd been toying with the idea ever since the children, who were no longer children, started to come in late night after night, and to lock themselves away in their rooms with the telephone, connecting with a world of their own, a world that was to be found on the other side of the street door, a world to which she would never belong. She realized that this wasn't a source of pain for her but was instead something of a relief, as were the frequent disappearances of her husband who, upon his return, enveloped in a cloud of someone else's perfume, would use the excuse of a business meeting, even though she never asked him about such things because she wasn't the slightest bit interested. She withdrew further and further into herself, finally conquering a land that only existed in her imagination and yet made more and more insistent claims on her as the days went by. With nothing to do, she would issue vague instructions to the cleaning lady and lock herself away in her bedroom — which was only hers when he wasn't there and when the children didn't come in asking for things — in the early days switching on the little television set that was kept at the foot of the bed and mindlessly watching

---

[42]   **Mallorca** and **Bailén:** names of two streets in Barcelona.

cualquier cosa que pusieran, aunque poco a poco adquirió seguridad y comprendió que se sentía igualmente bien si la pantalla estaba apagada; tumbada primero encima de la colcha, y más adelante metida entre las sábanas, protegiendo sus sueños despiertos, como si estuviera enferma. Cuando ellos volvían y la encontraban en bata y pijama no les extrañaba, al fin y al cabo era ya tarde y nadie, durante el día, la podía fiscalizar. A la mujer de la limpieza todo le daba igual: atendía la casa con la misma indiferencia con que ella la descuidaba.

Todo esto ocurrió durante la primera etapa, que más tarde, mirando atrás, ella llamaría de calentamiento, porque en aquella época ni siquiera sabía lo que quería hacer.

La segunda etapa se inició cuando la mujer se vio a sí misma en el metro, como si estuviera contemplando a otra, sentada a prudente distancia, precisamente, de la asistenta, a quien había seguido cuando terminó su jornada. Bajó tras ella las escaleras del suburbano y se introdujo en el mismo vagón, que afortunadamente estaba lleno de gente sudorosa que miraba sin ver y en silencio. Cuando la otra se apeó en una lejana estación, la mujer no hizo ningún gesto, y siguió el trayecto hasta que el tren se detuvo durante largo rato y todos salieron excepto ella, que regresó al punto de partida sin moverse. Otro día salió al mismo tiempo que su asistenta, siguiéndola a distancia hasta la cola formada en una parada de autobús. Después de casi una hora, la otra descendió del vehículo, y ella también lo hizo, pero no se atrevió a continuar y la vio perderse en una calle bulliciosa en cuyos escaparates había prendas de vestir que no se parecían en nada a las que ella guardaba en sus armarios. Entró en una de las tiendas y compró, compró mucho, como si no tuviera nada que ponerse. Al volver a su casa, lo escondió todo en una maleta, debajo de la cama.

Y entonces comenzó la tercera etapa, que consistía en vestirse con las prendas ocultas y vivir en ellas mientras los demás no estaban en casa. Aquellos jerséis gruesos, tejidos con trenzas, y aquellas faldas acrílicas, y los zapatos de medio tacón, e incluso los abalorios con que se adornaba, collares de colores agresivos y pendientes estrafalarios, determinaban en ella una nueva forma de caminar, de moverse, e incluso de hablar, porque iba de un lado a otro manteniendo imaginarias conversaciones con gente inventada. Siempre se cambiaba antes de que regresara su familia, salvo en una ocasión, en que olvidó quitarse el moño laqueado y su marido le dijo qué horror, vaya pinta que tienes esta noche.

anything that was on, although she gradually acquired a sense of security and realized she felt equally good if the screen was blank, at first lying on top of the bedspread, later slipping between the sheets, protecting her day dreaming, as if she were unwell. When they got home and found her still in her dressing gown and pyjamas they weren't surprised, after all it was already late and nobody could keep an eye on her during the day. The cleaning woman couldn't care less, looking after the house with the same degree of indifference with which she neglected it.

All this happened during the first stage, the one, looking back on it, she would call the "warm up phase", because in those days she didn't even know what she wanted to do.

The second stage began when the woman caught sight of herself on the Underground, as if she were looking at somebody else, sitting at a discreet distance, in fact, from the cleaning lady, whom she'd followed when she'd finished work. She followed her down the steps of the subway and got into the same carriage, which fortunately was full of sweaty people gazing with unseeing eyes and in silence. When the cleaning woman got off at one of the stations near the end of the line, she remained impassive and continued her journey until the train stopped for a long time and everybody got off except her. Without moving, she travelled back to the station she'd set off from. On another day she left at the same time as the cleaning lady, following her from a distance as far as the queue at the bus stop. After almost an hour, the cleaning woman got off the vehicle, and she did the same, but she didn't dare go any further, and she saw the other woman melt into a bustling street whose shop windows displayed garments unlike anything hanging in her wardrobes. She went into one of the shops and bought some things, bought a great deal in fact, as if she had nothing to wear. When she got back to her house, she hid it all in a suitcase under the bed.

And then began the third stage, which consisted of dressing herself up in the hidden clothes and living in them when there was nobody else in the house. Those thick cable-knitted jerseys, those acrylic skirts and the shoes with the medium heels, and even the glass beads, the necklaces in garish colours and the outlandish earrings with which she would adorn herself, would make her try a new way of walking, of moving around, even of speaking, because she would walk up and down holding imaginary conversations with people she'd made up. She always changed before her family came home, except once when she forgot to brush out the lacquered hair she'd swept into a bun on top of her head, and her husband said, for God's sake, you look a sight tonight.

Y un jueves, en que él le comunicó que tenía que pasar fuera de casa el
fin de semana porque la empresa iba a impartir un cursillo en un hotel de
Toledo, la mujer inventó sobre la marcha que una nueva amiga, una catalana
a quien había conocido en la escuela de repostería, la había invitado a pasar
con ella unos días en Barcelona. A su marido le pareció bien, y el viernes se
marchó despues de besarla en la mejilla. Los niños, que ya no eran tan
niños, estaban durmiendo cuando ella dejó sigilosamente el piso y diecisiete
años de vida matrimonial detrás, con el desayuno para sus hijos preparado
en la mesa y una nota para que no olvidaran apagar el gas por la noche.

Primero fue a un hotel, dio su nombre y colgó en el armario la ropa
clandestina, que ahora ya no lo era y verdaderamente le gustaba. Paseó
durante el fin de semana, y por último, el lunes, echó a andar con la maleta
por la calle Mallorca hasta Bailén y poco después se instaló en un piso
grande, con galería interior en la que colgaba la ropa, como el resto de las
mujeres, antes de salir a fregar pisos y regresar de noche, agotada, para
dormirse ante el televisor.

Y ahora estaba en un estudio, rodeada de focos y de gente, con unos
desconocidos que la besuqueaban y decían que eran su familia y ella sentía
una pereza absoluta, pero todos, incluido el simpático locutor, parecían tan
felices.

And one Thursday, when he told her he was going to have to spend the weekend away from home because the company was holding a short course at a hotel in Toledo, the woman had there and then made up some story about how a new friend of hers, a Catalan she'd met at her baking class, had invited her to spend a few days with her in Barcelona. This suited the husband fine, and on the Friday he had set off after giving her a peck on the cheek. The children, who were no longer so little, were sleeping when she crept out of the flat leaving seventeen years of married life behind her, with the children's breakfast left ready on the table and a note to remind them not to forget to turn off the gas at night.

She went first to a hotel, gave her name and used the wardrobe to hang up the clandestine clothing that was now no longer clandestine and which she really did like. She went out for walks over the weekend, and finally, on the Monday, she set off again on foot, suitcase in hand, along Calle Mallorca as far as Bailén, and shortly afterwards she settled in a large apartment which had an interior courtyard where she would hang up her clothes to dry, like the other women, before she went off to clean flats and return at night, worn out, to fall asleep in front of the television set.

And now here she was in a studio, surrounded by lights and people, with some people she didn't know covering her with kisses and saying they were her family, and she felt that she couldn't be bothered with it all, but everybody else, including the nice presenter, seemed so happy.

SOLEDAD PUÈRTOLAS

SOLEDAD PUÉRTOLAS was born in Zaragoza in 1947 but is now based in Madrid, where she went to live at the age of fourteen. She graduated in Journalism and later received an M.A. in Spanish and Portuguese Literature from the University of California, Santa Barbara (USA). She writes literary criticism for Spanish newspapers and, like some of the other authors selected for this anthology, combines creation with analysis. An excellent example of her personal and incisive reflections on literature is *La vida oculta* (1993), which was awarded the Premio Anagrama de Ensayo. She has also delivered a number of papers on the subject of her own fiction and some of them have been published, such as 'Las historias secundarias', in *El oficio de narrar* (1990), and 'Pauline a la luz del día', in *El personaje novelesco* (1993), both edited by Marina Mayoral. Other interesting articles are 'Los detectives de Hammet', *Revista de Occidente*, 44 (1985), 164-177 , and 'La gracia de la vida, la inmortalidad', on the *cuento* genre, in *Lucanor*, 6 (1991), 172. Mainly known for her novels and short stories, Soledad Puértolas is widely considered as a well-established literary figure.

Her first two novels, *El bandido doblemente armado* (1980), which won the 1979 Premio Sésamo, and *Burdeos* (1986), have in common a similar short story-like fragmented structure. The narrator of *El bandido doblemente armado* is an evasive young man, who is fascinated by his friend Terry's family, the wealthy Lennoxes. In *Burdeos* we find a detached but omniscient voice who, in three different chapters, narrates instances of crisis and realization in the lives of the three main characters, who are vaguely related through secondary characters. Both novels also share the influence of American thrillers – mainly Raymond Chandler, a favourite of Puértolas – in the meticulous way the stories are told.

Puértolas's next two books also have several features in common. They are both well-paced, densely-plotted novels set in contemporary Madrid; they have a similar first-person narrator who in both cases offers a self-consciously limited vision of the world around them: a young professional man in the case of *Todos mienten* (1988), and a young professional woman in *Queda la noche* (1989). Although they both play crucial roles in the development of events in their respective novels, the characters adopt a detached and somewhat passive attitude that links them not just to the narrator of *El bandido*, but also to some turn-of-the-century characters from the novels of Baroja or Azorín. *Queda la noche* won the 1989 Premio Planeta, the

literary award that embraces the whole Spanish-speaking world and makes its winners immediate best-sellers.

Queda la noche introduces some secondary characters that reappear in some of Puértolas's later books. This self-reflexive literary device can be seen in *Días del arenal* (1992), a novel where the city of Madrid, also the setting for the previous two, becomes the central *locus* of memory and action. Her following novel, *Si al atardecer llegara el mensajero* (1995), although dealing with the same concern for the human condition, is a complete departure from the more realist substance of her other work. Tobías Kaluga, a dissatisfied inhabitant from heaven, is sent to earth to ascertain whether it is better for people to know when they are going to die; his mission proves to be an impossible one, however, as the novel becomes a string of conversations on death, time, eternity, dreams, sex, etc., between Tobías and his many interlocutors.

Puértolas has returned to more familiar ground in her latest novel, *Una vida inesperada* (1997), in which the detached voice of a female narrator looks back on five crucial moments of her life.

Two recent books collect her latest journalistic work: *Recuerdos de otra persona* (1996), with articles of an autobiographical nature, and *La vida se mueve* (1996).

Puértolas is also an engaging and prolific short-story writer. Her first published *cuento* was 'A través de las ondas', in *Doce relatos de mujeres*, edited by Ymelda Navajo (1982), which paved the way for her first collection, *Una enfermedad moral* (1982). This enigmatic title belongs to one of the stories and to the book in general, since its characters, whether owing to their melancholy, unfulfilled desire or bold ambition, all seem to encounter moral ambivalences along the way.

Her second collection of stories, *La corriente del golfo* (1993), offers an impressive display of characters who seem to be waiting to be rescued out of their mediocre lives and achieve their epiphanic moment. *Madres e hijas*, edited by Laura Freixas (1996), has included her latest short story to date, 'La hija predilecta'.

Soledad Puértolas has also published two books for children, *La sombra de una noche* (1986) and *El recorrido de los animales* (1988), both recently reprinted together (1996), with illustrations by her husband, the painter Leopoldo Pita.

FURTHER READING ON SOLEDAD PUÉRTOLAS

Acín, Ramón, 'Soledad Puértolas', in *Los dedos de la mano: Javier Tomeo, José María Latorre, Soledad Puértolas, Ignacio Martínez de Pisón* (Zaragoza, 1992), 75-103.

Alborg, Concha, 'Cuatro narradoras de la transición', in Ricardo Landeira and Luis T. González del Valle (eds), *Nuevos y novísimos. Algunas perspectivas críticas sobre la narrativa española desde la década de los 60* (Boulder, COL, 1987), 11-27.

Amorós, Andrés, 'Penútimas novelistas', *ABC*, 19 September 1981.

Asís Garrote, Ma. Dolores de, *Última hora de la novela en España* (Madrid, 1996).

Ayala-Dip, J. Ernesto, 'Conciencia y espíritu. Los ángeles y las batallas de los humanos', *El País* (Babelia), 25 February 1995.

Basualdo, Ana, 'Soledad Puértolas: una noche en *Burdeos*', *La Vanguardia*, 24 June 1986.

Bayón, Miguel, 'Mujeres escritoras: la mirada que ve desde el rincón', *Cambio 16*, 24 November 1986, 149-52.

Bellver, Catherine G., 'Two New Women Writers from Spain', *Letras Femeninas*, 8/2 (1982), 3-7.

Camarero Arribas, Tomás, 'Lógica de una narrativa en *Una enfermedad moral* de Soledad Puértolas', *Ventanal: Revista de Creación y Crítica*, 14 (1988), 133-57.

Carmona, V., J. Lamb, S. Velasco and B. Zecchi, 'Conversando con Mercedes Abad, Cristina Fernández Cubas y Soledad Puértolas: "Feminismo y literatura no tienen nada que ver"', *Mester*, 20/2 (1991), 157-65.

Carrillo, Nuria, 'La expansión plural de un género: el cuento 1975-1993', *Ínsula*, 568 (1994), 9-11.

Castro, Antón, 'Itinerarios hacia lo inaccesible', *El Día*, 5 March 1989.

Catelli, Nora, 'Soledad Puértolas', *El Urogallo*, 6 (1988), 43.

—————, 'Los rasgos de un mestizaje. (La actual novela en castellano)' *Revista de Occidente*, 122-3 (1991), 135-47.

Cruz, Juan, 'Soledad Puértolas: "*Queda la noche* es mi novela más reflexiva"', *El País* (Libros), 17 October 1989.

DiNonno Inteman, Marguerite, *El tema de la soledad en la narrativa de Soledad Puértolas* (Lewiston, Queenstown and Lampeter, 1994).

Echevarría, Ignacio, 'La tristeza redimida: el talento narrativo de Soledad Puértolas al servicio del relato', *El País* (Babelia), 18 September 1993.

Encinar, Ángeles, 'Escritoras españolas actuales: una perspectiva a través del cuento', *Hispanic Journal*, 13/1 (1992), 181-91.

Fajardo, José Manuel, '"Escribo lo que puedo, no lo que quiero"', *Cambio 16*, 6 November 1989, 138-9.

Fernández, Daniel, 'Alrededores de la novela', *El País*, 19 November 1989.

Galán Lorés, Carlos, 'Los más jóvenes de los jóvenes', *Ínsula*, 512-513 (1989), 14-5.

Gascón Vera, Elena, 'La subversión del canon: Rosa Montero, Pedro Almodóvar y el postmodernismo español', in *Un mito nuevo: la mujer como sujeto/objeto literario* (Madrid, 1992), 39-59.

González-Arias, Francisca and Darío Villanueva, 'Soledad Puértolas: La ciudad de las almas', in Darío Villanueva (ed.), *Los nuevos nombres: 1975-1990*, vol. IX, *Historia y Crítica de la Literatura Española*, ed. by Francisco Rico (Barcelona, 1992), 371-5.

Ingenschay, Dieter and Hans-Jörg Neuschafer (eds), *Abriendo caminos. La literatura española desde 1975* (Barcelona, 1994).

Lottini, Otello, 'Il segni del tempo: la letteratura spagnola del post-franchismo', in *Diálogo. Studi in onore di Lore Terracini* (Roma, 1990), vol.I, 311-26.

Martín, Salustiano, '*La corriente del golfo. La vida oculta*. Encontrarle un sentido a la vida', *Reseña*, 245 (1993), 34.

Mattalia, Sonia, 'Entre miradas: Las novelas de Soledad Puértolas', *Ventanal: Revista de Creación y Crítica*, 14 (1988),171-92.

——————, 'Vidas morosas, la parodia de la aventura', *Ínsula*, 526 (1990), 26-7.

Mora, Marimont (1989) 'Soledad Puértolas/Premio Planeta a *Queda la noche*', *Tiempo*, 23 October 1990, 186-8.

Murillo, E., 'Prólogo', in Soledad Puértolas, *Todos mienten. Una enfermedad moral* (Barcelona, 1988).

Navajas, Gonzalo, 'Una estética para después del postmodernismo. La nostalgia asertiva y la reciente novela española', *Revista de Estudios Hispánicos*, 25/3 (1991), 129-51.

——————, 'Narrativa y género. La ficción actual desde la mujer', *Ínsula*, 589-590 (1996), 37-39.

——————, *Más allá de la posmodernidad. Estética de la nueva novela y cine españoles* (Barcelona, 1996).

Obiol, María José, 'Un habitante del cielo llamado Tobías Kaluga. Entrevista con Soledad Puértolas ante su nueva novela', *El País* (Babelia), 25 February 1995.

——————, 'Artículos para oír y leer' *El País* (Babelia), 3 August 1996.

Ortega, Carlos, 'La vida invertebrada', *El Urogallo*, 94 (1994), 57-8.

Pérez, Janet, *Contemporary Women Writers of Spain* (Boston, MA, 1988), 167-8.

Piñol, Rosa María, '*Todos mienten* es la historia de una imposibilidad', *La Vanguardia*, 1 March 1988.

Recio Baladiez, A, 'El tiempo detenido', *El País*, 21 August 1986.

Riera, Miguel, 'El fluir del tiempo', *Quimera*, 54-55 (1986), 107.

——————, 'Los vacíos del tiempo: Entrevista con Soledad Puértolas', *Quimera*, 72 (1987), 42-8.

Roldán, Concha, 'Soledad Puértolas: Sugerencias', *Heraldo de Aragón*, 14 April 1989.

Sanz Villanueva, Santos, 'Generación del 68', *El Urogallo*, 26 (1988), 28-60.

——————, 'Intrigas y amores', *Diario 16*, 16 September 1989.

Scarlett, Elizabeth A., 'Nomads and Schizos: Postmodern Trends in Body Writing' in *Under Construction. The Body in Spanish Novels* (Charlottesville and London, 1994), 166-85.

Sturniolo, Norma, 'Sobre la edición infantil y juvenil en España. 1989-1990', *El Urogallo*, April (special issue, 1990), 4-11.

Suñen, Luis, 'Los pasos de un año discreto', *El País* (Libros), 1 December 1980.

Talbot, Lynn K., 'Entrevista con Soledad Puértolas', *Hispania*, 71/4 (1988), 882-3.

Treacy, Mary Jane, 'Soledad Puértolas', in Linda Gould Levine, Ellen Engelson Marson and Gloria Feiman Waldman (eds), *Spanish Women Writers: A Bio-Bibliographical Source Book* (Westport, CT and London, 1993), 397-403.

Tsuchiya, Akiko, 'Language, Desire, and the Feminine Riddle in Soledad Puértolas's *La indiferencia de Eva*', *Revista de Estudios Hispánicos*, 25/1 (1991), 69-79.

Valls, Fernando, 'El renacimiento del cuento en España (1975-1990)', *Lucanor*, 6 (1991), 27-42.

Tales from the Past

Viejas historias

Original Spanish text from
La corriente del golfo (Barcelona: Anagrama, 1993), 93-106.

Viejas historias

Ernesto, el ex marido de mi hermana pequeña, me llamaba frecuentemente por teléfono para ponerme al tanto de las crisis nerviosas de mi hermana, se desahogaba conmigo y me acababa pidiendo que tratara de calmarla a ella y de comprenderle a él, que hacía dos años que se había separado legalmente de Alicia y que no conseguía vivir sin su vigilancia. Su vida se estaba convirtiendo en un infierno.

Ernesto vivía con Rosana, una chica que por aquel entonces quería ser actriz y que años más tarde, también ella separada de Ernesto, lo consiguió. Vivían en Avilés desde hacía un par de meses porque, huyendo de mi hermana, Ernesto tenía un nuevo trabajo, dirigía el laboratorio de una de esas empresas que contaminan el ambiente. Realizaba estudios ecológicos, lo que para Ernesto era algo así como su caballo de batalla, y para la actriz, y para mi pobre hermana. En eso coincidían todos. Tenían razón, a pesar de su tono misionero. Pero si se ponían a hablar todos a la vez, tuvieran o no razón, yo era capaz de llevarles la contraria.

Eran escenas que habían tenido lugar antes de que se trasladaran a Avilés, y que cerraban las visitas de mi hermana, que se abrían con violencia y lamentaciones, pero que concluían siempre en una amigable conversación sobre la necesidad de preservar las zonas verdes del planeta. La menos amigable en aquel momento era yo, no porque estuviera en profundo desacuerdo con ellos, sino porque me irritaba aquella repentina transformación, esa súbita reconciliación basada en una idea general y humanitaria que los unía después de haber gritado y llorado (Alicia y Rosana lloraban, las dos, muy espectacularmente, como si se tratara de una competición), haberse insultado y haberse maldecido, sin que aparentemente

Tales from the Past

Ernesto, the ex-husband of my younger sister, would often phone to bring me up to date on my sister's latest nervous crisis, pour his heart out and end up asking me to try to calm her down and to understand him, this man who had been legally separated from Alicia for two years now, and who was unable to live without her keeping an eye on him. His life was turning into a hell on earth.

Ernesto lived with Rosana, a young girl who at about that time wanted to be an actress and who, years later, she too separated from Ernesto, achieved it. They'd been living in Avilés[43] for a couple of months or so because, in running away from my sister, Ernesto had landed a new job, in charge of the laboratories at one of those companies that pollute the environment. He was involved in ecological research, which was something of a hobby-horse for Ernesto, as well as for the actress, and my poor sister. On this at least they were all agreed. And they were right, in spite of their missionary tone. But when they all began to talk at once, irrespective of whether they were right or not, I was quite capable of taking the opposite point of view.

Before they moved to Avilés my sister's visits used to conclude with one of these scenes. The visits would begin in violence and wailings, yet would always end in a friendly conversation about the need to preserve the green zones of the planet. In those days, the least amicable one was myself, not because I felt I was in strong disagreement with them, but because that sharp transformation used to irritate me, that sudden reconciliation based on some general and humanitarian notion that brought them together again after they'd been shouting and weeping (Alicia and Rosana, the pair of them, crying in the most spectacular way, as if in competition with one another), after having insulted and cursed each other, without, apparently, there being

---

[43]   **Avilés:**   industrial and maritime city in Asturias, northern Spain.

nada quedara en pie entre ellos. Pues bien, quedaba eso: su loable preocupación por la escalada de destrucción que estaba sufriendo la madre naturaleza. Y aunque todos sabemos que una cosa son las ideas y otra los sentimientos, no dejaba de desconcertarme, y de irritarme, que se produjera aquel desfase tan absoluto entre unas y otros y hasta llegaba a pensar que en algún momento mentían, porque no podía darse tanta radicalidad: o no se odiaban tanto, o las cuestiones ecológicas les importaban bastante poco. Algo tenía que fallar, algo había allí que no encajaba y que yo no conseguía ver. Era así, en aquel estado de perfecta connivencia e idílico acuerdo, como yo me los encontraba cuando, después de recibir la llamada desesperada de Ernesto, iba a recoger a Alicia, y nunca dejaba de pensar, inquieta y atemorizada, que en aquella ocasión me tocaría presenciar los gritos, las lágrimas, las violentas escenas que Ernesto me había contado por teléfono, pero nunca fue así, y aunque en sus caras se podían ver los signos de aquella explosión emocional— los ojos de Alicia y de Rosana estaban francamente rojos y sus maquillajes corridos; eran, inequívocamente, dos mujeres después de una batalla—los tres estaban tranquilamente sentados alrededor de la mesa baja del cuarto de estar, con una bebida entre las manos, preocupados, dadas las proporciones, alcance y dificultades del asunto que comentaban, pero plácidos.

El mismo Ernesto, con quien había hablado media hora antes y que me había pedido que fuera a ayudarlo a sacar a mi hermana de su casa, parecía no tener ya ningún deseo de poner punto final a aquella reunión. Me ofrecía una copa, se sentaba en el sofá, nos contemplaba con satisfacción y exponía sus teorías, encantado al parecer de encontrarse entre un público femenino tan incondicional. Tres mujeres que le miraban atentamente. Porque, hora es ya de confesarlo, Ernesto era un hombre que nos gustaba a las tres. Había sido yo quien se lo había presentado a mi hermana, como había sido ella quien había cometido tal vez aún mayor error al presentárselo a Rosana, y estábamos, las tres, a nuestro pesar, perfectamente convencidas de que Ernesto se merecía nuestra devoción. Sus ojos brillaban al mirarnos y se diría que existía en él un constante, puede que inconsciente, deseo de conquistarnos.

Cuando al fin bajamos Alicia y yo en el ascensor, ella, ligeramente más achispada que yo, declaraba que nada de lo que había pasado le importaba mucho porque lo único que necesitaba para seguir viviendo era poder ver a Ernesto y atreverse a pensar que él todavía sentía algo por ella, y yo la entendía y la disculpaba, aunque no se lo decía, porque hasta yo podía sentir

any common ground left between them. Well, there was just one thing: their commendable preoccupation with the escalating destruction being suffered by Mother Nature. And even though we all know ideas are one thing and feelings another, I was continually disconcerted and irritated that such an absolute imbalance should exist between one and the other, and I even came to believe that at times they were lying, because such a radical about-turn was not possible: either they didn't hate each other as much as they pretended, or the environment didn't matter that much to them. Something had to be wrong, there was something there that just didn't fit, that I wasn't able to see. Thus it was that I would find them, in that state of perfect collusion and idyllic accord, when I went to collect Alicia, after receiving Ernesto's desperate call, and I never stopped thinking, so worried and scared was I, that that would be the day it would be my turn to witness the screaming, the tears, the violent scenes that Ernesto had been telling me about over the phone, but it was never like that, and even though you could see the signs of that emotional outburst written all over their faces – Alicia and Rosana's eyes obviously red and their make-up all smeared; they were, unmistakably, two women after a battle – the three of them were sitting peacefully round the coffee table in the living room, a drink between their hands, worried, given the extent, the range and the difficulty of the subject they were discussing, but placid.

Ernesto himself, with whom I had been talking just half an hour before and who had asked me to go and help him get my sister out of his house, now appeared to have no desire whatsoever to bring the meeting to an end. He would offer me a drink, sit down on the sofa, look at us in a satisfied way and begin expounding his theories, apparently delighted to find himself before such a captive female audience. Three women all looking at him attentively. Because, and the time has come to confess the fact, Ernesto was a man that all three of us fancied. It had been I who had introduced him to my sister, just as it had been she who had made perhaps the even greater mistake of introducing him to Rosana, and all three of us were perfectly convinced, in spite of ourselves, that Ernesto was worthy of our devotion. His eyes shone as he looked at us and it might be said that there was in him an ever present, perhaps unconscious, desire to seduce us.

When at last Alicia and I went down in the lift she, slightly more tipsy than I, would declare that none of what had happened mattered very much because the only thing she needed to carry on living was to be able to see Ernesto and dare to think that he still felt something for her, and I understood her and forgave her, although I didn't tell her so, because even I was capable

algo parecido, mucho más tibio y controlado, pero sabía, como ella, que Ernesto era irresistiblemente atractivo y, sabiéndolo también él, todavía jugaba con nosotras, sin querer descartar del todo la posibilidad de un reencuentro, una reconciliación, por muy fugaz que fuera, por mucho dolor que nos causara después. Bastante más sensata que Alicia, mayor y más experimentada, yo conseguía ahogar aquel atisbo de esperanza sin excesivas dificultades, sin desmedidos esfuerzos, pero mi pobre y obstinada hermana se quedaba encasquillada, atrapada, y desde ese momento se iba preparando para la próxima escena. Se miraba en el espejo del ascensor y sin duda daba a su propia imagen una cita, todavía no determinada pero cierta, en aquel mismo lugar. Nos volveremos a ver.

Pero no estaba demasiado convencida del fundamento de sus ilusiones y no quería ir sola a su casa, de forma que me pedía que la dejara dormir en la mía, aunque fuera en el sofá, para evitar volver a pensar en Ernesto, para estar rodeada de gente, para no sacar las peores conclusiones sobre su vida. Ajena al orden y a las costumbres de mi casa, repentinamente olvidada de todo, se daba un baño y se paseaba por la casa, canturreando, envuelta en uno de mis albornoces, gastándoles bromas a mis hijos y a mi marido, y ya para entonces sus turbulencias emocionales parecían perfectamente superadas. Pero así era Alicia, y yo no podía asombrarme. Lo que no conseguía era convencer a mi marido de que su estado era crítico, porque él no acababa de creer que Alicia fuera capaz de violencias. Y yo misma terminaba concluyendo, cuando al día siguiente Alicia se despedía, bien arreglada, perfumada y maquillada, camino de su oficina, que todo aquello no tenía ninguna importancia y que debía dejar que mi hermana y su ex marido arreglaran sus problemas solos y, sobre todo, no sobresaltarme, porque cada vez que Ernesto me llamaba, en aquel tono marcadamente trágico, llegaba a pensar que Alicia había perdido la razón y mientras me dirigía hacia su casa en su búsqueda me decía que era ya hora de tomar una medida, de consultar a un médico.

Tantas veces se había dado esa situación y tantas veces la había arrojado de mi cabeza, que creo que ya estaba un poco inmunizada, aunque confieso que la decisión de Ernesto de trasladarse a vivir al norte me alivió. Al menos, ya no sería para Alicia tan tentador presentarse en su casa, y si lo hacía, a Ernesto no se le podía ocurrir llamarme en busca de ayuda, porque

of having similar feelings for him, albeit much more lukewarm and restrained, even though I knew, as she did, that Ernesto was irresistibly attractive and, being aware of this fact himself, would still play with us without wanting to rule out forever the possibility of a further encounter, a reconciliation, however fleeting it might be, however much pain it might cause us later on. Somewhat more sensible, older and more experienced than Alicia, I managed to stifle those first stirrings of hope without too much difficulty, without disproportionate effort, but my poor, obstinate sister remained stuck in the groove, trapped, and from then on she would spend her time preparing for the next scene. She would look at herself in the mirror in the lift, doubtless planning a rendezvous, not yet finalized but nonetheless certain, in that same place, with her own reflection. We'll see each other again.

But she wasn't too sure of how well-founded her dreams were and she didn't want to go home alone, so she would ask if I'd let her sleep at my house, even if it were on the sofa, to stop her thinking about Ernesto again, so that she could be surrounded by people, so that she wouldn't draw the worst conclusions about the way her life was going. Being a stranger to the arrangements and customs of my house, her mind suddenly oblivious to all that had happened, she would take a bath and wander through the house, humming, wrapped in one of my bathrobes, joking with my children and my husband, and by then her emotional storms appeared to have been perfectly overcome. But that was Alicia for you, and I couldn't claim to feel any surprise. What I failed to do was to convince my husband that her condition was critical, because he never showed any real signs of believing Alicia capable of violence. And when, on the following day Alicia took her leave of us, beautifully turned out, wearing perfume and make-up, on her way to her office, even I was left with the conclusion that none of it meant anything and that I should just leave my sister and her ex-husband to sort out their problems on their own and, above all, that I shouldn't be alarmed, because every time Ernesto called me in that oh-so-tragic tone of voice, I'd end up thinking Alicia had lost her mind and while I was on my way to his house to fetch her I'd tell myself the time had come to do something about it, to consult a doctor.

This situation had arisen so many times before and I had put it out of my mind so many times that I think by now I was a bit immune to it, although I must admit Ernesto's decision to move away and live in the north came as a relief. At least it wouldn't be so tempting for Alicia to just turn up at his house, and if she did, Ernesto couldn't possibly think he could call me up

Avilés estaba lo bastante lejos como para que esa petición resultara excesiva.

Fue Alicia quien me lo comunicó, y percibí que, a pesar de sus quejas, en lo más profundo de su ser aprobaba la decisión de Ernesto, consciente de que la distancia entre dos personas que no han conseguido, para la desesperación de una de ellas, la armonía en el amor, es indiscutiblemente terapéutica. Tal vez estaba ella cansada de sufrir, de llorar, gritar y reconciliarse al fin hablando de ecología, de venir a casa después de las peleas para bromear con mis hijos como si nada hubiera pasado y ella fuera la tía soltera y alegre de las novelas rosas. Esas escenas debían parecerle, al fin, unas iguales a otras, y debían dejarle la sensación de una repetición absurda, casi aburrida. Sin duda, ella también admitía la conveniencia de esa medida, que nunca se hubiera decidido a tomar, pero que la beneficiaba. Ahora empezaba su verdadera separación, ahora tenía que adaptarse a su nueva vida y tomar medidas para no dejarse hundir. Ernesto quedaba fuera de su alcance.

En todo caso, fue Alicia quien me dio la noticia. Ernesto no tuvo la delicadeza de llamarme para despedirse de mí. Sus llamadas respondían sólo a la urgencia, a la desesperación. Cuando se fue, en una huida que a todos nos pareció muy razonable, no consideró necesario hacérmelo saber.

No fui consciente de esa época de paz, porque es difícil valorar la calma cuando se tiene. Se añora en el mismo momento en que se pierde, y sólo entonces parece el mejor don que pueda obtenerse sobre la tierra. Entre tanto, no se piensa en ella porque ése es su regalo. En la verdadera calma no cabe el análisis. Pero me temo que estoy, ya, hablando de otra cosa: estoy hablando de mí.

No sé el tiempo que transcurrió hasta que volví a escuchar la voz de Ernesto. Lo primero que me asombró fue que aquel timbre tan conocido no sonara con ansiedad, no era un grito, una llamada de urgencia. Tenía una cadencia lenta, de cansancio, de contenido temor.

—¿Sabes dónde está Alicia? —me preguntó, después de interesarse brevemente por mi existencia.

—Supongo que estará en su casa —dije, comprendiendo de inmediato que él ya habría intentado localizarla allí.

—No está —confirmó—. Llevo días buscándola. No ha ido a trabajar desde hace cuatro días y su teléfono no contesta. Por eso te llamo.

—Puede que esté de viaje.

looking for help, because Avilés was far enough away to make such a request unreasonable.

It was Alicia who told me about it, and I could see that, in spite of her protests, deep down she agreed with Ernesto's decision, aware of the fact that putting a distance between two people who have, to the despair of one of them, failed to achieve harmony in love, is undoubtedly therapeutic. Perhaps she was tired of suffering, of crying, of screaming, of finally making up by talking about ecology, of coming home after the fights to joke with my children as if nothing had happened and as if she were the unmarried, merry aunt of sentimental novels. Those scenes must finally have all looked very much the same and must have left her with a feeling of absurd, almost boring, repetition. Doubtless she too could see the convenience of that move, which she herself would never have decided to undertake, although it was good for her. Now she started her real separation from him, now she had to adapt to her new life and to take steps to ensure she didn't let herself be overwhelmed. Ernesto was beyond her reach.

In any event, it was Alicia who told me the news. Ernesto didn't have the decency to call me to say goodbye. His calls came only in times of emergency and despair. When he left, making an escape that seemed highly reasonable to all of us, he didn't think it necessary to let me know.

I wasn't aware of that period of peace because it's difficult to put a price on calm when you have it. You long for peace of mind at the very moment that you're losing it, and only then does it seem like the greatest gift this earth has to offer. In the meantime you don't think about it, because peace of mind is its own gift. Analysis has no place in real peace of mind. But I'm afraid I'm talking about something else now: I'm talking about myself.

I don't know how long it was before I heard Ernesto's voice again. The first thing which surprised me was that his so familiar tone didn't sound anxious, it wasn't a shout, a cry for help. It had a slow, tired cadence to it, a note of controlled fear.

"Do you know where Alicia is?" he asked, having asked briefly after me.

"I assume she'll be at home," I said, realizing straight away that he'd already tried to track her down there.

"She's not there," he confirmed. "I've been looking for her for days. She's not been in to work for four days and her phone isn't answering. That's why I'm calling you."

"She could be away on a trip."

—En la oficina no saben nada. Pidió unos días de vacaciones, pero nadie sabe dónde está. Creí que teníais mucha confianza. —Ahora su voz cansada cobró un matiz de irritación, de reproche.

—Alicia es bastante mayor. No suele darme explicaciones de su vida —me defendí—. Y siempre ha hecho lo que le ha dado la gana, como seguramente sabes.

Una de las cosas que había hecho era quitarme el novio y casarse con él sin mostrar jamás el menor remordimiento por ello. Supuse que Ernesto sabía a lo que yo me estaba refiriendo.

—¿La crees capaz de cometer una tontería? —me preguntó.

—¿Qué quieres decir?

—La última discusión que tuvimos fue bastante fuerte. En realidad, le dije cosas que no siento. Ya sabes cómo acaban esas peleas, uno acaba sacando lo peor, sólo por fastidiar, por hacer daño. De repente, todo se convierte en una cuestión de honor, de amor propio. Lo único importante en ese momento es vencer, humillar. Creo que me pasé de rosca.

—¿Cuándo fue eso?

—El viernes pasado.

—¿Fue Alicia a Avilés?

—Sí. Me quedé asombrado. Nunca pensé que vendría hasta aquí. Se presentó con una maleta y dijo que se quedaría en casa hasta estar perfectamente convencida de que no había nada entre ella y yo. Que necesitaba esa prueba antes de decidirse a olvidarme. Cielos, a veces pienso que está loca —suspiró—. Por eso me preocupa. —Al fin, salía ese verbo: preocupar, que estaba al fondo de la conversación.

—¿Cuánto tiempo se quedó?

—Muy poco. Yo estaba solo. Rosana estaba en Madrid, haciendo unas pruebas. Supongo que eso fue lo que me empujó a insultarla. Pensé que Alicia estaba enterada de la ausencia de Rosana, que, desde Madrid, nos seguía espiando. Me llené de ira. La insulté y la eché de casa. Le puse la maleta en la puerta, la cogí del brazo y la saqué al descansillo. Cerré la puerta y ya no la volví a abrir, aunque ella siguió tocando el timbre. Al fin, pidió el ascensor y se fue. Al poco tiempo, empezó a sonar el teléfono, pero no lo cogí. Y eso es todo lo que sé. —Volvió a suspirar—. Rosana vino el domingo y me hizo llamar a Alicia. En realidad, creo que Rosana siente simpatía por ella. No le pareció bien que la hubiera tratado así. Pero ya no

"They don't know anything at her office. She asked for a few days holiday, but nobody knows where she is. I thought you two were very close." His tired voice now held a trace of irritation, of reproach.

"Alicia is a big girl now. She doesn't usually tell me what's going on in her life," I countered. "And she's always done whatever took her fancy, as you must surely know."

One of the things she had done was to take away my boyfriend and marry him without ever showing the slightest remorse for having done so. I supposed that Ernesto knew what I was talking about.

"Do you think she's capable of doing something silly?", he asked me.

"What do you mean?"

"The last row we had was pretty bad. To tell you the truth, I said things to her I don't really feel. You know how these fights end up, you show your worst side, just to upset or hurt the other person. It all suddenly becomes a question of honour, of pride. The only thing that's important at the time is to win, to humiliate. I think I went too far."

"When was this?"

"Last Friday."

"Did Alicia go to Avilés?"

"Yes. I was astonished. I never thought she'd come up here. She turned up with a suitcase and said she'd be staying at the house until she was thoroughly convinced there was nothing left between herself and me. That she needed proof of that before deciding whether to forget me. Honestly, sometimes I think she's crazy," he sighed. "That's why I'm worried." At last it had come out, that verb: to be worried. It was at the very root of the conversation.

"How long did she stay?"

"Not long. I was on my own. Rosana was in Madrid auditioning for a couple of parts. I suppose that was what drove me to insult her. I thought Alicia knew about Rosana's being away, that she'd been spying on us from Madrid. I got very angry. I called her names and threw her out of the house. I took her suitcase to the door, grabbed her by the arm and pushed her out onto the landing. I slammed the door and refused to open it again even though she kept ringing the bell. She finally called the lift and went. A little while later the phone began to ring, but I didn't answer it. And that's all I know." He sighed again. "Rosana came back on the Sunday and made me call Alicia. To tell you the truth, I think Rosana rather likes her. She didn't think it was right that I should have treated her like that. But then we

pudimos encontrarla. La estamos buscando desde el lunes. ¿Dónde crees que puede estar? ¿No te parece extraño que no te haya dicho nada?

Me resistía a inquietarme, pero tampoco sentía ninguna necesidad de tranquilizar a Ernesto, cuyas llamadas nunca habían sido tranquilizadoras.

—Voy a intentar buscarla —dije.

Pero cuando colgué el teléfono comprendí que no sabía cómo hacerlo. No sabía mucho de la vida de mi hermana y no quería asustar a mis padres, que eran los únicos que tal vez tenían algunos datos sobre sus actuales amistades. Me las arreglé para sacarles un par de nombres sin levantar demasiadas suspicacias, pero volví a encontrarme en un punto muerto. Nadie sabía nada.

Ernesto me volvió a llamar.

—¿Crees que debemos acudir a la policía? —me preguntó.

Yo tenía la mente paralizada y su sugerencia me sorprendió.

—Supongo que sí —dije—. Hazlo tú, por favor. Es algo que me impresiona demasiado.

Me telefoneó en cuanto la policía hizo sus investigaciones. Ni en las comisarías ni en los hospitales se sabía nada de mi hermana, y eso era todo lo que podía hacerse. Si tenían otras noticias, nos las comunicarían de inmediato.

Pero no nos llamaron.

Alicia apareció el lunes siguiente. Lo supimos porque le telefoneamos a la oficina. Cuando hablé con ella, acababa de hablar con Ernesto.

—No entiendo por qué os habéis preocupado tanto —dijo—. Me he ido de viaje.

—Pero no se lo habías dicho a nadie.

—Soy ya bastante mayor, ¿no crees?

Algo parecido le había dicho yo a Ernesto hacía unos días.

—¿Fuiste sola?

Se rió.

—Ya que me lo preguntas, me fui con un chico.

Parecía bastante contenta, y me alegré. Tal vez había encontrado ya la forma de consolarse.

Sucedió otro período de calma, sin que yo dedicase mucho tiempo a las vicisitudes amorosas de mi hermana. Y una tarde de invierno, sonó el timbre de mi puerta de una manera insistente. Era Ernesto. No quiso pasar, sólo pidió por favor que lo acompañara a un bar porque quería hablar conmigo a solas.

couldn't find her. We've been looking for her since Monday. Where do you think she could be? Don't you think it's odd that she hasn't said anything to you?"

I refused to start worrying, but neither did I feel any need to calm Ernesto down; his phone calls to me had never been reassuring.

"I'm going to try to find her," I said.

But when I hung up I realized I didn't know where to start. I didn't know very much about my sister's life and I didn't want to alarm my parents who were the only ones who might have any information about her current circle of friends. I managed to get a couple of names out of them without raising too many suspicions, but I ran up against another dead end. Nobody knew anything.

Ernesto called me again.

"Do you think we should call the police?" he asked me.

My mind had gone blank and his suggestion took me by surprise.

"I suppose so," I said. "Please, you do it. I'd find it too upsetting."

He called me as soon as the police had carried out their enquiries. None of the police stations or hospitals knew anything about my sister, and that was all they could do. If they had anything further to report, they'd get in touch with us straight away.

But they didn't call.

Alicia turned up the following Monday. We found out about it because we phoned her office. When I spoke to her, she'd just been talking to Ernesto.

"I don't understand why you were so worried," she said. "I've been away."

"But you didn't say a word to anybody."

"I'm a big girl now, aren't I?"

I'd said more or less the same thing to Ernesto a few days earlier.

"Did you go on your own?"

She laughed.

"Now you ask me, I went with a male friend."

She sounded quite happy, and I was glad. Perhaps she'd already found a way of consoling herself.

There ensued another period of calm during which I paid little attention to the amorous vicissitudes of my sister. Then one winter's evening my front doorbell started to ring insistently. It was Ernesto. He didn't want to come in, he only wanted to ask me to go to some bar with him because he wanted to talk to me privately.

—Aquí no —dijo—. No quiero molestar. Sois una familia.

Temblaba, no se había afeitado, me miraba fijamente bajo el mechón de pelo mojado que cubría su frente y parte de sus ojos. No di muchas explicaciones y me fui tras él. Anduvimos bajo la lluvia fría —yo sostenía el paraguas contra el viento y Ernesto no hacía nada por cubrirse— hasta encontrar un bar que le gustara. Éste no, decía, tiene demasiada luz, aquí hay demasiada gente, éste es horroroso... Al fin, se decidió, un poco resignado, y entramos y nos sentamos y pedimos algo de beber. Yo le observaba, esperando que empezara a hablar, ¿qué podía preguntarle?

Bebió, se pasó la mano por la cara, miró la superficie lisa de la mesa.

—Me ha dejado —dijo—. Se ha ido definitivamente.

—¿Quién?

Me devolvió una mirada de asombro, vacía, como si no me entendiera.

—Alicia —susurró.

—Creí que eras tú quien la habías dejado.

Negó con la cabeza, volvió a restregarse la cara mojada.

—Cielos, no lo sabía, te lo aseguro, no me había dado cuenta. Es la única mujer a la que he querido. No soporto perderla. No quiere verme. Dice que nunca nos volveremos a ver.

Se puso a llorar. Sacó un pañuelo y se limpió la cara.

—Es tan raro todo esto, tan extraño.

—Has necesitado que Alicia te dejara para darte cuenta de que la querías —le dije, y supongo que era un reproche, por Alicia y tal vez por mí, que nunca le había dejado.

—Soy un estúpido, lo sé —dijo—. Pero estoy desesperado. Nunca volveré a tenerla.

—¿Para qué querías verme? No puedo hacer nada por ti.

Volvió a dedicarme una mirada de desconcierto.

—No lo sé —balbuceó—. De repente, me vi frente a tu casa. Supongo que eres la única persona a la que puedo decir esto.

—Siempre acudes a mí —dije, con mi viejo resentimiento—. Cuando Alicia te molestaba y querías que se fuera de tu casa, me llamabas para que me la llevara a la mía. Ahora que no quiere verte, me llamas para llorar sobre mi hombro. ¿No crees que eso es muy cómodo? Yo siempre estoy ahí, para ayudarte. Te saco de apuros y te consuelo. Deberías preguntarte

"Not here," he said. "I don't want to bother you. You have a family."

He was trembling, he hadn't shaved, he was staring at me from under a lock of damp hair that had fallen across his forehead and part of his eyes. I didn't say much by way of explanation and set off behind him. We walked along in the cold rain – I was holding my umbrella against the wind but Ernesto did nothing to cover himself up – until we found a bar he liked. Not this one, he'd say, it's too bright, there are too many people here, this one is awful .... He finally made up his mind, somewhat resigned, and we went in, sat down and ordered something to drink. I kept my eyes on him, waiting for him to start speaking. What could I ask him?

He took a drink, wiped his hand across his face and looked at the smooth surface of the table.

"She's left me," he said. "She's gone for good."

"Who?"

He answered me with an astonished, vacant look, as if he didn't understand my question.

"Alicia," he whispered.

"I thought it was you who'd left her."

He shook his head and went back to mopping his wet face.

"Heavens, I didn't know, honestly, I didn't realize. She's the only woman I've ever loved. I can't bear to lose her. She doesn't want to see me. She says we'll never see each other again."

He started to cry. He took out his handkerchief and wiped his face.

"This is all very odd, very peculiar."

"You needed Alicia to leave you to make you realize you loved her," I told him, and I suppose it was a reproach, for Alicia and perhaps for me, who had never left him.

"I know I'm being really stupid," he said. "But I'm desperate. I shall never have her again."

"Why did you want to see me? I can't do anything for you."

He gave me another disconcerted look.

"I don't know," he stammered. "I suddenly found myself outside your house. I suppose you're the only person I can say this to."

"You always turn to me," I said, feeling my old resentment. "When Alicia used to bother you and you wanted her out of your house, you'd call me so I'd take her to mine. Now she doesn't want to see you, you call me to cry on my shoulder. Very handy, don't you think? I'm always there to help you. I get you out of tight spots and comfort you. You should ask yourself

por qué lo hago. Aunque ya es tarde. Me parece que me he cansado de ayudarte.

El vacío de sus ojos se convirtió en pánico y, a mi pesar, sentí compasión. No podía ayudarle, pero todavía me conmovía, y me acordé de Alicia cuando, después de una de sus violentas escenas y posterior reconciliación, se miraba en el espejo del ascensor de la casa de Ernesto y se decía que él la amaba y que ella no podía renunciar. Al fin y al cabo, ahora se demostraba que tenía razón.

—Lo siento —murmuró—. Pero ne te vayas. No puedes fallarme.

Decidió sobreponerse a su temor y se echó a reír. Fue entonces cuando comprendí que estaba verdaderamente borracho.

—Vámonos —le dije—. Prefiero andar bajo la lluvia.

Al ponerse de pie, empujó la mesa y su vaso cayó al suelo. Me excusé con el camarero, cogí a Ernesto del brazo y lo saqué a la calle. Al otro lado de la puerta de cristal del bar, el camarero se inclinó para recoger el vaso roto.

Anduvimos mucho rato, cobijados bajo mi paraguas, envueltos en el ruido de la lluvia, hablando cada uno sin escucharnos demasiado, contando retazos de vida y de ilusiones, sosteniéndonos mutuamente.

—¿Cómo va a terminar esto? —preguntó Ernesto.

De vez en cuando lo decía, como una frase de la que uno no se puede desprender, que termina por perder su verdadero significado y se convierte en algo desconocido, ajeno, salvador, una respuesta.

why I do it. Even though it's a bit late now. I think I've grown tired of helping you."

The emptiness of his eyes turned to panic and in spite of myself I felt sorry for him. I couldn't help him, but he still moved me and I remembered how Alicia, after one of their violent scenes and subsequent reconciliations, would look at herself in the mirror in the lift at Ernesto's house and tell herself that he was in love with her and that she couldn't give him up. And when all was said and done, it turned out she was right.

"I'm sorry," he murmured. "But don't go. You can't desert me."

He made up his mind to overcome his fear and burst out laughing. It was then I understood he was completely drunk.

"Let's go," I said. "I would rather walk in the rain."

As he got to his feet he knocked against the table and his glass fell on the floor. I apologized to the waiter, took Ernesto by the arm, and led him out into the street. On the other side of the glass door to the bar the waiter had bent down to pick up the broken tumbler.

We walked for a long time, sheltering under my umbrella, enveloped in the noise of the rain, each of us talking without listening very much to what the other was saying, relating snippets of our lives and our hopes and dreams, giving each other mutual support.

"How's this all going to end?", asked Ernesto.

From time to time he'd say the same thing, like a phrase you can't get out of your mind, that ends up losing its real meaning and becomes something unknown, foreign, a life-saver, an answer.

MARÍA EUGENIA SALAVERRI

MARÍA EUGENIA SALAVERRI was born in Bilbao in 1957. A journalist by profession, she is currently the deputy producer of a discussion programme on Basque Television. She has been a regular contributor to many newspapers and periodicals, among them *La estafeta literaria, ABC, Cuadernos Iberoamericanos, Pérgola, Tribuna Vasca* and *La Gaceta del Norte.* Her first book, *Retrato de un pájaro*, was a volume of poems. Later, she published *Un tango para tres hermanas* (1991), a beguiling collection of short stories in which she reveals her talent for charging a perfectly ordinary situation with a hint of nightmare. The main characters in the ten stories of *Un tango para tres hermanas* are all female and constitute an impressive and variegated collection of self-seeking women. They all seem to be driven by their instinct to survive and fight, often against each other, in a world where men have been pushed to the background. Some of the characters travel from one story to another, giving the book a purposeful sense of unity in spite of the diversity of literary strategies it deploys (diaries, letters, stories told by different kinds of narratorial voices, etc.).

A multifaceted writer, María Eugenia Salaverri also lectures on creative writing and in the last two years she has become a successful cinema scriptwriter. The first of her scripts has already been made into a film soon to be released.

Still relatively unknown outside the Basque Country, María Eugenia Salaverri is now preparing a new book of short stories (in which the one selected for this Anthology, 'Cirugía plástica', will be included) that could very well be the breakthrough she fully deserves.

Plastic Surgery

Cirugía plástica

Original Spanish text from
Joseluís González and Pedro de Miguel (eds),
Últimos narradores:
Antología de la reciente narrativa breve española
(Pamplona: Hierbaola, 1993), 179–190.

Cirugía plástica

En Francia anochece antes. Eso es así. A mí no me gusta hablar mal de este país porque a fin de cuentas si estoy aquí lo menos que puedo hacer es ser agradecida, pero las cosas como son: en Francia anochece antes y ésa es una de las tristezas de vivir aquí, que a eso de las nueve de la noche no hay un alma en la calle.

Nosotros tenemos un bar. Fran y yo. Abrimos hace ya tres años. Hacemos cocina vasca. Ponemos pinchos al mediodía y luego tenemos un menú con comidas normales, de las que hemos comido siempre, bacalao, pochas, arroz con leche. A los franceses les gustan mucho. También damos cenas, pero a la noche viene menos gente porque aquí todo el mundo se acuesta más temprano que allí. Así que a eso de las nueve, cuando comienza a flojear la clientela, yo suelo aprovechar para ponerme a limpiar. Limpio todo, la barra, los anaqueles, los vasos, pero sobre todo me aplico bien en las botellas, que se ven mucho. Soy muy limpia, pero la verdad es que no les saco brillo sólo por eso, sino sobre todo porque aquí piensan que los del otro lado de los Pirineos somos todos unos guarros. Bueno, y también para dar ejemplo y que me vea Simone, que en cuanto nos quedamos sin clientes se va al extremo de la barra, donde se sienta Fran a leer el periódico, y comienza a darle palique sobre cualquier tontería. Generalmente Fran no le hace demasiado caso, es decir, no más que a cualquiera que entre y se ponga a charlar sobre fútbol o política o lo que sea, porque Fran es muy sociable y habla muy bien francés, pero a mí me molesta porque creo que no hace buen efecto entrar en un local y encontrarte al personal de cháchara, como si no tuviera nada mejor que hacer. Además hay otra cosa que me fastidia, y es que si Fran no está, Simone no se dedica a buscar temas de conversación para hablar conmigo,

Plastic Surgery

It starts to get dark earlier in France. That's how it is. I don't like to run down this country because, when all's said and done, if I'm here the least I can do is be grateful, but that's the way things are: it gets dark earlier in France and that's one of the sad things about living here, the fact is that by around nine o'clock at night there's not a soul on the streets.

We've got a bar. Fran and I. We opened it three years ago now. We serve Basque food. We do light bar snacks at midday and then we have a menu with the usual dishes — the sort of food we've always eaten — cod, pinto beans, rice pudding. The French like it a lot. We also provide evening meals, but not as many people turn out at night because round here everybody goes to bed earlier than they do there. So at around nine, when trade starts to slacken off, I usually seize the chance to get on with the cleaning. I clean everything, the bar, the shelves, the glasses, but what I pay particular attention to are the bottles, which are always on view. I'm very clean, although to tell you the truth that's not the only reason I leave them sparkling, no, it's because round here they think that all of us who come from the other side of the Pyrenees live like pigs. OK, it's also to set an example and so Simone can see me — as soon as the last customers leave she goes to the end of the bar, where Fran sits reading the paper, and she indulges in idle chitchat with him. Fran usually doesn't take much notice of her, I mean no more notice than he does of anybody else who comes in and starts nattering away to him about football or politics or whatever, because Fran is very sociable and he speaks very good French, but it bothers me because I don't think it creates the right impression for people to come into an establishment and find the staff chattering away as if they had nothing better to do. Besides, there's something else that annoys me, and that's the fact that if Fran isn't around, Simone doesn't spend her time searching for topics to make conversation with me, she obviously thinks what's the point,

pensará que para qué, que yo hablo un francés pésimo, o sea que es de esa clase de chicas que resultan muy simpáticas y muy dicharacheras si hay hombres cerca y que si no, no abren la boca, y a mí esa gente me revienta.

—Mira, Simone —solía decirle antes—, en un bar siempre hay trabajo para el que quiera trabajar, así que quien está mano sobre mano es porque le da la gana.

Y es cierto. Pero un día Fran me dijo que la dejara en paz, que ya cumple cuando tiene que cumplir, que muchos clientes vienen a verla expresamente a ella, y que si seguía asi terminaría por marcharse, así que ahora no le digo nada, simplemente quito el polvo de las botellas para que me vea y coja la indirecta y aunque es cierto que a veces alguien me ha dicho que cuando limpio parezco malhumorada y que aprieto los labios, yo suelo contestar que soy simplemente limpia y que si hago el trabajo a conciencia no voy a estar pendiente de qué cara pongo.

Así que esa noche, la noche de la que quiero hablar, cuando conocí a los Lucas, yo estoy limpiando botellas y Simone y Fran hablan en la esquina de la cafetera. Es Simone quien habla. Fran escucha y desde donde yo me encuentro puedo verle de perfil. Veo cómo se tira del labio inferior con los dedos una y otra vez, como si estuviera pensando en algo que requiriera mucha concentración, pero no logro ver la expresión de sus ojos. Posiblemente los tenga entornados, pienso, porque así es como suele mirar cuando hace ese gesto. Y entonces me acuerdo de que el día de nuestra boda también lo hizo. Fue precisamente en el momento en que le preguntaron eso de si promete honrarte y respetarte hasta que la muerte os separe. Bueno, pues sencillamente no contestó. Se quedó mirando al vacío, pellizcándose el labio de abajo como sí la cosa no fuera con él, como si estuviera esperando a un autobús en la parada o algo así. Yo estaba atónita. El cura repitió tres veces la pregunta y entonces le di un codazo y le dije "Fran", porque creí que no había oído. Pero no es que no oyera, lo que ocurría era que realmente se lo estaba pensando. Fue algo increíble. Allí estábamos los dos, de pie, delante de un montón de gente y él se lo estaba pensando. Ni siquiera se le ocurrió ponerse en mi lugar e imaginarse cómo podía sentirme allí plantada, esperando a ver qué decidía. Y en aquel momento me dije que no tendría nada de extraño si simplemente se diera la vuelta y se marchara. Con la cara que tenía hubiera resultado incluso normal. Pero de pronto giró la cabeza hacia mí, me miró a los ojos, parpadeó un par de veces y dijo "Sí". De eso hace ya siete años, aún no habíamos venido a Francia, pero se me

my French is very poor, in other words she's one of those girls who are very nice and chatty when there are men around, but if there aren't they don't open their mouth, and people like that really get on my nerves.

"Look, Simone," I used to say to her in the early days, "in a bar there's always work for those who want to do it, so when somebody sits twiddling their thumbs it's because that's what they feel like doing."

And it's true. But one day Fran told me to leave her alone, because when she's needed she does what she has to do, that a lot of customers come in expressly to see her, and that if I carried on like that she'd end up by walking out, so now I don't say a word to her, I simply wipe the dust off the bottles so she can see me and get the hint, and even though it's true that people sometimes tell me that when I'm cleaning I do look bad tempered and I purse my lips, I usually reply that I'm just a clean person and if I'm doing my job properly I don't have time to bother about the look on my face.

So that night, the night I want to tell you about, when I met the Lucases, I'm cleaning off the bottles and Simone and Fran are talking in the corner by the coffee machine. It's Simone who's doing the talking. Fran is listening and from where I'm standing I can see his face in profile. I watch how he pulls at his bottom lip with his fingers again and again, as if he was thinking about something that requires a lot of concentration, but I can't see the look in his eyes. Perhaps he's got them half closed, I think, because that's how he usually looks when he's doing that business with his lip. And then I remember that he did it on our wedding day too. It was at the precise moment he was asked if he promised to love and honour till death us did part. Well, he simply didn't reply. He just stood there staring into space, pinching his bottom lip as if it was nothing to do with him, as if he was queuing at a bus stop or something. I was amazed. The priest repeated the question three times and then I nudged him and said "Fran" because I thought he hadn't heard. But it isn't that he hadn't heard him, the fact of the matter was that he was thinking about it. It was unbelievable. There we were, the two of us, standing there in front of a crowd of people and he was thinking about it. It didn't even cross his mind to put himself in my place and imagine how I might feel, stuck there, waiting to see what he'd decide. And just at that moment I told myself I wouldn't be in the least bit surprised if he were simply to turn on his heel and walk away. Given that look on his face, it might even have been the normal thing for him to do. But he suddenly turned his head towards me, looked me in the eyes, blinked a couple of times and said "yes". That was seven years ago now, we hadn't yet come to France, but that moment was imprinted on my mind and

quedó grabado y siempre que le veo esa cara me pregunto qué estará pasando por su cabeza, porque creo que si algún día decidiera largarse sin más, sería después de haber puesto una expresión como ésa.

Pero esa noche, la noche en que después vinieron los Lucas, él parece de muy buen humor, y aunque escucha estirándose el labio, de pronto estalla en carcajadas.

—¿De qué habláis? —pregunto.

No me oyen, así que me quedo mirándoles e incluso sonrío mientras les miro. Luego pienso que sería más lógico que fuera Simone quien limpiara y yo la que estuviera acompañando a Fran, pero ya hace demasiado tiempo que las cosas están así y aunque meses atrás he decidido que esa situación no me gusta nada, tampoco sé qué hacer para cambiarla.

Entonces llegan ellos, los Lucas. Primero entra él. Avanza balanceándose sobre unas piernas cortas y combadas, lanza una mirada general y de pronto, abriendo los brazos, dice en voz muy alta que no está mal el tugurio. Lo dice en español. "Nada nada mal", repite.

Tiene unos treinta años y es de esa clase de tipos que son todo pecho, de esos que sentados parecen normales o incluso grandes y cuando se levantan tienen la estatura de un niño de doce años. Y ahí está, mirando el local con la misma satisfacción con la que lo miraría si fuera el propietario y sonriéndonos a todos con sus dientes mellados.

Fran se vuelve sorprendido, les mira, dice "vaya, vaya", abandona con lentitud el taburete y se dirige hacia ellos.

—Mira quién está aquí —dice cuando llega junto al hombre, mientras le da en el brazo un puñetazo suave y luego un abrazo.

La chica se ha quedado un par de pasos atrás y permanece con la vista fija en la puntera de su zapato, haciendo círculos en el suelo hasta que el hombre la toma por el codo y la acerca a Fran.

—Ésta es Rosa —dice—. Fran, Rosa. Rosa, Fran.

Ella extiende la mano y Fran, que ha avanzado un poco, como para besarla en la mejilla, cambia de idea y le estrecha la mano.

—Bueno, y ahora me presentarás a tu parienta, ¿no? —pregunta el hombre mirando fijamente a Simone.

Entonces me seco las manos, salgo de la barra y me acerco. Nos damos la mano y nos quedamos mirándonos. Tienen un aspecto chocante. Los dos llevan vaqueros y camisetas de algodón, pero aun así tienen un aire

whenever I see that look I wonder what's going through his head, because I think that if he were to decide to just clear off some day without further ado, it would be after wearing an expression like that.

But that night, the night on which the Lucases later turned up, he seemed to be in a very good mood, and although he's listening and pulling at his lip, he suddenly bursts out laughing.

"What are you talking about?" I ask.

They don't hear me, so I keep watching them and I even smile while I watch them. Then I think it would make more sense if it were Simone who was doing the cleaning and me who was sitting next to Fran, but things have been like this for a long while now, even though I made up my mind months ago that I didn't like the situation one little bit, nor do I know what I can do to change it.

Then they turned up, the Lucases. He comes in first. He comes in, swaying on short bandy legs, gives the place a general once over and then suddenly, throwing his arms open wide, he announces in a very loud voice that it's not a bad joint. He says this in Spanish. "Not bad, not bad at all," he repeats.

He's about thirty years old and he's one of those people who are all chest, the sort of person that looks normal, even big, when they're sitting down, but when they stand up they've got the stature of a kid of twelve. And there he stands, looking round the place with the same air of satisfaction he would have if he were the owner, smiling at all of us with his chipped teeth.

Fran turns round, surprised, looks at them, says "Well, well," gets slowly up from his bar-stool and walks over to them.

"Look who's here," he says when he gets up to the man, giving him a light punch on the arm and then hugging him.

The girl has stopped a couple of paces behind and stays there, her eyes fixed on the tip of her shoe, tracing circles on the floor until the man takes her by the elbow and moves her closer to Fran.

"This is Rosa," he says. "Fran, Rosa. Rosa, Fran."

She stretches out her hand and Fran, who has moved forward a little as if to give her a kiss on the cheek, changes his mind and stretches out his hand.

"Right, and now you'll introduce me to the wife, won't you", asks the man staring at Simone.

Then I dry my hands, come out from behind the bar and go over to them. We shake hands and stand there looking at each other. There's something odd about them. They're both wearing jeans and cotton T-shirts, but they still have a Sunday-best look about them, as if they've got dressed up

endomingado, como si se hubieran arreglado para la ocasión.   Tal vez no sea así, quizá él salga siempre a la calle con el pelo embadurnado en fijador y ella con esa diadema de perlas, pero la pinta que tienen es muy rara.   Ella lleva unos zapatos blancos, con lazos de raso.   Algunos de los lazos están deshilachados y me pregunto si se habrá comprado esos zapatos para su propia boda.

Fran hace las presentaciones.   Dice que se llaman Lucas y Rosa.   Yo digo "Irma", y ellos me miran y luego se miran entre sí, como si nunca hubieran oído que nadie se llame de ese modo.   Sonríen.   Todos sonreímos.   Fran explica que Lucas y él han hecho la mili juntos.

—Vi muchas fotos tuyas —comenta Lucas—.   Tenías una foto de ella con un gato.   Me acuerdo de aquel gato.   Recuerdo que era un gato muy bonito, blanco.   Aquella foto parecía un calendario.

No recuerdo haberme hecho nunca una foto con un gato, pero no digo nada.   En realidad odio a los gatos.   No me gustan los animales, pero supongo que podría haber salido en alguna foto con algún perro.   Mi hermana tiene uno.   Pero nadie que yo conozca tiene un gato y, aunque lo tuvieran, jamás me acercaría a él.

Fran endereza los hombros y suspira.

—Hace años de eso —dice.

Luego pregunta qué hacen ellos en Poitiers y como resulta que viven en Limoges, dice que tenemos que celebrarlo, que hay que sacar champán y festejar el encuentro.   Nos sentamos en la mesa del fondo y Fran le pide a Simone que traiga una botella de brut.   Hablamos del bar, de cómo se había enterado Lucas de la dirección por otro compañero de la mili y de las ganas que tenía de venir a vernos.

Mientras, Simone ha traído la botella de champán y las copas.   Nos sirve a Fran, a Lucas y a mí.   Rosa tapa su copa con la mano y niega con la cabeza.

—Yo prefiero agua —dice, y su cara se vuelve roja como la grana.

—Está embarazada —comenta Lucas pasándole una mano por el pelo—.   O al menos eso creemos, ¿verdad, Rosa?   Aún no lo hemos confirmado porque sólo ha tenido una falta, pero estamos seguros porque nos hemos empleado a fondo, ¿eh, Rosa?

specially for the occasion. Perhaps it isn't like that at all, perhaps he always goes out plastered with hair oil and she with that pearl-studded Alice-band, but there is a very strange look about them. She's wearing white shoes with satin bows. Some of the bows are beginning to fray at the edges and I wonder if she has bought those shoes for her own wedding.

Fran makes the introductions. He says they're called Lucas and Rosa. I say "Irma," and they look at me and then they look at each other, as if they'd never heard of anybody with such a name. They smile. We all smile. Fran explains that he and Lucas did their military service[44] together.

"I saw a lot of photos of you," remarks Lucas. "You used to have a photo of her with a cat. I remember that cat. I remember it was a very pretty white cat. That photo looked like something off a calendar."

I don't remember ever having my photo taken with a cat, but I don't say anything. To tell the truth, I hate cats. I don't like animals, although I suppose there could be a photo of me somewhere with some dog. My sister's got one. But nobody I know has a cat and even if they did, I'd never go anywhere near it.

Fran leans back and sighs.

"That was years ago," he says.

Then he asks what they're doing in Poitiers and how come they live in Limoges, he says we should have a celebration, that we must bring out the champagne and toast the reunion. We sit down at the table at the back and Fran asks Simone to bring a bottle of the best champagne. We talk about the bar, about how Lucas had tracked down the address through another friend who'd done military service with them and about how much he'd wanted to come and see us.

Simone, meanwhile, has brought the bottle of champagne and the glasses. She pours some for Fran, for Lucas and for me. Rosa puts her hand over the top of her glass and shakes her head.

"I would rather have water," she says, and her face turns as red as a beetroot.

"She's pregnant," remarks Lucas, stroking her hair with his hand. "Or at least, we think she is. Isn't that right, Rosa? It's still not been confirmed because she's only missed once, but we're sure because we've been trying really hard, eh, Rosa?"

---

[44]   **Military service:** compulsory enlistment of young men for a period of military service of approx. one year.

Rosa asiente varias veces. Al parecer tiene esa costumbre. Espera a que Lucas hable y entonces ella cabecea tres o cuatro veces, como esos perros que adornan las ventanillas traseras de los coches.

Lucas explica que trabaja en un taller de reparaciones. Antes pasó unos años en Barcelona, pero se quedó sin empleo y alguien le buscó trabajo en Limoges y se vino.

—He hecho de todo, tío, de todo —dice, y sus ojos se vuelven graves y tristes, como si fuera a confesar algo inconfesable. Pero de pronto cambia de expresión y pasando el índice por la mano de su mujer dice que ahora todo está bien. Después él y Fran comienzan a hablar de amigos comunes y a recordar anécdotas de cuando estaban en la mili.

—¿Tenéis hijos? —me pregunta Rosa de pronto.

Contesto que no. Luego miro a la barra. Han entrado clientes y Simone atiende a un hombre gigantesco que bebe cerveza mexicana con limón. Más allá una pareja formada por una rubia y un viejo están haciendo tonterías con la corbata del viejo. De vez en cuando se besuquean.

—No, todavía no —digo, pero Rosa no parece escucharme.

Hemos terminado de cenar y todos, excepto Rosa, estamos un poco achispados. Hemos comido como bestias. Tortilla, anchoas, tigres, champiñones, callos, queso, y todo regado con champán, lo que para mi gusto es un poco asqueroso y para el gusto de Fran, en estado normal, también. Pero hoy Fran no está muy normal que digamos. Ha bebido más de la cuenta y parece estar deseando hablar de cosas deprimentes. Ha contado con pelos y señales la muerte de su hermano. Su hermano se suicidó ahora hace un año tirándose al asfalto desde un puente. Fue algo terrible y Fran jamás lo menciona, ni siquiera conmigo, pero esta noche ha empezado a hablar de eso y luego se ha echado a llorar. Dice que muchas veces sueña que habla con su hermano y que al despertar le siente tan cerca como si pudiera tocarle.

—¿Es eso cierto? —pregunto—. ¿Por qué nunca me lo has contado?

Alza los hombros y se limita a jugar con una miga de pan. Entonces, no sé cómo, Lucas y él empiezan a hablar de coches. Lucas cuenta un chiste muy malo sobre Nicky Lauda y los dos se ríen. Se ríen muy alto y desde el

Rosa nods several times. It seems that this is a habit of hers. She waits for Lucas to speak and then she nods three or four times, like one of those dogs you see in the rear windows of cars.

Lucas explains that he works in a garage. Before that he'd spent a few years in Barcelona, but he lost his job and somebody found work for him in Limoges and so he came.

"I've done everything, man, everything," he says, and his eyes turn serious and sad as if he was going to confess something that could not be confessed. But his expression suddenly changes and drawing his index finger across his wife's hand he says that everything's fine now. Afterwards, he and Fran start talking about mutual friends and reminiscing about things that happened when they were doing their military service.

"Have you got any children?" Rosa suddenly asks me.

I answer no. Then I look at the bar. Some customers have come in and Simone is serving a huge man who's drinking Mexican beer with lemon. Further along a couple, a blonde and an older man, are doing silly things with the old chap's tie. Every now and again they start necking.

"No, not yet" I say, but Rosa doesn't appear to be listening to me.

We've finished dinner and everybody, except Rosa, is a bit tiddly. We've eaten enough to feed an army. Omelettes, anchovies, mussels cooked in spicy tomato sauce, mushrooms, tripe, cheese, and the whole lot washed down with champagne, which I find slightly revolting, as does Fran when he's in a normal mood. But today Fran is not, let us say, quite normal. He's had too much to drink and seems to want to talk about depressing things. He's given a blow-by-blow account of his brother's death. His brother committed suicide a year ago now by throwing himself off a bridge onto the road. It was terrible and Fran never mentions it, not even to me, but that night he started to talk about it and then he burst out crying. He says that he often dreams he's talking with his brother and that when he wakes up he feels he's so close he could touch him.

"Is that true?" I ask. "Why have you never told me?"

He shrugs his shoulders and restricts himself to playing with a crumb of bread. Then, I don't know how they got onto it, he and Lucas start talking about cars. Lucas tells a very sick joke about Nicky Lauda[45] and the two of them laugh. They laugh very loudly and from the other side of the table

---

[45] **Nicky Lauda:** former racing driver born in Vienna in 1949. He was three times world champion (1975, 1977, 1984). He survived a horrific crash at the Nurburgring (West Germany) in 1976, but did not retire until 1985, after 25 career wins.

otro lado de la mesa llega una vaharada de olor dulzón y picante de la loción fijadora de Lucas. Recuerdo que olí algo parecido hace mucho tiempo, pero aunque me esfuerzo no consigo recordar dónde fue.

—Pues yo no puedo dormir sola —dice Rosa de pronto.

Me está observando fijamente con sus grandes ojos negros mientras se retuerce un mechón de pelo con el índice. La miro extrañada porque nadie ha dicho nada sobre eso. Que yo sepa, estaban hablando sobre garajes. Estoy a punto de decírselo, pero en el último momento decido callar.

—Hasta que Lucas no llega, no me duermo —añade.

Parece esperar una respuesta.

—Caramba —digo. No se me ocurre nada mejor que decir.

Ella asiente tres veces.

—Pueden ser las cuatro, o las cinco, la hora que sea. Me da igual, no me duermo. Y si empiezo a dormirme, me despierto. Pienso cosas. Pienso que tal vez haya tenido un accidente, o que alguien le ha atracado o que ha perdido la memoria y se encuentra en medio de una calle sin saber hacia dónde echar a andar. Y me lo paso fatal. De verdad.

Lo ha dicho de corrido, pero ahora se detiene y nos mira con ansiedad.

—Pobrecita chiquitina —dice Lucas mirándole tiernamente y acercando su cara a la de ella, que se aparta hacia un lado.

—Así que no me extraña que sueñes con tu hermano, Fran. No me extraña nada. Te entiendo muy bien —añade con voz rotunda.

Fran echa atrás el cuerpo y su silla se balancea únicamente sobre las patas traseras.

—Ah... —dice. No dice nada más. Cruza las manos tras la nuca mirando al aire y se queda pensativo y silencioso unos instantes.

Yo podría contar que una noche Fran no vino a casa. Fue hace un par de meses y cada vez que lo recuerdo me siento enferma. Podría contarlo ahora. Podría contarlo perfectamente y todos dejaríamos de mirar a Fran como si se tratara de alguien sensible que sufre pesadillas. Podría decirles que yo tampoco dormí. Que creí que no volvería nunca. Que paseé por toda la casa encendiendo y apagando luces. Pensaba "vuelve, cariño, vuelve". Y luego pensaba "ojalá no me cruce nunca más contigo, cabrón de mierda, ojalá no vuelva a ponerte la vista encima porque te mato". Y otra vez le rogaba que volviera. ¡Se lo rogaba! Hablaba con él como si estuviera allí delante. Quiero decir que hablaba en alto. Llegué a convencerme de que

there comes a woft of Lucas's sickly sweet and racy hair lotion. I recall that I smelt something similar a long time ago, but try as I might I can't remember where it was.

"Well I can't sleep alone," says Rosa suddenly.

She's staring at me with her big dark eyes while she twirls a lock of hair round her index finger. I look at her in surprise because nobody's said a word about that. As far as I knew they were talking about garages. I'm on the point of telling her that, but at the last minute I decide to hold my tongue.

"I don't get to sleep until Lucas comes to bed," she adds.

She seems to be waiting for a reply.

"Well I never," I venture. I can't think of anything better to say.

She nods three times.

"It could be four or five o'clock, any time at all. It's all the same to me, I can't get to sleep. And if I start to nod off, I wake up. I think about things. I think that may be he's had an accident, or that somebody has mugged him or that he's lost his memory and he's in the middle of a street and doesn't know which way to go. And I feel ghastly about it. I really do."

She had gabbled all this out, but now she stops and looks at us anxiously.

"Poor little darling," says Lucas, looking at her tenderly and moving his face towards hers, which she turns away to one side.

"So it doesn't surprise me you have dreams about your brother, Fran. It doesn't surprise me at all. I understand you very well," he adds in a decisive voice.

Fran leans backwards and his chair is rocking on its rear legs only.

"Ah....," he says. He doesn't say anything else. He folds his hands behind his neck, looks into the air and remains silent, lost in his thoughts for a few seconds.

I could tell the story about how Fran didn't come home one night. It was a couple of months ago and every time I remember it I feel sick. I could tell the story now. I could very well do it and we would no longer be looking at Fran as if he were a sensitive person suffering from nightmares. I could tell them how I didn't sleep either. That I thought he'd never come back. That I went through the whole house switching lights on and off. I was thinking "Come back, darling, come back." And then I thought "I hope I never have to have anything more to do with you again, you bloody bastard, I hope I never set eyes on you again because I'll kill you." And then I begged him to come home. I begged him! I spoke to him as if he was there in front of me. I mean I was talking out loud. I ended up convincing myself that I'd gone

me había vuelto loca. Pero no. Simplemente sabía dónde estaba y con quién. Tiene gracia. Siempre se piensa que esas cosas no le van a pasar a una. Pero pasan.

Ahora los cuatro estamos en silencio. Simone retira los platos y se los lleva a la cocina, desde donde nos llega un estruendo de cubertería y vajilla estrellándose en el suelo. Sin embargo, ni Fran ni yo nos movemos para ir a ver qué ha ocurrido. Estamos bastante borrachos y nos da lo mismo. Al menos a mí me da igual. Estoy agotada y con gusto me iría a dormir ahora mismo. Me pesan los párpados y me siento envejecer por segundos. Es una sensación clarísima. Noto cómo me arrugo, cómo la piel se me vuelve fláccida y mate, cómo se descuelgan y derrumban los músculos, como si fueran los de una anciana decrépita. Apoyo la cabeza en la pared y cierro los ojos. Cuando los abro tengo la impresión de que ha pasado muchísimo tiempo. Creo que incluso he dormido. Pero ninguno parece haberlo advertido y supongo que si me hubiera dormido de verdad alguien diría algo. Necesito café. Pregunto a los demás y me levanto a poner tres cafés solos y un descafeinado para Rosa. Podría pedírselos a Simone, que sigue coqueteando con el gigante y agitando su melena rubia a diestro y siniestro, pero prefiero hacerlos yo para ver si así me espabilo.

Cuando vuelvo a la mesa, encuentro a Fran y a los Lucas muy animados. Les pregunto de qué hablaban y Fran dice que no estaban hablando, sino soñando.

—Soñamos con lo que pediríamos si se nos fuera a conceder el mayor deseo. Lucas se compraría una casa y un coche de carreras. Rosa quiere una habitación azul para su niño. Yo pediría un velero. ¿Y tú? ¿Qué pedirías tú, Irma?

Me quedo pensando. Es la primera vez que alguien me pregunta algo así y no sé qué responder ni por dónde empezar.

—Bueno —digo al fin—, una vez escuché una cosa muy curiosa que contó una mujer en la peluquería. Estaba bajo el secador, le hacían la manicura y ella hablaba alto mientras se miraba las manos. Dijo que había tenido un accidente. Su coche se incrustó en otro. Debió ser un golpe tremendo, porque la mujer se estrelló contra el cristal delantero y salió disparada hacia la carretera. La ingresaron en la uvi y cuando salió de allí estaba totalmente desfigurada. Así que la operaron. Le hicieron cirugía facial en la nariz, en los ojos, en la boca. Y cuando le retiraron las vendas la mujer se miró en un espejo y se encontró frente a frente con otra persona.

crazy. But no. I simply knew where he was and who he was with. It's funny. You always think these things will never happen to you. But they do.

By now all four of us had fallen silent. Simone clears away the plates and takes them into the kitchen, from where there comes the sound of china and cutlery crashing to the floor. Neither Fran nor I, however, make any move to go and see what's happened. We're quite drunk and we don't really care. At least I don't care. I'm absolutely exhausted and I'd happily go to bed this very minute. My eyelids are heavy and I can feel myself ageing by the second. It's a very clear sensation. I see how I'm getting wrinkled, how my skin is getting flabby and dull looking, how my muscles are drooping and collapsing as if they were the muscles of a decrepit old woman. I lean my head against the wall and close my eyes. When I open them again I have the impression that a great deal of time has passed. I think I might even have fallen asleep. But nobody seems to have noticed and I suppose that if I really had been asleep, somebody would say something. I need some coffee. I ask the others and get up to fetch three black coffees and one de-caff for Rosa. I could have asked Simone to get them – she's still flirting with the giant and tossing her blonde mane this way and that – but I prefer to get them myself to see if it will wake me up.

When I get back to the table I find Fran and the Lucases very excited about something. I ask them what they're talking about and Fran says that they weren't talking, they were dreaming.

"We're dreaming about what we'd ask for if we were granted the thing we wanted most in the world. Lucas would buy a house and a racing car. Rosa wants a blue bedroom for her baby. I'd ask for a sailing boat."

"And what about you? What would you ask for, Irma?"

I get to thinking about it. This is the first time anybody has asked me anything like this and I don't know what to say or where to begin.

"Well," I say at last, "I once heard something very strange, something a woman in the hairdressers' was talking about. She was under the dryer, they were doing her nails and she was talking loudly while was looking at her hands. She said she'd had an accident. Her car had smashed right into another one. It must have been a tremendous crash, because the woman was thrown against the front windscreen and hurled out onto the road. They admitted her to the intensive care unit and when she came out of there she was totally disfigured. So they operated on her. They gave her facial surgery on her nose, on her eyes, on her mouth. And when they took the bandages off the woman looked at herself in the mirror and found herself face to face with somebody else. It was somebody who looked about ten

Era algo así como diez años más joven que ella y también era más atractiva. Ella decía que lo que le habían hecho le hacía parecer mil veces más guapa. Así que todos sus amigos y su marido y sus hijos la felicitaban. Le decían que había tenido verdadera suerte con aquel accidente y que hay actrices que pagan millones para que les hagan algo parecido. Pero ella no se sentía a gusto con su nueva cara. Dijo que cada mañana, al despertarse, se preguntaba cuál de sus dos caras la miraría desde el espejo. Dijo que era una cosa muy extraña y muy desagradable tener dos caras diferentes.

Fran me mira con perplejidad. Parece molesto.

—¿Qué quieres decir? —pregunta—. ¿Qué tiene que ver esa mujer contigo? La verdad es que no entiendo nada. Estamos hablando de lo que nos gustaría hacer y tú sales con una historia que no tiene ni pies ni cabeza. Esa mujer estaba loca. Tendría que estar agradecida. Tendría que dar gracias a Dios de que en este país exista una seguridad social que te haga todas esas cosas. En otros países la hubieran echado a la calle con sus cicatrices y todo. En África. 0 en Asia. Diles a los africanos que no te gusta tu cara. Diles que estabas llena de ojales y que te han puesto una piel nueva y que no te gusta. Díselo y verás. ¿0 es que tú quieres que te hagan cirugía plástica? No entiendo nada. No sé si dices que quieres una nariz nueva o si estás diciendo que aquí hay alguien que tiene dos caras. ¿Es eso lo que pretendes decir? ¿Crees que yo tengo dos caras? Porque si es así, me gustaría saberlo.

—No es eso —contesto.

En realidad no tengo ganas de explicar nada. Lo que yo quiero, lo único que de verdad deseo es volver a mi casa. A veces cierro los ojos y me lo imagino. Imagino que he vuelto, que voy caminando y conozco los nombres de las calles, que cuando me hablan no tengo que esforzarme por entender qué dicen, que hay gente que me conoce y me saluda y con la que me paro a charlar un rato. Que no me encuentro tan sola. Hay mañanas que me despierto y siento que he vuelto a mi pueblo. Son sólo unos segundos, hasta que de verdad espabilo por completo y comprendo que no, que soy como la mujer del espejo, que tal vez nunca más volveré a ver mi verdadera, mi auténtica cara, la mía. Pero ¿cómo se explica algo así?

—No es eso —repito—.

Fran se levanta de la mesa.

—¡Mierda! —dice.

years younger than her and who was also more attractive. She was saying that what they had done to her made her look a thousand times prettier. So all her friends and her husband and her kids congratulated her. They told her that she'd had a really lucky accident and that there are actresses who pay millions to have something similar done to them. But she didn't feel happy with her new face. She said that every morning, when she woke up, she'd wonder which of her two faces would be looking back at her from the mirror. She said that it was a very odd sensation and very unpleasant to have two different faces.

Fran is looking at me, perplexed. He looks annoyed.

"What are you trying to say?" he asks. "What's that woman got to do with you? Honestly, I don't understand a word of it. We're talking about what we'd like to do and you come out with some story that doesn't make any sense. That woman was mad. She should be grateful. She should give thanks to God that there's National Health Service in this country that takes care of these things. In other countries she'd have been thrown out onto the street, scars and all. In Africa. Or in Asia. Tell people in Africa that you don't like your face. Tell them you were full of holes and they've given you a new skin and you don't like it. Tell them and you'll see. Or is it that you'd like them to do some plastic surgery on you. I don't understand it at all. I don't know if you're saying that you want a new nose or if you're saying that there's somebody here who has two faces. Is that what you're trying to say? You think that I have two faces? Because if that's what you think, I'd like to know about it."

"It's not that," I reply.

The fact of the matter is I don't want to explain anything. What I do want, to tell the truth it's the only thing I want, is to go home. Sometimes I close my eyes and I imagine it. I imagine that I've gone back, that I'm walking along and I know the names of the streets, that when people talk to me I don't have to make an effort to understand what they're saying, that there are people who know me and who say hello and who I stop and chat to for a while. That I don't feel so alone. There are mornings when I wake up and I feel I've gone back to my home village. It only lasts a few seconds until I wake up completely and I understand that no, I'm like the woman in the mirror, that perhaps I'll never see my true, my real face, my own face again. But how do you explain something like that?

"It's not that," I repeat.

Fran gets up from the table.

"Shit!" he says.

Le oigo trajinar detrás de la barra, a mi espalda. Oigo que saca hielos de la máquina y que los echa en la cubitera, pero no me vuelvo para verle. En cambio, me empeño en convencer a Lucas y a Rosa de que se queden a dormir en nuestra casa y mientras insisto, miro fijamente una única burbuja de champán que asciende continuamente por mi copa. Las demás se han muerto hace rato, pero ella sigue subiendo, recta y solitaria, desde el mismo punto.

Ahora los Lucas se han ido a buscar su coche. Finalmente han desistido de viajar de noche y van a quedarse en la habitación de invitados. Mientras les aguardamos, Fran barre y yo recojo las sillas, las copas y el cenicero. Después me desmaquillo ante el espejo del baño. Pienso en lo que ha ocurrido esta noche, pienso en lo que ha dicho Fran, en lo que he contestado yo, pero ya no sé si las cosas han sucedido como yo creo o de otro modo. Tampoco sé si a estas alturas eso importa. Me cepillo bien las uñas. Me peino. Me miro y veo que estoy igual de horrorosa que antes de peinarme. Luego abro la puerta.

—¡Lo prometiste, Fran, lo prometiste! —escucho decir a Simone.

Me quedo clavada en la puerta. Oigo que Fran contesta algo, pero no entiendo qué.

¡Pero tú lo prometiste, Fran! —repite Simone.

Fran hace "Sshhh" y lanza una perorata en un francés rápido y nervioso.

Entonces vuelvo a entrar en el baño, cierro con el pasador y apoyo la espalda en la puerta. Intento pensar. Intento concentrarme y pensar, pero veo mi cara en el espejo y continuamente me viene a la cabeza la mujer de la peluquería así que apago la luz y me quedo quieta en la oscuridad sintiendo cómo me tiemblan las piernas.

Cuando Fran llama a la puerta no contesto. Le oigo mover el pestillo y llamarme, pero no contesto. Él comienza a aporrear la puerta y pienso "Vete. Vete, Fran. Márchate. Por favor, vete", pero tampoco digo nada.

Y entonces él pregunta:

—Irma, ¿estás bien? ¿Te encuentras bien, cariño? Dime, ¿estás bien?

I hear him bustling about behind the bar, behind me. I hear him getting ice cubes out of the machine and throwing them into the ice bucket but I don't turn round to look at him. Instead, I try to persuade Lucas and Rosa to sleep at our house and as I keep trying I stare at a single champagne bubble which is continually rising up through my glass. The rest died out some time ago, but this one keeps on rising, following its straight and solitary course, from the same point.

The Lucases have gone to look for their car now. They've finally given up the idea of driving through the night and are going to stay in our guest room. While we wait for them, Fran sweeps up and I put the chairs on the tables, and collect the glasses and the ashtray. Afterwards, I clean off my make-up in front of the bathroom mirror. I think about what has happened tonight, I think about what Fran has said, about what I said in reply, but now I don't know if things happened the way I think they did or in some other way. Nor do I know whether that matters right now. I give my nails a good scrub. I comb my hair. I look at myself and see that I'm just as much of a mess as I was before I combed my hair. Then I open the door.

"You promised, Fran, you promised!" I hear Simone saying.

I stand frozen in the doorway. I hear Fran say something in reply, but I can't make it out.

"But you promised, Fran!" Simone says again.

Fran goes "Shhh" and launches into some long-winded spiel in rapid, nervous French.

Then I go back into the bathroom, I close the door and turn the lock and lean back against the door. I'm trying to think. I'm trying to concentrate and to think, but I see my face in the mirror and the woman in the hairdressers' keeps popping into my head, so I switch off the light and I stay there motionless in the dark, aware of how my legs are trembling.

When Fran knocks at the door I don't answer. I hear him trying the latch and calling out my name, but I don't answer. He starts pounding on the door and I think, "go away, go away, Fran, clear off, please, just go away," but still I don't say anything.

And then he asks:

"Irma, are you OK? Are you feeling OK, darling? Tell me, are you OK?"

Vicente Blasco Ibáñez

The Holding (*La Barraca*)

'Another excellent offering from Aris & Phillips in their bilingual Hispanic Classics series [provides] help in the development of linguistic skills by students of Spanish by introducing them to the literature of Spain.' *British Bulletin*

'This bilingual edition of the classic text of Spanish Naturalism is to be welcomed. [...] The editor pursues a good range of themes and is particularly incisive on the religious and political echoes in the novel.' *Forum for Mod. Lang. Studies.*

Antonio Buero Vallejo

The Shot *(La detonación)*,

'Johnston and his publisher are to be applauded for their efforts at bringing a major Spanish playwright to the attention of the English speaking world.' *Estreno*

A Dreamer for the People *(Un soñador para un pueblo)*

'The English translation is sufficiently idiomatic and colloquial to be used for stage performance, while being as faithful as possible to the original text.' *British Bulletin*

'This translation with its introduction will become a necessary set text in all English-speaking universities where Spanish theatre is studied and it is to be hoped that directors and producers will decide to use it when offering what would be a very welcome production of *A Dreamer for the People*.' *Forum for Mod. Lang. Studies.*

Ramón María del Valle-Inclán

Lights of Bohemia *(Luces de Bohemia)*

'The excellence of the translation and its accompanying explanatory materials will be invaluable to anyone interested in staging this play.' *BHS*

Mr Punch the Cuckold *(Los cuernos de Don Friolera)*

'This masterful version of *Los Cuernos* is indeed a welcome addition[...] Keown and Warner are to be commended for doing justice to the overall tone of Valle's farce, for not losing sight of the ambiguities contained in both structure and content and for opening up such an important work to an even vaster audience than before.' *BHS*